Dark Advent

~ Petra Piitalaat Jensen Books 1 & 2 ~

THE CALENDAR MAN and THE TWELFTH NIGHT

by Christoffer Petersen

Dark Advent

Published by Aarluuk Press

ISBN: 978-87-93680-24-1

Original Cover Photo Annie Spratt
@anniespratt (Unsplash)

www.christoffer-petersen.com

Conceal me what I am, and be my aid
For such disguise as haply shall become
The form of my intent.

— *Twelfth Night, Act I, Sc. II*

William Shakespeare (1564-1616)

Introduction

~ *This is not a book* ~

The Calendar Man is, however, a complete story, and you can read it like a book, from start to finish, one chapter after another. Or, if you're feeling festive, you can read it in the way it is intended, as a Scandinavian *Julekalender* – a story told over twenty-four days, from December 1st to Christmas Eve on December 24th, the night Greenlanders and Scandinavians celebrate Christmas.

Scandinavian *Julekalendere* (plural) have been a part of the Scandinavian Christmas tradition and culture for decades, and the first *Julekalender* aired on Danish television in 1962. Greenland also has a tradition for *Julekalender*, and I saw one of the first Greenlandic-produced Christmas Calendars called *Ammartagaq* in 2010.

The classic format of the Scandinavian Christmas Calendar tells a story over twenty-four television episodes. The action occurs over the course of each day, and as the month progresses it looks increasingly unlikely that there will be a Christmas this year. This is a common theme in many Christmas stories and films with many variations.

The Calendar Man is my version of a *Julekalender* set in Greenland in the year 2042. It is not science fiction, and there is very little technology or technobabble to distract from the story. However, some current issues, such as Greenlandic independence, the Chinese interest in Greenland's minerals, and the threat of rising sea levels, do play a part, and it was fun to imagine a future Greenland including characters from my existing series of books.

True to the nature of a Christmas Calendar, *The Calendar Man* is episodic, with new events and discoveries that drive the investigation towards its dramatic climax. But unlike Christmas Calendars in Denmark and Greenland, the elves have been replaced, and it is up to the police, and Police Commissioner Petra Jensen, to save Christmas.

The Calendar Man is a Dark Advent story with elements of the

Greenlandic Christmas tradition woven into the story.

Whether or not you are familiar with my Greenland crime novels and stories, *The Calendar Man* can be read independently of the other books. Some reference, however, is made to earlier stories, without spoilers, for the sake of continuity.

Remember, it's not a book. Try to limit yourself to one chapter a day.

Merry Christmas!

Chris
December 2018
Denmark

The Calendar Man

A Scandinavian Dark Advent novel set in Greenland

~ Petra *Piitalaat* Jensen Book 1 ~

Ataasinngorneq

Monday, 1st December 2042
Nuuk, Greenland

Chapter 1

Memories, I think, are like icing sugar. Add too much water, or *time*, and the icing is thin and diluted, but add too little and it is thick and unmanageable, something you can barely stir with a spoon. My memories of David Maratse are like the icing sugar I am mixing together with Iiluuna's daughter Quaa: so thick I can barely move the spoon. I need time. Not so much that I will forget him, but just enough to spread the memories a little more evenly, thick enough to enjoy, thin enough to breathe. Quaa is watching me again, her mother's strange new friend. I should add a little more water so that I can stop crying and we can finish icing the Christmas cookies before she has to go to bed.

David's funeral was just last month, and now we have begun the darkest month of the year. We need something sweet to take the edge off the bitter night, and we need light to brighten even the darkest corners. I smile when Iiluuna lights a candle and places it on the table. I smile at Quaa, encouraging her to dip her finger in the icing. She licks the tip of her finger, and her eyes shine in the candlelight.

"It's ready," I say.

Iiluuna makes cocoa as we paint half of each cookie with a thin layer of icing sugar. I can hear her cursing the milk she burns on the bottom of the pan, and I can hear Quaa swallow as she sticks the tip of her tongue between her lips and concentrates. It's moments like these when I wish David and I had had a child. But then that chance was taken from me so many years ago. And now, so many years later, he is gone, and I have adopted the daughter he never had, and her child who he never saw. This is my family now – small and compact, manageable, my sanctuary from the streets of Nuuk.

"What are you going to do?" Iiluuna asks.

She places the cocoa in a glass jug on the table beside the candle. The light reflects and shines on the plain walls, glitters on the frosted window. There are tiny white lights hanging from the ceiling, strung from the corners on nails, draped over the light fixtures and fittings. We are elves in a grotto. We could be in the mountains, or in one of David's science fiction stories that he loved. But we are barely above street level in a city that has doubled in size since David and I moved here eleven years ago. The Chinese arrived a few years before we did and expanded the iron ore mine in the very north of *Nuup Kangerlua*, the fjord above Nuuk. They needed a town for so many Chinese workers, and they built it – Chinatown, just south of Qinngorput to the east of the city centre, together with the new harbour and airport. The first climate immigrants came next when Pipaluk Uutaaq, then minister for Housing and Infrastructure, saw an opportunity to boost Greenland's economy. The opposition parties and the media were sceptical, but when the Dutch arrived and began work on Little Amsterdam, Pipaluk was praised for her foresight, and Mitsimmavik, south of Chinatown, was transformed into a pretty colony that van Gogh would have died for. According to the media. David wasn't so sure, but we took the bus there on Saturdays when he was strong enough, stronger than his cancer, and we walked along glittered paths with granite trees cut and chipped from mountain roots. He liked the *stroopwafels*. He liked anything sweet.

"Petra?" Iiluuna says.

That's right. I must make a decision. I can only stretch my compassionate leave for so long. Not long enough.

"I could retire," I say. "David and I talked about it. I have a good pension. I have a nice apartment. I might even travel a little. Berlin, perhaps."

"You can leave it all behind?"

"Police work?"

I laugh. It is a strange sound, but it feels good.

"Yes," I say. "I can leave all that behind."

I wouldn't miss it and I have given so much of my life to the job already, so many years – from Constable to Commissioner, as a detective and a victim. Without David to come home to, I'm not sure I can cope with the street, the suffering, and the evil that lies in those dark corners without light. People think being a Police Commissioner is all about administration and politics, which it is, but a good Commissioner is never far from the street. Not in Greenland.

Without David, I think. Without him I am struggling to sleep alone in my apartment, forcing Quaa to share her mother's bed as I sleep in hers, staring at her pop posters and ornaments, waking at the beep of her new mobile phone. I laugh at the thought of how David struggled to keep up with even the most basic technological developments, at how old-fashioned people thought his books were, and how he revelled in reading them to me, his brow creased by candle-light, during winter power cuts.

"Yes," I say. "I will apply for early retirement, just as soon as I return to the office."

"When?"

I have been waiting for her to ask. It is the season of giving, but I cannot continue to just take, I can't deprive Quaa of her bed and her room any longer. I think I knew I would leave as soon as we started on the icing, the first drops of water brought the tears, as I realised that I was going home tonight, back to the apartment, to the smell and the sights that I associate with David. But not the sounds. The apartment is silent now, like the earth in which he lies, beneath the rocks and stones in one of the last reserved spots in Nuuk's city graveyard.

I take a breath and then I reach across the table to brush crusts of icing and biscuit crumbs from Quaa's cheeks.

"You can sleep in your own bed tonight," I say, as I force a smile.

Quaa's long black hair tumbles from her shoulders as she looks at her mother and I nod.

"Yes," I say. "I'm ready."

"If you're sure?"

"You've both been very kind, but it's time."

My phone buzzes and I show them the screen.

"And work calls," I say.

The intrusion is welcome, and the urgent message from the station hurries me out of Iiluuna's apartment, into my winter clothes and onto the street. They have sent a patrol car, and I climb inside, a second or two after it hums along the street and stops where the tyres have compacted the snow into a curb. Nuuk police have three of these electric SUVs, with two more arriving on the first ship in spring. They are as quiet as they are spacious. Comfortable too. I nod at the Constable behind the wheel and he pulls away from the curb.

I scan the message as he drives, teasing out the details of the text and wondering why they have called me at such a delicate time. The photos embedded in the message provide some answers, and I gasp at the sight of the banded fingers on the dead body, naked and stiff, tied with plastic ties to the railings outside the new community centre.

"Are you alright, ma'am?"

I place my mobile on my thigh, screen down, reminding myself that he is kind to ask, and that he deserves an answer.

"Have you seen the body?" I ask.

"Yes, ma'am."

"The fingers are banded," I say, and turn the screen upwards. "It might be tattoos, and if so, then…"

I sigh as he waits for me to continue. He is too young to push, but I see him glance at my bare hands.

"Yes," I say. "It's true, the backs of my fingers, between the joints, are banded with tattoos – stick and poke from a fish hook."

He would be too young to have followed the case in the media, but not so young he wouldn't have heard the stories about the Commissioner, back when she was a victim. It helps to think of that time in the third person, as if I can remove myself from the memory. But that is why they called, dragging me out of my grief only to compound it with traumatic memories. If nothing else, it makes me even more determined to retire.

The Constable parks the patrol car and escorts me to the body. The area is cordoned off, the shoppers guided around the scene by blue and white tape and gentle commands, the kind that are difficult not to understand.

"Keep moving," the police officers say. "No pictures."

Someone thought to hang a tarpaulin from the covered walkway above. It flaps with crisp crackles in the chill wind blowing between Nuuk's oldest supermarket and the entrance to the new community centre. There are people pressed to the glass of the walkway above, and I whisper to the Constable that I am fine, and perhaps he can find a colleague to clear the walkway. They have a direct view of the body, and I wonder if they can see something that the officers on the ground cannot. Perhaps I should go with the Constable, but then a deep voice and a gentle touch on my arm suggest I am wanted here. There is no escape.

"I'm sorry," Sergeant Aqqa Danielsen says, as he guides me towards the body. "It's so soon after the funeral, but when I saw the fingers, I told them to call you."

I nod as he lets go of my arm and I crouch beside the body of a young man, a Greenlander, naked and stiff in the cold, palms upwards, fingers blue and banded. It couldn't be the work of the man Aqqa and I knew, but it is plain to see that someone has been inspired by that man's work. I glance at my fingers and then search for a thin pair of gloves from the pockets of my police jacket. I pause at the touch of a length of bailing twine and the cold plastic shell of a lighter. This is not my jacket. And I remember it was one of three things I took when I left my apartment after the funeral – my phone, an overnight bag, and David's old police jacket. There are no gloves. He never used them. I tuck my hands inside the pockets, clasping the twine and the lighter like tiny talismans, and wait for Aqqa to continue his report.

"The man was strangled," he says. "We need to get the body to the morgue before we'll know more. But there's something else."

I follow Aqqa to the back of a patrol car. The swirl of blue emergency lights flash across the faces of the crowd. The Danes and the Dutch immigrants are barely indistinguishable, the Greenlanders and the Chinese more so, but mostly by the clothes they are wearing – the Chinese are layered with chicken-feathered duvet suits, loose feathers drift in the cold air above them when they move.

"This was strung around his neck," Aqqa says and hands me an advent calendar inside a large plastic evidence bag.

Father Christmas in his *Coca Cola* suit is on the front, and all but one of the windows is closed. I turn the calendar in the light.

"Today is the first of December," I say.

"*Aap.*"

"But the window that is open," I say and turn it towards Aqqa. "Is the sixteenth."

"I have no idea," he says. "But I'm pretty sure we were meant to find it. Oh, and the First Minister wants to talk to you. She's waiting in her car."

"She's here?"

Aqqa points around the patrol car and I nod as the driver of the luxurious government vehicle gets out and waves me over.

"You've finished with the scene?" I ask Aqqa.

"We were just waiting for you."

"Okay, I say. Carry on and I'll see what the First Minister wants."

The driver opens the passenger door as I walk over, and I climb inside. The interior is lit with soft lights, and Pipaluk Uutaaq looks radiant. I wonder, just for a second, what she might think of David's jacket, decorated as it is with the spots and smears of fishing and hunting adventures. She seems not to notice and offers me a drink from the cabinet beside her seat as the driver closes the door. I shake my head and wait for her to speak.

"You've seen the advent calendar?" she asks.

"Yes."

"And do you know what happens on the sixteenth of December?"

"Forgive me, First Minister. I've been a little preoccupied."

"I'm sorry. My condolences," Pipaluk says and takes my hand. "The sixteenth is the day Greenland votes for independence," she says. "You do remember?"

Despite turning off the radio, avoiding the television and the streaming media, and hiding in Iiluuna's apartment, even I cannot pretend that I don't know Greenland is set to vote, again, for independence from Denmark, again.

"We're going to get it this time," Pipaluk says. "So, you can imagine I am very concerned about the dead body in front of the community centre. It's the most central voting station in Nuuk. My father worked hard for this, she says. And we're so close."

"You think this is related?"

"Don't you?"

Pipaluk looks at me in such a way that I know all thoughts of early retirement are about to be postponed, indefinitely, at least until Greenland has cut its colonial ties.

"I want you to investigate this case personally, Commissioner."

"First Minister, with respect, I have many competent investigators. All of whom can investigate this case."

"But I want you."

"You can't tell me what to investigate, or even how I should conduct investigations," I say.

"Petra," Pipaluk says with a pat of my hand. "I just did."

Marlunngorneq

Tuesday, 2nd December 2042

Chapter 2

The apartment is as silent as I remember. I don't hear the crash and thump of the neighbour's children, nor the raised voices of the couple arguing, the distorted music of the drunk fiddling with the volume of his stereo or the sudden scream, the percussive crash, or any of the other sounds associated with apartment life in the city. All I can hear is the silence of empty space where he should be. All I can see are his books, lining the shelves – they are full of words and yet they don't speak.

Spineless.

After a moment at the door I manage to close it, but I won't remove his jacket. Not yet. I kick off my boots, but I unzip and curl the jacket around my body, pressing my fingers into the corners of the pockets, zip overlapping as I pad across the floor of the living room, ignoring the books, and pressing my face to the window, it is cool on my brow. I close my eyes. I can feel my breath against the glass, cooling; it cools my chin and my cheeks. I know the bed is made, but I haven't the strength to face it. It is after midnight, but I can't go into the bedroom.

"Just a few minutes more," I say. "Then, I promise, I will go to bed."

Tomorrow I will file for retirement. Pipaluk can find another Commissioner. If not from Nuuk, they can send a temporary replacement from Denmark, until a new one can be appointed. I don't need to do it.

Piitalaat.

I don't look around. I know it's not him. If I just press my head a little longer against the glass, if I look out across the bay and remember the view is the reason we chose to keep the apartment, even after my promotion, then he will return to the land, he will sink to rest, peacefully, beneath the snow and the rocks.

Stop it, Piitalaat.

"Stop what?" I say, as I turn around, eyes wide, searching the black corners of the room.

Let me go.

"You're the one talking."

Eeqqi, Piitalaat. It's not me.

I know it. Of course, I do.

I look at the shelves again. There are fewer books than the smallest book shelves in a Danish household, but in some parts of Greenland, in the small hunting and fishing communities, David's three shelves of science fiction books were the equivalent of the national library. And still they don't speak. Perhaps if I opened one of them, took it to bed with me, then maybe...

I let the thought hang in the air as I pull my hands out of David's deep pockets. I grab an armful of books and carry them into the bedroom, kicking the door with my heel to open it. I dump the books on the bed and return for the next shelf, and again, until his side of the bed is heavy with books. I will have to tug at the duvet to cover my body, just as I did every night, even when he was weak, and my complaints at him *hogging the duvet again* became code for *I love you* and *don't leave me*.

I take off the jacket and cover the pillow with it, crawling under the duvet in my winter salopettes and fleece. I can smell the north pressed between the fibres of his jacket as I lay my head on the pillow, and I can feel the wind's teeth and the dogs' claws in the scratches and tears of the stiff cotton and greasy flaps covering the pockets.

Sleep, Piitalaat, he says, and I let him.

There is a practical part of my nature that takes over when it feels my emotions are getting the best of me. It's almost as if I am torn with internal jealousy. I can almost hear *practical me* sighing and shaking her head. Colleagues in the past have wondered at it, although, to be fair, there are very few police officers who haven't experienced their own *practical me* when dealing with difficult scenes and investigations. So, I'm not so special after all, and I remind myself of that as I shower, dress, and get ready to walk down the long hill from the apartment in Qinngorput to the bus stop across from the school. I could take a taxi, call for a patrol to pick me up, or even drive my own car. But today I want to see the people of Nuuk, feel them bustle and bump against my shoulders in the early morning standing-room-only bus.

I feel stronger now that I have survived the first night alone in what was *our* bed and is now my own. I have decisions to make, and that one night's sleep has given me the strength to make them.

I will go north, back to Inussuk, for a little while at least.

I should have buried him there, in the tiny graveyard on the mountainside, above the settlement. But I didn't. I will visit instead.

The short walk from the bus stop to Nuuk Police Station is just enough to colour my cheeks as I open the doors and climb the stairs to the Commissioner's office. My office. My assistant, Aron Ulloriaq stands to greet me as I hang my jacket on the rack and peel off my salopettes.

"You walked?" he asks.

"I took the bus."

Winter clothes are like a chrysalis, and as I straighten my black tie I am ready for the day.

"Is there any coffee?" I ask.

"Of course."

It is a distraction, and I almost feel guilty, but while Aron pours me a fresh mug of coffee I find the necessary paperwork in the filing cabinet by his desk. So much of our daily life is paperless, and yet some things require a formality that can be felt, as if the weight of the paper itself and the gravity pulling at it make it more important. I tuck the papers into an empty brown file and carry them into my office, slapping them on the desk as Aron brings me my morning coffee.

"What about breakfast?" he asks.

He knows I haven't eaten, and that I won't touch anything before ten o'clock. But he asks anyway, just as he has asked every morning since he started in August.

"Maybe later," I say.

He's hovering by the desk, and I am uncertain if he wants to ask about me, about the body with the banded fingers – which is also *about me*, really – or if there is something else.

"There was a call," he says. "Just before you got in. It was the doctor in the morgue."

"Dronning Ingrid's Hospital?"

"No, Kong Frederik's."

That's the new hospital, the modern one, and yet not so modern it could save David's life. I prefer to work with the staff at the old hospital. They at least don't pretend they can work miracles.

I wait for him to leave and then the light glows on the handset of my office phone. He has already patched me through. Doctor Bendt Hersholt's voice has a touch of morning grit about it, or perhaps it is late night gravel and he is annoyed at the overtime and the urgency of the dead.

"This is Commissioner Jensen," I say.

"Petra?"

I have noticed that ever since I was appointed to the post of Police Commissioner doctors prefer to use my first name, as if I have joined their ranks. Or perhaps, even after so many years, it has something to do with my sex and the reluctant acceptance of men – still – to accept that the position was something earned not rewarded.

"Doctor," I say.

"You sent me a body late last night."

"Yes."

"Cause of death was strangulation."

I want to ask why he is telling me, why not the officer assigned to the case? Sergeant Danielsen perhaps. Then I remember that the First Minister assigned me to the case. I'm sure she called the doctor too, I can hear as much in his tone of voice. He must have worked through the night.

"Anything else?" I ask.

"You saw the fingers?"

I turn the palm of my left hand upwards – trauma tattoos, a physical reminder of what I carry on the inside. David helped me heal, and *practical me* told me to get over myself and get on with life. It took a few years, but I listened, to both of them. And now I have to listen to him, the doctor, as he tells me something I already know. I'm tempted to ask him his age but bite my tongue instead. I can taste the blood as he speaks.

"The tattoos are old and crude. I think he might have done them himself."

"What's his name?" I ask.

"That's what I can't give you, not yet. We're still trying to merge the records from Dronning Ingrid's into our new system."

I let him rant for a few seconds, as I study the bands across the joints of my fingers and swallow the blood in my mouth. I close my hand around the coffee mug to hide my fingers as I rinse the blood with coffee. Right on cue, the doctor has finished, and I swallow and speak.

"You'll let me know?"

"Yes," he says.

I put the phone down when I hear him take a breath. I'm not

normally so rude, but I can see Aron hovering at the door. Sergeant Danielsen is behind him.

"Come in," I say.

"We've got another one," Danielsen says.

He steps into my office and shows me the screen of his mobile. The body is charred as if it has been burned. He swipes the next photo onto the screen and shows me the advent calendar. It is identical to the first, and the window for the ninth day of December is open.

"Have we got forensics on this?" I ask.

"They are at the scene."

"Take me there," I say.

Danielsen has a *new-car* grin and he wears it well. He owns the driver's seat, filling it with a middle-aged stomach and backside that could be the result of patrol snacks or home cooking. I have met his wife, the lovely Kuuka, and I imagine it is a bit of both. The SUV purrs along the snow-packed road and I almost wish we could just keep driving. The roads in Nuuk have expanded with the city, there is even a bridge spanning *Kangerluarsunnguaq Fjord*, east of the city, providing access to the United States Coast Guard Station Nuuk. An imaginative name for a high-security foreign base. No-one travels across the bridge because the Americans won't let them. They prefer to remain secluded and secretive, just one of the conditions for their substantial contribution to the new harbour. They won't be visiting anytime soon, and neither will we.

And just like that, the journey is over, and so too are my plans for early retirement, as soon as I see the body. Practical me steps aside for my emotions as I see what I failed to notice in Danielsen's photograph – the charred body is too small for an adult.

This part of Nuuk has escaped the developer's eye. The concrete walls of the courtyard and the apartments above are fatigued, like the occupants. I can feel the chill wind press and flap the fabric of my trousers as it blows from the road, swirling snow over my boots, and dusting the black with a layer of fine white sugar. I should have worn my salopettes. I thought this would be a quick visit to the crime scene, before I told Danielsen to carry on, and then returned to the office. I know Aron has a backlog of paperwork for me to see to but is too polite to say so.

I crouch beside the body, see the charred remains of a wooden chair and the streak of black that has burned through the snow from an empty fuel can.

"We're not sure if it is a child or someone very small."

"Look at the size of the hands," I say. "And the head."

Practical me is back, and I'm almost embarrassed. But years of police work attune the eye to some things that others might not see, at least not to begin with. Someone was burned to death – a child or a small adult – and the papers and streaming media have another body to report.

"Show me the advent calendar."

Danielsen taps one of the technicians on the shoulder and they fetch the calendar from the van. The technician's eyes are obscured by the mask, and his or her clothes are hidden beneath protective overalls. I can't tell if it is a man or a woman, but the eyes, what I can see of them, are all business. I nod my thanks and turn the calendar in my hands.

It is a duplicate of the first, and I imagine there will be more. Twenty-four in all, if that's what this is – the first two murders in a series. But if the open windows on the advent calendar are significant then they need to be studied, and the other windows need to be opened. I press the calendar into Danielsen's hands.

"Congratulations, Aqqa," I say. "You're the lead investigator."

"But the First Minister…"

"Does not decide how we work. I'll stay close, but I won't get in your way. Oh, and you'll need a task force. Any thoughts?"

"Atii Napa is just back from leave."

"Good. Call her. Get her up to speed as soon as you get back to the station."

"You don't want a ride?"

"No," I say. "I'm still officially on leave. I'll make some calls, from home and assemble the team. I want everything ready by first thing tomorrow morning. I'll see you then."

Pingasunngorneq

Wednesday, 3rd December 2042

Chapter 3

I waited until they were settled, and Aron had finished handing out the breakfast rolls. It was one of those moments when, from a distance, one might worry that the tone was too light and cheery for a murder investigation. The collegial small talk while buttering rolls, or the humorous jibes that inevitably follow a small mistake, or perhaps even a romantic rebuff from the weekend. But it is these small inappropriate things that make the difference when working within and for the community, from the inside, often isolated like the Americans on the base across the fjord.

I let them chatter a few minutes more as I observe the team Danielsen has put together. There is Atii Napa, bronzed and beaming from her short break in Greece. She is two years younger than me, but one could be forgiven for thinking it wasn't at least ten. I think of my old colleague and friend Gaba Alatak and smile at the image of him running his own company and getting the boys ready for school while Atii, his wife and former patrol partner, cruise the streets at night in one of the new SUVs. She was ready to cancel her trip to Greece with her sister when she heard about David's death. I'm not sure she has forgiven me for ordering her to go on holiday, but it was the right thing to do. David wouldn't have wanted the fuss.

I don't know the man sitting next to her, but I have read his file, and can understand why Danielsen wanted him on the task force. Ooqi Kleemann is from Upernavik, and I know David would have liked him. He has the quiet smile of shy intelligence that you often see in the smaller towns and villages. His glasses are thick, and I wonder if it is because he has spent more time in front of a computer screen than he has on the ice? His file says he is an IT specialist, and the attached notes show a record of pre-teen hacking that was expunged prior to him starting high school. Someone is looking out for Ooqi, and I decide that I will do the same.

Expunged.

I'm lost in the word for a moment, until Danielsen coughs and beckons me to the front of the room. I said he was the lead investigator, but he seems reluctant to start. A quick look over my shoulder suggests why, and I present my best thin-lipped smile to Greenland's First Minister.

"Don't mind me," she says.

But we do mind, and I whisper to Aron to find her a chair, as I walk to the front of the room. I amend my opening speech for her benefit and begin.

"Thank you, Aqqa," I say, as he sits down. "You're a small team, but you've got the full weight and cooperation of the department behind you. It's true; we're still short-staffed. We needed more police officers before the Chinese arrived, fourteen years ago, and we still needed them when the first Dutch immigrants began work on Little Amsterdam. I expect to reach out to the Chinese and Dutch security staff after this meeting, but I just wanted to get you started, and to hand over to Aqqa. He'll walk you through what we know."

"I thought you were leading the investigation?" Pipaluk says from her seat behind the task force. "That was what we agreed, Commissioner."

The image of her father, the late Malik Uutaaq, flickers through my mind as I return the look she casts from the back of the room. He was a popular figure in Greenlandic politics, but he must have loaded his genes with power and persuasion when he created her. She is twice the politician he was, and twice as popular. He helped sow the original seeds for Greenlandic independence, but she has nurtured them, and soon, according to the opinion polls, they will bear fruit.

"I will be monitoring progress on a daily basis," I say.

"Closely?"

"Very."

"And who will report to me?"

"I will," I say, as I move to lean against the wall.

Danielsen takes his cue, rises from his seat, and turns to face the small task force, while I work on *expunging* the last few minutes from my mind.

He really has put on weight, I think, as Danielsen runs through what we know of the two murders. It helps, I realise, to think about such things, and to be back at work again. The problem with the new pay system that Aron told me about this morning, the dead battery in the newest SUV, Aqqa's gut, and the crime scene photos he flashes onto the wall all help to push thoughts of David to some quiet part of my mind. I can revisit them later, as I did last night when the weight of David's books fooled me into thinking he really was hogging the duvet.

Piitalaat.

"What?"

Focus.

"Do you have anything to add?" Danielsen asks.

"Remind me again."

"We're waiting for a positive identification of the victims, and we were talking about the calendar. The sixteenth is the referendum," he says with a nod towards the back of the room. "But we've got nothing on the ninth."

"That's not completely true," Atii says and stands up.

Danielsen moves to one side as she casts a file from her mobile to the wall screen with a flick of her finger. Atii slips her finger and thumb inside two thimbles, clicking them together to highlight boxes of text on the screen, and pointing with the laser bead embedded in the thimble on her finger. I smile at the memory of the day I told David we were getting digital thimbles on trial.

Focus, he says, and I send him a mental roll of the eyes. Although, it is nice to be working with him again. I catch myself and process the thought as Atii runs through a few associations with the number nine.

"According to Norse Mythology, there are nine worlds connected by the world tree Yggdrasil. Odin hung from the tree for nine days before he gained knowledge of the runes."

"You're looking at myths?" Pipaluk says.

"We're looking at links," Atii says. "Anything."

"Keep going, Atii," I say.

"Odin and Yggdrasil might be relevant if the suspect is a Dane, but the Chinese have a lot more nines in their culture, mostly associated with the dragon, its nine forms, and nine children. The number nine is lucky in Chinese culture."

"And do we have any Chinese festivals coming up?"

"*Aap,*" Atii says. "Dongzhi is the Chinese celebration of the Winter Solstice."

"When is it?" I ask.

"The twenty-third of December."

"*Lillejuleaften,*" I say, remembering the Danish term for the night before Christmas Eve. If I remember correctly, that was a night to be celebrated because all the preparations for Christmas Eve should have been completed, the last presents bought and wrapped, food and last-minute decorations ticked off the list. "That might be something. But I'll call the Chinese as soon as we're done."

"There's one more thing," Atii says with a look at Danielsen. At a nod from him she continues. "The ninth letter of the alphabet is *I*."

I wait as Atii glances at Danielsen.

"The sixteenth letter is *P*," she says.

"I'm listening," I say, as my stomach grows heavy and cold.

"The bands on your fingers," Danielsen says. "I'm sorry, Commissioner, but I was there. I remember."

And so do I.

"That's why I called you. I knew you were still on leave, but…"

"It's okay, Aqqa," I say. "Please, continue."

"The tattoos on your fingers are the same as the dead body from the community centre. The First Minister thinks the sixteenth window has something to do with the referendum, and she might be right, but *P* is the first letter in your name."

"But the second is *E*," Pipaluk says. "The Commissioner's name is *Petra*."

"That's not what Maratse called her," Danielsen says.

He catches my eye and I nod that I'm okay.

"What?"

"David called me *Piitalaat*," I say. "It's the Greenlandic spelling of my name."

"It's just a theory," Danielsen says. "We don't have a lot to work on at the moment."

"But if you're right," I say. "Then it's personal."

"Yes, ma'am."

"Alright." I walk past Danielsen and Atii to the wall. The glare from the screen is warm on my skin as I breathe, slowly, knowing what I have to do. "Ooqi," I say, as I turn around. "Danielsen has chosen you as the tech specialist. Is that right?"

He nods.

"Then I'm giving you permission to open the old files. You'll need a codeword clearance for some of them. Or not," I say and frown at the colour rising in Ooqi's cheeks.

"When I saw the tattooed fingers," Danielsen says, "I asked Ooqi to see what he could find." Danielsen shrugs. "He's pretty good, ma'am."

"That's why he's on the team," I say and smile at Ooqi. His

cheeks flame and I find that despite the personal nature of the task force's theory, I almost feel sorry for him. "I'll be in my office," I say, as I excuse myself.

Pipaluk glares at me as I walk out of the room, and I can still feel her eyes on my back as I enter my office. It must be ten o'clock, I realise, when I see the buttered roll on a plate on my desk. I'm not hungry, but Aron will know if I don't eat. I take a bite and wash it down with a swallow of fresh coffee. I buzz for him to come in as I sit down behind my desk.

"I need to call the Chinese," I say. "What was the name of their security liaison?"

"Tan Yazhu," Aron says. "Yazhu is his first name."

I frown at the nagging thought that the name is new to me.

"He arrived shortly before the funeral," Aron says. "He is the new liaison."

"What happened to the last one?"

"Recalled," Aron says and shrugs. "We never met that one either."

"Well, see if you can put me through to Tan Yazhu. I'll take it here."

I pick up the phone a few seconds later but am distracted by the new position of the folder containing my retirement papers. A quick glance through the glass wall of my office at Aron's desk reveals nothing. Perhaps he looked. Perhaps he didn't. I might ask him later, but the voice on the other end of the line pulls me back into the investigation.

"Tan Yazhu?"

"*Shì.*"

"This is Commissioner Jensen, from Nuuk Police."

"*Shì.*"

He sounds distracted and I wonder if I have caught him in a meeting.

"I'd like to meet with you, as soon as possible."

"We can meet," he says. "But not right now."

"Are you alright?" I ask.

"You say you are police?"

"That's right."

"Then maybe you should come. We have found a body."

"Where are you?"

"Chinatown, of course. Apartment nine…"

I don't hear the rest, and I will have to call him back as I let the phone slip from my ear. It could be a coincidence, but if Atii and Danielsen's theory is to gain traction it needed another number, and a second number nine provides the third letter *I* of my name.

Piitalaat.

"Ma'am?" Aron says, as he enters my office.

"Yes?"

"I've just talked with the Chinese Liaison. Tan Yazhu?"

"Yes."

"He said you were talking, but that you were cut off." Aron walks around the desk and takes the handset gently from my hand. "I've sent a patrol car," he says. "And Danielsen."

"That's good, Aron."

"Are you sure you're alright? You're very pale."

"I'll be fine," I say, as I stand up. "I just need a minute."

I run a basin of cold water in the washroom. The bands on my fingers are refracted as I plunge my hands into the water. I try to lift them to my face, to clear my mind, but they don't move. I don't know how long I have been standing there, but it is Atii's face beside mine in the mirror.

"You've got a lovely tan," I say, as she smiles and smooths my hair from my cheeks.

"Gaba says you should come for dinner."

"That's nice," I say. "Soon. Maybe."

"Are you alright?"

"Yes, of course," I say.

She steps back as I force my hands to my face and wash the tears from my cheeks.

Sisamanngorneq

Thursday, 4th December 2042

Chapter 4

The books weighing down the duvet are not heavy enough and I can't sleep, neither am I alone. I know there is a patrol car parked outside, special duty, something Danielsen arranged with the Deputy Police Commissioner. *He* might be on a course in Copenhagen, but Danielsen must have briefed him and requested the security detail. I think it's an overreaction, of course, but Danielsen is right about the links to my past. I think about this as I dress and leave the apartment, startling the police officer in one of the older Toyota's when I knock on the window.

"Let's go for a ride," I say, as I open the passenger door and settle in beside him. The car is cramped and familiar compared to the new electric models.

"Yes, ma'am." He starts the engine; it coughs and splutters in the cold. "Where to?"

"Downtown."

The tyres squeal in the snow as we pull out of the car park by my apartment in Qinngorput. The air has sunk inside the wheels with the cold and it takes a kilometre to warm it up. The *thud thud thud* of the triangular wheels smooths into a regular rumble by the time we reach the first roundabout.

"What's your name?" I ask.

"Nikolaj Valkyrien," he says.

Valkyrien. The name is familiar, and I try to remember where I have heard it before as we drive past the five-pointed paper Christmas stars lit by soft bulbs in the windows of the apartments – almost every apartment – on the way into town. There are no Northern Lights in the sky tonight, and the cloud is heavy with snow. Nikolaj turns up the heat as we head up Nuuk's main street *Aqqusinersuaq*, past Hotel Hans Egede, now fifty-three years old. *Just three years older than me*, I think. But that wasn't what I was trying to remember.

"Your mother was a police woman?"

"Yes," he says. "In Denmark."

"What is her name?"

"Ada."

"That's right. I remember now."

"Did you meet her?"

"Once. She helped a friend of mine."

Nikolaj says nothing more and I don't pry as we slow by the new housing and office development area overlooking the fjord at the southern tip of the city. The office windows of the Nuuk Media Group are lit and there is activity beneath the bright lights behind the Christmas stars. Nikolaj slows as I point at the car park.

"I'll be about an hour," I say, as I get out of the car.

Nikolaj follows me inside the building, hovering a respectful distance behind me as I sign in with the Âmo Security Guard. The uniform is familiar, and the guard catches me staring at the logo on the patch on his arm.

"It's Âmo, the shaman's familiar," he says, as I frown at the creature in the logo. The head is massive, and the long arms wrap around the company name. "The boss makes sure we know. It's part of the training."

"Your boss?"

"Gaba Alatak."

Of course. I should remember. It's almost as if my memory has been shattered since David's death and I am gathering the pieces, turning and fitting them in my mind each day, rebuilding my memory and clearing my vision. I'm not sure I am fit for duty, not yet. I wonder if I will ever be.

But I do remember the day Gaba saw an opportunity to create a private security company when the government announced that the first Chinese workers would be arriving within the year. Fourteen years ago. Gaba left the police a few months later, took out a loan and started recruitment for Greenland Private Security. I had forgotten when and why he had changed the name – something about being more Greenlandic, perhaps. I would have to ask him the next time we saw each other.

"Is Qitu Kalia in the building?" I ask.

"He's in his office. They're putting the paper to bed," he says. "Digitally. Qitu never leaves until all the top stories are ready." The guard grinned. "He sleeps here a lot."

"Can you let him know I'm on my way up?"

The guard nods and waves us through the security entrance. It must be Nikolaj's first time at Nuuk Media Group and I watch as he admires the thick glass, cameras and heavy locking mechanisms on the inner door.

"Qitu has a reputation for exposing powerful people and underground movements," I say, as the guard buzzes us into the building. "Is this your first time in Nuuk?"

"My first time in Greenland," Nikolaj says. "I'm covering someone's maternity leave."

"Right," I say, as I wonder who it might be. I really have lost touch, although, to be fair, the department is twice the size it once was when I was a Sergeant.

Qitu meets us outside the elevator. His hug is tight like the arms of the shaman's familiar, protective and sincere. I step back when he lets go so that he can read my lips – he stopped using hearing aids a long time ago. *That* I do remember.

"You're busy," I say, and gesture at the journalists hunched over their desks.

"We're working on *The Calendar Man*," he says. "It's big news, Petra."

"I wish it wasn't." I can feel my brow knitting. "How do you know it's a man?"

"It's an educated guess. We don't have all the answers, just a lot of questions. But that's why you're here."

I nod and gesture towards his office. "Can we talk?"

"Sure."

"I'll be a little while," I say to Nikolaj. "I'll find you in the canteen when I'm done."

I wait for Nikolaj to nod, pointing him in the direction of the canteen before following Qitu to his office. I realise now why he chooses not to wear his hearing aids, even with computers and soft keypads, the noise and chatter between the desks is overwhelming. I relax once we are inside his office. The door closes with a soft hermetic sigh. Qitu pours coffee and we sit in the comfy chairs around a small table in the corner of his office, a few metres from the clutter of his desk.

"You've seen the similarities," I say, choosing to launch straight into the details of the case I wish didn't exist.

"Your tattoos," Qitu says, as he glances at my fingers.

"And the calendar windows," I say. "The three dates match the letters of my name."

"Three?"

"Three numbers." I pause for a moment as I consider my history with Qitu, and how much I should reveal at this moment. I trust him, I realise, and then the decision is made. "There was a body found in Chinatown last night. No calendar, but the apartment number was number nine. Danielsen found fake snow sprayed around the number, dashed with the victim's blood." Qitu reaches for the notepad on the table and I stop him with a shake of my head. "Please, let us release a statement first," I say.

"Okay," he says. "And the third number would be?"

"Another *I*. So, now we have *PII*."

"Piitalaat," he says, and for a second, I think it is David's voice. They both have such soft voices.

"It's a theory. And that's why I'm here, Qitu. Who would know about me? I don't remember you writing about me in your article."

"I never mentioned you," he says.

"And the man who did this is dead," I say, as I look at my palms. "*Aap.*"

"Pipaluk thinks it's a scare tactic, to keep people indoors and stop them voting on the sixteenth. What do you think?"

"I think she could be right, but…"

"Qitu?"

"If your theory is right."

"Danielsen and Atii's theory," I say.

"If they are right, then it could have more to do with you, and maybe Maratse."

"David is gone. This can't have anything to do with him. And the scare tactics seem plausible. What we don't yet know is the identity of the victims. The young man with the banded fingers has yet to be identified, and the charred body of the small person – perhaps a dwarf – is proving difficult. They are looking at dental records, but you know the history of dentistry in Greenland. They still have problems recruiting dentists in the smaller towns and settlements. We might never find any records."

"And the third victim?"

"Chinese. We're waiting to hear more. But then, if we ignore the number on the door, there doesn't seem to be any connection. Although, we know that nine is a lucky number in China."

"Not for the victim," Qitu says.

"No. I suppose not."

The coffee is cooling in the mug and I force myself to take a sip as my mind whirls with possible links and connections.

"I have another number for you," Qitu says with a smile.

"What's that?"

"Today is December the 4th. It's the one hundred and eleventh anniversary of the first screening of Boris Karloff's *Frankenstein*. They're showing it tonight at the cinema. We should go."

"A horror movie?"

"From the 1930s, Petra." Qitu laughs. "You need a distraction, and it's science fiction. David would have gone."

"He read books, Qitu. He didn't watch movies."

"Only because he didn't have a television. Come with me. It will be good to get out."

"I am out," I say.

"Before breakfast. It doesn't mean you are *out*, it just means you can't sleep. Why don't you call in sick? Go home and rest. I'll pick you up later."

"I'm the Commissioner, Qitu. I can't call in sick."

"You're still on compassionate leave. Aren't you?"

"You've been talking to Danielsen."

"*Aap*. And he tells me he has a task force now. Take the day. I will pick you up, and we can watch the movie."

"I'm not sure, Qitu. A horror movie?"

"It's a classic. Lots of overacting. I'll buy the popcorn."

"Popcorn?"

"Definitely."

"Fine," I say. "But we will need three tickets." I nod in the direction of the canteen. "I have a chaperone. Danielsen's orders."

I think about cancelling at least three times during the day, but Qitu has conveniently turned his phone off. I give up, and concentrate on relaxing, showering, and tugging on a pair of jeans and a baggy sweater. Nikolaj is in plain clothes when I meet him at the door, just as Qitu arrives in his Tesla SUV.

The cinema is almost empty, but Qitu spots someone he thinks I should meet as we carry our popcorn from the counter to our seats.

"This is Geert Aalders," he says in English, as he introduces me to a short man with a finely-trimmed beard. "He was the one who told me about this special screening of *Frankenstein*."

"It's just possible I gave the cinema manager a tip, in the hope he might show one of my favourite films," Geert says. "It's far too festive for my liking."

"You don't like Christmas?" I ask.

"I think it's possible to overdose." He laughs. "However, tomorrow is *Sinterklaas*. I'm excited about that."

"You're Dutch?"

"You didn't guess?" Geert smiles. "It's alright; there are lots of foreigners in Nuuk these days. But some of us live here now. I am assistant to the Jonkheer, Coenraad Kuijpers. I think your Sergeant has scheduled a meeting for tomorrow morning." He leans closer for a second and lowers his voice. "We're quite concerned about the murders."

"I meant to call yesterday," I say. "But something came up."

"Yes," he says. "We heard about the body in Chinatown."

"Come on," Qitu says. "Let's find our seats, enjoy the movie."

I watch as the monster is winched up into the electrical storm and lowered again to the laboratory floor. The doctor's passion is alarming, and I wonder what David would have thought about it. I see that Nikolaj is watching me, while Qitu and his Dutch friend are mesmerised by the black and white drama playing out on the screen.

"Do you want to go, ma'am?" Nikolaj says.

I nod and follow him out of the cinema. Reanimation is perhaps too strong a subject for someone who has just buried a loved one, and the young constable recognised what the film buffs did not.

"Thank you," I say.

I am about to suggest coffee in the café while we wait for Qitu, but my mobile buzzes in my pocket and I recognise Danielsen's number.

"Aqqa," I say, as I answer it.

"Where are you?"

"With Frankenstein's monster." I laugh.

"Then you know?" he says.

The undertone in his voice suggests I have made an inappropriate joke.

"Know what?"

"We had a call from the morgue. Someone has taken parts of the victim's bodies."

Tallimanngorneq

Friday, 5th December 2042

Chapter 5

"I want more officers on the street," Pipaluk says, as she walks into my office. "And I want you to put a muzzle on Qitu Kalia." She snaps the paper edition of *Oqaasaq*, the Nuuk Media Group's expensive and limited print edition of its online newspaper. I think the Lapland rosebay flower logo is pretty, and a perfect choice for a newspaper that investigates important issues concerning Greenland and its people. Of course, there are times when I wish it didn't; now being one of them.

"I can't spare any more officers."

"Give them overtime."

"On what budget?"

"Yours, of course," she says.

"That's a problem," I say. "Until Greenland is officially independent of Denmark, the Police will continue to fall under Danish administration. The budget is decided in Denmark…"

"Based on your recommendations."

"Yes, to a degree."

"Surely you can demand more money when situations demand more resources?"

"If it was only about the money," I say. "But I only have so many officers. They can't work twenty-four-hour shifts. Most of them have families. And there are a lot of married couples within the department." I stand up and knock on the window, cupping an imaginary mug of coffee to my lips when Aron looks up from his desk. "First Minister," I say, and gesture to one of the chairs around the table. "Perhaps we can find another solution."

"Body parts were removed from the morgue, Commissioner," she says, as she sits down. "I want a police officer on the door to the morgue."

"There are better things – more urgent things – for a police officer to do than guard the morgue," I say. "Besides, the hospital should have a security budget. They could use Gaba's company."

"Âmo? We have them in the parliament building."

"Exactly. Now, if you were to suggest to the hospital administration that they beef up their security, perhaps we can avoid another incident like this one."

"And Qitu? According to his paper, The Calendar Man is

building Frankenstein's monster."

It is a sensational headline, and a far cry from Nuuk Media Group's investigative background.

"It sells papers and subscriptions," I say.

"And frightens people off the street."

Pipaluk waits as Aron places coffee and buttered rolls on the table. It must be ten o'clock, already. I take a roll as Pipaluk adds milk and sugar to her coffee.

"I share your concern, First Minister, but I can't spare any more officers. I simply don't have them, even if I could pay them. But, if you're concerned…"

"Aren't you?"

"Yes, of course. I'm just saying that you could talk to Gaba, and maybe find the resources to put his security guards in key places. It would make the people feel safer. In the meantime, I can increase the frequency of patrols, and make the police officers I have more visible."

"You should have done that already."

She's right. Perhaps I would have if I was thinking straight.

"It's only been four days," I say. "We are reacting, and already have a task force in place. There's only so much we can do, until we catch a break, as they say."

I relax as Pipaluk's shoulders sag and she leans back in her chair. Aron appears at the door and I wave him in.

"The Jonkheer has arrived," he says.

"Would you like to sit in on the meeting, First Minister?" I say.

"You're going to talk about security?"

"I'm sure that's his main focus, yes."

"Then I'll stay."

"More coffee, Aron," I say, as I stand up to greet the Jonkheer of Little Amsterdam.

I recognise Geert Aalders as he walks behind the taller and better dressed Jonkheer. Coenraad Kuijpers is older than me, but not yet sixty. He is taller than most of the Greenlanders I know, with the exception of Gaba. The Jonkheer's handshake is firm, warm and dry. *A little too dry*, I think, as I notice the pink rash of eczema on his knuckles.

"It's the cold," he says, when he sees me look at his hands.

"You'll get used to it."

"I suppose we will." He steps to one side to let Geert into the office. "You've met my assistant?"

"Yes, last night," I say. "Shall we sit at the table?"

I wait as Pipaluk stands up to shake the hands of the Dutchmen and Aron brings more coffee. Geert is the first to sit. He pulls a small tablet out of his pocket and opens a new page for notes.

"Do we say Merry Christmas?" I ask.

"Ah, *Sinterklaas*," the Jonkheer says and smiles. "I'm impressed."

"Don't be. Geert mentioned it last night. I imagine that's why you want to meet today."

"Yes, we're concerned about the situation. This *Calendar Man*, it's not pleasant and we are worried." He pours a cup of coffee. "There are roughly three thousand Dutch citizens in Mitsimmavik, or *Little Amsterdam* as you call it. We have a small local constabulary, as approved under the initial agreement with your government," he says and looks at Pipaluk, "and brokered with Anna Riis from the Danish government. I think we have ten officers in total."

"Eight," Geert says. "Two of them are away on training at the moment in the Netherlands."

"So, not many," the Jonkheer says. I believe the Chinese have their own security measures. Is that right?"

"Yes," I say. "Although, their numbers are more fluid as they change with the number of workers they have at any one time. I think they have thirty security personnel at the mine, and fifteen in Chinatown."

"*Chinatown*," he says.

His eyes glitter in the light and I decide that I like this Jonkheer better than the first one.

"Greenland is a big country," I say, "but we have very few people. When the city expanded, and we got our own Chinatown and Little Amsterdam, it made Nuuk feel like New York."

"Just colder," he says.

"Yes."

I notice that Pipaluk has little to say, and I wonder if I have missed something. She seems to struggle to look at the Jonkheer and avoids looking at Geert altogether. I should remember the details about the agreement, but like a lot of things since David's death, I have a lot of pieces of the puzzle, but need to put them back together again to make sense of them. It feels like the ice forming on the sea, small plates and pancakes fusing as the water temperature drops, drifting apart with the warmer winds, and then merging and freezing to create a solid, tangible whole. At least, that was how it once was further north when we lived in Inussuk, but now the ice is less certain. Climate change hasn't just affected the Dutch, the whole world has had to adapt to changing environments, new threats and new opportunities.

"We have a small celebration this evening, in the administration building," the Jonkheer says. "We want our people – all the people in Nuuk – to feel safe, and I want to ask if you will be increasing your patrols this evening?"

I struggle for a moment to remember what we did last year, and the Jonkheer sees it.

"Last year was different," he says.

"Yes, it was."

"Perhaps you can send a couple of officers to the celebration. It will be entertaining for them and reassuring for us."

"And a few extra patrols during the night," Geert says. "It would be useful to know where they will be and at what time so that we can coordinate with our own constabulary."

I glance at Pipaluk, anticipating her reaction when I agree to double the patrols in Little Amsterdam tonight, but she excuses herself to answer a call on her mobile.

"I'll have my watch officer contact your constabulary," I say.

"*Hartelijk bedankt*," the Jonkheer says, and I can see that he means it. "And perhaps you will come too? It will be a very pleasant evening, I am sure."

"Of course," I say.

I think of Nikolaj as the Dutch prepare to leave, and hope that he is sleeping as it seems we are going out again this evening.

"If there is anything we can do to help," the Jonkheer says, as he steps into the corridor. "You only have to ask."

"And I will," I say.

I watch them leave and then sit down at my desk. Aron clears away the coffee and rolls. He hovers at the door, hands full of plates and cups, and an apologetic look on his face.

"Aron?"

"I just wanted to say I'm sorry."

"About what?"

"I thought it was something that I needed to file," he says. He nods at the folder on my desk. "I haven't told anyone."

"And I haven't signed it yet," I say.

"It's not my place, ma'am, but I would hate to see you go."

"I appreciate that, Aron. Thank you."

His cheeks regain some of their colour and I smile again.

"There's something else, isn't there," I say, as he seems reluctant to leave.

"There's a man outside. I said you were busy, but he said he would wait. I couldn't get rid of him."

"You tried?"

"He's pretty big for a Greenlander."

I only know one *big* Greenlander, tall, powerful, confident and arrogant. Aron couldn't know that the big Greenlander waiting to see me is an ex-cop and an ex-lover.

"Send him in," I say, as I try to not to smile.

The cups rattle in Aron's hands as he calls to the man.

"Do you want me to stay?" he asks.

The cups rattle for a second time in tune to the heavy footfalls landing on the floor of the corridor outside my office.

"If you think it's best," I say, and then I laugh as Aron shrinks against the door to make room for Gaba Alatak. The image is priceless, and my cheeks ache as he enters the room.

"Gaba," I say, as I walk around my desk and wrap my arms around him. He hugs back, resting his head on top of mine. I can feel the muscles barely contained inside the sleeves of his jacket, and I hear the muffled rattle of cups as Aron leaves the office and closes the door.

"He's new," Gaba says.

"And very young," I say, as I press my hand on Gaba's cheek, smiling at the white stubble outnumbering the black. "I'm pleased you came."

"Atii said you were back at work. I would have come sooner, but I've been busy, and the boys are..."

"Gorgeous. I've seen pictures."

"I was going to say frustrating. Miki has just discovered girls. He's never home."

"Were you any different?"

"Probably not." Gaba pulls out a chair and sits at the table. "You disappeared after the funeral."

"I know," I say, as I sit down. "I met a woman at the funeral. David helped her when she was a child. I kind of moved in with them for a few days. Silly really, but I felt closer to him when I was with them."

"It's not silly if it makes you feel better."

"I could have called," I say.

"You don't have to do anything. Only when you're ready. I'm surprised you're back so early. It's The Calendar Man, isn't it? Atii told me about…"

"The tattoos?"

"And her theory." Gaba taps the table with a thick knuckle. "What are you doing about protection?"

"I've got Nikolaj."

"Who's he? Do I know him?"

"He's a constable from Denmark. Danielsen arranged it."

"Where is he now?" Gaba says and makes a display of turning his thick bald head to scan the room. "I don't see him, Petra."

"He's sleeping, probably. He's been sitting in a patrol car outside my apartment the last two nights."

"Not good enough."

"Gaba," I say and reach for his hand. "You're sweet. You always have been, but it's not your job to protect me. It wasn't then, and it isn't now."

He grips my hand and looks away. I squeeze his fingers as he starts to tremble.

"I almost lost you once," he says. "It won't happen again." He looks at me and I can see the energy in his eyes, can almost feel the heat. "I can't let it happen again. I promised Maratse."

"I know."

Gaba lets go of my hand and pushes his chair back. "Eat with us tonight," he says, as he stands up. "Bring this Nikolaj."

"So, you can vet him?"

"Sure," he says.

"You're impossible."

"*Aap*. That's my job. Speaking of which," he says and looks at his watch. "I have a meeting with the First Minister."

"Well, you'd better go," I say. "But I can't come tonight. I've been invited to *Sinterklaas* in Little Amsterdam. It's a Christmas celebration," I say, as Gaba frowns.

"Lots of people? I don't like it."

"You don't have to like it. I'm going, and I have Nikolaj with me, plus the extra patrols we're adding to the night shift."

I stand up to give Gaba a last hug, only to pause when Danielsen appears at the door. He is out of breath, and I wonder if it is the stairs or the reason he needs to see me. I realise it could be both.

"Gaba," he says, with a nod. "I need to speak to the Commissioner."

"I was just leaving," Gaba says. He squeezes my hand as he leaves.

"What is it, Aqqa?"

"*Sinterklaas* has been cancelled," he says.

"That was fast. Why?"

"They found the missing body parts," Danielsen says and takes a breath. "They were stitched to a fourth body and left on a chair inside the Dutch administration building. Atii is there now. I came to tell you."

"Alright," I say. "Let's go."

"*Naamik*," he says shakes his head. "I've called Nikolaj. You're going home."

I almost laugh, but I can see that he is serious.

"I don't think you can make that decision, Sergeant."

"Probably not, but, officially, you are on compassionate leave until Monday. The Deputy Commissioner gave me explicit instructions to make sure you stay at home this weekend."

"Aqqa, are you putting me under house arrest?"

"If I have to, ma'am," he says.

Arfininngorneq

Saturday, 6th December 2042

Sinterklaas

Chapter 6

Danielsen said nothing about finding an advent calendar on the Frankenstein victim and it bothers me as I lie under one half of the duvet and pretend that the weight of the books tugging the other half is David. I should get up, and my curiosity about the case finally pulls me out of bed and I put on a pot of coffee. It is dark outside. It won't be light before mid-morning, and I can see Nikolaj's patrol car pulling out of the parking area. He stops beside the day shift and I get a sudden shiver of guilt as I realise I didn't think about Nikolaj sitting in the cold through the night. His relief has one of the new SUVs and I wonder if it is warmer than the older Toyota.

I carry my coffee to my desk and open the computer with a few curt voice commands, followed by an iris-check to access the secure department server. I open the task force folder and decide to start with the first victim, the one linked with my own past. The notes attached to the file indicate that he is still unidentified. I fetch more coffee from the kitchen, pull thick woollen socks over my feet, and David's old police jacket around my shoulders. There is a faint smell of fish and dog from the jacket as I work my way through the first victim's file.

I concentrate on the bands between the joints of the victim's fingers. They are like my own, but the ink is lighter, or perhaps it is the contrast in the photograph. I press my nose into the shoulder of David's jacket, drawing in the strength to dig deep and recall what I know of the bands on my fingers. I can see that Ooqi has merged my file with the first victim's and I nod at the highlighted reference to the *loyalty card* as each band represented an act, and once the fingers were full of bands the person was rewarded. In my case and the case of a young man called Salik Erngsen from Uummannaq in the north, freedom was the promised reward. I was rescued. Salik was murdered. But we were both freed, from *him*. As far as I knew, I was the only survivor.

The man's fingers provide a link that suggests someone knows what happened to Salik and me twenty-four years ago. Alternatively, the young man found dead outside the community centre has links to my past, but the killer doesn't. the computer mistakes my sigh of frustration as a command, and I have to scroll back down the page to Atii's follow-up notes and an additional photograph. The young man's lower left leg and foot, together with his right forearm have been removed. There is a second photograph of a bloody bone saw on the metal gurney beside the victim. I look at my arm and my leg and wonder if the thief carried them off in a sports bag, a backpack or a shopping bag. An additional note from Atii spoils any hope of finding out if the thief was caught on camera – the firmware for the security cameras was being updated on the night of the 4th December.

Now, is that a coincidence? Is it convenient, or was it contrived? Either way the thief or the killer, likely one and the same, had access to the security system, or knowledge of the update. A quick check of Atii's notes confirms that she has considered the same thing and a profile of the so-called *Calendar Man* is emerging.

He or she works in hospital security, works for the security contractors, or knows someone who has access to the camera systems.

And, it's possible, I think, *that he knows about me.*

Another note reveals that the contractor for the cameras is based in Nuuk and that Atii has pinned a meeting in her activity log.

"Why didn't she send Ooqi? He's the tech guy." I wonder, and the computer beeps and flashes a window that suggests I rephrase the question. "Never mind," I say, and take a sip of coffee. A text message scrolls across the screen as I swallow.

CAN I HELP YOU, MA'AM?

"Ooqi?"

AAP.

There are four victims and I only really know about the first and the second, and only a little at that. I wonder if Ooqi knows any more.

"What do we know about the body in Chinatown?"

MALE. NAME: HUANG FEN. MINER. FORTY-THREE. FAMILY IN CHINA.

"Any record of any kind?"

GAMBLING. REGULAR CLIENT AT MINING PLEASURE HOUSE.

That's right; the Chinese workers rotating through Nuuk and the mine include administration and logistical staff, miners and entertainment specialists – also called whores. The only Greenlanders employed at the mine are cleaners and one translator.

"But no criminal activity?"

NONE.

"What does Tan Yazhu say?"

THE BODY HAS BEEN PROCESSED, READY FOR RETURN TO CHINA.

"But no motive for the killing?"

POSSIBLE GAMBLING DEBT. HE IS INVESTIGATING.

"He doesn't think it is related to our investigation?"

HE HAS NOT SAID SO.

David's jacket slips from my shoulders as I reach for the coffee pot. I fill my mug halfway, pausing as another message from Ooqi appears on the screen.

DANIELSEN IS CHECKING IF CHINESE BODY IS MISSING PARTS.

"Okay."

ATII IS MEETING WITH CONTRACTOR.

"Good. What about you?"

There is a pause and I put the coffee pot down on the desk.

DO YOU REALLY WANT TO KNOW?

This is one of those moments when I realise that the quiet ones on the team are often the most dangerous, or the ones most likely to create problems, if not handled correctly. I should shut down the link, or visit the station, but Ooqi short-circuits my procrastination with a new window of text. It reads like a passage of Latin before the letters rearrange into something that could be very old English, before settling into Danish.

LOTS OF ACTIVITY FROM JONKHEER'S OFFICE COMPUTER. I AM MONITORING. SAY "OK" IF I SHOULD PROCEED.

"Okay," I say, before I can talk myself out of it.

The window dissolves into the screen and Ooqi's activity icon flashes to inform me he is AFK. I press the hint button on the screen and discover that it means he is *away from keyboard*. I just don't think it is likely and imagine him pulling out a second keyboard or working on another terminal or whatever he uses when he doesn't want to be traced. I decide that, given the circumstances, it is important to gather as much information as fast as possible. Whatever lead Ooqi is following, I trust him to be discreet. In the meantime, I could use a break.

I can feel a familiar sadness settling on my shoulders and I need to get out of the apartment. I call Iiluuna and smile as Quaa answers her mother's mobile.

"What are you doing today?" I ask.

"We're going to the Christmas Market."

It sounds like a good idea, and I arrange to meet them there as soon as Iiluuna joins the call. The sky is brightening, and I think I can see the sun as I finish the call and start to dress. Danielsen has provided me with a security detail and I think it is time to use him. I lock my apartment and take the stairs to the parking area. I wave to the police officer as I approach the patrol car, pausing at the passenger door as I notice a car parked with the engine running just a few cars away. The two men inside watch me as I climb into the passenger seat of the patrol car. They pull out of the parking space and follow us as we drive down the hill.

The officer assigned to me today is a young woman, and I am pleased that I remember her name.

"Natuk," I say, as she slows for the roundabout, "are we being followed?"

She looks in the rear-view mirror as she accelerates onto the road leading into town. She says nothing for a few moments, and then nods, just once.

"I think so," she says. "Do you want me to stop and find out?"

Even in the new Nuuk, with its expanded road system and new housing areas and communities, there is still very little road compared to towns and cities of a similar size in the rest of the world. To follow someone discreetly on vacant streets is an art form. The men in the car behind us are not artists, and when Natuk slows to a stop, snow crunching beneath the SUVs tyres, the men behind us stop too. The dilemma then is what to do next.

"I'll call for back-up," Natuk says, and reaches for her radio.

"No," I say. "Take me to the market. We have extra patrols there, today. I don't want us to pull any unit away from their assigned duties."

"But Danielsen said…"

"Yes, Natuk, I'm sure he told you to respectfully ignore my commands if my personal safety was at risk. But I am with you, inside a fast car, and they haven't broken the law yet. Let's keep going and see what happens."

"I'm not sure."

"Then call it in and tell the station where we are going."

I say nothing more until Natuk has talked with the duty officer back at the station, and we have pulled out into the road. The car behind us follows; matching our speed and parking close by when we enter the parking area of the old sports hall. I tell Natuk to relax as we leave the car and walk past the first market stalls inside. I smile as I remember that this was one of David's favourite places in Nuuk. The craft stalls with grotesque figures – *Tupilaq* carved from whalebone, and knives with ivory handles, brought the hunting culture of Greenland to the capital, as did the narwhal curry and sealskin furs. It wasn't quite the same, he would say, but we spent hours each Christmas at the market, haggling about prices with hunters and artists, sampling everything there was to eat, and quietly doing the rounds of the different stalls as David and I remembered the north, and our time in the settlement of Inussuk.

I let Natuk keep an eye on the men following us as I look for Iiluuna and Quaa. I feel safe around so many people, and I smile at the police officers in each corner of the sports hall. And then I feel Quaa's warm hand tickle my own, and she pulls me over to a stall to find her mother.

"This is Natuk," I say when I see the frown on Iiluuna's brow. "She is spending the day with me."

I smile again as Iiluuna wonders why Natuk is with me and then I feel a hand grip me by the arm. Stronger than Quaa's, I realise it is Natuk and she pulls me through the crowds, away from Iiluuna and towards the police officers close to the entrance.

"Reports are coming in of Calendar Man sightings in the city. We have to go," she says with a nod to the men following us. "The police in the market will stop them, and we'll go back to your apartment."

"That's not what I want to do," I say, but it is no good. I can feel Natuk's urgency through her fingers gripping my arm. I look around and try to catch Iiluuna's eye to say sorry, or Quaa's to reassure her that everything is alright, but Natuk pulls me into the cold Nuuk air, and a few seconds later we are in the car.

"They're going to stop them," she says, as she accelerates onto the road back to Qinngorput and my apartment. "Nikolaj will meet us at your apartment."

"Nikolaj? Didn't he have the night shift?"

"He's working overtime," she says. "We all are."

"Because of me?"

"Because of The Calendar Man."

It is confirmed then. Once my own officers start to use the media's name for the killer, he or *she* has become a legend, and the curse of Christmas.

Natuk turns up the volume of her radio as reports of suspicious activity at the market, and at other locations in the centre of Nuuk compete for space on the airwaves. It appears that a manhunt is underway as Natuk speeds me back to my apartment.

"This is ridiculous, Natuk. I am the Commissioner."

"Yes, ma'am."

She says nothing more until I am inside my apartment.

"Please lock the door, ma'am. Nikolaj will be here soon."

I am prisoner in my own apartment, while The Calendar Man has the run of the city.

Sapaat

Sunday, 7th December 2042

Chapter 7

I don't know how much of it is my fault, but I am starting to feel mollycoddled. Danielsen has effectively locked me in my apartment until my compassionate leave is officially over. Meanwhile, my police officers are racing back and forth across the city chasing a killer. They've been at it all night, and, according to the reports I can hear on Nikolaj's radio, they have found nothing. They might as well be chasing a ghost.

It's going to be okay, Piitalaat.

"No, David, it's not. If I'm stuck here I can't do anything. Can I? And you know how that feels."

"Ma'am?" Nikolaj asks, as he taps my bedroom door with his knuckle. "Are you alright?"

"I thought you were asleep on the couch?"

"I heard voices."

"It's just me, arguing with a ghost."

"Ma'am?"

"Don't worry about it. I'll get up and make breakfast soon."

"Okay," he says, and I hear him drift back to the lounge, together with the frustrated radio chatter.

I wait a moment to hear if David has more to say and then pick up my phone and log in to the police server. There are no new updates, and the task force activity icons show that Danielsen and Atii have, finally, gone home. There's no sign or record of Ooqi's activity, but I know he is there.

"Ooqi?"

A new window loads onto the screen, together with the false text. This time it is a passage from the bible that rearranges itself into a text from a popular novel before Ooqi's message appears and I lower my voice to a whisper.

"Anything new?"

AAP.

"Okay. Tell me."

LOTS OF EMAILS FROM THE JONKHEER TO THE DANISH OMBUDSMAN.

"Anna Riis?"

AAP. JONKHEER IS CONCERNED ABOUT REFERENDUM. WANTS ASSURANCES.

"What kind?"

WANTS TO KNOW IF CURRENT ECONOMICAL AGREEMENT WILL BE SAME UNDER GREENLANDIC RULE.

I think back to the meeting in my office and recall that the First Minister struggled to look the Jonkheer in the eye. I remember Pipaluk Uutaaq receiving lots of praise for her negotiations, and that the Dutch rental payments for the land outside Nuuk would be a significant contribution to the Greenlandic economy. In a curious twist of fate, Greenland's most valuable resource is not the minerals buried beneath the land but the land itself. Of course, no-one knows the details of the negotiation, nor the actual sum to be paid by the Dutch.

SOME CONCERN ABOUT RELATIONS, TOO.

"Explain."

CULTURAL DIFFERENCES. RACISM. WHAT HAPPENS IF DANES LEAVE.

It must be difficult for the Dutch. The Greenland colony is just an experiment, a toehold for the people of Holland, as their own country is threatened by the rising water levels that no dike can withstand. The world is warming, and the sea ice is melting, but it doesn't change the fact that Greenland is located at a much higher latitude than the Dutch are used to. The warmer climate has brought more snow, and the hours of light have not changed. It is just as dark as it ever was each winter, just as light in the summer. And then there is the language and the spontaneous nature of the Greenlanders that befuddled the Danes long before it confused the Dutch. I smile at the thought, as a new message from Ooqi flashes onto the screen.

NO MENTION OF CALENDAR MAN OR FRANKENSTEIN BODY.

Now that is curious, and I try to picture the Jonkheer, in his trim suit, and his warm hands, slightly chapped. He was concerned when we met, and the whole purpose of the meeting was, as I understood it, to request additional security at the *Sinterklaas* celebration. Perhaps it would be useful if Ooqi could look at the Dutch constabulary's communications.

THEY HAVE ARRANGED TO MEET TONIGHT.

"Okay," I say. "What about other mails and correspondence?"

YOU WANT ME TO LOOK AT THE CONSTABULARY?

"Haven't you already?"

There is a long pause and I wonder if Ooqi is hacking into the constabulary's server as I speak, and, if he hadn't before, did I just order him to do it? I'd like to blame it on Danielsen, to say that I was forced to seek alternative sources of information when my own police department kept me out of the loop. But I realise they haven't, there is just very little to report. Besides, whether Ooqi had already hacked into their server, or if it he was doing it for the first time, both were just as illegal, and whether I ordered it or not was immaterial. Maybe I wouldn't have to retire after all? Perhaps matters would be taken out of my hands and I would be dismissed, as soon as Ooqi and I were exposed.

"I trust you, Ooqi," I whispered.

AH, MAYBE YOU SHOULDN'T.

It occurs to me that I have yet to hear his voice, and that, online at least, the shy police technician is quietly confident.

VICTIM: BENJAMIN DE KLOET. FIFTY-THREE. NO RECORD. MISSING FOLLOWING LIMBS: LEFT LEG AND FOOT. RIGHT FOOT. RIGHT FOREARM. LEFT HAND. CONSTABULARY INVESTIGATION ONGOING. SEARCH FOR MISSING LIMBS ONGOING.

"And the other body parts? Stitched to the body found in the Dutch administration building?"

CHARRED RIGHT FOOT. CHARRED LEFT HAND. TAKEN FROM BURNED BODY AT MORGUE.

"From Kong Frederik's Hospital."

AAP.

The window on the screen flickers with another cycling of fresh text before Ooqi returns.

SHALL I KEEP DIGGING?

"Yes," I say, and log out of the server.

I might still be grieving and locked up, but I intend to get back into the game. After all, the First Minister made a personal request for me to take responsibility for the investigation. By midnight tonight I will be officially back on duty, and despite his best intentions, Danielsen or my deputy police commissioner, won't be able to do anything about it. But I need to be prepared, and I need more information.

Nikolaj averts his eyes as I pad out of my bedroom in my

pyjamas, but I have no time for his subordinate sensibilities, we have work to do.

"What were Danielsen's latest instructions?" I ask.

"Regarding you, ma'am?"

"Yes."

"I was to remain here and accompany you to work tomorrow morning."

"And I'm not allowed to leave my apartment?"

"Not without sufficient back-up," he says.

"Even shopping?"

"Not without back-up."

"Okay," I say, as I walk to the window.

The roof of the apartment block opposite steams in the midday sun, and the ravens spread their wings in the warm air. It is still chilly on the street, and I can see breath condensing on the windscreen of the car parked to the right of Nikolaj's patrol car. It is difficult to see the men's faces, but there are two of them, like before, but whereas the last two were of equal height, one of these men is significantly shorter than the other.

"Back-up you say?"

"Yes, ma'am."

I grab my phone from the bedroom and walk to the kitchen window, dialling as I stare at the car. I watch as the taller of the two men pulls a mobile out of his pocket and presses it to his ear.

"Brunch in ten minutes," I say. "And bring your friend."

I wave and end the call, smiling at the sigh I caught on the other end of the line as Gaba Alatak answered the call.

"Ma'am?" Nikolaj asks, as he hovers in the kitchen.

"Eggs in the fridge. Bacon and baguettes in the freezer," I say. "I'm going for a shower."

The pressure in the shower is good. Another reason we didn't move. The water drums on my body and I almost don't hear him.

Piitalaat.

"Yes, David?"

Having fun?

"I'm about to."

Be careful.

"You know I will." I smile as a thought occurs to me. "Past, Present or Future?"

What?

"Which ghost are you? Christmas Past, Present or…"

Just David.

We leave it at that and I turn off the shower as Nikolaj answers the door. When I step outside Gaba is making coffee as Nikolaj finishes the eggs. There is a bemused Greenlander in the hall, and I brush past him to change in my room. He is still there when I come out again, but this time he is holding a bacon and egg baguette in one hand, and a mug of coffee in the other. I smile and walk into the kitchen.

"What about yesterday?" I ask Gaba as he pours me a coffee. "Were they your men?"

"*Aap.*"

"You couldn't have told me?"

"I thought about it."

"You pushed my security detail into overdrive," I say. "Nikolaj was pulled in to do an extra shift."

"And my men spent the night outside your apartment," Gaba says, as he sits down; the chair creaks beneath his muscled frame. But he looks tired and I wonder when he started the morning shift.

"If I'd known," I say.

"You would have called and told me to send the men home."

"Yes."

"I'm not going to do that, Petra."

"But this isn't about me; it's about Nuuk, or the referendum. You're wasting resources."

"The men are getting paid."

"And you?"

Gaba gives me the look that he often wore as a police Sergeant, the one that doesn't invite any further comment.

"Fine," I say. "But I'm going nuts here. I've even started talking to David."

Gaba's look softens beneath his frown, the one that threatens to wrinkle his bald head.

"Stop that," I say. "It's just a calming device I'm sure. Nothing to get worried about."

"If you say so."

"I do, and once you're all finished with brunch, we're going out."

"Danielsen said…"

"Nikolaj," I say, as he protests. I point at Gaba. "Let me introduce you to Greenland's former head of the Special Response Unit, Gaba Alatak. If he isn't back-up, I don't know what is."

"But he's not on the force."

"No, he's not."

"And not armed."

"Nikolaj," Gaba says.

"Yes?"

"Constable?"

"That's right."

"This is your first time in Greenland?"

"Yes."

"Then you have a lot to learn. We might have tightened up on gun control over the past few years, but you can still buy a pump-action shotgun over the counter at the supermarket. Without a hunting licence. Don't make the mistake of thinking we're not armed. In Greenland, in the city, the towns and the settlements, you're never more than a few metres from a gun. Remember that."

"Alright, stop scaring him, Gaba," I say. "We're going out."

"Where?"

"The morgue, the supermarket, and then Little Amsterdam."

"The supermarket?"

"Yes, we're going to need supplies for the stake-out."

It feels good to be doing something. To be talking charge again. Catching the doctor off guard at the morgue was a bonus. I let him talk us through the bodies, pre-mutilation, while Gaba's man waits outside the door. There is something familiar about the face of the young man, and it has nothing to do with the tattoos on his fingers. I take a long breath and feel Gaba's reassuring grip on my arm. I lean against his body as I breathe out.

"And the age of the burned body?" I ask. "Any ideas?"

"I'm not a forensic dentist," the doctor says, "but I can say that it was a woman, in her twenties. The number of cavities in her teeth is typical for Greenlanders living outside of the city, and those who can't afford private dental care. She was short for her age. She was not a child."

"Have you seen the Chinese body?"

"Haven't seen it. Haven't been asked," he says. "I'm not

surprised. It's rare that they involve us in any medical emergencies."

"But it does happen?"

"Not yet."

"And the Dutch?"

"What about them?"

"Do they ask for help?"

"Yes, if they need it. Part of the climate colony deal was providing health care," he says. "We have some regular Dutch patients, and we visit the outpatient clinic in Little Amsterdam."

"And do they contact you in the event of a death?"

"There hasn't been one yet, but I imagine they would. Why?" The doctor flicks his gaze from me to Gaba. "Am I missing something?"

"Thank you for your time, doctor," I say.

Gaba walks beside me on our way out of the hospital with his man in front of us and Nikolaj three steps behind.

"What now?" Gaba asks.

"We get supplies for our stake-out."

"You're enjoying this?"

"I'm enjoying being active, Gaba. It stops me feeling sad."

Apart from discussing what to buy in the store, I say little until we find a spot to park two cars in Little Amsterdam and we settle in for a cold night with a good view of the Dutch administration building.

"Why here, Petra?" Gaba asks when he calls my mobile.

"It's a hunch," I say. "I want to see who goes in after hours, and if they come out again."

"And this is related to The Calendar Man?"

"Quiet, Gaba. Someone's going inside."

Ataasinngorneq

Monday, 8th December 2042

Chapter 8

I'm still stiff from sleeping in the car through the night when I walk to the screen in the room set aside for the task force, but it feels good to be *doing something*, and I smile as I bid everyone good morning. I linger for a second or so before starting as I catch Ooqi's eye. He has yet to say a word, but I feel as though I know him best, at least where this investigation is concerned.

"Yesterday was the second day of advent," I say, "and, as far as we know, it passed without incident."

Atii nods and Danielsen shifts on his chair in search of a more comfortable position. They both look tired, and Aron's arrival with the coffee is well-timed.

"Aqqa is still in charge," I say, with a nod to Danielsen, "but I wanted to just go through a few things before we begin, just to catch us all up, and to let you know of a potential development in the investigation."

I pause to slip the digital thimbles over my thumb and index finger, and then I start casting images and the relevant notes onto the wall screen behind me.

"Victim one, unidentified, has some links to my past, but until we discover who he is, I think we need to shift our focus." I glance at Danielsen and wait for his reluctant nod. "Victim two, female, in her twenties, also unidentified. I think discovering their identity is key, and we need to focus – stop chasing ghosts, and jumping at shadows. The suspect – whoever he or she may be – has us running all over Nuuk, reacting to the next sensational act or murder. We have to stop that. We have to start anticipating what might be next, and where, and we need to be smart about how we do that. Any ideas?"

"About identifying the bodies – the first victim at least," Atii says. "I appreciate you don't want us to focus on you, but have you explored the link? Do you have any ideas how you might do that?"

"One," I say, and I am surprised I haven't thought about it before. "I'll look into it as soon as we are done. What about the young woman? Do we have a missing persons report that we might have missed?"

Many years ago, that was my job, handling the missing persons cases, the most sensational being the Tinka Winther case when the daughter of the then First Minister went missing, and Maratse found her body. It feels like such a long time ago.

"That sounds like a job for Ooqi," Danielsen says, as he turns in his chair to look at the younger police officer.

"No, I have a job for Ooqi," I say. "Perhaps you can follow up on that, Aqqa?"

"Alright," he says, but I can see he is not wholly convinced.

"Unless you have another lead?"

"I was going to check in with the Dutch constabulary."

"No need," I say. "The victim was Benjamin De Kloet. I plan on meeting the Jonkheer either today or tomorrow. I'll follow up on that."

"Missing persons then," says Danielsen.

I almost smile. It's the same with a lot of the police officers who come from the settlements. The idea of spending a day inside with the computer feels like torture. David was the same, although Sergeant Aqqa Danielsen is far more computer proficient than David ever was.

"Thank you," I say. "Is there anything else? Atii?"

Atii stands up and joins me at the front of the room. She double-clicks her own thimbles and takes command of the wall screen. A few clicks and casts later and the screen is filled with a temporary profile in bullet form. She talks us through it.

"The Commissioner is correct, we don't know the sex of the suspect, or even if there is more than one, but if we assume there is only one, then we believe they are physically strong due to the lifting and positioning of the bodies, and they are most definitely smart – they either have knowledge or are able to act on knowledge that they have access to. For example, I have to go back to the IT contractors today to interview one of the employees who was sick. Based solely on the morgue robbery, the suspect either had knowledge of the camera systems upgrading or they knew they would be offline and planned accordingly. The suspect is also quick to react to local events, such as the screening of Frankenstein. If you've read the media coverage of the robbery at the morgue, and the *monster* discovered in Little Amsterdam, you'll agree that the suspect knows how to inspire the media to achieve his or her goals."

"What about motive?" I ask.

"I think the alphabet theory was a good one and discovering the first three letters of your name – plus the tattoos on the first dead body – it made sense, ma'am."

"And now?"

"It seems that the best motive might be the referendum after all. That the suspect is intent on creating a level of fear among residents in Nuuk, enough to keep them indoors and stop them from voting."

"And yet there were plenty of people at the market on Saturday," I say.

"Because we had plenty of police available. Visible, and tired," she says. "I think the suspect has been quiet these past few days to wear us down, have us chase our own tails, so he or she can plan the next move. A few prank calls were all it took over the weekend to stretch all the patrols to the limit."

"And you think something is coming?"

"*Aap.*"

"I agree," I say. "So, let's get out there and chase our leads, feed the information into the server, and meet back here first thing tomorrow morning, unless something breaks, of course."

I shake my head as Ooqi stands up and ask him to wait with a discreet wave of my hand, not discreet enough to escape Danielsen's eye. He frowns for a second before he strolls out of the room. I shut the door when he and Atii have left.

"I saw the Ombudsman go into the Dutch administration building late last night," I say to Ooqi. He presses his glasses further up his nose, and I smile at the fact he could easily have his eyesight adjusted, and then I realise the glasses are more than just a physical aid, they function as his covert computer terminal. He nods for me to continue, and I see a stream of date reflecting from the lens of his glasses onto the surface of his eyes. "Can you confirm it?"

"*Aap.*"

His voice is soft, almost inaudible.

"And can you see if there has been any activity, any record of what they discussed."

"Not possible," he says.

"What would you need to do to find out?"

Ooqi reaches into his pocket and pulls out a tiny disc. He places it on the desk between us.

"I need to get that close to the Jonkheer's computer. Within a metre. He has some new firewalls I can't get around."

"And this," I say, as I pick up the disc, "will give you access?"

"*Aap*," he says. "Maybe you can do it?"

I thought he might say something like that. Regardless of the ethics surrounding bugging the Dutch administrator's office, or, rather, bugging it even more, I can't see another way of exposing what could be a motive to disrupt the Greenlandic vote for independence. If the Jonkheer truly was worried about the future of the Dutch climate colony and the survival of his satellite community, then the question was just how far would he go?

"I'm not sure," I say.

"It will help with the investigation."

"I know. I want to see the Jonkheer anyway. Perhaps he will give me the information willingly."

"Maybe."

"I'll think about it," I say, as I slip the disc into my pocket.

I give Ooqi's shoulder a squeeze as I walk towards the door. It could have been collegial, or even motherly, and I decide it is a squeeze of concern, and I follow it up with a question.

"Are you sleeping, Ooqi?"

"*Aap*," he says. "A little."

"Make sure it is enough," I say.

We all need to sleep more, I think, as I see yawns stifled behind folders and hands as police officers pass me in the corridor. Even Aron looks tired as I enter my office.

"The First Minister wanted you to see this," he says, as he scurries from his desk with a folder in his hand. "She has found sufficient funds to put private security guards on all public buildings."

"Gaba will be pleased," I say, as I read the note. "Starting immediately, I can see."

"Yes, ma'am."

"Good." I give Aron the folder. "Do you drive, Aron?"

"Yes, ma'am."

"Right then. Get a car from the pool and meet me at the entrance in five minutes. We're going to pay the Jonkheer a visit."

Aron pales and I wonder if he knows what Ooqi wants me to do in the Jonkheer's office. But his innocent face and gentle nature are the perfect foil. *Besides*, I think, *the Jonkheer brought his assistant to a meeting, why can't I take mine?*

The thought niggles as Aron drives to Little Amsterdam, and then I feel a little rush of something that feels like adrenalin, more than I am used to of late. I can also feel David's voice ready to issue his warning, but as much as I love him, and miss him, I can't take him with me inside the administrator's building. I need to be clear-headed, and I need to leave my ghosts in the patrol car.

It has to be done, and it has to be done now. I get out of the car and zip my jacket up to my neck, trapping a few strands of my long black hair in the plastic teeth of the zipper. It takes forever to tease them free, and by then we are inside the building and I am roasting in the Dutch heat. It seems that they have yet to find a happy medium between freezing and fiery temperatures. The Jonkheer's secretary is in short sleeves, and the sight of her pale arms brings a little colour to Aron's cheeks. *Finally*, I think, but I keep the thought to myself. As for my own cheeks, I am sure the word guilty is spelled across both of them, but I regain a moment's composure when the secretary brings us tea and small *stroopwafels*, David's favourite.

"He'll see you now," she says when we have finished our tea.

"Thank you for the tea," I say.

"Did you like it?"

"It's unusual, but pleasant."

"It's Rooibos," she says, as she presses two envelopes of tea into my hands. "Good for the heart and against colds and influenza."

"Thank you," I say.

I slip the tea into my pocket and follow the Jonkheer's secretary to a thick panelled door. The office is empty as we walk in and the secretary shows us to the chairs in front of the Jonkheer's desk. She leaves us, and I almost place Ooqi's disc beneath the stand for the Jonkheer's computer screen, but I am distracted by a large photograph on the wall of the Jonkheer and two children. They have his eyes, the girl especially.

"That's Esmée on the right," the Jonkheer says as he enters the room. "She's the oldest. And that's her brother, Hugo. A little scamp. Three years younger than his sister. Esmée is fourteen."

"Are they in Holland?" I ask.

"For the time being, yes. They are in one of the Vaalserberg towers, built on the highest point of Holland. I agreed with their grandparents that they should come once we have settled in."

"And your wife?"

"No," he says, as a sad smile flattens his lips. "She passed away some time ago." He gestures for me to sit down. "I understand you have also lost someone close to you. How are you doing?"

"Better each day," I say, and I wonder if that is true. "It helps to keep busy."

"Yes, I know," he says. He nods at Aron and then sits behind his desk. "Of course, we are very busy at the moment. You heard about the incident around *Sinterklaas*?"

"Yes, but we haven't been given any details."

"That's my fault. I was in shock. I wanted to handle it quietly, but I forget that this is such a small town in a small country. You can't hide something like that."

"No, you can't."

I slip my hand inside my pocket and pinch Ooqi's disc between my fingers. There is a space between the cushion of my chair and the wooden frame. We are sitting so close to the Jonkheer's desk that I can kick it. Well within one metre. I can easily press the disc into the gap if I lean forwards. But I pause as the door opens and the little rush of adrenaline peaks as the Ombudsman Anna Riis enters the Jonkheer's office; she has a stack of books in her arms.

"Commissioner," she says. "This is a surprise."

"Yes," I say. I stand to greet her and she drops one of the books on the floor.

"*Twelfth Night*?" I say. "That's Shakespeare."

"My favourite bard," she says, as she picks up the book. "I was going to lend it to the Jonkheer, but perhaps you would like to borrow it instead."

"Oh, I'm not a reader."

"You might find it useful."

"Useful?"

"Interesting. That's what I meant to say." She presses the book into my hands and walks around me to the Jonkheer's desk. "I've something a little heavier for you, Coenraad. Julius Caesar, as promised."

It's suddenly awkward, and I nod to Aron that we can leave.

"Petra," the Jonkheer says. "I'm pleased you came."

"Me too. I'm hoping we can start again," I say, "and that you will be ready to share what you know as soon as possible."

"Yes, yes," he says.

"Well, I just wanted to check-in and to see if you were alright."

"Thank you."

There is an awkward pause as the Jonkheer and the Ombudsman wait for Aron and me to leave.

"Your office is always welcome to contact us. You know Aron," I say, as he stands up. "He's my personal assistant, and you only have to call."

I'm rambling, and it's time to leave. I see the Jonkheer glance at my chair, and the adrenalin that I found so weak before, spikes to embarrassing levels.

"You dropped something," he says and walks around his desk. "Ah, Rooibos. Good for colds." The Jonkheer smiles as he hands me the tea. "I will be sure to have the constabulary contact you first thing tomorrow with an update on the body."

"Thank you," I say, as my heart recovers after another spike of excitement.

Aron is the first to reach the car and he opens the passenger door for me to get in.

"Back to the station?" he asks.

"No, take me home," I say. "I think it's best to quit while I'm ahead."

"Ma'am?"

"Don't worry about it, Aron. Just drive."

I'm sure Ooqi can find another way to listen in to the Jonkheer.

Marlunngorneq

Tuesday, 9th December 2042

Chapter 9

The brief lull in the Calendar Man's activity passes the moment Nikolaj knocks on my door and tells me he is taking me to meet Danielsen at Atuarfik Samuel Kleinschmidt, the school closest to the centre of old Nuuk town. It is also close to the parliament buildings and the refurbished police station. It's within short walking distance of everything, and now it's on the map of crime scenes chosen by the Calendar Man to strike fear into the people of Nuuk. I can see it has worked, too. The children huddle together with parents and teachers as we arrive and the head teacher declares the school is closed for the day. Head teachers have rarely needed an excuse to close a school for the day in Greenland, but in this case, I have to agree with him. I wait in the car until the children have dispersed and then Nikolaj takes me to the school entrance.

I recognise the advent calendar taped to the window at once, the fingers and toes in the snow beneath it are unfamiliar, although I have an idea where they might have come from.

"The toes came out of the twentieth window," Danielsen says. "The fingers were behind the fourth." He pauses as the head teacher hovers just behind us.

"I'll be in my office," the head teacher says. "At least for the next twenty minutes."

He stumbles over the ice in front of the door and I nod for Nikolaj to go with him.

"Go on," I say to Danielsen.

"I think we both know where the fingers and toes came from, but we'll check them for fingerprints, and get the doctor to match them with the body parts we recovered in Little Amsterdam."

"We have the body?"

"*Aap*. The Dutch Constabulary brought it to the morgue just before we got the call from the school." Danielsen's breath mists between us as he sighs. "The numbers," he says.

"Yes?"

"Four is the letter *A*. And twenty is *T*."

"Alright, Aqqa, what does that give us?"

"Including the number nine on the apartment door in Chinatown?"

"Yes, including that."

"Including that we get *PIITA*."

"That's Piita," I say. "Or *Peter*, if you spell it in Danish."

"It's also the first five letters in your name, ma'am."

"Oh, come on, Aqqa. This isn't about me," I say, and wave my arm at the advent calendar and the blood freezing to the window. "It's a coincidence."

"But the tattoos on your fingers…"

"A coincidence, Aqqa. And until we know who that man is, it will remain a coincidence. That's all."

I wonder if it's fair to let go at Aqqa like this. He's doing his job, and he's looking out for me, his boss, the Police Commissioner. I have to remind myself of the title, more and more with every new day in December. The department is overworked. Half of them are worried about me, and the other half thinks it is because of me.

"I should have retired, already," I say.

"What's that?"

"Nothing. You didn't hear that." I scuff at the snow beneath my boots, stamping it into a hard triangle before looking at Aqqa. "Alright," I say. "Let's move on. Next step."

"Identify the fingers and toes, as far as possible."

"Agreed."

"Find Piita."

"Definitely. Most definitely agreed. He could even be our first victim. Wouldn't that be a break, eh?"

"Yes, ma'am."

"Okay," I say, as Nikolaj walks out of the school building.

He turns and locks the door with a key from a large bundle at the end of a sealskin cord.

"The head teacher gave me the keys," he says. "What do I do with them now?"

"Leave them with me," Danielsen says. "And then take the Commissioner to the station."

"Not home?"

"No," I say. I'm almost tempted to stamp my foot. I look at Danielsen. "Call Atii and have her find Piita. You take care of the fingers and toes."

"Agreed."

I turn to head for the car but stop as soon as I see Danielsen reach for Nikolaj's arm.

"No," I say. "No more counter-orders. I'll dig into my past, these tattoos," I say, as I hold up my hands. "And we'll see you back at the station."

"Where are you going, ma'am?"

"Nuuk Media Group," I say. "You know the way, Nikolaj."

I'm quiet in the car, and the sound of the tyres rumbling across the compacted snow jars my thoughts into order. I'm not angry at Aqqa. I would never be angry at him. But this case is proving impossible. We need a break. Perhaps the killer has given us one? But then the question would be *why*?

I tell Nikolaj to wait in the car, or the canteen, but to give me some space. He might have heard stories about my past, but he doesn't need to know all the details. Few people do. Aqqa knows a little, Gaba a little more, but only two men know the full story. One of them cared for me and loved me until the day he died. The other is the director of Nuuk Media Group, and he clears his schedule a few seconds after I knock on his door.

"I need to know what you discovered twenty-four years ago. Anything that might be relevant to this case."

"You mean what I published?" Qitu asks.

"Let's start with what you didn't," I say, as I remove my jacket and flop down into one of Qitu's comfy chairs.

"I published almost all of my notes, edited of course. But one thing I never revealed had to do with Tertu."

"Tertu?"

The name is familiar, and I remember something about her being on television, an interview, together with Qitu. She even met with the Minister for Education, Culture, Church and Foreign Affairs – Malik Uutaaq, Pipaluk's father. It was his big break and a significant comeback from the scandal surrounding his involvement in the disappearance of Tinka Winther. The other details are sketchy, and I have blocked out even more than that.

"Tertu was my source on the story about the man who gave you those tattoos," Qitu says. "She even lived with me for a while. She and her baby."

"She was pregnant? Who was the father?"

Qitu says nothing, and, as much as I don't like to imagine it, I know it before he says the name.

"The man who gave you those," he says.

I rest my hands in my lap and stare at my palms. Qitu presses his hand on my shoulder as he walks to the other side of his office to make coffee. A sadist gave me these tattoos, and years' worth of counselling, nightmares, and anxiety. It was David that pulled me through, and I can feel the sadness welling up in me as I am forced to revisit the events surrounding my abduction.

I'm here, Piitalaat.

"No, David," I whisper. "Not anymore. You can't help me anymore. I have to do this alone."

I press my lips together and close my hands into fists as Qitu places a mug of coffee on the table in front of me. He is quiet. He watches and waits. Ready to speak and I nod for him to continue.

"Tertu decided to keep the baby. She said it was worth it, as if one good thing could erase so much pain. That's what she said."

I understand, more than I think Qitu could know, perhaps even more than David did.

"You were with her when she gave birth?"

"*Aap.*"

"And she stayed with you?"

"Until the boy was about ten months old. And then she just disappeared. I went to work one day, and the spare keys to my apartment were in the door when I came home. She was gone."

"A boy?"

"*Aap.*"

"What was his name?"

"I never found out. She didn't name him while he was an infant."

I look at my hands again.

"Did Tertu have tattoos? Did *he* give them to her?"

"She had tattoos before him," Qitu says, as reaches out to take my hand. "Her fingers were covered like yours, except her thumbs. She managed to run away before he did them."

"That's good," I say, as I gently tug my hand out of Qitu's.

Qitu waits as I drink my coffee. It's quiet in his office, such a contrast to the bustle I can see between the desks through the thick glass of the office window. A wild thought occurs to me and I glance again at the thick rectangles inked into the joints between my fingers. It's just possible that they were done out of love. I don't mean by *him*, the very thought creases my lips, stirring Qitu into a concerned fidget.

"What would Tertu tell her son, do you think? About his father?"

"I can't begin to imagine," Qitu says.

"But if she wanted her son to grow up thinking he was loved, do you think she would tell him everything, or just the good things – if there were any – about his father?" I put my mug on the coffee table and study my hands. Qitu moves his head for a better view of my lips. He reaches out to brush my hair to one side, and I lift my head. "Sorry," I say. I often forget he is deaf.

"What are you thinking?" he asks.

"I think her son might have tattooed his own fingers," I say. "Out of love, for his mother. Do you think that's possible?"

"It's possible. Of course."

"The problem with this case – The Calendar Man – is that my officers, the ones closest to me, keep trying to link everything to me. I just need to prove it's not about me."

"Why?"

"Because if I don't, then we will never solve the case. We will be looking in the wrong direction. It's all misdirection," I say, as I stand up, quickly. *Too* quickly. Qitu steadies me as blood and bad memories rush to my head.

"Petra?"

"Yes?"

"Sit down."

I let him lower me into the chair, and I smooth my palms on my thighs, backwards and forwards. I stop when I feel myself rocking. I can almost see David by my side, uncertain as to what to do as I rocked back and forth with the pain of rehabilitation.

"I think he would have done it," I say. "I think her son would have tattooed his fingers just like his mother's, if he loved her enough."

"I'm sure he did."

"It would have been a while ago, when he was young and impressionable. Perhaps he was hurting?" I say. "What happened to Tertu? You never said."

"I never saw her again, but I did get a call from a hospital in Denmark. She had named me as next of kin. When they found her body, they called me."

"She's dead?"

"An overdose. They never said anything about her son. It's a few years ago now. He would have been about fifteen."

"Then he would have been in the system. Maybe in a Children's Home in Denmark."

"Or in Greenland," Qitu says. "I'm sorry; I don't have any more information."

It was enough, I thought, and convenient if the killer was attempting to deceive us with misdirection. If he found Tertu's son, and if he was the first victim. A lot of *ifs*.

I almost miss Atii's call as my thoughts reel inside my head. I feel the vibration of my mobile humming through my jacket pocket and into the chair. I swipe my thumb across the screen as soon as I have the phone in my hands.

"Atii?"

"*Aap*," she says.

"You've found something?"

"Danielsen told me to dig through the missing persons files looking for a man named Piita."

"Yes?"

"I found two, in Nuuk, and I've talked with both of them today."

"You've talked to them?"

"*Aap*. One was missing earlier in the year; he was on a hunting trip near Kangerlussuaq. The other one was missing for three days. Drunk, at his girlfriend's house. She was drunk too."

"Any deaths? I mean dead *Piita*s?"

"*Naamik*, but Ooqi ran a quick search of the Children's Homes in Greenland."

"Yes?"

"A thirteen-year-old boy called Piita was admitted to the Children's Home in Maniitsoq in 2032. His record shows he self-harmed, something about his fingers. He pricked them with a fishing hook."

"Piita? You found him, Atii," I say. "That's our first victim. I'm off the hook."

Pingasunngorneq

Wednesday, 10th December 2042

Chapter 10

I sit at the back of the room as the Calendar Man task force work through the latest developments. Atii has a lead on Piita and wants to visit Maniitsoq, a small town north of Nuuk. It's an hour or so by plane – still the most effective and cost-efficient way to get around Greenland, and I think she should go. Danielsen is not so sure, and I wait as they discuss the pros and cons of sending one of the task force out of the city. I have decided to be nicer to Aqqa and give him more control of the daily running of the task force. Of course, it could be that I'm just relieved that the links between me and the murderer are becoming increasingly tenuous. My phone shivers with a message and I realise I never did explain to Iiluuna what happened at the Christmas Market, and why I had to leave so suddenly. I accept her invitation to dinner tonight, and then sip my coffee as Danielsen relents, and Atii makes travel arrangements.

"She'll be gone two days, weather permitting," Danielsen says aloud. I nod, and he continues. "I want to do a wider search for information. Go door to door at each crime scene, starting with the school – we'll work backwards."

Now that Gaba's security guards have taken some of the weight off the department, Aqqa has more officers at his disposal. Going from house to house will also make us more visible, and hopefully calm the people of Nuuk as well as giving us more information to sift through. I glance at Ooqi as he casts a map onto the wall screen and Aqqa circles the locations with a beam from the thimbles. Each area is marked, working backwards from the school, the Dutch administration building, the apartment in Chinatown, the empty lot by the housing block, and the steps outside the community centre opposite the supermarket. Five locations, four bodies, and assorted bits.

"What about the morgue?" I say. "That's also a crime scene."

"*Aap*," Danielsen says. "But the doctor has already told us as much as he can about the robbery."

"But maybe he has more information about the bodies." I put my cup on the tray at the back of the room and stand up. "I'll go and see him."

"Do you have time, ma'am?" Danielsen asks.

He's right to ask, of course he is, and I know that Aron is

thinking the same thing – the daily stack of administration tasks is piling up. It was substantial before David died, and despite Aron's best efforts, the daily reports, intelligence, budget approvals and requisition orders have accumulated, especially with the Deputy Commissioner away on a course. But I have discovered that if I am active – no matter how disturbing the case – then I can get through the day without thinking too much about David. This is all part of the recovery process, I tell myself. I still need time. I need to ease myself back into the job. If I can do something useful at the same time, contribute to the investigation rather than slip into another bout of grief as I pore through reports at my desk, then the admin can wait. Besides, the First Minister wanted me personally involved.

"I have the time," I say. "But I want to talk to Ooqi before I leave."

Danielsen's frown is deeper this time, but he shrugs it off with a question.

"You'll take Nikolaj?"

"Yes, Aqqa, I will take Nikolaj."

He is satisfied, and the meeting is over. Ooqi follows me to my office. He waits by the door as Aron presses a few papers and a digital pad under my nose. I sign and give my thumbprint on three of the more urgent items and ask Aron to leave the rest on my desk. Ooqi closes the office door as Aron bustles into the outer office.

"I failed, Ooqi. You know that."

"Yes, ma'am."

The corners of Ooqi's mouth begin to crease and I realise he has found another way past the firewalls.

"You're in, aren't you?"

"*Aap.*"

I knew it, of course, but I sigh for effect, playing the role of the exasperated Commissioner.

"And?"

"Not much. An email to his mother asking about the children."

"Nothing to the ombudsman? No reply from Anna Riis?"

"Not yet."

I'm disappointed, and I slump into my chair. I'm taking a chance with this line of inquiry. It is both daunting and exhilarating, but less so when nothing happens, when there is nothing to report. However, if there was, I would have to decide just how to share it with the group. I look at Ooqi. Maybe he has an idea about that, a way of casually slipping the information into the collective pool of data.

"Danielsen is suspicious," he says. "He thinks you are withholding information."

"I am, sort of."

"He blames me."

"Ah," I say. "Is that a problem, Ooqi?"

"Not yet."

"Alright. Well, so long as you do your other tasks…" The thought makes me pause. "What other tasks are you doing?"

Ooqi's cheeks colour as he shifts from one foot to the other.

"Ooqi? *Constable?*"

"The Chinese are a little more alert than the Dutch," he says.

"What does that mean?"

"They discovered someone snooping inside their system and they have taken steps." Ooqi shrugs. "I'm locked out."

"And Danielsen?"

"Heard me curse at my desk the other day, and he guessed what I was doing."

"What did he say?"

"Nothing. Yet."

Ooqi gestures at the door and I nod that he can go. I watch as he stops by Aron's desk, just for a second, but enough to suggest that the two shiest officers in the Nuuk Police Department have something in common. They might even be friends. I realise how little I am aware of the social relations between my officers, and I decide that I must do more, that I must get back in the game, as it were.

Piitalaat.

I've been in the office too long. I text Nikolaj and arrange to meet outside the station. I don't know how much he has slept since the beginning of December. We make a good pair.

Nikolaj parks outside Kong Frederik's Hospital and I follow him to the morgue. The walls are panelled with wood, pine, like the thick façade and beams of the outside of the building. Danish architects have won awards for their Greenlandic buildings. The designs incorporate a lot of wood – which Greenland doesn't have – and huge glass windows to let in the precious light at the cost of large surface areas susceptible to heat loss. Greenlandic buildings then, are a constant paradox of aesthetic design, politics and pride, often at the sake of practicality. I don't mind, the building is pleasing to the eye, and the pleasant interior has a calming effect. But I'm pleased I don't see the hospital's budgets, and I shudder to think of the running costs. Nothing is cheap in the Arctic. Something the Chinese and the Dutch are learning daily.

One of Gaba's security men stands outside the morgue, and a technician – perhaps one of the Nuuk contractors – fiddles with a wide-angled camera above the door. He steps to one side as we walk in. I glimpse the patch on the security guard's shoulder and think once again of Âmo and the spirit's long protective arms curling in from both sides. I wonder just how far they reach.

"Petra," the doctor says, as we approach his desk. "I was going to call you."

"Oh?"

"Yes. I found something of interest." He pauses. "I admit, I didn't think to check – what with the robbery and all the media. I have been a bit distracted. I apologise."

"What have you found, doctor?"

"The age of the burned victim."

"Yes."

"She's three weeks old. Three and a half, to be precise."

"Three and a half weeks?"

"Give or take a day or two. Actually, we can pinpoint the day, if I am correct."

I don't mind the doctor using my first name, but I don't care for his riddles. But, for the sake of cooperation and positive relations between our organisations, I try to smooth the crease I can feel on my brow.

"The victim was not burned at the scene," he says.

"We found a can of fuel and burn marks," I say.

"Yes. That's right. I'm sorry, the victim was *burned* at the scene, but that's not where she died." He pushes back his chair and stands up, turning screen on his desk towards us. "I won't bore you with the science of carbon dating, but I can say there has been significant progress in allowing for and eliminating radiocarbon levels in the environment, to use forensic carbon dating to determine the age of a body, and, in this case, the degradation of the skin." He walks over to one of the freezer doors in the wall and opens it, pulling the corpse of the charred woman into the room with a soft rumble of oiled wheels. "The skin was already burned before it was burned at the crime scene."

I lean over the corpse as the doctor points at the area where the arm was removed prior to being stolen.

"It was after the robbery that I could see a difference in the tissue." He grins, clearly pleased with himself. "The killer's first mistake," he says.

Killer. I'm beginning to wonder.

"When I started to look more closely, and after applying rudimentary carbon dating methods, I sent a sample to the university – the archaeology department. I even invited some geologist friends from the natural resources office to have a look."

"And?"

"We all agree. The victim died in a fire three and a half weeks ago. She did not die at the crime scene."

"You're certain?"

"Yes."

"And the cause of death?"

"Smoke inhalation followed by trauma associated with the flames. She burned to death."

I step back as I try to think where I was three and a half weeks ago. It was before David's funeral. We had just decided that he should rest, and give up the fight, no matter the cost. I couldn't go on seeing him in such pain, and when I realised he was fighting for me – always for me, never for himself – I told him to let go, so that we both could.

"Ma'am?" Nikolaj says with a soft touch of my arm.

"Yes?"

"Are you alright?"

I'm not, but we need to move on.

"When did you arrive in Nuuk?"

"Late October," he says.

"And do you remember a fire, in Nuuk?"

"I know when it was," the doctor says. "That's how I can be so precise."

He beckons for us to follow him to his computer and clicks on a headline from *Oqaasaq*. The fire occurred inside an older workshop used to paint vehicles. The sprinklers were clogged with paint, the article says, and the base coats and the clearcoats burned with surprising intensity.

Who was surprised, I wonder. I glance at the woman's corpse and realise she would have been overcome very quickly.

"No casualties," the doctor says. "According to the article."

"So, her body was removed."

"Yes."

"During the fire?" I say. I tap the screen and highlight the word *intensity.* "If she was an employee, she would be missed."

"The fire occurred at night."

"Then she was there out of hours."

"Maybe she broke in," Nikolaj says. "Together with the killer."

"Killer," I say. "In this instance, he is an opportunist, until we can prove otherwise." I look at my watch. I have somewhere I need to be. "Let's get this information to Danielsen and Ooqi. We'll add the workshop to the list of scenes to investigate, and interview anyone connected to it. Thank you, Bendt," I say, and he seems pleased at the familiarity. He's earned it.

Nikolaj drops me off at Iiluuna's apartment. He is reluctant to leave, and I'm forced to order him to drive home and rest. He waits until Iiluuna answers the door and seems satisfied when she hugs me and draws me into the cosy interior that smells of cinnamon and candle smoke. Nikolaj drives away as Iiluuna closes and locks the door.

Quaa's hug is tight enough to bring tears to my eyes, and I clutch her to my stomach as she stands on tiptoe to reach around my neck. Her fingers slip, and I lift her, just enough so she can clasp her fingers and complete the hug. Kicking off my boots and walking into the kitchen is a challenge, but neither of us want to let go.

"Quaa has something to tell you," Iiluuna says, as she sets the table.

"Really?" I press my lips against Quaa's head and whisper. "What is it? Are you going to get a puppy?"

"*Naamik,*" Quaa says, and giggles.

"A new pair of ice skates?"

She shakes her head.

"Then I don't know," I say, as she lets go and slips out of my grasp. I feel a slight tug of sadness as she runs to her room, but then she returns, just as quickly, carrying something behind her back.

"Put it on," Iiluuna says.

Quaa lifts a green wreath onto her head, fiddles with a button at the back, and then beams as four digital candles flicker and twist between the pine needles. Quaa's brown eyes twinkle in the light and I struggle not to cry, again.

"You're going to be Lucia," I say.

"*Aap.*"

"Sankta Lucia," Iiluuna says. "And not just at her school. She is going to be Sankta Lucia in *Katuaq*, at the Christmas concert. The First Minister is going to be there."

"Saturday," I say, as Quaa sits at the table.

Iiluuna dims the lights and we eat roast seal and rice with a thick brown sauce. David would love it, and I hope he'll forgive me, but when Iiluuna suggests it, I agree to spend the night.

Sisamanngorneq

Thursday, 11th December 2042

Chapter 11

Iiluuna's apartment is near the centre of Nuuk, and within walking distance of the police station. I can still smell the sweet cinnamon rolls and see the candlelight flickering in Quaa's earthy brown eyes as I dip my chin inside the high neck of my jacket and brush wayward strands of my black hair beneath my wool hat. Breakfast was a delight, and I was actually hungry, sipping my coffee and eating toast as Quaa sat on my lap at the kitchen table. We parted half an hour later as Iiluuna walked Quaa to school and I went the other way towards the station. With no new bodies, Nuuk Media Group had little to worry the city with other than the latest speculative polls and concerns that the supermarket is running out of sugar. The same happened last year when the Greenlanders competed with the Danes and the Dutch for Christmas ingredients. Vanilla was in short supply too, but not cinnamon. It seems we will never run out of cinnamon. Although, as I round the corner and check for traffic before crossing over to *Aantuukasiip Aqqutaa*, it looks like someone has spilled a bag of cinnamon in the snow.

Except it isn't cinnamon, it's blood, and there is more than a bagful.

I follow the trail of blood-drenched snow all the way to the body of an elderly woman, Greenlandic, maybe seventy years old. Her arms are stretched straight above her head, hands tied. Her legs point at ninety degrees from her waist. A closer inspection shows the ankles are bound too. I call the station on my phone and try to corral the stream of pedestrians to the opposite side of the path. I try to keep them moving. I fail.

It's not far to the station, I can almost hear the cough of one of the old Toyota's as the engine starts and it drifts out of the car park and around the block. The patrol car's blue lights reflect across the pale faces of the onlookers as they squint into a new swathe of snow that dusts the body on the ground and obscures the camera lenses of their mobiles. I'm less worried about the mobiles, and more about the advent calendar that I spot tucked beneath the victim's head. Whoever left her here was worried about the wind blowing the calendar away. I wait until the evidence team has photographed and bagged the calendar before looking at it. The window for December twenty-second is open.

"I'll put it with the others," the crime scene investigator says.

"They're in the evidence room?"

"Yes."

"I can see them?"

"We've got them laid out on a table along the far wall. You can't miss them."

"Thanks."

I see Natuk talking with the pedestrians. All of them arrived at the scene after I did, but I let her work the line. Perhaps someone knows the victim. There is no mortuary ambulance service in Nuuk, not currently, and I walk beside the paramedics as they are reduced to porters, their life-saving skills are not needed. It's a shame, I think, as I study the victim's face. The soft lines of her cheeks are filled with a dusting of snow. She must not have seen her attacker, or he was too fast for her to react.

I'm making assumptions again. When did the attacker become a *he*? Is that Qitu's fault when NMG dubbed the killer *The Calendar Man*? And is *he* really a killer, or simply an opportunist with an agenda?

Without thinking, I reach out and squeeze the old woman's hand, just before the paramedics load her into the back of the ambulance. Atii is following up on the first victim, Piita, while Danielsen directs officers to explore the crime scenes. I found this little old lady, and I decide that she will be my responsibility, as I push thoughts of paperwork to one side, again, and choose to work on my rehabilitation. I find it hard to believe that no-one knows this latest victim. I'll contact the local artist we bring in for sketches and have her work with the photos from the crime scene. Qitu has a new headline, but I want this lady's face on the front page. I intend to find out her name before the end of the day.

I wait until the paramedics have gone, and then I walk towards the station, tugging Natuk gently by the arm as I walk past her.

"I want you to work with our artist," I say. "And have Qitu put her picture in the paper. He can stream it as soon as we send him the file."

Natuk nods and makes a new note in her notebook. Digital pads and tablets don't always work in the cold, and a pencil and pad of paper are required tools even in 2042. Some things don't change.

"I'll be in the evidence room," I say, as Natuk tucks her notepad inside her jacket pocket. "Meet me there when you are finished with the artist."

"Yes, ma'am."

We part company just inside the door, and, when I'm finished banging the snow from my boots and dusting it from my shoulders, I take the elevator down to the basement, and sign-in to the evidence room with a thumb scan. The lights flicker out of hibernation into a working intensity, and I see the calendars laid out as the officer had described on a long table at the end of the room. The light catches small pools of wet snow on the floor. The evidence team have already been here.

The long walls to my left and right are concertina cupboards on rails that open with a winding handle, or the press of a button. I ignore them and concentrate on the calendars.

There are five advent calendars including the latest one I found this morning. The numbers are sixteen, nine, twenty, one and twenty-two. If I add the number nine from the Chinatown apartment between the second and the third calendar, I get the following letters:

P I I T A V

There is a roll of wrapping paper and a thick marker at the end of the table. This must be the table they use to prepare evidence that needs to be transported. I tear off a square of paper for each calendar and write the letter associated with the number on each one, adding an extra *I* as agreed with the task force between calendars two and three. I finish as Natuk enters the evidence room with a folder under her arm.

"That was quick," I say, as she shows me the artist's sketch of the victim.

"It's a preliminary drawing before she feeds it into the computer. I thought you'd like to see it."

"Thanks." I nod at the folder. "What else have you got?"

"A few images from the scene. The body and the calendar." Natuk hands me the folder and walks up and down the row of calendars. "Why have you put a letter *I* between these calendars?"

I forget that she has not seen all the evidence and explain about the supposed link between the apartment door in Chinatown and the Calendar Man.

"And you're using the alphabet."

"It's Atii's theory," I say.

Natuk takes the folder from my hand and shuffles the photos at the end of the table. She shows me the image of the woman and traces the letter *L* with her finger.

"The shape of her body," she says. "Do you see it?"

"Yes."

"So," Natuk says, as she writes the letter on a new square of paper. "It goes at the end." She steps back and reads the letters aloud. "P I I T A V L."

"It used to spell *Piita*," I say.

"Hmm," Natuk says, as she looks at the photo again. She swaps the *L* and the *V*.

"Why did you do that?"

"The calendar is under the woman's head," she says. "The killer wanted us to see the body first."

"I thought it was because of the wind."

"Maybe. But the wind was light this morning. It hasn't really blown for a few days."

She's right. But switching the last two letters doesn't give the word anymore sense.

"P I I T A L V," I say. "It's just as meaningless as before."

I watch as Natuk studies the photograph; almost smile at the way the tip of her tongue peeps through her lips as she works. It reminds me of Quaa and the icing sugar. But I stop smiling as Natuk slowly turns the letter *V* upside down.

"It's an *A*," she says with a triumphant smile. "Look. The calendar was upside down." She points at the woman's head in the photo and taps the calendar. "Santa's feet are pointing up the way. He wanted us to turn the letter around." Natuk grins and then places the photo on the pile at the end of the table.

I know I should praise her analytical skills, and even suggest that she looks at the other evidence we have on the task force wall, but I can't quite distract myself from the new arrangement of letters. The *P* and the two *I*s followed by the other four letters of my nine-letter name.

Piitalaat.

"Yes," I say, more to David than Natuk, but she seems pleased that I agree.

Natuk steps back to take a photograph with her mobile, but I stop her with a light touch on her arm.

"For the files," she says. "I can cast it to your wall."

"Not yet," I say.

"I don't understand."

"I know, but I want you to trust me. Let's see if Qitu has published the sketch yet. I just want to know her name, or if anyone is missing her. You can send the picture to Ooqi or Danielsen after that. Okay?"

"Yes, ma'am."

Natuk is a pretty young Greenlandic woman, and the puzzled lines around her mouth complement her. She is still wearing them as we leave the evidence room and enter the elevator. Aron is waiting in the hall as the doors open, and the sight of the papers under his arm and the tablet in his hands almost distracts me from the Natuk's interpretation of the latest piece of the Calendar Man's puzzle.

"Can it wait?" I ask Aron.

"This?" he says, with a quick glance at the folder. "Yes, this can, but there's a call for you. It's Qitu at NMG."

"In my office?"

"Yes," Aron says, as he shuffles alongside us as we walk along the corridor to my office. "He says he knows who the woman is. That she died last night in the retirement home."

"How does he know?"

"Qitu has an aunt in the next room. He was visiting her last night when the woman passed away. He saw her face as the staff prepared her body for the family to see her. They are flying in today. There is a chapel in the retirement home, and she was put there for the night."

"There are no guards at the retirement home?"

"No, ma'am. They're only in public places," Aron says. "Places open to the public," he adds. "The retirement home is only open to staff and relatives of the residents."

"Natuk," I say.

"I'll go straight there."

"Thank you."

I watch her leave and hope she remembers our deal. I want the victim's name before my own is dragged back into the investigation.

"Is everything alright, ma'am? Can I get you some coffee?"

"Hot water," I say. "For tea. Use the bags we got from the Dutch secretary."

I walk into my office and hang my jacket on the back of the

chair. There is a light flashing on the telephone and I pick up the handset.

"Qitu?" I say. "It's Petra."

There is a delay, and I picture Qitu reading the transcript of my voice on the screen of his phone before he replies.

"I know the woman's name," he says. "She is Ivaana Qaavigaq. She was seventy-five."

"And you saw her last night?"

"I saw her after she passed. I have seen her a few times, each time I visited my aunt."

"Do you think her death was natural?"

"I can't say, Petra."

"But there was no sign of a struggle while you were with your aunt? The staff didn't say anything?"

"They said they had been expecting it. So, I suppose it was natural then."

"I suppose so."

I let the phone slip down my cheek as I think about the woman passing away peacefully in her own bed, only to have her body desecrated by a coward. An opportunistic coward. That's what I think of him now. He isn't worthy of the title *killer*. But he has to be stopped all the same. If there is a connection between him and I, if it isn't just misdirection, perhaps there is a way to expose him, and bring him out into the open.

"Petra?"

"The referendum," I say.

"*Aap?*"

"You have not mentioned much about it in the paper."

"The Calendar Man has taken up a lot of column space, that's true."

"Save some space for me in the next edition," I say. "I promise you an exclusive."

"Petra," Qitu says and laughs. "That's sweet, but NMG has a monopoly on the news in Greenland these days – both the sensational and the investigative pieces."

"As a favour then," I say, as I put the phone down.

Tallimanngorneq

Friday, 12th December 2042

Chapter 12

Atii is due to report in and I wait as Ooqi sets up the wall screen. Aron brings in the breakfast rolls and a plate of *klejner* – they remind me of twisted donuts, but denser. Another seasonal cinnamon creation we have inherited from Denmark. Another fried pastry to plague Danielsen's waistline. He catches my eye as he takes one and I wonder if Natuk has told him anything. The softness in his eyes suggests that she has, which I should have expected, but that he cares, which I should accept. But what I can't accept is the so-called Calendar Man's methods which I find as cowardly as they are repugnant.

"Atii's ready," Ooqi says and we turn to face the screen.

The image of Atii's face moves as she jogs through the snowy streets of Maniitsoq. The sky is lighter already here in Nuuk, but it feels as though Atii is working in the night. There is a police officer slightly ahead of her, and the shadow jostling in and out of the camera's vision on her right suggests there are at least three of them.

"Atii?" Danielsen asks. "Are you there?"

"*Aap.*"

"And what are you doing?"

"Following a lead," she says. Her breath mists in clouds in front of the camera and the view bounces as she increases speed. Her words come in waves as she runs down the street. "We're going to pick up a captain of a fishing trawler."

"Why?"

"He had Piita's body on ice," she says. "For over a week."

"On the boat?" I ask.

"*Aap.*"

We can see the docks now, and the pancake ice bumping in the water. Another week of low temperatures and it might be strong enough to walk on, if it wasn't for the fishing trawlers doing their best to keep a channel open.

"Piita was working on a trawler," Atii says. "Some of the men, including Piita, got drunk, and there was a fight. One of the crew strangled Piita. The captain put Piita's body in the hold, with the fish, on ice."

"In Maniitsoq?"

"*Aap.* But the boat was in Nuuk at the end of November." Atii pauses at a signal from the police officer in front of her. They slow, and we see the Maniitsoq police officers draw their sidearms. Atii lowers her voice to a whisper. "We arrested the crewman in a bar last night. He confessed to killing Piita but knows nothing about what happened to the body. He hasn't talked to anyone. Now we want to pick up the captain. He sleeps on the boat."

"Atii," I say. "Was Piita's body on the fishing trawler when it came to Nuuk?"

"We think so. But the crewman – the one who killed Piita – was kicked off the boat. He's a cousin of the captain."

"And the captain was protecting his cousin."

"*Aap*." Atii adjusts the camera angle so we can see her face. "The captain is known to be violent, and we believe he is armed. We're going in now."

Atii clips the camera to her vest. The sights of her pistol are just visible as her body stiffens at a quiet command from the Maniitsoq police sergeant. We can hear them breathing. Aron opens the door and steps into the room. Danielsen hushes him with a look.

"That's it," Atii whispers. "We're going in."

It's been a while since I was a part of a team tasked with picking up a suspect and I grip the edge of the desk in front of me. I hold my breath as Atii's camera shudders on her vest and we can hear boots slipping and stomping across the hard snow. She turns, and we see the hull of the trawler. We see the railing as she climbs over it and hear the soft thud as she lands on the deck.

I remind myself that Atii spent several years on the Special Response Unit when Gaba was her boss not her husband. She is a competent officer and an excellent shot, but she has two boys now, and I worry suddenly that she is in danger. So are the other officers, but I don't know them. And yet, I am equally responsible for them. I snap out of my thoughts as one of the police officers shouts a warning to the occupants of the trawler. We can see his hand on the door handle.

"Police," he shouts. "We're coming in."

Atii moves into position, her hand slips into view as she presses it onto the shoulders of the officer in front of her, just as he opens the door. My vision is fixed on the sights of Atii's pistol. It is as if the pistol is glued to her body and her head as she moves through the wheelhouse of the trawler to the stairs leading below decks. We hear something rattle and thump in the darkness as Atii follows the police officer into the trawler's kitchen. A sudden flash of orange and an explosive boom makes me jump, and then we hear three shots, we see three bursts of white, and then we follow Atii as she steps over the police officer on the deck in front of her, kicks a shotgun to one side, and presses her knee on the body of a man bleeding at her feet.

"Suspect secure," Atii says, and I am amazed that her voice is so calm.

I want to know about the police officer from Maniitsoq, the one who disappeared beneath the flash of the captain's shotgun.

"Status?" Atii says.

It takes three or four long seconds before we hear the officer's voice.

"I'm alright," he says.

Atii turns and we see the third officer help his Sergeant to his feet.

"Danielsen," Atii says.

"Go ahead."

"The captain is dead. I'm sorry." There is a crackle of static as Atii removes the camera from her vest and looks into the lens. "I'm going to have to stay another day or two to write this up."

"Understood."

"Atii," I say.

"Ma'am."

"Good work."

"Not so good, I think. I had some questions I hoped the captain could answer."

"I understand, but you're unhurt. That's good. And you have confirmed Piita was dead before he was dumped outside the community centre. That's important information. We can use that to move the case forwards."

"How, ma'am?"

"We're going to draw him out," I say. "Write up your report and get back to us as soon as possible."

Ooqi casts the case notes and images onto the wall screen as Atii closes her camera link. I study the notes for a second and then step up to the screen.

"Piita was dead before the perpetrator used his body. Based on Atii's report and her interview with the crewman, I think we can assume that Piita's body was taken from the fishing trawler when it was in Nuuk."

"The Calendar Man must have known it was onboard," Danielsen says. "He must have known the captain or someone on the crew." He pauses for a second. "It's not a very big trawler. The crew might have been just two or three men."

"Piita, the captain and his cousin," I say.

"And the captain won't be able to tell us anything," Danielsen says. "We need to check with the Nuuk harbour records, and see when the trawler was here, and who was onboard."

A window pops up on the wall screen as Ooqi opens a link to the Nuuk Harbour administration office.

"What do you mean when you say you want to draw him out, ma'am?" Danielsen asks.

"I'll come back to that," I say, as I swipe the image of the second victim into the centre of the screen. I drag the image of the elderly woman alongside it. "Both these victims were dead prior to being used by the perpetrator. Based on this evidence, I don't think we can refer to him as a killer. More an opportunist and a coward with an agenda." I can feel the curl of my lip and I'm a little shocked at how personal the case feels. It's getting harder and harder to remain objective.

Focus, Piitalaat.

"I am focused," I say.

"Ma'am?"

"What?"

"Your focus?" Danielsen says. "It's the three victims. What about the Chinese body or the one found in Little Amsterdam?"

"If I'm right, then I'm sure we'll find that they died prior to being used by the Calendar Man – if they are related. The Chinese victim's body is probably already in China by now, and the Dutch have been slow to report any details," I say. I glance at Ooqi and he shakes his head, just slightly, but enough to suggest that we will have to use the official channels to find out more.

"And if they were dead already?" Danielsen asks.

"Then we need to force his or even *her* agenda. We need to know what the motive is. We need to take the initiative. Qitu is saving us some column space in the next edition of *Oqaasaq* – online and print. The news has been dominated by the Calendar Man, with very little reporting on the referendum. We need to change that and see if that is the driving factor."

"Unless you are, ma'am."

It's not clear to see, but I guess that Natuk has talked to Danielsen, or that he has been down to the evidence room and seen the calendars. I smile at the thought of Nikolaj bursting through the door at any minute, dragging me to a safe room at a nod from Danielsen.

"If I am," I say, as I walk away from the wall screen and sit down on the nearest chair, "then I think we need to use that. I want to make a statement. I want to be the one quoted in the media."

"What do you intend to say?"

I realise that I haven't thought that far ahead, but I remember Iiluuna saying that the First Minister was going to be at the Sankta Lucia Christmas celebration, and it occurs to me that I should talk with Pipaluk. She wanted me to take personal responsibility for the case. Perhaps it is time to show a united front, standing side by side on the stage tomorrow. I make a rule of leaving the majority of the press conferences to the media officer, or the investigator in charge of the case, but for once I think it is time to mix policing with politics, and to reassure the people of Nuuk with a more personal presence.

"It's risky, ma'am," Danielsen says.

"I'm willing to take that risk. You can double my protection if you feel it is necessary."

"Actually," he says, "I was thinking of the risk to the general public. What if you force his hand? What if he actually kills someone as a result?"

"Aqqa," I say. "We have doubled our patrols, to the limit of what the department can bear. The First Minister has contracted Gaba's security company, and he has guards all over the city – even the retirement homes, since yesterday. We have the city all but locked down. With the cooperation of the Chinese and the Dutch, we're making it increasingly difficult for anyone to do anything without being seen or stopped. It's time to up the ante and make a move."

"I'm not sure, ma'am."

"You don't have to be. I take full responsibility."

Aron shuffles to my left and I turn to look at him.

"I can set up a meeting with the First Minister," he says.

"Good," I say. "Invite Qitu to the same meeting."

Aron slips out of the room and the door sighs to a close. It is the last sound we hear for over a minute, although I'm sure I can hear Danielsen thinking.

"It's dangerous," he says.

"And necessary."

He sits down and taps his fingers on his thighs.

"I talked to Natuk. She showed me the calendars, and the letters beneath them. I think her interpretation is right," he says, and nods for Ooqi to cast the image onto the screen. "It's your name, ma'am. It has to be."

"But why?" I say. "If this is about me and my past, surely the only link was Piita – the son of the man who gave me these." I lift my hands to reveal the bands across my fingers. "Revenge died with Piita."

"Maybe it's not about revenge," Danielsen says.

"What then?"

"I don't know," he says, but I can see a shadow of an idea in his eyes.

"Aqqa? Say it."

There is another pause followed by the sigh of the door as Aron leans into the room to confirm that the meeting is set for tomorrow morning. Danielsen looks at Aron and waits for him to leave.

"If it's not revenge," he says, as the door closes, "it could be infatuation."

"That's ridiculous," I say.

"Maybe, but I think we need to dig deeper into your past, or maybe something more recent," he says, with another glance at the door.

Arfininngorneq

Saturday, 13th December 2042

Sankta Lucia

Chapter 13

The first time I met Pipaluk Uutaaq was in a mountain graveyard above the remote settlement of Inussuk overlooking Uummannaq fjord. She stood between her mother and brother as her father, Malik Uutaaq, took a non-partisan decision to join with the then First Minister as she buried her daughter on the mountainside. It was a unifying moment for the two political parties, during a period when Greenlandic culture and identity had more to do with the language one spoke than the country one was born in. I remember being moved by the First Minister's speech, when she repeated it in Danish. I remember holding David's hand as I felt what I believed to be the beginning of a new era of acceptance and opportunity for the people of Greenland. It was Malik Uutaaq who forged a new, more sustainable approach to Greenlandic independence, but following his death it would be his daughter who made it happen.

If, I think, *the people come out and vote.*

Pipaluk is thirty-seven now, and, if I admit it, slightly intimidating. She has an eye for fashion, projecting power and confidence through the colour and cut of her clothes. She captures her identity in the creamy curl of her narwhal earrings, and hints at her agenda in the shade of her lipstick and the delicate highlights on her cheeks and around her eyes. For my part I left David's jacket at home and smooth the crisp lines of my uniform with my hands as we sit at the distressed pine conference table in the room beside Pipaluk's office. Qitu wears the wrinkles and scents of another late night at the office, and he slumps in the chair opposite me.

Aron hovers at the end of the room beside Pipaluk's assistant. I smile at him as I scan the artwork on the walls, rough, like the conference table. There is a driftwood feeling in the room that has more to do with a fishing trawler than a government office, and it offsets the smoothly tucked hems of Pipaluk's sealskin trousers and black blouse. Like her clothes, the room signals identity. She is grounded, at one with the sea and the land, and my thoughts are drifting, bobbing from one image and association to another, a tide of memories as I try to avoid a niggling thought that bubbles to the surface each time I look at Aron.

Infatuation.

But that's not what this meeting is about, and I clear my mind as

Pipaluk speaks.

"The doors open at four. The choir will sing two carols and then the children will walk in bearing candles – digital wicks, of course. Once the children are arranged in front of the stage…" Pipaluk pauses as she wipes the screen on the next page. "Then I will make my speech. Petra," she says.

"Yes."

"The speech is in two parts. Once I am finished with the festive address, I thought I would invite you to stand beside when I talk about the importance of the vote and the safety measures the city has put in place."

"Of course."

"Good."

Pipaluk's smile softens her professional demeanour, and I wonder if she has practiced it. It is strong enough to rouse Qitu into a more upright position.

Piitalaat. Focus.

He's right. I need to think, although thinking is what kept me up half the night.

"First Minister," I say.

"Yes, Petra."

"I'd like to add something to the speech. It's the reason I arranged this meeting."

"The speech is locked, *Commissioner.*"

"It's just a comment I'd like to add, in connection with assurances we are making regarding safety."

I wait for her to respond, trying not to place too much weight on her use of my title, not my name, or the tiny wrinkles on her top lip as she straightens her smile.

"Go on," she says.

"It's nothing much, more of a continuation of the piece Qitu is streaming just after lunchtime today." I wait for Qitu to nod. "We've decided that each time we talk about the so-called Calendar Man, we use the words *coward* and *cowardly.* Together with the article we're working on changing the image of fear to pity and disgust, and we'd like you to do the same, First Minister."

"*We,*" she says, and points a manicured finger at Qitu and me.

"The department, and *me*, specifically."

"You want the killer…"

"Coward," I say.

"You want him to think *you* are calling him a coward. Why?"

"Him or her, yes," I say.

I try not to glance at Aron, but I can feel him staring at me. It's difficult to determine how he is looking at me, as concern could so easily be mistaken for *infatuation*. Regardless of how I interpret my assistant's look, it is the First Minister's reaction that is more important.

"You're making yourself a target."

"Yes."

"I don't understand. Is it for the good of the people, to save the vote, or do you have information you're not sharing with me?"

"It's too early to tell," I say.

"So, you're testing a theory?" Pipaluk looks at Qitu, waits for him to focus on her lips. "You haven't said anything yet. What do you think?"

"I think," Qitu says, "that the Commissioner is making a mistake. Two mistakes." Qitu sighs as he looks at me. "I think you're underestimating the Calendar Man and underestimating the impact any link – tenuous as it may appear – may have upon you."

"I have to know," I say.

"But goading him puts you in danger. Danielsen agrees with me."

"Ah, you've talked to Aqqa," I say. I'm tempted to laugh, but instead I point at the shadow of Nikolaj just visible through the glass in the door. "Danielsen is the reason that poor officer isn't sleeping."

"You still haven't heard from the Chinese or the Dutch," Qitu says.

"No. I was hoping the First Minister could apply some pressure," I say.

"What do you need?" she asks.

"They have yet to confirm if the two bodies – one in each district – died of natural causes or if they were victims of the Calendar Man."

"What about the others?" Pipaluk leans forwards. "Have I been kept in the dark? I thought we agreed that you report to me directly."

"I'm here, First Minister."

"Barely. Your mind seems to wander in between, and now Qitu says you have failed to take the situation seriously. Where is the Deputy Police Commissioner? Should he be here instead of you?"

Like the surf receding from the shore, I feel as though the

purpose of the meeting is slipping through my fingers, and I am losing control, or I am about to.

"First Minister," I say.

I want to say more, but Aron cuts me off.

"I have sent daily briefings to your assistant, as per the Commissioner's request," he says, as he turns the tablet in his hands. Pipaluk's assistant confirms with a quick nod of her head.

"I see," Pipaluk says.

"While some aspects of the case have been unfolding, I have provided you with a full report, each day, following the Commissioner's instructions."

Aron glances at me, and I decide the earlier look in his eyes was in fact, and could only have been, concern. Nothing more. I would be foolish to think I have suppressed David's shadow. I am still grieving. Perhaps Pipaluk is right to infer I should be replaced.

"The Deputy Police Commissioner is in Denmark. He is on a course, after which he is taking leave, and will be in Denmark over the holidays. He will return just before New Year," I say. "However, if you feel that a replacement is necessary…"

"No." Pipaluk shakes her head. "I've been busy meeting with ministers. I confess I have followed the investigation in the media rather than your reports. I will be sure to take the time to study them once the Sankta Lucia celebration is over. Perhaps we should get ready? I'll leave the wording of your part of the speech to your discretion," she says, as we stand. "But, Petra, please do listen to your colleagues." She glances at Nikolaj and Aron. "They seem to have your best interests at heart."

I whisper my thanks to Aron as we leave the conference room and Nikolaj leads us out of the parliament building. He stops as Qitu catches my arm, just before we cross the parking area to the police station entrance.

"You're sure about this?" he asks.

"Yes," I say. "The referendum is three days from now. We have to force his hand, give him a chance to make a mistake."

"And then?"

"Then we find the coward and stop him."

I have a good view of the centre aisle from where I stand in the shadows behind the podium. The choir is split in two sections, framing Quaa and the children walking with the halting step of Saint Lucy, their white gowns trailing on the floor, candles in their hands and a flickering crown on Quaa's head. It is a struggle, but I manage not to cry, and then I think of Iiluuna, and hope she is taking lots of pictures.

The children's voices sing the last refrain of Sankta Lucia and the audience settles in their seats, just as Pipaluk steps onto the stage. I have seen the Danish copy of her speech, and I follow her Greenlandic as best I can, using the speech as a guide. I know she will repeat it in Danish, but I want to be ready to step onto the stage on cue. I'll miss it if I am listening to what she says.

I feel a tug at my arm and turn to see Qitu. He leads me backstage and I nod at his friend Geert Aalders waiting by the door.

"Qitu, I'm on soon," I say.

"I know. I just wanted you to know that the article has been read over a thousand times since we posted at one o'clock. The comments are ticking in, and I have a team sifting through them. This one," he says, as he shows me his tablet, "is written in English."

"English?"

"A neutral language, perhaps. When you read the comment, you'll understand why."

I can just hear Pipaluk begin the Danish part of her speech, and then Geert interrupts us, as I take the tablet from Qitu."

"I'm going to find my seat," he says.

Qitu nods and I read the comment.

Caesar said: a coward dies a thousand times before his death. You, Commissioner, taste of death but once.

"We've traced the comment to a user account created for the purpose of leaving that one comment." Qitu takes my hand as I return the tablet. "It's a death threat, Petra."

"No," I say, as I force a smile. "It's Shakespeare." I glance over my shoulder. "I have to go, Qitu."

"Petra. Don't go out there. What if he's in the crowd? You've just made him mad enough to try and kill you."

"Mad enough to make a mistake, and then we'll catch him, Qitu. Thank you," I say, as I slip free of his hand and walk onto the stage.

The lights are brighter now. Less atmospheric, more political. I smile as Pipaluk steps to one side so that we can share the podium. I know what I am going to say, but I can see a copy of my part of the speech on the podium's screen. I plan to start by thanking the children and the choir, and then the First Minister, but the crashing of emergency doors and the sight of Gaba's security men ushering people out of their seats and into the lobby pushes the speech out of my thoughts. The First Minister's security team remove her next, as the audience begin to murmur, and the parents ignore the guards and grab their children from the stage. I look for Quaa, to see if she is with her mother, and then my view is blocked by Nikolaj's black jacket and all I can see is his body, as he presses me to his chest and drags me off the stage, through the backstage access and across the snow to one of the spacious SUVs humming in the snow outside the back entrance.

"What's going on?" I ask, as Nikolaj bundles me into the back of the SUV.

"Drive," he says, as he gets in beside me.

"Nikolaj?"

"Bomb threat," he says, as the officer behind the wheel weaves through the crowds fleeing the cultural centre. "Someone called it in as you were walking on stage."

"Stop the car," I say. "Turn around. We have to help these people."

"No, ma'am. I'm to get you home. Those are my orders."

Sapaat

Sunday, 14th December 2042

Chapter 14

They have been here all night and I can't remember how many times I heard them make coffee or knock softly on my door to hear if I was alright. I am being handled by Danielsen, riding high on some supposed authority the Deputy Commissioner has given him. Gaba isn't much better, as he plays the *old friend* card, together with his resources that he threatens to arm – within his rights – and turn Nuuk into a militarised state of martial law. They let me watch coverage of the fallout following the bomb threat at least. I still can't shake the images of people fleeing what should have started out as one of the more charming and festive Sankta Lucia celebrations I can remember. I excused myself after midnight and locked myself in my room to read the message from Iiluuna.

Her mobile needed charging, she wrote. She was sorry she couldn't message me earlier.

But you're safe? Both of you?

Aap.

That was all I needed. Confirmation that they are home. That the doors are locked. Quaa's big day has been spoiled, but it is a day she will never forget. No-one will. And it is all my fault at least that's what Danielsen insinuated, despite Gaba's more vehement conclusions that suggested the opposite.

When does Atii get back, I wonder, as I hear his raised voice once more. *Who is looking after his sons?*

They have turned my living room into ground zero, demanding regular updates from the station and fielding calls from the First Minister's office. At least I'm not alone. She is under lock-down too.

I'm frustrated and angry. I just don't know who to direct it towards. Me or him? The Calendar Man. I think it is a *he* now, ever since reading the quote from Julius Caesar. It's such a masculine thing to quote. So dramatic. I'm tempted to look at it again, for the twelfth or thirteenth time tonight, but as I pick up my mobile, a new window flashes onto the screen. More encryption followed by the familiar ALL CAPS text.

COMMISSIONER?

"Ooqi?" I say, and picture the young officer typing in some dark corner of an even darker room.

AAP.

"What's going on? At the station?"

LOTS OF ACTIVITY. KIND OF FORGOTTEN ABOUT ME.

They have underestimated him again. The thought makes me smile.

"Anything new from the Dutch or the Chinese?"

STILL LOCKED OUT OF THE CHINESE SYSTEM. BUT HAVE ACCESSED DUTCH SERVER. MAN DIED OF HEART ATTACK. WAS BEING TREATED FOR HEART CONDITION.

"That's four out of five," I say.

AAP. IS THERE ANYTHING I CAN DO?

"Do you still have access to the Jonkheer's computer and mail?"

AAP.

"Anything of interest?"

NOT YET.

"And nothing more from the ombudsman, Anna Riis?"

NOTHING.

"Okay. Let me know the minute you get something."

I slip my phone between David's jacket and my pillow and lie down. My hair catches in the thick weave around the pockets of David's jacket, and I can smell him again, the smell of the north.

Piitalaat.

"Not now, David," I say. "I need to think."

It occurs to me that the Calendar Man is somehow plugged in to the life and, more importantly, the deaths in the city. He might be reluctant to kill his victims, but he is not squeamish about working with the dead. He has knowledge of butchery, which means he could be a hunter. I almost laugh at the thought of how unhelpful that it is – almost every man in Greenland is a hunter, and most women know how to butcher a seal. At least in the settlements. So, the Calendar Man might be from the north, or the east of Greenland. The population is greater on the west coast and in the south, with a higher percentage of non-hunters as generations of Greenlanders continue to adapt to city life and the service industry.

Focus.

"I will if you stop interrupting."

I bite my lip. I don't mean that. I wish he was here to interrupt. I wish he had never left. I want David by my side, not a pile of books weighing down the duvet. I want *him* hogging it, snoring, keeping me awake because he is here, not just because I miss him. And I do miss him. Terribly.

I feel the sudden need to visit his grave, and I peel David's jacket from my pillow. I slip my legs over the side of my bed and pause, pressing my toes against the floor; I can feel the rough fibres of my socks against my skin.

"None of the victims had been buried," I say.

The victims were either in the refrigerator at the morgue, in the cool chapel, or even on ice, as Piita was aboard the fishing trawler. The Chinese man's apartment was cold – he had stopped paying his bills, and the windows were open in the Dutch administration building.

"They weren't buried but they were all chilled, one way or another."

I don't know how important it is, but it's a fact, and I grab my phone and add a note to the file on the server. We can talk about it, if Danielsen ever lets me out of my room.

I return to my earlier thought and wonder how the Calendar Man is getting his information. He is scouring the city for dead bodies, so it makes sense if he has access to institutional records. But that doesn't explain how he knew Piita's body was in the hold of the trawler, or that the young woman burned to death in the fire at the workshop. We still don't know her name, but I have an idea that she knew Piita, or the Calendar Man. Perhaps both.

We need a new break in the investigation, and we're not going to get it stuck inside my apartment. I pull on David's jacket, stuff my mobile into the pocket and open my bedroom door. It's still dark outside, and the men in my living room look tired. None of us has slept, although Nikolaj looks like he might have tried from where he is slumped on my sofa.

"Petra?" Gaba says. "Are you alright?"

"Nothing happened, Gaba," I say, with a look at Danielsen. "Nothing."

"I had to take precautions, ma'am. We saw the comment on the article, and then the bomb scare…"

"Misdirection," I say. "I'm still not convinced this is about me. But he's done it again – the Calendar Man. We're looking in the wrong direction, again. The First Minister has been saying it from the start – this has to be about the referendum. But we're not going to convince people of that from my living room."

"You can't leave your apartment, ma'am," Danielsen says.

"No?"

"You're a target."

"With the luxury of knowing where I go and when I go there, before he does." I frown as I look around the room. "Where's Aron?"

"I thought it best to leave him at the station," Danielsen says. He looks at his watch. "Of course, he'll be off duty now."

"He's my personal assistant, Aqqa."

"I know."

"And now he's a suspect?"

Danielsen glances at Nikolaj as he stands up. He gestures for him to sit down again with a wave of his hand.

"Under the circumstances..."

"You've made an assumption. I suppose you've taken him off the task force too?"

"I may have suggested he concentrate on clearing the paperwork on your desk."

"These are my decisions, Aqqa."

I never would have believed it before, but it seems clear now. There might be a reason Danielsen has been communicating so closely with the Deputy Police Commissioner. I would never call Danielsen a coward, but I recognise an opportunist when I see one.

"What has he offered you?" I ask.

"Who?"

"The Deputy Commissioner. Has he given you the nod for his position, when he takes mine?"

"Ma'am?"

"Is that what this is all about? This whole theory of yours about the calendar numbers being letters. Natuk had to turn one of the letters from a *V* to an *A*. It wouldn't have fit otherwise."

"Petra," Gaba says, as he takes a step towards me. He stops as I clench my fists at my sides.

"You've been shoe-horning this theory of yours into the investigation from day one, Aqqa. How do I know you're not trying to manipulate the investigation for your own personal gain, and the Deputy's?"

"That's not what I'm doing, ma'am," Danielsen says.

I don't hear him. Suddenly I'm reeling, and the kitchen is hotter than it was a second ago. Maybe it's David's jacket. He always wore it outside. It must be warm. I'm warm. I'm hot, and I'm starting to sway. I feel Gaba's hands on my shoulders as he guides me to a seat at the table. He presses a glass of cold water into my hand, smooths his palm over my brow and helps me out of David's jacket.

"I'll stay," he says to Danielsen. "You can leave an officer at the door, but the two of you should go home."

"You're not a sergeant anymore, Gaba," Danielsen says. "You can't tell me what to do."

"You don't think so?"

I reach out for Gaba's hand, squeeze it until he stands down, and Danielsen slowly, quietly nods for Nikolaj to follow him out of my apartment. I wait until I hear the door close with a soft click, and then I let go of Gaba's hand.

"I'm alright, Gaba."

"No, you're not. I just don't know if it's because of Maratse or if this case, the links to you…"

"Can't it be both?"

I take another sip of water and then lower the glass to the table. The chill water condenses the glass, and my fingers are wet. I wipe them on the table and Gaba watches me.

"I don't know what the next move is," I say. "I feel as though I'm barely functioning as a police officer, and certainly not as Commissioner. I don't think I care if Danielsen has career ambitions. It might even be best for him to step up. He's making more decisions than me now anyway, and my assistant is covering the paperwork. Perhaps I should just step down."

"I don't think so, Petra. Not yet."

"Why? Because of this case?"

"It's high-profile. It needs someone at the top. Someone with a title. You can put Danielsen there, but he'll still only be a Sergeant. Even if the Deputy was back, he would only be a leader by default. You are the Commissioner, Petra, and Nuuk needs to see you. You need to be visible. If you were to slip away now, if Danielsen keeps you trapped inside your apartment, then this Calendar Man has won." Gaba reaches for my hand and it is his turn to squeeze. "You might not feel strong right now, but you can be strong again. I've seen you bounce back from much worse than this. I know you're hurting, and that you miss Maratse."

"I really, really do, Gaba."

"I know. But he would tell you the same if he was here, and he would do what had to be done if you were gone. He would hate it, but he would do it."

"This is your pep talk?"

"It's one of them," Gaba says and laughs. "Did I ever tell you why I changed the name of my company to Âmo?"

"You wanted to make it more Greenlandic?"

"It's a little more than that."

Gaba lets go of my hand and opens my fridge. He pulls out two bottles of beer and opens them. I don't remember buying them, but the beer tastes good and I smile as Gaba sits down.

"Âmo is the shaman's familiar spirit," he says. "You know when the shaman is inside the turf hut or the igloo, or whatever it was that our people lived in back then..." Gaba pauses for a swallow of beer. "Well, he's just got the whole crowd on the edge of their seats, the lights are low, it's warm, and his soul is just about to take flight, that's when Âmo comes in. He's got these long arms, and he wraps them around the people inside the hut, igloo..."

"Tent."

"Whatever. Anyway, he's got them there. It's Âmo that keeps them on the edge of their seats; he's protecting them while the shaman is off in the underworld, or some other magic place. Âmo makes sure the people are still there when the shaman gets back. They're trapped. Under his spell. And I like that. The idea that someone has got the shaman's back, while he is off solving problems, combing Sedna's hair for the sake of the hunters, or chasing down some mean old angry *tupilaq*. That's what I imagined. I mean, I loved being a police officer, but who looked after the police when they were off solving problems?"

"The police are the shaman in this story?"

"*Aap.*"

Gaba shrugs as he takes another swallow of beer.

"What are you trying to tell me, Gaba?"

"I'm trying to tell you not to worry. I'm trying to tell you to start doing your job. The people of Nuuk need you, and," he says and smiles, "I've got your back."

It's a stretch. I can't quite imagine the Commissioner as a shaman, but the thought that Gaba is looking out for me, an old, reliable friend in uncertain and unruly times, is enough to finish what I've started. The coward may have many deaths before he dies, but with Âmo by my side, I'm willing to taste death if it means I can get my life and my job back. On this second Advent of Christmas, it's time to stop hiding and start hunting.

Ataasinngorneq

Monday, 15th December 2042

Chapter 15

It takes a lot of convincing, but as soon as Gaba proves his kids are sleeping at his parents' house I let him sleep on the couch. Danielsen has a patrol car outside my apartment, anyway. But I can't sleep, and I pick up one of David's books and read the first few pages. It's clear that we had our own interests outside of work, and, after all these years, I can't see what he saw in science fiction stories. I admit, I don't read for pleasure, and I believe the smartphone was invented just for me. The new integrated models that they developed over the years are more intuitive, even more invasive, and so much more fun than David's books will ever be. I decide they are better as bed ballast, the physical weight of my thoughts, and a constant reminder. I close the book and place it on top of the pile on his side of the bed.

I liked it when he read to me, and I miss the rasp of his voice after he was finished with a chapter. That was when I was sick. It was therapy, and I remember those horrible moments when David realised he had forgotten to bring a glass of water to my bedside. His mouth would be dry, and I remember him fidgeting as he wondered if I would notice if he went to the kitchen and brought back something to drink. That's when, eyes closed, I would reach for him, and clasp his fingers between mine. I wouldn't let him go, and he would start another chapter, reading until his tongue stuck to the roof of his mouth, trapping the words behind his teeth. I didn't need the words so much as I needed to hear his voice, or just his breath. I needed to feel his weight on the mattress, and the rough scratch of his skin on my hands. It would take months before I actually listened to the stories.

That's all we have now – stories, the memories of what we did together. The things that happened to us, the decisions we made, and the way each story shaped our lives. David is gone, but I still have stories to tell. I'm saving them up for when I see him again.

I hear the sofa creak as Gaba crawls out of it. It's still dark, but I have survived yet another night without David. I dress for the day and when I smell fresh coffee I walk out of my room and join Gaba in the kitchen.

"Do you have a plan?" he asks, as he fills the toaster with thick slices of rough-hewn bread.

"To show my face. I thought about calling Pipaluk Uutaaq. I'll ask her if she'll join me on a walk along Nuuk's main streets."

"You're campaigning?"

"She can campaign all she wants. I just want to be seen, not hidden away. Will you walk with me?"

"Sure."

"I'll make the arrangements while you butter the toast. Bring some for the day shift too."

I press my phone to my ear to blot out the vigorous scraping of butter across thick toast. I laugh as I wait for my call to connect. There is little that Gaba doesn't do *vigorously*. I walk into the lounge and stare across the bay as I invite the First Minister to a walk through town.

"Security won't be a problem," I say, as Pipaluk hesitates.

I can hear her advisors in the background, but her sighs suggest she is just as frustrated as I am. We agree to start at the cultural centre, and then it's just a matter of convincing Danielsen's police officers that they still answer to me. Gaba's presence and reputation helps, and it's not long before we are parked beside the First Minister's car.

"I invited the Jonkheer," she says, as we greet each other in the parking area. "I hope you don't mind."

"I think it's a good idea," I say, despite the flush of adrenaline I feel as I think about Ooqi's illicit monitoring of his computer, the parts he has access to.

I recognise Geert Aalders as he gets out of the passenger side of the Dutch administration's saloon. He looks untidy when compared to the sleek form of the Jonkheer, Coenraad is taller than Gaba, but the slim fit of his winter jacket presents an almost willowy figure beside Gaba's robust form. Together with two Dutch Constables, a handful of Âmo security personnel, and my own close-protection team, the pedestrianised streets running through the centre of Nuuk feel suddenly narrow, and our entourage presses the shoppers and office workers to both sides of the street. We are more of a nuisance than a reassurance, and I split our group into three, with enough space between each group to allow pedestrians to slalom between us like a steam of fish through a coral reef. The First Minister's group is in front, and when she stops, we all stop.

"She's quite the showstopper," the Jonkheer says, as he walks towards me. "I thought we could talk for a moment while we wait."

"I'd like that," I say.

"But first," he says, "I have something for you." The Jonkheer takes a package from Geert and hands it to me. "*Stroopwafels*," he says, as I unwrap it. "I heard that you liked them."

"Yes," I say. "And a friend of mine – he was very fond of them."

"Ah, yes. My condolences. I heard about your friend. David, was it?"

"David Maratse. He was my partner."

"Partner? Not Married?"

I tuck the Jonkheer's gift inside my jacket pocket and start to walk as the First Minister's group moves along the street. The sky is light enough for the street lights to react, but still dark enough that the neon lights of the shops, offices, and apartments of Downtown Nuuk give a Tokyo-sheen to the snow-lined streets.

"We talked about it, but there were complications," I say. I can see Gaba a few paces behind us talking with the Jonkheer's assistant. "I was kidnapped in the beginning of our life together. David rescued me, but the following years were dark, and…" I stop myself as I wonder why I am saying this, but the Jonkheer wears a look that is a sympathetic as his clothes are sophisticated.

"Please, continue," he says. "If you want to." He gestures at the First Minister's group just ahead of us. "Pipaluk needs this, and the people need to see her. We have plenty of time."

"Alright," I say, as Pipaluk's group moves on and we meander behind them. "I suppose we had been through so much together that marriage felt too formal. It wasn't necessary, so long as we had each other."

The Jonkheer stops and reaches for my hand. "When you were kidnapped, is that when you got these… tattoos?"

"Yes," I say, and draw my hand back into my pocket.

"Forgive me," he says. "It's just I have been briefed by my senior constable. Your Sergeant…"

"Danielsen."

"Yes. He has been very forthcoming with information. And our own studies have concluded that there are many links between you and this Calendar Man. Do you agree?"

"There are some similarities," I say.

"More than a few, according to my men, and the evidence. We have been trying to establish the link between the Dutch victim and the others." He lifts his hands for a second. "I must apologise for our tardiness. Your department has shared information, whereas we have been silent."

"We did notice."

"And yet, you have exercised such professional restraint. I admire that. For our own part, I think we found the whole thing abhorrent to the degree that we were paralysed." He lowers his voice." You've seen the body?"

"Yes."

"Such horror. A real Frankenstein's monster. It was shocking. We were stunned, to tell you the truth."

"And now?"

"Now we have had time to collect our thoughts and process our data. My Senior Constable is meeting with your Sergeant today, but I wanted to tell you what we know, and what we have surmised."

I'm tempted to patch Ooqi into the conversation but decide to let Danielsen handle it. But I'm curious and almost impatient when the First Minister interrupts us.

"We're going to continue through town and on to the community centre," she says. "My assistant has called the media and they are setting up now. Will you join us?"

"Of course," I say. "We'll follow you."

The Jonkheer continues as soon as she is gone.

"Benjamin De Kloet died of natural causes. He had a heart condition, and was struggling to adapt to the cold, and a new lifestyle. I would never have put him on the list. He would have been better off and better suited to life in one of the Vaalserberg Towers, but he had some political sway, and climbed to the top third of an exclusive list."

"And he died of complications?"

"We believe he died as a result of his condition. It cost him his life."

"And he was treated by the colony doctor?"

"Yes. Benjamin called the doctor earlier in the day before he died. According to the doctor's records he arranged a visit and then cancelled it later. The post mortem of his body, carried out by the same doctor, determined that he was dead an hour or two prior to his body being mutilated." The Jonkheer stops as we near the entrance to the community centre. "The doctor has been quite disturbed by all this. He feels responsible, despite our best efforts to convince him otherwise."

I wait as the Jonkheer talks with his assistant. It strikes me again how the Calendar Man must have access to medical journals and information to find the bodies necessary to wage his terror campaign. The Jonkheer knew of Benjamin de Kloet's medical condition. What else does he know, and about whom? But even if he has access to the Dutch colonists' medical information, he can't possibly know about the Chinese or the Greenlanders. Not without some form of bugging device. I watch as Geert Aalders gives the Jonkheer something. Geert catches my eye as the Jonkheer walks back to me.

"Sorry, I was just talking with Geert about returning to the office." He points at the community centre. The light from the digital frieze casts stars across his dark blue eyes. "We won't be voting tomorrow. No matter what might have been agreed, and whatever we signed, we still consider ourselves guests in your country."

"It's your country too," I say.

"Yes," he says, and turns something small within his fingers. "And yet, we are still foreigners and I suppose it will take some time, perhaps even years, before we are able to trust one another. This doesn't help," he says and places a slim disc into the palm of my hand. "The cleaners found it last night," he says. "We don't know how long it has been there." He turns it in my palm. "If you look at the markings – very small, at the edges – they look like Chinese characters to me."

"Chinese?" I say, and I wonder if he can hear my heart thumping inside my chest.

"Yes." The Jonkheer lowers his voice. "I appreciate that we arrived after they did, but perhaps we can talk about this at another time. At your convenience, of course."

"Of course," I say, grateful for the splash of blue from the frieze above my head. It changes the hue of my cheeks from an embarrassed red to a healthy glow.

"Once again," he says, "please forgive us for our tardiness. I promise it will never happen again, and if we uncover any further evidence that will help in your investigation, you will be the first to know."

"I look forward to that."

"Yes," he says, with a glance at the community centre. "You

must catch this man, before he ruins what we have all worked so hard to achieve."

We shake hands and I watch him leave, pressing the disc into my pocket as the Jonkheer's assistant catches my eye for a second time, staring until the Jonkheer steps between us and the Dutch contingent walk back to their vehicle.

"Petra?" Gaba says. "What was all that about?"

"I think I just dodged a bullet," I say.

"Really?" He points at the retreating figure of the Jonkheer's assistant. "Not from where I was standing."

Marlunngorneq

Tuesday, 16th December 2042

Chapter 16

Aron shuffles a stack of folders in his arms at the rear of the assembly hall as the duty officer briefs the day shift. It is voting day, and all leave has been cancelled, bonuses promised, and favours cashed-in. I wait for him to finish with the practical details, and then join Danielsen at the podium. He starts with a profile of the Calendar Man.

"We're looking for a male, in good physical shape. We don't believe he is Chinese. We honestly don't know if he is Greenlandic or European. He's intelligent, and motivated. He's also an opportunist and experienced in low-cost disruption. We're not trying to anticipate what he might do. We believe that if we do our job right. Look in all the usual places, check the back entrances regularly, and basically use common sense policing, we will foil all but the most elaborate plan. As for a description, based on the nature of his activity, he is likely to be wearing practical clothes." Danielsen pauses at a shuffling of feet and a few suppressed laughs. "You're right; he'll look like everyone else on the street. But pay attention to his hands – if he's wearing gloves, they are more likely to be insulated work gloves than fleece. He'll be wearing a backpack, big enough to fit one of these," Danielsen says and holds up one of the advent calendars inside its plastic evidence bag. "The last calendar was left with the body of an elderly woman close to the shopping mall. The calendars have been left with bodies, or they have contained body parts – I'm referring to the advent calendar left at the school." Danielsen pointed to where Atii and Ooqi stand at the rear of the room. Atii will be in one of the SUVs reserved for reports concerning the Calendar Man. Ooqi will be coordinating everything via uplink, and we want you to feed relevant data directly to him. Contact Atii directly with sightings and critical incidents. Ooqi will be patched into her channel and will collate everything, pushing data to your patrol tablets with priority messages if there is an incident." Danielsen takes a step back from the podium, and then remembers something. "Oh, and I'll be with the Special Response Unit on standby here at the station."

"Thank you, Aqqa," I say, as I step up to the podium.

I can see fifty police officers in front of me, and the duty officer has confirmed that another thirty are already on the street, at the close of their shift. Twenty more police officers are at home, or relaxing, voting, shopping and enjoying their day off, but ready to respond, should it be necessary. I hope it won't be. We're already stretched thin and eating into the next year's budget. Or was it the following year? I don't remember. But it should be the last thing on my mind as I look at the men and women waiting for me to speak.

"There's been a lot of speculation," I say, "as to the Calendar Man's motives, and even his target. It has been suggested, several times, that it has something to do with me. And, several times, I have believed that to be the case. Some of you have felt that more than others, pulling extra shifts to provide protection – for me. Or responding to incidents at the very end of their shift – because of me. Well, now that we've established who's to blame…" I pause for a few laughs and many tired smiles. Too many. "It's only fair that I ask you to do one more thing. Not for me this time, but for your country. Today Greenland votes, one more time – perhaps the very last time – on its future. Today, what you do, *everything* you do, is for Greenland. To give the Greenlandic people the chance to vote, not just for their future, but yours, our children's future, for every child from this moment forwards. Now, if this sounds a little dramatic, then allow me to be selfish, and angry for just one moment, because this is not about me." I take a step towards Danielsen and pluck the advent calendar from his hands. "One cowardly opportunist, no matter his motive, is not going to stop the people of Greenland making a decision on their future. We're not going to let him. *You're* not going to let him."

The first sporadic claps echo around the assembly hall as I press the calendar into Danielsen's hands. I raise my own hand for them to stop clapping as I step up to the podium.

"One more thing," I say, as the men and women of the Nuuk Police Department clasp their hands behind their backs. "I'm not going to tell you how to vote today, but I am going to remind you to *remember* to vote. This is your day too. Now, go make it safe for everyone."

I catch a few words and comments as the officers disperse and get ready to hit the streets. It feels good to see them straighten tired shoulders, to clap each other on the back as they leave the assembly hall. I feel like a Commissioner again, for the first time in a long time, certainly the whole of December. I turn as Danielsen and Atii approach the podium and I wave to Aron that I will be with him in a moment.

"Nice speech, ma'am," Atii says.

"Thank you. It's good to have you back. Now, what are you going to do about Gaba?"

"Ma'am?"

"He seems duty-bound to sleep on my couch."

"*Aap*, we talked about that."

"And?"

"He stays until we catch the Calendar Man," Atii says. "No discussion."

"Atii…"

She shakes her head. "It's either Gaba or Danielsen."

I start to say something but stop as soon as Atii starts to laugh.

"I think it's best I stay with the task force, ma'am," Danielsen says. "If you don't mind."

"That'll be fine." I can see he has something else to say. "Aqqa?"

"I checked your schedule with Aron. I just want to be sure you are staying in the office today."

"Yes. Although I plan on voting around lunchtime."

"They say that will be the busiest time, ma'am," Aqqa says with a frown.

"Yes," I say. "Will it be Nikolaj, again?"

"And whoever else I can find."

Danielsen swears under his breath, but he hasn't tried to stop me, and I take that as an encouraging sign. With Gaba's security guards, extra police officers on duty, and the Dutch constabulary pulling double shifts, there is a uniform of one description or another on almost every corner, at the door of every public and vulnerable building, and beside every voting booth. Even the First Minister has noticed, and I think of her public address on the radio at breakfast as Danielsen calls for Aron to join us.

"I want you to stay with the Commissioner all day."

"Alright."

"Nikolaj will be with you too.

"Yes, Sergeant."

"You never leave her side," Danielsen says, with a glance at me.

It would almost be endearing if it wasn't so frustrating. But I'm still on a high following the assembly. I can't remember the last time I spoke to the whole department. It feels good. The whole day feels good, and I take a step back to send a message to Iiluuna, to coordinate our vote. I realise we haven't talked about what we actually want. Thoughts of an independent Greenland, many years ago, were plagued with poisonous agendas that split the country. For Greenlanders such as me, who never learned to speak Greenlandic, our place in our own country, culture and society was questioned. Those were dark times, plagued by corruption at a local and government level. David was stubbornly apolitical, and I remember that it infuriated me. But I wonder what he would have voted for today, if he had the chance.

"Commissioner?" Aron says, and I realise we are alone.

"Yes, Aron."

"Perhaps we could go to your office? I have a few things you need to look at – before you vote."

"Lead the way," I say, but I am slow, as I have to check Iiluuna's message. Aron holds the elevator and I step in beside him. "Two o'clock," I say. "That's when we'll vote. At the community centre opposite the supermarket."

"Is that safe, ma'am?"

"What do you mean?"

"It was the place the Calendar Man left the first body," he says, with a glance at my hands.

"And probably more secure than the police station right now. See how quiet it is."

The desks in the outer office are empty and dark except for a lamp on Aron's desk. The Christmas Stars in the window cast a red glow into the room, and I hesitate to flick the switch for the main lights. It's not often you can call a police station pretty, but there is a thick layer of snow on the window ledges, and flowers of frost on the glass. The administration staff has done their best to compete with the other departments and units, and I see, for what feels like the first time, the effort they have made to decorate the office, and to spread a little Christmas cheer.

Only one thing is missing.

I can't see a single advent calendar on any of the desks.

We have more than enough in the evidence room, I think.

But with only eight days until Christmas, it's beginning to feel festive, as if Christmas will come despite the Calendar Man and his best efforts to ruin it, for me, for the people of Nuuk, and for

Greenland.

"It must be ten o'clock," I say.

"I'll make coffee," Aron says, as he dumps the files on his desk. "Unless you want tea, ma'am?"

"Coffee will be perfect, thank you."

It occurs to me that Danielsen has let him off the hook, and that the young man's supposed infatuation, is nothing more than genuine loyalty and concern. Nothing more dangerous than that.

"Sit with me, Aron," I say, as he brings the coffee and rolls into my office. "The paperwork can wait for a moment. Let's just sit for a minute." I pull out a chair and gesture for Aron to do the same. "Tell me about yourself. You arrived during a difficult time for me – David got really sick just after the summer. I feel as though you have been here forever, but I forget it is just a few months, really. Tell me where you come from, and what you will do for Christmas?"

It's a classic case of too much, too soon. Aron splashes the coffee on the table as he pours, and I pull my hand back quickly to avoid hot splashes of coffee on my skin.

"Aron?"

"Sorry, ma'am," he says. He settles once the coffee is poured.

"Christmas?" I say, with a gentle smile.

"With *anaana*, my mum. In Sisimiut."

"Just the two of you?"

Yes," he says. "I never knew my dad, and my sister committed suicide when I was twelve."

"I'm sorry," I say.

It's a sad story, but all too familiar. Suicide clouds nearly every family in Greenland, leaving few untouched, and far too many missed.

"We've accepted it now," he says. "I have, at least."

Aron is quiet for a moment and we sip our coffee. When I put my mug down, I see that one of the Christmas Stars is glowing brighter than before. The red and orange light flickers upon the glass, and the flowers of frost are lit with golden threads. I'm amazed at the detail, the magic of Christmas. I want a closer look, but the pounding of feet in the hallway and the crash of someone slapping the door to one side as they charge into the office dispels the last of the Christmas cheer with a crash of metal and wood as the door slams into the wall and the glass in my office window shakes.

Aron spills his coffee as he reaches for the pistol holstered at his waist, and then he stops, and we both stare at Nikolaj as he slows outside my office. He must have taken the stairs, and he takes a few quick breaths before speaking.

"It's the parliament building," he says, and points towards the Christmas Stars in the windows. "There's a fire. A big one. We have to evacuate."

"Evacuate?"

"We're too close. They want us out."

"Where are we going?" I ask, as I grab my jacket.

"Danielsen is setting up a command centre in the sports hall."

"A command centre? Nikolaj," I say, as I grab his arm. "What's going on?"

"More fires, all over the city."

"How many?"

"Three, maybe four."

"The voting centres?"

"Yes." Nikolaj guides me to the stairs. "We have to go, ma'am. Nuuk is burning."

Pingasunngorneq

Wednesday, 17th December 2042

Chapter 17

The latest reports come in after midnight, by which time the voluntary fire service confirms that the fire at the government building is under control, and that we can return to the police station in the next few hours or wait until mid-morning when it will be safer. We've been here all night, and the grey light of dawn is pressing against the windows of the sports hall. I stand to one side as Danielsen receives reports and updates from across the city.

"Ooqi is offline," he says to me during a brief lull.

"That's unusual."

More than that, I think. *It's unheard of.*

"His activity icon has gone dark. Maybe he was thrown off the server when we evacuated the police station. I don't know." Danielsen sighs as he sees the Chinese representative, Tan Yazhu, walking towards us.

"I'll talk to him," I say. "Just get Ooqi back online."

Tan Yazhu meets me in the middle of the sports hall and we find a place to sit along one of the walls. There is some glitter left over from the Christmas market on the table and I brush it to one side with my hand as Tan Yazhu sits down.

"We are very sorry about the vote," he says.

Initial reports suggest that no-one was hurt at any of the fires at the voting centres, but that voting was disrupted, and the decision of Greenland's independence has been postponed. A brief article I read in *Oqaasaq*, stated that if Greenland doesn't vote before the end of the year, it will be another two years before Denmark will be willing for them to have another referendum. I don't pretend to understand the politics, but I know the fallout will be great, and I feel sad for my country and my people.

"Thank you," I say.

"And the fires. We are sorry for you about them too."

"Yes. But they are under control now. I understand you sent a team of miners to help. We appreciate that."

"*Shi.*" Tan Yazhu bows his head. "You're welcome."

"How can I help you?"

"This Calendar Man. Do you think you can catch him?"

His question makes me hesitate for a second. I suppose I have never imagined that we wouldn't, that it was only a matter of time.

But perhaps time is running out. If this was the Calendar Man's final act, to prevent the vote from happening, then he could just disappear. Perhaps we will never catch him. I can almost feel the tattoos on my fingers burning and I realise that I want him caught, at all costs.

"Yes," I say. "We will catch him."

"When?"

"That's difficult to say, Tan Yazhu."

"Before Christmas?"

"Ideally, I would like to catch him tonight, but I don't know…"

"Before December twenty-three."

"I don't know."

"It's important, lady Commissioner. December twenty-three is *Dongzhi*. The Winter Solstice. It is very important to us. There will be big celebrations in Chinatown. Already, the Dutch have missed *Sinterklaas*. Ruined with a monster man left in the administration building. We do not want this to happen to *Dongzhi*. The miners have been working very hard, very hard all year, and they need *Dongzhi*. It is very important. I have promised them everything will be alright. Now you must promise me."

"I cannot promise anything."

"Then we will take matters into our own hands. And you must step aside."

He folds his arms across his small chest. He is smaller than me, smaller than a lot of Greenlanders, but the intensity in his eyes, the way he looks at me, makes him seem twice as tall. Dangerous and committed.

"Tan Yazhu," I say. "You are the Chinese security representative."

"*Shì*."

"And your official title?"

"That's not important. I am the boss. I am responsible." He stabs the table with his finger. "I will find this man, if you cannot."

"Perhaps we can find him together? I'm sure if we shared our information, then maybe we could help each other."

"Sharing information? Is that what you call hacking our computer?"

I was afraid of this. Ooqi had warned me, but with no communication from the Chinese, zero cooperation, they left me with little choice and I turned a blind eye to Ooqi's search for information. I could even deny it, and I try.

"Could you be more specific, Tan Yazhu?"

"How about this?"

He places a small disc on the table. I recognise it instantly. Although, on closer inspection, the Chinese symbols I saw on the disc the Jonkheer gave me are missing.

"It is a bugging device. I found it in the crack between the leg and surface of my desk. Can you explain?"

"No, I can't."

I really can't. I'm tempted to look at Danielsen, to see if he has established contact with Ooqi, but I think it's best to play ignorant. It's not difficult.

Tan Yazhu stands up and I realise the meeting is about to end.

"You catch him before December twenty, or I will."

"Tan Yazhu…"

"No, lady Commissioner, say nothing more. Just catch him."

"It would help if you shared information about the dead miner. We can use that to help us find the Calendar Man."

Tan Yazhu waves his hand, as if it is irrelevant.

"He was drunk. He died in his apartment. Choked on his own vomit. I sent his body back to China. Good riddance. He was bad worker."

"Thank you," I say, as I think about the opportunistic nature of the Calendar Man. Or was it just a coincidence and the apartment – number nine – was just a number, nothing more.

Tan Yazhu barely even nods before marching with short urgent strides to the entrance. I watch him leave and consider the diplomatic implications of being caught snooping on the Chinese, and the more pressing concern about Tan Yazhu carrying out his own investigation to catch the Calendar Man. I don't want to imagine the methods he might employ, but I can't help wondering if they might produce results, faster and more conclusive than our own.

A shout and a series of quick commands from Danielsen pull me back to the moment, and I watch as the SRU team run towards the door. Danielsen follows at a slower pace and I catch him before he leaves the sports hall.

"What's going on?"

"We've got a sighting, ma'am. A positive identification. Two officers are chasing a man with a backpack towards the docks. I have three police cars en route and the SRU…"

"I'm coming with you," I say. "No discussion. Let's go."

I reach the door of the SRU vehicle before Danielsen, and the team of four heavily-armed officers make space for me in the middle of the passenger area, as Danielsen climbs into the seat beside the driver. The driver accelerates onto the road as the men shut the doors.

"Suspect is medium height," Danielsen says from the front seat. "Medium build. Carrying a black backpack. He's wearing tan coloured work gloves and has a wool hat."

The men wait until Danielsen has finished speaking before they make a last check of their gear, apologising as they bump padded shoulders with me as the driver slings the SRU vehicle around the bends, drifting across the ice before accelerating along the straight sections, siren wailing, lights flashing.

David loved this – the speed, the lights, the excitement and the adrenaline. He pretended he didn't, but I could see it in his eyes every time a patrol car raced past us on the streets. It was even more evident in the final months before he died, when our walks were precious, and he savoured everything he could including the sights, sounds and smells of Greenland's rapidly expanding city. I wish he was here now, and I'm ready for him to just appear on the seat beside me, flashing a toothy grin and gripping my hand at all the excitement. But the man beside me is all but hidden beneath his helmet, behind the mask. I can't see his face, and neither can I pretend he is David. But just one word could make all the difference. David's voice, the one inside my head.

Focus, Piitalaat.

Apparently, I can conjure him on command, and I smile as I kid myself that David's ghost is with me, travelling right beside me as we fly down Nuuk's streets and the driver downshifts the gears and slows at the top of the slope leading down to the docks. There is a bump and a curse as the vehicle shimmies into a snowdrift, followed by a gasp of cold air as the four-man team open the doors on each side of the vehicle and race down the street towards a police officer waving his arms and pointing towards the rocks to the right of the road.

"That way," he shouts. "Fifty metres."

"Ma'am," Danielsen says, as I leap out of the vehicle.

I haven't worn a pistol for over a year, and I feel naked all of a sudden. The thought chills me more than the bite of cold air that tickles my skin and freezes my breath onto the tips of my hair. I can feel the cold pinch my cheeks as I race after the SRU team. I'm almost giddy, invigorated by the pursuit. Danielsen won't catch me, his midriff and the ice coating the rocks will slow him down. I don't care about slipping. I can hear the SRU team begin to shout, ordering the suspect to get down and stay down. I press the soles of my boots into the prints left by the team in the snow. I can see them now, their submachine guns pointed down at a man on the ground, his black clothes, backpack, and hat dusted with snow. I arrive just as the team leader presses his knee onto the man's back, secures his wrists with plastic shackles, and pulls the man onto his knees.

"Just a minute, ma'am," one of the SRU officers says, as he steps in front of me, slowing me down and shielding me from the suspect. "We need to make sure he's alone."

He is. I'm sure of it.

I nod, and then step to one side. I need to see his face. But I can feel the cold pinch my brow as I see the man – younger than I imagined him to be, with the wispy beard and bushy black eyebrows so typical of Greenlanders.

"It's not him," I say, as Danielsen wheezes to a stop behind me.

"We need to talk to him," he says, between gasps of breath.

"He can't help us."

"We don't know that."

I'm disappointed. Perhaps it is the anti-climax of the chase, the adrenaline evaporating from my body, drawing the heat from my head, and turning my hair white with breath and dismay. I thought we had him. I thought it was over.

I walk away, back towards the road, convinced that we have been on yet another elaborate wild goose chase, with little to show for it. I was so eager, and I wonder if it was because of Tan Yazhu, or the referendum, or just the simple fact that I want this to end so that Nuuk, and me, can get through the darkest month of the year, and just enjoy Christmas. I want to spend Christmas Eve with Iiluuna and Quaa, to watch them open their presents, give them something to show how much they mean to me, and how much they have helped me through my grief.

But no. It was all for nothing. The hunt is still on, and we are desperate for leads.

"Ma'am," Danielsen says, as he catches up to me. His breathing is normal now, but his cheeks are rosy red, complementing the flash of blue emergency lights.

"I'm sorry, Aqqa. I thought we had him."

"We might still," he says. Danielsen pauses to take a breath. "He has a message, from the Calendar Man."

Sisamanngorneq

Thursday, 18th December 2042

Chapter 18

There is no darkness, only ignorance. The Calendar Man's message was the first, the last and the only thing the man told us. Danielsen interviewed him through the night while the city held its breath. If I look out of the office window, I can see the charred façade of the government buildings. I can hear about the fire on the radio or read it in the first few pages – streaming and paper editions – of *Oqaasaq*. I imagine Qitu steering his reporters along different avenues of inquiry, exploring leads and receiving tips as the people of Nuuk weigh in on the activity of the past few days. Gaba wrote a report for the First Minister and sent me a copy. I skimmed the summary with my first coffee of the day, but I am distracted, and I feel the need to look at the evidence again. The paperwork can wait.

"Aron," I say, as I stand at the door to my office. "Can you find Natuk and tell her to meet me in the evidence room."

"Yes, ma'am."

He hesitates, and I know why. It's the end of year budget approval that I have been ignoring, along with several other administrative tasks that need a final signature or a few lines of comments and amendments. I would like to think that these things can wait, but I know that I'm just pushing them, one day at a time.

"I know about the budget," I say. "I promise to look at it later."

What Danielsen and I thought might have been an unhealthy infatuation, turns out to be one of Aron's endearing qualities – a sense of loyalty and responsibility. It will get the better of him one day, I'm sure of it. But one more day won't kill him, and I have other things to deal with, at the personal request of the First Minister. Her voice follows me back into my office as I open a new search page on my browser. There's still no sign of Ooqi, although Danielsen assures me he is looking into it. He is probably exhausted. I don't remember seeing him take a break or a day off. He is always online or at his desk. But without him, I have to do some of the leg work myself.

Danielsen plugged the message into a search engine almost as soon as the man in custody said it. Some of the results were random, others were Shakespearian. He was never on the Greenlandic school curriculum, but the Danes know a little about him. I remember Hamlet having something to do with Denmark, and then there is the Ombudsman's fascination with Shakespeare.

Danes and Shakespeare.

I leave the browser open as I look through the few shelves on the wall of my office. I slipped the Ombudsman's book somewhere between books on law and conduct after a glance at the back cover suggested it would be just as interesting. I don't read books. I know few Greenlanders that do. David was an exception to the rule, but I don't remember him ever reading Shakespeare. I pull the thin volume off the shelf and read the title: *Twelfth Night: Or,What You Will.*

I feel a slight thrill, a subtle crackle of energy in the air as I remember Danielsen's notes, something about the quote. He thinks it could be related to *Twelfth Night,* and he found it in Act IV, Scene II. The message is paraphrased, but clear to see, spoken by a clown and a character called Malvolio. It means nothing to me, but when Aron confirms that Natuk is on her way I take the book with me to the evidence room.

It's curious that the Ombudsman should have an interest in Shakespeare, and that the Calendar Man's message is taken from the very play she suggested I read.

"It's a Christmas story," she had said.

I prefer something cosier, and in a language I understand, but Shakespeare has a new-found meaning, and if it can give us a lead then, no matter how archaic the language, I'm going to have to read it. Of course, if David was alive, I could have asked him to read it to me, as I curled into his body.

Focus, Piitalaat.

"I will," I say, as I scan my thumb and open the door to the evidence room. "I promise."

Natuk is waiting at the table, studying the calendars. I smile as she turns, and I am reminded of a younger version of myself. She has the same oversized police jacket, the boots that give her at least one more inch in height, and the soft eyes that have seen too much suffering already, and yet not so much that the light is fading into shadow. She has a keen mind too, and I want to put it to work.

"We need to start again," I say. I press the book into Natuk's hands and gather up the letters printed on squares of paper beneath each calendar. "Imagine that it has nothing to do with me. We've spent too much time on that already."

"Ma'am?"

"Misdirection. I think we leaped at the chance to find meaning in

Piita's body. Following that line of inquiry just got us stuck in the mud. We need to think differently, attack this differently."

"And the book?" Natuk says, as she turns it in her hands. "Shakespeare?"

"The Ombudsman, Anna Riis, lent it to me. Danielsen thinks the message from the Calendar Man might have come from there. Act four, scene two: *There is no darkness, only ignorance.*"

"I've found it," Natuk says. "Sort of. It's not a direct quote, ma'am."

"No. it's not. But if we imagine it is relevant," I say, and gesture at the calendars. "How does it apply to these?" I smile at the furrow deepening on Natuk's brow. "That's why you're here. Have a think about it, and I'll call Aron for some coffee."

It could be an abuse of power, but Aron was with me when Anna Riis gave me the book. If I ask him to bring coffee, I might jog his memory. It feels good to be contributing again to the investigation. Danielsen is occupied with the interview and Atii is sifting through the crime scenes. With no sign of Ooqi, the task force has been diluted. So, the budget can wait, and I can reassign assets such as Natuk and Aron.

Aron responds to my text, and I slip my mobile into my pocket, standing quietly beside Natuk as she flips through the pages of *Twelfth Night*. She stops after five minutes, takes a closer look at the calendar, and taps her finger on her bottom lip.

"Natuk?"

"There are five calendars," she says.

"Yes."

"There are five acts in the play."

"One calendar for each act?"

"I thought so, but then the number for each window is wrong."

"In what way?"

Natuk flips through the pages of the book and turns it towards me.

"There are five scenes in the first two acts, four in the third, three in the fourth and only one in the fifth."

"And those numbers in the margin. What are they?"

I turn at the sound of Aron struggling to enter the evidence room and carry the tray of coffee, mugs and breakfast rolls. I don't have to look at my watch to know it is ten o'clock, or thereabouts. I leave Natuk with the calendars and help Aron come through the door.

"Thank you, ma'am," he says.

He puts the tray down to one side of the calendars and turns to leave.

"While you're here, Aron," I say. "Why don't you help us a little? The budget can wait."

"If you're sure?"

"That's a loaded question," I say. "How about you give me half an hour of your time, and I'll do the same."

"Alright," he says.

The sight of Aron relaxing makes me feel guilty, as if half an hour of my time is more than he could have hoped for. Since he arrived, I have been preoccupied with David's illness, followed by grief, and now a case that has had me at odds with my staff, and under house arrest. It's a wonder he has managed to get anything signed or processed since he began work as my assistant. But he has a keen mind behind that mask of worry and concern. He could be as sharp as Natuk, if given half the chance. According to our deal, he has half an hour.

Aron leans over the book and traces the lines with the tip of his finger. "The numbers," he says, "correspond to the lines. They are line numbers, that's all."

"It's that simple?"

"Yes, ma'am."

Natuk steps closer to the table and lays the book flat on the surface. She turns the pages to the first act as Aron and I join her at the table.

"Calendar one is Act one," she says. "Do we agree?"

"We do," I say.

"The first window was sixteen, and line sixteen is…"

"*Will you go hunt, my lord?*" Aron reads. "Spoken by Curio. Who's that?"

Natuk flips to the character list at the front of the book.

"An attendant to the Duke. Gentleman. Male."

The way she says it, it sounds like a brief profile of a suspect, and I catch myself smiling. Perhaps there's a reason Shakespeare isn't required reading at the Police Academy.

"How about the second calendar," I say. "What does that give us?"

Natuk turns the book towards Aron as he makes a note on his tablet. He finds the task force server and shares it to the case folder.

"Act two, line nine," Natuk says, as she turns the pages. "*Let me yet know of you whither you are bound,*" she reads. "And that makes no sense."

"It might not have to," I say. "Keep going."

"Act three, line twenty." She pauses and shows the book to Aron.

"What's wrong?" I ask.

"The line starts and finishes on the lines above and below. Do we take the whole sentence?"

"No," Aron says and presses his finger onto the page. "Just take this bit. It makes the most sense."

"*...indeed, words are very rascals,*" Natuk reads. "That makes *sense* to you?"

I let them argue for a moment as I step away from the table. The concertina cupboards of the evidence room allow for plenty of space to wander, unless they are in use. I pour a cup of coffee, blowing on the surface as I think about the words, the very rascals. It's a stretch, but the first quote from the first calendar makes some sense – the beginning of the hunt for the Calendar Man. Is he goading us? He wouldn't be the first. If it is aimed at us, then the second quote fits too, as he wonders where we are going, what leads we are following. I wonder if he knew just how confused we were, and, if that is the case, then he is mocking us with the quote from the third calendar, as the words lead us nowhere. Or perhaps he means the evidence, or even the motive. We were focused on me, then back to the referendum. But we had no idea that he was communicating with us, that he had opened an avenue of dialogue – the calendars were less about days and more about communication. But what is he saying?

"What is he saying in calendar four?"

"*Saying,* ma'am?" Natuk says.

"The line, the quote. What is it?"

"*Will you make me believe that I am not sent for...,*" she says. "The clown said it. Is it important who says it?"

"It could be."

But I'm not worried about that. This line is more direct. More sinister. On one level, it suggests that what he is doing is justified, and, on another, that he is here at someone's request. But who? Someone from my past? I don't want to go there. What if it is bigger than him, or he *thinks* it is bigger than him. Does he think Greenland *sent* for him? Or is it Denmark?

"The last calendar is another fragment," Natuk says. "*...my friends, and the better for my foes...*"

I hear Aron tap the last quote into his tablet with soft thuds of his fingers on the glass, and Natuk closes the book with a snap. It was the last calendar, his last words of communication before the referendum and the message delivered by his courier.

There is no darkness, only ignorance.

Is ignorance better than darkness? Are things better now that the referendum is postponed? It will be if it is not held before the end of the year. Is that the result the Calendar Man intended, to put things off for at least another two years?

If the calendars are meant to be interpreted, and we have done it right this time, then the Calendar Man has been sending messages from day one. It's time we sent one back.

Tallimanngorneq

Friday, 19th December 2042

Chapter 19

"I'm sorry we couldn't meet yesterday," Pipaluk says, as she welcomes me into her suite at Hotel Hans Egede. "It's been hectic, and we're still trying to discover what we have lost, since the fire."

"It's only been three days," I say. "I understand completely."

"Do you?" she says, as she sits down.

She seems sterner than usual, with a more aggressive cut of her clothes that extends to the straight and firm set of her jaw. I decide it is the shock of the fire and the failed referendum and let her comment pass.

"I've seen the fire chief's report. He says you should be able to move back into your office before Christmas."

"I've seen it too. The fire was superficial. The walls are a bit black on the outside, but the damage is irreparable."

"You mean the referendum?"

"Is there anything else more important at the moment, Commissioner?" Pipaluk clenches her fists and presses them on the table as she leans towards me. "I asked you to see to this case, personally, Petra. That was all. And yet, you deferred to some Sergeant from one of the settlements."

"Sergeant Danielsen has an exemplary record, First Minister."

"That's touching. He no doubt holds you in the same high regard, which is why he wasted time protecting you, and let this Calendar Man run riot through the town and tear down the foundations of Greenland's future with a few dead bodies and a handful of advent calendars."

I honestly thought this meeting was going to be better than this, but I had forgotten how important the question of Greenlandic independence is for Pipaluk Uutaaq, how personal it is for her and her family – the living and the dead.

"Sergeant Danielsen was reacting to the information we had at the time."

"Information interpreted by your own officers." Her heels bite into the carpet as she stands up and walks to the window. She stands close to the glass and stares down at Nuuk's main street. "This is our country," she says, her voice almost a whisper. "I don't think you understand how important it is to be allowed to govern what is ours, to make our own mistakes. I've met people in the small towns who are ready to work two, maybe even three jobs if they think it will make a difference, if it might help the economy – our economy. We've been under the Danish thumb for far too long. And now these climate immigrants…" She turns to look at me. The sneer on her lips is as sharp as ice. "It's just another colonial foothold, reminding us that we had better tow the line, do as *they* say. That we will never make it on our own."

"I thought you signed off on the Dutch agreement?"

"I signed it; I didn't *sign off*, Petra. There's a difference."

"But the money that they pay to the state…"

"Is just another grant, a lump sum to keep us content. It should have made us better off, but the Danes just adjusted their contribution to allow for it. We're no richer, no poorer, and no closer to economic independence."

"That's not what you said," I say.

"No?" Pipaluk laughs. "After all you've been through, Petra, after all these years, I never expected you to be so naïve. But then, you are the token Greenlander in a very public position. What? That surprises you too? You're a political pawn, Petra. Just like me."

Perhaps I have been naïve, but when I was encouraged to apply for the position of Police Commissioner, I honestly thought it was the natural step up the ladder after many years of service on the force. I managed to distance myself from the politics, and maybe that was my first mistake.

It is time to make amends.

"Earlier," I say, "you asked me if I understand. I think what you really want to ask me is how I would have voted, if I had had the chance."

Pipaluk crosses her arms as she waits by the window. Her jaw has softened, only a little, but enough to reveal her curiosity. She wants to know. And I'm ready to tell her.

"I would have voted *yes*," I say. "Yes, for an independent Greenland. Does that surprise you?"

"Honestly, it does."

"Because I don't speak Greenlandic."

She laughs. "You're confusing me with my father. I don't care what language you speak, Petra. But I didn't think you would vote for independence, because I don't think you want to fight." She raises her hand as I start to speak. "Don't mistake me. I know you're strong, and you've had your battles, tougher than anything I have experienced. But I think you're ready to stop. To let life continue on around you. I think you're looking for peace, something you've earned, but a vote for independence is not the peaceful choice. It's going to be tough, and I didn't think you wanted to fight."

"Then we have something in common, First Minister."

"What's that?"

"We both underestimate each other."

I stand up and walk to join her at the window. The midmorning sky is lightening, and the Northern Lights are barely visible. This city, taller than it once was, has grand ambitions. She's not wrong, I do want a peaceful life, but I don't think I'll ever stop fighting. Not really. I pull a folded piece of paper from my pocket and press it into her hands.

"What's this?"

"Something I want you to work into your speech."

"My speech?" she asks, as she frowns at the words I have written on the paper.

"The one when you announce a new referendum, on the twenty-third of December."

"The night before Christmas Eve? It can't be done."

"I think it can. You just need to convince your staff." I smile as the frown ruins her otherwise perfect composure. "What was it you said? Something about people doing two or three jobs to make things work, to achieve an independent Greenland. A new referendum won't make that a certainty, but it will give the people of Greenland a chance to do something about it, to fight for it – with their voice, of course. They will be heard."

"And the Calendar Man? He's achieved his goal. Won't this just incite him?"

I tap the paper in her hand.

"You're going to send him a message, First Minister."

"*Be not afraid of greatness?*"

"And the next bit," I say.

"*Fate, show thy force.*" Pipaluk folds the paper into her pocket. "What message, exactly, am I sending, Commissioner?"

"You're calling him out, so that we can catch him."

"I'm not just painting a target on my chest?"

"You've had one from the day you entered office, First Minister.

I don't think a few more days are going to make a difference."

"I suppose not."

I leave her by the window. How she works Shakespeare into her speech is up to her and her staff. How I catch the Calendar Man is up to me.

I smile at Nikolaj as I open the suite door, and we walk quietly along the carpeted corridor to the elevator. Gaba's security guards are everywhere. I nod at one of them as Nikolaj presses the button for the elevator and the door opens.

"You're not coming with me?" I ask, as he waits in the corridor.

"Natuk will meet you in reception. I've been assigned to the First Minister." Nikolaj can't quite hide the smile on his lips. "Better hours," he says, as the door closes.

I should warn him about the sleepless nights Pipaluk has ahead of her, but I have a childish urge to giggle instead, and I allow myself that little pleasure from the top floor to reception.

Piitalaat.

"I know," I say, as the elevator bell rings once prior to the doors opening. "I'll behave. I promise."

"What's that, ma'am," Natuk says, as I walk out of the elevator.

"Nothing important. Let's go back to the station."

"We can't," she says, as she opens the door of the SUV parked at the entrance. "Danielsen needs you to see something."

"What?"

"It's best you see for yourself," she says, and closes the passenger door.

It's hard not to feel optimistic when the sun shines in the winter in Greenland. The towns, villages and settlements further north won't see the sun for another few weeks, longer in Qaanaaq at the very top of Greenland, but Nuuk and the south enjoy lower latitudes. I pull down the sun visor as Natuk accelerates.

"He said it was urgent, ma'am," she says, when I glance at the speedometer.

I'm curious and tempted to suggest we turn on the emergency lights and siren. For David's sake, of course. Although, the smile on Natuk's face suggests she is not immune to the thrill of a rapid response.

"It's nearly Christmas, Natuk. There are a lot of people about."

"Ma'am?"

"Turn on the siren. It will be safer."

And more fun for Natuk, I think, as she pushes the new electric SUV to an appropriate, if slightly elevated speed. I glance at the graveyard and send a thought to David as we flash past it.

The fun stops as Danielsen waves us over to the side of the road and Natuk parks beside the SRU patrol vehicle in the parking area below one of Nuuk's older residences – a grey apartment block devoid of Christmas Cheer.

"Danielsen?" I say, as I tug at the collar of my jacket and join him by the side of the SRU vehicle. The four SRU officers are wearing body armour and ballistic helmets. Their submachine guns are trained on the windows of the building, and a quick glance to the left and right reveals more officers in armour in strategic positions. The building is surrounded.

"You've found him?" I say, and I clench my fingers inside my jacket pockets as they begin to tremble.

"*Naamik*," Danielsen says. "It's not him."

"Then who?"

"Atii responded to a call this morning. Four men armed with what could be Chinese bangsticks."

"I don't know what they are."

"Basically, a simple explosive device at the end of a rod, that can be fitted with charges or other attachments. Harpoons, for example. The men inside the building were seen carrying at least two each. Atii is inside negotiating, but they won't come out. One of the men says you promised him something. And, according to him, you have the rest of the day to do it."

"Who is she talking with?"

"Tan Yazhu," Danielsen says. "He says you promised to catch the Calendar Man before the twentieth of December. And if you don't, then he and his men will carry out their own investigation, starting at dawn tomorrow."

"But they're surrounded."

"I don't think that was part of the plan, ma'am."

"We don't have time for this," I say.

I imagine that Pipaluk will arrange a live interview on the early evening news. As soon as she makes it known that there will be a new referendum, the Calendar Man will be forced to act.

"We can't have our men tied up here," I say.

"I agree, ma'am." Danielsen tugs the radio from the clip on his jacket. "Atii has been briefed about the First Minister's speech and the new referendum. She knows what to do."

"She's ready to go in?"

Danielsen nods.

I wonder if this is what the First Minister imagined when she wondered if I was ready to fight for my country? Coupled with the thought that I am a Danish-speaking Greenlander in a very visible public office, I am tempted to call her, and postpone the announcement. But that would mean postponing the referendum and sabotaging a last attempt to allow the people to vote for their future. The towns, villages and settlements outside Nuuk might have escaped the Calendar Man's campaign of terror, but turnout to the polls was limited by the drama playing out on the radio and streaming media. The digital booths could be reset, but the people still had to visit them.

"Ma'am?"

"This might be my last order as Police Commissioner," I say.

"It might." Danielsen lowers his hand, the stubby radio antennae scratches against the rough weave of his trousers. "It might also be the most important."

"What would you do, Aqqa?"

"Me?"

"You might be in this same position one day. What would you do?"

"In the same situation? A terrorist on the loose a few days before a new referendum to vote on our independence, when foreign investment will play a critical role in our economic future."

"Yes."

"And you're about to storm a building to pacify four armed foreign nationals, whose country is one of Greenland's greatest investors."

"That's about the size of it, Aqqa," I say. "What would you do?"

He laughs. It's contagious.

"*Be not afraid of greatness*," he says. "Apparently, that's Shakespeare. Whoever he was."

"I prefer the other line," I say. "*Fate, show thy force.*"

And in that moment, I know what I have to do.

"Tell Atii to keep negotiating."

"And if it doesn't work?"

"You go in at dawn," I say. "That's an order."

Arfininngorneq

Saturday, 20th December 2042

Chapter 20

Natuk picks me up one hour before dawn. In the north of Greenland dawn is still months away. For Tan Yazhu and his team of three security guards, we chose four o'clock in the morning. I need the SRU team and rest of the department rested and ready to respond to the Calendar Man's reaction to the First Minister's announcement. To put it bluntly, the Chinese are in my way. Regardless of politics and international relations, it is bad timing.

Natuk is quiet as we drive. I turn on the radio, hear a repeat of the closing remarks of the First Minister's speech, and smile at the familiar words.

"That could be a first, you know," I say.

"What's that, ma'am?"

"A Greenlandic politician quoting Shakespeare."

Natuk says nothing more until we can see the police cordon around the grey concrete residence. She parks beside Danielsen's patrol car.

"I'm worried about Ooqi," she says. "No-one has seen him. He hasn't called in."

"Perhaps he has taken a day off. He's been working all week."

I should know, or at least find out, but I am distracted. I'm also impatient to get out of the car and be present when the SRU team storm the residence. I reach for the door handle but relax my grip when Natuk speaks.

"I think he's involved in something," she says. "He's been quiet for months now. Ever since the summer. We used to talk. Nothing more than that, but he was pleasant to be around. Now he's quiet and withdrawn."

"Involved in something?"

"Or taking something. Have you noticed that he doesn't look you in the eye?"

"He doesn't say much, but I don't remember thinking he was avoiding me or any of the task force."

"It could be drugs," Natuk says. "I wouldn't have said anything, and I don't want him to get into trouble. But if he's already in trouble, I want to help him."

"Let's find him first. It might just be his day off, and he has gone on a fishing trip in the fjord."

"You don't know Ooqi," she says. "He's too moody to fish. Since the summer, at least."

I should ask more, show a little more support at the very least, but Danielsen has waved twice now. They are ready. He doesn't need a command from me, but I want to be there, to be visible – visibly fighting for Greenland.

"Find him, Natuk. If he needs help, I'll do all that I can."

Natuk stays in the car as I jog to Danielsen's position. He gestures for me to crouch behind a large ballistic shield. The glass in the shield's bulletproof window is sticky with frost and he wipes it clean with his elbow.

"Atii is on the roof with the team making the entry. They will rappel down the sides and enter through the windows. We have units with shields at all the exits."

"And the negotiations failed, I gather."

"Atii tried until early evening. She took a break for a few hours while one of the Danish officers tried a new tack – he said he had some experience, and I thought it couldn't hurt."

"It's fine, Aqqa. I left you in charge."

"Yes, ma'am." He shifts to a more comfortable position. "But it didn't help."

"We're sure they're still inside?"

"Absolutely. There's no way out. We've got the cellar covered and they can't dig through granite." He takes a breath. "They've had their chance, ma'am. Now it's up to the SRU to bring them in without any casualties. They'll use flashbangs."

"And the media?"

"One of Qitu's journalists is on the other side of the cordon, down there," he says and points to a police car at the opposite end of the street. "But I think they are too busy speculating over what will happen now the First Minister has announced a new referendum."

"They're not the only ones."

Danielsen lifts his finger at a double-click from his radio.

"That's it."

I look through the glass and can almost see the rapid descent of three of the SRU officers from the roof to the windows of the apartment the Chinese have occupied. I hear a splinter of glass and I'm blinded by the magnesium flash of light from the windows, and my ears are ringing from three concussive blasts. I can't imagine what it must be like inside the apartment.

The thunder in my ears settles and I hear shouts and cries in Chinese, commands in English, and a muffled explosion.

"Bangstick," Danielsen says.

I worry that the next sound will be the rapid stutter of one of the SRU's silenced submachine guns, but the night is still once more, and then I hear Atii's voice on the radio.

"Four subjects detained," she says. "One injury."

"Who?" Danielsen asks.

"One of the Chinese. A bangstick discharged as he reached for it. I've sent a medic in. It's not life-threatening."

I realise I am holding my breath, and I breathe as Danielsen sends his congratulations to the team. I spare a thought for Aron as I realise the incident might be over, but the paperwork is just about to begin.

"Well, that's it," Danielsen says.

"Have you been here all night?"

"I had a break for a few hours. I came back at midnight."

"I'll send Natuk home, if you'll let me buy you breakfast," I say.

"I'd like that, ma'am."

Natuk hasn't moved, and I see the blue glow of her mobile lighting her face. She starts as I tap on the window.

"I'm sorry," she says. "I thought it was over."

"It is, and I want you to go home. Get some sleep, and then I want you to find Ooqi. You're right to be concerned. Keep me updated."

"I'm your protection, ma'am."

"Sergeant Danielsen is relieving you."

"Okay," she says.

I wait for her to pull away and then join Danielsen in his patrol car. There are more cafés in Nuuk today than there have ever been, which means there are about twelve, and three of them are open all night. Danielsen groans as I suggest we go to *Tupilaq*.

"What's wrong with that?"

"The music," he says. "It's seventies."

"Greenland's favourite soundtrack."

"Yes, ma'am."

Tupilaq has a certain vibe about it, even at five o'clock on a Saturday morning. It is far enough away from Nuuk's bars and nightclubs to put off hungry revellers, but the menu and the very early morning specials, encourage some people to stay up half the night to try *Huevos Rancheros* or *Cowboy Scramble*. The secret is the eggs, and where they get them from. David loved it here, and, when he was in too much pain to sleep, he would dress quietly, leave a note, and slip out of the apartment. I usually caught up with him at the end of the road, pretending that I couldn't sleep, and that breakfast at two in the morning was just what I wanted. It was easier in the summer, when it was light all night. But the winter dark was another matter.

"My treat," I say, as we find an empty table and I gently push thoughts of David to the back of my mind. I'll revisit them later, but, for now, I think I need to repair my relationship with my Sergeant.

"What's good?"

"You've never been?"

I catch myself before I glance at Danielsen's waistline. He takes off his jacket and his uniform blue sweater bulges over his utility belt.

"My wife's cooking," he says and pats his belly. "Good Greenlandic food. I never eat out."

"I thought you had filled out a bit recently."

"*Aap.*"

"Then I'd go for the scrambled eggs, on thick toast. Canadian style."

I order for both of us, and then, as the waitress brings us coffee, I decide to apologise.

"I understand why you might think this case was all about me, Aqqa," I say. "And I'm sorry I gave you a hard time about it."

He sips his coffee, but his eyes never leave mine, and then he raises his eyebrows in a classic Greenlandic *yes*.

"And I'm sorry I went behind your back to the Deputy Commissioner."

"I'm sure I would have done the same," I say.

"Maybe."

The waitress returns with a double order of scrambled eggs on toast, and we say nothing more until we are both finished eating. Danes would have talked the whole way through the meal, but I relish that part of our culture. Somehow, we still manage to hold onto the sacred peace around mealtimes.

But it is technology that disturbs the peace as the waitress refills our coffee mugs. The beep of an incoming message on my mobile seems loud, but after reading it, the second beep feels louder than one of the SRU's flashbangs.

YOU SHOULDN'T HAVE DONE THAT, MA'AM.

"Ooqi? What shouldn't I have done?" I say with a glance at Danielsen.

FATE, SHOW THY FORCE.

"He's quoting Shakespeare," I whisper to Danielsen. "From the First Minister's speech." I hold my mobile closer to my lips. "Where are you, Ooqi?"

YOU DON'T WANT TO KNOW.

"Why? What are you doing?"

YOU DON'T WANT TO KNOW, BUT YOU WILL, SOON ENOUGH.

"Ooqi," I say. "Listen to me. People are worried about you. Natuk is worried about you. I think you're tired – we're all tired. Tell me where you are. I can come and get you."

YOU SHOULDN'T WORRY ABOUT ME. YOU DON'T HAVE TO THINK ABOUT NATUK.

"Is she with you?" I press the phone to my body and whisper to Danielsen. "I told her to find Ooqi."

Danielsen nods as he stands up and moves away from the table. He pulls out his mobile. *Atii*, he mouths as he dials.

"Ooqi, listen..."

NAAMIK. YOU HAVE TO LISTEN.

A blurred image flickers onto the screen. It sharpens as it increases in size. It's a child, a girl, she's in a kitchen, looking away from the camera, her chin is pointed down, she's laughing, her teeth bright. I recognise the cut of her hair, the glow of her skin. If I could see her soft brown eyes, I know they would be shining with candlelight.

SHE'S IMPORTANT TO YOU?

"Yes," I say, my voice little more than a breath, softer than the beat of my heart, quieter than the blood pulsing through my veins.

THEN STOP THE REFERENDUM.

The screen flickers and he is gone, and he has taken the image of the girl with him.

"Atii is at the station. She'll meet us there," Danielsen says, as he walks to our table. "Ma'am? Petra?"

"We can't go to the station."

"I think it best if we do. We need to dig into Ooqi's background. We need to know everything about him. Then we'll find him, and Natuk."

"He hasn't got Natuk," I say, as I press my hand over my mouth. I turn my head to look at Danielsen, peel my fingers from my lips, and force myself to say it. "It's Quaa. He's got Quaa. You have to take me to Iiluuna. Now, Aqqa. We have to go now."

The next steps are the hardest. From the café to Danielsen's patrol car. I'm on autopilot as he races through the streets. There are no smiles at the swirl of emergency lights, and I can't hear the sirens. I can only see her face – sweet, innocent Quaa, crowned in a wreathe with candles flickering, her bright white teeth flashing. I can feel her weight on my thighs as she eats breakfast. I can smell her hair – coconut shampoo – as she sits beside me and leans over the cookies, decorating them with icing sugar – it's thick, it requires all her concentration to paint it onto the baked dough.

I see and smell all these things, but I taste nothing, my mouth is dry, as I realise that I did this.

This is my fault.

Iiluuna is at the door. Her fingers are white around the door frame as she steadies herself. She lets go when we arrive, and I hold her tight as she shakes until Danielsen suggests we go inside, into the kitchen.

The First Minister wondered if I was strong enough to fight for my country, or would I choose the peaceful alternative. I made a decision then, in her office, when I suggested what to say and another outside the residence before ordering armed police to storm the building. It seems I am good at telling others what to do. As for fighting, when it's personal and the stakes are higher than those on the political and international agenda? That's something else altogether. If the First Minister was here, if she saw me now, I don't think she would question if I was prepared to fight. I don't even think she would recognise me.

Sapaat

Sunday, 21st December 2042

Chapter 21

Danielsen left me with Iiluuna, promising regular updates, and to send someone to pick me up in the morning. I don't remember much of the night, and Ooqi was silent and invisible. The most notable update was when Danielsen informed me he had seconded Aron to the task force. Apparently, my personal assistant has undiscovered talents.

"Ooqi helped me out every now and again," he says, when I arrive at the station. "I paid attention. It wasn't too hard."

"And Ooqi is out of the system now?"

"We can't know that for certain, ma'am," Danielsen says. "It's probably best to assume he still has full access."

"There's nothing we can do?"

Danielsen looks tired, which is to be expected, but there is a spark in his eyes that gives me hope, and it lifts his shoulders a couple of inches.

"Aron thinks we can use it, to mislead him."

"It's an idea," Aron says. "But Ooqi will know that we know he could still be in the system. He will have thought of that." Aron lowers his voice. "He's very clever."

"You looked up to him," I say.

"Yes, ma'am. I'm sorry."

"There's nothing to be sorry about. I confided in Ooqi," I say with a glance at Danielsen. "He had access to the Dutch, and the Chinese – for a limited period. My guess is that he has had access to almost everyone for longer than we can imagine."

"But why?" Danielsen says. "I mean, we know his agenda, but what's his motive?"

"That's what we have to find out," I say. "Aron, I want you to scour the server for everything we know about Ooqi, his personal life and his career. Talk to Natuk. I think she knows more about Ooqi than any of us."

The wall screen flickers behind me as Aron casts clumps of text, scanned documents, images and video clips into a collage of Ooqi's life. I glance at the wall and feel a surge of strength as we begin to compile the most complete profile of the Calendar Man to date. I need every ounce of strength and energy I can muster. I have to be strong for Iiluuna, determined and undaunted for Quaa.

"Aqqa, I know you're tired, but I need you to coordinate the search for Quaa."

"*Aap.*"

"Atii," I say, as she enters the room. "Good work last night."

"Thank you, ma'am."

"I want you to meet with Qitu at NMG. I have a feeling he will have access to information not on our servers. Qitu has made a lot of enemies in the past, and I know his systems are protected, probably better than ours. There's a chance Ooqi has not accessed them. Anything you find might give us an advantage."

I stop for a moment as Aron casts an image of Ooqi onto the screen. He is wearing swimming trunks and standing next to a Greenlandic girl of about the same age, only a little shorter than he is. Their facial features are almost identical. In the background I can see a beach, and what look like red brick buildings on the other side of the dunes. It looks like Denmark.

"Aron, can you send me a copy of that?"

I feel my phone vibrate as Aron shares the image with my account.

"Where will you be, ma'am?" Atii asks. "If we need to contact you."

"I'm going to visit the Ombudsman, Anna Riis. And, I'd like to borrow your husband."

It's the last advent of Christmas before Christmas Eve and the Ombudsman's house is a picture-perfect example of the Scandinavian wooden house in the snow, red paper stars glowing in the windows, and lanterns pressed into black buckets of sand either side of the thick green door. I can see movement inside the house from the window of Gaba's car.

"Who's the guy," Gaba asks, as he fiddles his glasses out of the case. He pushes them onto the bridge of his nose with the tip of his finger.

"When did you start wearing glasses?"

"Funny, Petra." He stabs a thick finger towards the house. "Who's the man in the kitchen?"

Whoever he is, he's smartly dressed, and I realise it is the Dutch Jonkheer. Ooqi failed to read the Jonkheer's mails to Anna Riis. At least, that's what he told me.

"It's Coenraad Kuijpers. You've seen him before, when we waited outside his office."

"*Aap.*"

"And she showed up, very late."

"Coincidence or something more carnal?"

"His wife passed away. His children are in Denmark. He is probably lonely."

"And how does he know her?"

"She brokered the deal for the climate colony," I say.

Gaba sighs and shifts in his seat, stretching his long legs and pressing the caps of his boots against the wheel arch.

"Do we wait for him to leave?"

I look at my watch. The short day will turn grey and then black within the hour – one more hour of terror for Quaa. I tug the Ombudsman's copy of *Twelfth Night* from the pocket of my police jacket and open the car door.

"I trust you can convince him to come back later," I say, as I step out of the car.

The snow crunches beneath our boots as we walk to the green door. Gaba holds up his hand for me to wait as I reach for the door knocker. He slips his glasses inside the case and into his pocket and nods.

I take a breath. It's the calm before the storm. I have a theory that the Ombudsman knows something about Ooqi, and I'm hesitant, wondering about the best way to approach her. Gaba takes the initiative, places his hand over mine and lifts the door knocker. He knocks three times, letting go as we hear footsteps on the other side of the door.

"You were dawdling," he says and takes a step back.

"Commissioner Jensen," the Ombudsman says, as she opens the door. "It's Sunday."

"And urgent. Can we come in?"

Anna looks over her shoulder. I can just see the Jonkheer's jacket hanging over the back of one of the kitchen chairs. Her grey hair is tied up neatly, and her cardigan is trim and fashionable, the colours are from the designer winter collection, I remember the catalogue left on our doormat, a few days before I took David to the hospital, and he never left. I give the thought a gentle push out of mind and focus instead on the framed photograph of two young Greenlandic children posing in front of an animal enclosure at the zoo. We don't have any zoos in Greenland, and I'm tempted to compare the picture of the boy and girl with the one Aron sent to my mobile.

"It's really not a good time," she says.

"Yeah, we don't care about that," Gaba says. He leans around me and slaps the door inwards with his arm. "After you, Commissioner."

"This is not acceptable," Anna says, but I am already in the hall, and Gaba is banging the snow from his boots as the Jonkheer steps out of the kitchen.

"Is everything alright, Anna?"

His English is clipped and cultivated, whereas Gaba's is blunt with the potential to get bloody. There's a reason I *borrowed* him from Atii.

"Go back in the kitchen, sit down and shut up, sir," he says.

"You do realise who I am," Anna says.

"You're the one people complain to when they have a beef with the government," Gaba says, as he guides Anna into the living room with a firm grip of her elbow.

"And if you're here in an official capacity…"

"We are," I say, as Gaba helps the Ombudsman into one of two padded armchairs. I sit in the one next to her. Gaba stands in the centre of the room where he can keep an eye on the kitchen. "A girl has been abducted, and I have some questions."

"You can't possibly think that has anything to do with me, Commissioner."

"Perhaps not directly." I press her copy of *Twelfth Night* onto the arm of her chair. "Why did you lend me that?"

"This is what links me to your missing girl?"

"Just answer the question," Gaba says.

Anna picks up the book and flicks through it. I marked several pages with strips of paper, and they slip out of the pages as she turns them.

"You've read it?"

"I've skimmed it. But you haven't answered the question."

Anna looks at Gaba, and then slowly turns her head to look at me.

"It's a Christmas story," she says. "A comedy – tragic in many respects. A classic. I thought you might enjoy it."

"No," I say. "There's more to it than that. I think you gave it to me for a reason."

"You're digging for something, Commissioner. Why don't you just tell me why you think I gave you the book?"

"So that I could communicate, with the Calendar Man."

Anna closes the book and places it on her lap. She smooths the crease of her wool skirt and then clasps her hands on top of the book. She could be just another well-dressed grandmother if her flint-like eyes didn't spark when I looked at her.

"And did you?" she asks. "Communicate?"

"We tried."

"Not very well, and far too late."

Gaba shuffles his feet and I lift my hand, gesturing for him to stand down. I'm tempted to tell him to wait in the kitchen, but I'm concerned that the Jonkheer might incite him to violence. Gaba is not a violent man, but his strong-handed tactics can be misinterpreted. I already have one international incident to deal with. I don't need another.

"Please explain," I say.

"I don't believe I am required to explain anything. I lent you a book. A seasonal story. That's all."

"And right now, an eight-year-old girl is in danger. That book provides a link to the man who has abducted her, and I think you know who that is. I also think you gave me the book so that I might be able to decipher some of the man's messages, I just don't understand why."

"I'll arrange for you to speak with my lawyers in the morning. You'll have to be up early, of course, their head office is in Denmark."

"We don't have time for this," Gaba says. He takes a step forwards and I meet him halfway, pressing my hand to his chest and shaking my head.

"It doesn't matter," I say, as I turn to look at the Ombudsman. "You've obviously washed your hands of your son. You're abandoning him."

"My son? I don't have a son."

"No? A foster child then. Someone you care about – or pretended to, until he was no longer of use to you."

Anna's frown is so deep it looks like a gash in her forehead. It could be the light casting shadows, but I can see she is starting to crack.

"Coenraad," she says, and I hear the kitchen floorboards creek as the Jonkheer crosses the floor.

"Gaba."

"Got it."

I swear he lives for this, but he has learned, over the years, to hide his enjoyment, and his smile is thin and unimpressive, unlike the look of shock on the Jonkheer's face as Gaba meets him at the living room door and invites him to go back to the kitchen with a single slap to the chest. Anna starts to rise at the sound of a chair crashing to the floor, but I stop her with a firm grip of her shoulder. I show her the image of the children playing on the beach in Denmark, and she sinks into the armchair, clutching the book to her chest like a shield.

"It's Ooqi, isn't it?"

"Yes," she says, her voice barely a whisper.

"When?"

"The summer of 2026. He was nine."

"And the girl? Who is she?"

"Oh, I think you know her too, Commissioner. Her name is…"

"Natuk," I say, but I can barely hear my voice.

"You think Ooqi is dangerous?" Anna laughs, and lowers the book-shield, just a little. "You wait until you see what she is capable of. Of course, now that her bother is exposed, she'll be gone. You'll never find her, unless she wants you to."

"Brother and sister."

"Yes," Anna says. She puts the book down and beckons for me to follow her to the wall opposite the window. "They came to me when they were both seven years old. They are twins, but you wouldn't know it. Not since puberty. Natuk is so much more mature than her brother, she always has been. Probably due to what her father did to her. Ooqi was lucky, he was only beaten. They were born in Denmark, and they came to me when the social services stepped in. Far too late if you ask me." She points at a picture of a double birthday. "Ah, this was their twelfth," she says. "January 6th, 2019."

"The twelfth night."

"That's right. *Hellige tre konger* or Epiphany if you prefer it in

English."

"And you read the book to them?"

"I've always been a Shakespeare fan. Imagine what fun I had trying to explain what the bard was talking about. I mean, Greenlanders are so visual. If you say it's raining cats and dogs they will look outside and call you a liar, but Shakespeare's play on words and multiple hidden meanings and deception... Well, it took a long time for Natuk and Ooqi to understand any of it."

"I think they got the hang of it," I say, as I think of how Ooqi had us running in circles across the city. *And now he has Quaa.*

"Here's another birthday photo," Anna says. "I gave them each a computer that year. They were coding after only two months."

"I'd like you to come with us, back to the station," I say. "We need to find Ooqi, and the little girl, and we need to gain a better understanding of who he is and what motivates him."

"Oh, I can't help you with that, Commissioner. Not until he has finished what he has started. There's far too much at stake."

Ataasinngorneq

Monday, 22nd December 2042

Chapter 22

I don't remember much of the night, only that the sofa in the staff lounge is more comfortable than it used to be, and that Aron's coffee gets stronger by the hour. The Ombudsman said nothing more until just after five o'clock in the morning, the start of a new working day in Copenhagen, four hours ahead of Greenland. Aron woke me to take the call and pressed a mug of coffee into my hand as he guided me into my office.

"Anything new?" I ask, as I slump into my chair.

He shakes his head. I don't think he has slept, and he certainly hasn't been home to change his shirt. Neither have I.

"They're on hold," he says. "Just push the button when you're ready, ma'am."

I'm not ready, but the coffee helps.

I reach for the phone and my hand brushes a note taped to the receiver – something about a meeting with a representative for the Chinese at nine o'clock, Greenlandic time.

"This is Petra Jensen," I say, as I press the handset to my ear. "Police Commissioner." It's almost an afterthought.

"You do realise what you've done?" the lawyer says. I didn't catch his name.

"I've taken Ombudsman Anna Riis into custody in connection with an ongoing case of terror, referendum manipulation and kidnapping."

"You're charging her with *all* that?"

I can hear the lawyer laugh and I grip the phone in my hands.

"I'm interviewing her about *all* that. So far she is saying nothing."

"And she won't, until she has legal representation."

"We can provide a lawyer."

"She has a lawyer, and you can wait until we get there."

"And when will that be?"

"Two days before Christmas, Commissioner? I think you know the answer to that."

Clearly, he doesn't understand the situation, and neither does he care. I take a breath as I try to formulate a more professional response than the one I want to give him, when Aron appears at the door. I can just see the Jonkheer behind him in the outer office. The lawyer can wait, and I slam the handset onto the receiver.

"The Jonkheer wants to see you, ma'am."

"Let him in," I say, with a brief wave at the table. "And stay with us, Aron."

Aron waits by the door as the Jonkheer smooths the lapels of his jacket with slim hands. His fingers are trembling, and he looks as though he has slept less than I have.

"Commissioner," he says.

"Yes?"

"I need to know what I can expect."

He grips the back of a chair. I think he might fall without it.

"I don't know what you mean."

"I have information, and if I share it, I would like to know if I am… If that will be favourable… If I will be treated favourably, I mean."

"Why don't you sit down," I say.

Aron slips out of the office and brings the Jonkheer a mug of fresh coffee. It occurs to me that we wouldn't have got through the month without it.

"Thank you," the Jonkheer says.

"Why don't you start again."

"Yes, I'm terribly upset about this. As you know, I am a father. And it was never meant to happen like this. I was assured that no matter how gruesome, no-one would get hurt, and there was never talk of children – never children."

Aron slips his phone onto the table as I sit down opposite the Jonkheer. At a nod from me he presses the record button.

"Are you saying you know what's going on?"

"Yes," he says. "But you must understand. We are in such a precarious position – my countrymen, and I. In desperate times one does unimaginable things. The Netherlands have been under the shadow of climate consequences – climate change – for as long as I can remember. My parents' generation knew it too. Even as we built the Vaalserberg Towers, we knew it was a symbolic gesture, one life raft for a whole nation. That's when we looked to the former colonies, and to other countries willing to take us in. But we were not refugees, not yet. We wanted some assurances, and your government agreed to terms that would allow us not only to relocate huge numbers of our people, but to preserve our culture for future generations with a small village built after our own design."

"This was the deal brokered by Anna Riis?"

"Yes. And it was favourable to us, and the Danes. Perhaps less so to your government. But I was assured it would never be a problem. But in the three years we have been in Greenland, the question of independence has grown to alarming levels. We were so concerned we took steps – through official channels, of course. But since Anna Riis left the government to take up the position as Ombudsman here in Nuuk, our voice was drowned in the Danish government, not unlike our people back home in our shrinking country. But Anna did not desert us. She knows what is best for Greenland, Denmark and my own people."

"What exactly are you saying?"

The Jonkheer glances at Aron's mobile and presses his palms upon the table, gaining strength as he stills the trembling in his fingers.

"Nothing more, until I am sure we can make a trade."

"A trade?"

"I give you information, and you protect me – as a witness."

"What kind of information? More details about the Calendar Man?"

"Yes," he says. "And something more. I know where he girl is."

"She's in the workshop," I tell Danielsen over the phone, as Aron slips through the gears and accelerates between the warehouses and stacks of shipping containers on the perimeter of the new harbour. The emergency lights flash across the corrugated metal sides of the container, and I reach across the dashboard to turn them off. "Slow down, Aron," I say, as we approach an icy corner in the road. "Stop here."

The tyres crunch in the snow as we stop just above the charred roof of a car workshop. It has been abandoned ever since the fire. Insurance has always been a luxurious concept for many Greenlanders, including the owners of the workshop. It will rot, slowly, like many privately-owned buildings and houses dotted around the coast of Greenland, until an outside investor sees potential in the space and pulls it down.

I scan the surroundings and see a small path beaten through the snow to the back door. It leads all the way to the road. I can see the start of the path in the beam of the patrol car's headlights.

"Ma'am," Danielsen says. "Where are you?"

"I'm looking at the workshop. I left the Jonkheer in one of the cells at the station."

"Wait there. We're coming to you."

I lower the phone as I squint at thin lines of light seeping through the black timber walls of the workshop.

"Someone's inside," I say.

"And we're coming to you."

The back door opens and the light floods out onto the snow, illuminating the figure of a man dressed in a black police uniform.

"Aron," I say. "The lights."

It's too late. Ooqi slams the workshop door and the light is extinguished.

"Commissioner?" Danielsen's voice recedes as I lower the phone and reach for the door handle. "Petra?"

"Aron, give me your gun," I say, as I open the car door.

"Shouldn't we wait, ma'am?"

"Just give it to me."

It might be the adrenaline coursing through my body, but it feels like he is too slow, and I snatch the Glock pistol from his hand as I step out of the car.

"Stay here and wait for Danielsen," I say, as I tighten the elastic securing my hair in a ponytail.

I can hear Aron's mobile ring as I turn mine off and stuff it into my pocket. The snow is slippery at the top of the path, and I slide into the drift to one side, scramble to my feet, switch the Glock to my right hand, and run down the path. I slow to a walk, arms extended, both hands around the pistol, as I approach the back door of the workshop.

I can smell the burned wood, and something else, like cooking odours through the timbers. I reach for the door handle with one hand and open it, just an inch, and then three more. It's black like a winter sky inside, as I open the door just wide enough to step inside.

My heart is beating so fast it feels like the echoes are bouncing off the black blistered walls, pummelling my body as I move further into the workshop. I bump a desk with my thigh and something rolls off and thuds on the floor. I freeze, press my hands around the pistol grip, and slowly lift my foot to take another step.

I don't know how I turned it on, but *practical me* runs through a quick assessment of what I know about Ooqi, and what he is capable of. Taking Quaa was a rash move, something I forced him to do. All the other victims had already suffered. They were already dead. I once called the Calendar Man an opportunistic coward, but I realise now that I was wrong. There was nothing *opportunistic* about Ooqi's actions and *coward* doesn't seem to fit either. If what the Jonkheer said is true, Ooqi was following orders, using a recipe designed to achieve the greatest effect at a minimal cost.

An effective, rational, deliberate and cool campaign.

I only hope he will remain cool, now that I have pushed him off course. Now that he has Quaa.

The timber floor cracks beneath my boot and I jump at the sound. My sudden movement draws a figure out of the shadow and I feel a whoosh of air a second before something heavy slams into my shoulder and I spin onto the floor. My left hand submerges through a film of litter and ash, as I break my fall. The Glock is heavy in my right hand, and I turn it in an arc, following the sound of someone crashing through the debris on the workshop floor. I squeeze the trigger safety, squeezing further until I fire the first bullet, followed by a second and a third, shattering the silence and splintering the walls of the workshop. I hear a shout, a curse, and the back door as it is kicked open and he is gone.

My boots slip in the debris as I pick myself up. I'm tempted to run after Ooqi, but a cry from above stops me, and I pull out my phone to use it as a torch. There is a metal staircase to my right, the steps creak as I climb it, drifting the light from my phone ahead of me as I carefully place my feet.

When my light catches the sooty face of a young girl, I lower the Glock, stuffing it into my jacket pocket as I pick my way across broken floorboards, avoiding the ragged holes in the floor until I am right in front of Quaa.

"It's okay," I say, as I hold out my hand. "I've got you. You're okay now."

I press the tips of my fingers into the dirty blanket covering her body, and then I press my hand around her arm and pull her to my body. Quaa flings her arms around my neck and presses her face into my cheek. I can feel snot and tears on my skin as I clasp a hand behind her head and another beneath her bottom, tugging her into my chest as I work my way to the stairs.

"I'm going to take you home, Quaa. Okay?"

I pause at the top of the stairs as lights flicker in solid beams of white through the workshop below. The lights mounted to the SRU's submachine guns pick through the ash and dust until they find us, and I turn my face into the beam, so they can see it is me. I turn around and the light catches Quaa. A second later and the first of the SRU officers is on the stairs and I let him guide us down and through the workshop door and around the front to where Danielsen is waiting. He walks beside us as a paramedic gently plucks Quaa from my arms to examine her, while his partner turns me in the light to look at my cheek.

"I'm alright," I say. "He hit my shoulder."

"We need to look," the man says.

I smile at Quaa as I follow her inside the ambulance. Danielsen waits at the door.

"Aron said he heard shots," he says.

"Yes. I fired three times."

"That explains the blood in the snow." He points at the path leading to the back of the workshop. "You must have hit him."

"Yes."

"And did you see his face? Was it Ooqi?"

"I think so. He was wearing a police uniform. But I didn't actually see him."

Danielsen nods as Atii jogs across the snow from the workshop to the ambulance. She removes her ballistic helmet and mask and lets the submachinegun dangle from the sling around her chest.

"It looks like he's been here a lot," she says. "We need more light, but we found three chest freezers in the back. They're not plugged in, but there are body parts in one of them, and a bloody knife on a workbench. There's also a stack of advent calendars."

"The Commissioner says she shot him," Danielsen says.

"I think it was him," I say.

"Okay." Atii waves one of the SRU officers over. "Start the search from here and put units on all the roads." She looks at the black water and then at the lights of Chinatown glowing on the other side of the fjord. "Get a water unit here too. He might have a boat."

"What about Natuk?" I say.

"No sign of her yet," Danielsen says.

"We need to find her."

"*Aap*. But right now, we need to get you and Quaa home. You need some rest. I'll call you the minute we hear anything."

"The very minute…"

"Yes, ma'am," he says. "Aron will follow you in the patrol car."

I reach out for Quaa as the paramedic closes the door. There is a faint trace of coconut in her hair as I press my lips to her brow.

"You're going to be okay, Quaa. Let's get you home."

Marlunngorneq

Tuesday, 23rd December 2042

Chapter 23

Greenlandic culture is full of powerful creatures, beasts and spirits. The Danish Christmas tradition is heavily influenced by *nisser*, Christmas elves in all nuances of good and evil to the downright mischievous. The Greenlandic Christmas tradition includes a bit of both, but I have never imagined Christmas to be a time of dragons. But when Danielsen calls from the patrol car on the street outside Iiluuna's apartment, I look out of the kitchen window and I can see Tan Yazhu sitting in the passenger seat.

"Iiluuna," I say, as I finish the call. "I have to go."

Quaa is sleeping on Iiluuna's lap on the sofa. She is safe now. One of Gaba's security men is in the hall outside the apartment, and I must leave. If it is possible to save one more person before Christmas, I owe it to Ooqi to at least try.

"Will you come back?"

"As soon as I can."

"*Aap*," she says. "I meant will you come for Christmas Eve?"

Quaa stirs on her mother's lap and opens one of her soft brown eyes.

"Yes," I say. "There's nowhere else I would rather be."

Quaa smiles and I fix her image in my mind as I grab my jacket and leave the apartment. It's only when I stuff my hands into the pocket and feel the twist of twine between my fingers that I realise it is David's. I can't remember how long I have been wearing it, if I had it on when Gaba and I were at the Ombudsman's house, or if I wore it when I shot Ooqi. Appearances don't matter, I realise. All that matters is that he is with me.

Danielsen meets me on the path to the street. He stops me with a nod towards the patrol car.

"There's been a sighting in Chinatown, and I thought he might come in useful."

"He's not armed?"

"No, and he's willing to drop all charges and pretend it never happened. I think someone has leaned on him from above."

"Lucky for us."

"*Aap*. But we're not done yet. Atii has Chinatown locked down, and Gaba's men are all over Nuuk and Little Amsterdam." Danielsen shakes his head. "I don't know where he gets them from. They're like *nisser.*"

"It's Âmo," I say. "He's looking out for us."

"Whoever and however, the First Minister is happy, and voting has begun."

"And Natuk?"

"Still no sign. If she's involved and if she's smart…"

"She'll be long gone," I say. "What are the chances of both of them joining the force and keeping their family relationship secret?"

"Good, apparently, ma'am."

"Yes," I say, and take a step towards the car. "Let's go and get him."

Atii's security cordon is tight, with a ring of Âmo security around the first perimeter of armed police officers. There is a team of SRU officers standing in front of the perimeter and six long flame-bright dragons weaving through the crowds. There is a second when I wonder if Atii's perimeter is for Ooqi or to prevent the dragons from slipping out of Chinatown. Under different circumstances I might be tempted to think it was the latter. But bullets and ballistic shields won't stop the Chinese dragon – nothing can.

"Ma'am," Atii says, and pulls me to one side.

"Where is he?"

"He was spotted here," she says, raising her voice over the Chinese horns, drums and gongs as she pulls up a map on her tablet. "He's still in uniform, and he bluffed his way into the Chinese medical centre. They treated him for a bullet wound to the left arm. He said he was shot by the Calendar Man, if you believe that."

"Right now," I say, with a second glance at the dragons, "there's very little I don't believe. But there's only one thing I want to know – what is he going to do?"

"Hard to say, ma'am. He knows he's surrounded, and it's unlikely that he's going to get away. It's just a matter of time before we pick him up." Atii curses as a tall man pushes through the police cordon. "I said no, Gaba," she says.

"And I remember disagreeing."

"He does this all the time, ma'am," Atii says. "He still thinks he's head of the SRU, and that he's still my boss."

"We're married," Gaba says, and shrugs. "Of course, I'm the boss."

"Let's save this for later, and let the Commissioner decide."

"Decide what?"

"Gaba thinks that Ooqi will give himself in, if you talk to him."

"It makes sense, Petra. He has been through your files. He used your past to mislead the investigation…"

"Helped by his sister," I say.

"*Aap*. But nonetheless, there is a connection there. And," Gaba says with a smile, "you shot him."

"Gaba thinks he'll talk to you, if you're alone – no visible police presence. Danielsen and I agree, reluctantly."

I look over my shoulder and see Danielsen fastening a bulletproof vest around Tan Yazhu's body. He nods and points at two more vests on the roof of the SUV.

"And you have a plan?"

"Tan Yazhu will take you into Chinatown, through the festival to the location where Ooqi was last seen."

"The medical centre?"

"A noodle bar, just in front of it," she says. "Gaba has forced me to agree that he should go with you."

"For old time's sake," he says, and grins. "And, I'm bored."

"I left you in charge of the kids," Atii says.

"They're teenagers. They don't need me anymore, babe."

I let them quarrel as I walk back to Danielsen. He hands me a vest and I remove David's jacket and pull the vest over my head.

"I recognise this jacket," Danielsen says, as he helps me with the vest.

"You've seen me wear it before."

"*Aap*. But I never thought about it. It's Maratse's, isn't it?"

I nod. "It makes me feel safe."

I zip David's jacket over my vest and wait as Danielsen explains to Tan Yazhu the very limit of his involvement.

"Aqqa," I say, when he is finished. "I need to know – you've done everything you can to keep me out of harm's way, right up until this moment. But now, you're just going to let me walk in there? Why?"

"Because no matter what he's done, ma'am, and for whatever reason, Ooqi is one of ours, and I think you can bring him home." Danielsen removes his pistol from the holster at his belt and presses it into my hand. "Besides, I know you can take care of yourself," he says. Danielsen looks at Gaba. "And he'll never let anything happen to you."

"That's a lot of responsibility, Aqqa."

"It goes with the title," he says.

"You don't want to be Commissioner?"

"Never have, never will." He pats his belly and laughs. "Besides, my wife would never let me. The hours you keep…"

I stuff Aqqa's pistol inside my jacket pocket and dip my head, just once.

"I'll be here when you get back," he says.

Tan Yazhu walks beside me to the edge of the police perimeter. His eyes are fixed on the dragons, and the end of the street where a little slice of his home country is nestled between the granite rocks of Greenland. Gaba presses the Velcro straps of his vest into position and lifts the flap of a canvas holster attached at an angle to the front of the vest.

"What's that?" I ask, as he winks at Atii and we move through the cordon and into a corridor of flame and dragons.

"A shotgun," he says.

"You're armed."

"It's legal. It's for hunting."

"You've sawn off the stock and shortened the barrel, Gaba."

He shrugs. "It didn't fit in the pouch."

"This way," Tan Yazhu says, as he weaves around the dragons swirling in the street.

I can feel the beat of the drums through the asphalt, and the echo between the tall buildings, brushing at the snow on the roofs. The beat makes it difficult to think, and I worry that I'm not prepared, that I can't help Ooqi after all, and that he is beyond reach. But there is no more time to think, as Tan Yazhu raises his hand and points through the crowds towards the noodle bar at the edge of the street. The bright plastic tables shine in the light of Chinese lanterns, and the snow is coloured in reds and yellows, the colours of flame and fire. Between the flames I see Ooqi. I see the bandage around his arm, the sling around his neck, and the empty sleeve of his jacket dangling at his side.

"Danielsen say I must stop here," Tan Yazhu says. "But I will come if you want me to."

"No," I say. "You've done enough."

"You will stop him," he says. "I trust you now."

Gaba waits until he is gone and then points to a position close to Ooqi's table.

"I'll stay close," he says.

"I know."

I can't hear my words for the beating of the drums. Or is it the thumping of my heart? It beats faster as Ooqi turns his head and catches my eye. I'm close enough to see his eyes flicker behind the lenses of his glasses, and I wonder if he is online, if he is connected with Natuk, and if this is all a trap. He could be streaming it. This could be his last chance to strike before voting is over, but there is something else in his eyes. Sadness.

Piitalaat. Focus.

I wondered when David would come. I know it is me, that I am projecting what I want to hear, but it gives me the courage to take the next step, and the one after that until I am standing at Ooqi's table, and he invites me to sit down.

"Just a second," he says, as his eyes flicker. He removes his glasses and puts them on the table. "That was Natuk. She's gone. You have to promise you won't try to find her."

"Is she involved?"

"No. It was all me."

He's lying, of course he is. The twitch beneath his eye that shudders through his soft, young cheek betrays more than the lie. I can see his love for his sister, and he's willing to make that last sacrifice. I realise I might never know about her role in the Calendar Man's campaign of terror. At least, not from Ooqi.

"I need to know why," I say.

"Why?"

"Why did you try to stop the vote?"

"You have to ask?" He gestures at the festival behind us, raises his voice over the beat of the drums. "Do you think we can negotiate all this? You think we can decide our own future?"

"I think we have the right to try."

"You're wrong," he says. "Think about it. Greenland never had an industrial revolution. We haven't had a gradual progression from one technology to the next. We went from turf huts to apartment blocks, from hunting with harpoons to checking the weather on our smartphones. Greenland went global too fast too soon." He shakes his head. "We can't process this. We don't have the experience. We can't do it alone. We need help."

"Then we ask for help."

"And whose help will we get? Who will help us to understand the nuances of a seventy-page contract in a foreign language?"

"You sound like your foster mother. That's what she would say."

Perhaps he doesn't know that we have her in custody, or perhaps he doesn't know that the Jonkheer is ready to make a statement detailing how the Ombudsman Anna Riis had a plan to spoil the vote and ensure that Greenland remained a part of Denmark for the foreseeable future. But he's still ready to fall on his sword for her. I can see it in his eyes.

"She's got nothing to do with this," he says.

"Ooqi," I say. "I understand that she helped you. She helped both of you. And I realise how loyal that makes you feel, that you owe her. But you don't, Ooqi. You don't have to take responsibility for this, just to protect her."

"No-one was hurt," he says.

"You terrorised the people of Nuuk and frightened the whole country."

"No-one died. There were no victims, I made sure of that."

"Victims? What about their families, their friends? What about Quaa?"

"No," he says, as he pushes back from the table. "That was your fault. I was done. The referendum was finished. But you, you had to ruin *everything*."

Ooqi's last word turns the heads of the people eating at the next table. It snaps Gaba to attention and he reaches for the flap covering the shotgun on his vest. There is a flash of dragons reflected in the window of the noodle bar behind Ooqi, and I'm distracted by the beat of the drum. I don't see Ooqi pull the pistol from his holster, not until it is inches from my face. The diners at the nearby tables spill their noodles as they flee into the street. There is a scream, almost swallowed by the drum and the dragon, but then the crowd withdraws, the beat slows to an echo, and it's just Ooqi, Gaba and me.

"Ooqi," I say. "Please."

"I thought you would understand," he says. "I read your file. I've seen your hands. You've suffered. More than me, maybe more than

Natuk. I thought you would know that we need someone strong to take care of us. We can't do this alone. We shouldn't be alone."

"Being independent doesn't mean we have to be alone, Ooqi. Whatever she told you, whatever she taught you, you're not alone."

"You leave her out of this." Spittle flies from Ooqi's mouth as he stands and jabs the gun closer to my face. "She saved us. And this," he says, waving the gun at the terrified people on the street. "It was the least I could do."

I glance at Gaba. He has the shotgun out of the holster and his fingers curled around the grip. Ooqi twists his head to see where I am looking, and then lurches backwards. I grab for his jacket, tug at the loose sleeve. Ooqi spins and twists out of his jacket. His pistol thumps into the snow at his feet as he pulls his arm free. He reaches for it.

"Leave it," Gaba yells, as he moves to within just a few feet of Ooqi.

I pull the pistol from my pocket and walk around the side of the table.

"Ooqi," I say. "This is my friend, Gaba. He used to be a policeman. He's one of us. He won't hurt you. I won't let him. Just move back, away from the gun."

I relax my grip and lower Danielsen's pistol, just a little, as Ooqi looks into my eyes, and then past me, towards the table. I turn my head a fraction and see the reflection of the Chinese lanterns in Ooqi's glasses. He nods once, and then reaches for the gun.

"No," I shout, as he curls his hand around the pistol grip and raises the barrel towards me.

No drum is louder than the simultaneous blast of the two shells in Gaba's shotgun, and a bullet from the pistol in my own hands. But I wish the drums would beat, and the dragons roar, because the silence is killing me just as I killed Ooqi.

In that minute I don't care about the vote, and I don't care about Greenland, because all I can think about is that I only had one thing to do, and I failed. I failed to bring him home.

Pingasunngorneq

Wednesday, 24th December 2042

Christmas Eve

Chapter 24

If I open my eyes, I can see the red glow of the paper star in Quaa's window. *If* I open my eyes. I don't want to, but I have slept too long already. I can hear Iiluuna preparing a late breakfast in the kitchen, and Quaa's voice – higher than her mother's – asking if *now* was a good time to wake Petra. I suppose now is as good a time as any, and I open my eyes.

It's better than I thought. Quaa's room is familiar – the posters on the wall, the toys she says she is too old for, the clothes she should have tidied away, the smell of the duvet – soft and warm. Everything is reassuringly familiar, and very far from the blood red snow outside the noodle bar in Chinatown.

I checked with the duty officer shortly before I crawled into Quaa's bed. Even after the death of her foster son, Anna Riis remains silent, and I suppose she will stay that way until her lawyers arrive sometime after Christmas. The Jonkheer's statement provided just enough evidence to keep her in her cell until they turn up. The duty officer promised to keep me updated through the day.

It's time to get up.

I have some clothes in the bottom drawer in Quaa's room, and I dress in the soft glow of the star. The Northern Lights are bright, drifting and twisting above Nuuk in greens and pale blues. If we're lucky we might get a little red light, just for Christmas. Beyond the city I can just see the black fjord, the icebergs in the bay, and a single fishing trawler returning to the harbour with the last catch before Christmas.

Quaa skips across the kitchen floor in bare feet as I open the door and step out of her room. She wraps her arms around my waist, and I smooth her hair – she is coconut clean for Christmas. And she is wearing her crown of pine and candles. She is transformed from the girl Ooqi held captive in the ashes and black timbers of the workshop. Quaa tips her head back and starts talking. I don't hear the words. Instead I search for some sign of trauma, but she is giddy with Christmas and I have to see the tree.

She tugs me into the living room, her small hand clasping my fingers, and she presents the tree, only slightly taller than she is.

"It's very pretty," I say, as she turns on the lights – small white buds between the baubles and the paper streamers of Greenlandic flags.

There is a star on top.

It makes me think of Ooqi, and David, and I bend down to hug Quaa, so she can't see my tears.

There's more to see, and I let her lead me around the apartment, pointing out various ornaments and the all-important *nisser*, tiny felt or plastic Christmas elves peeking out from behind picture frames, tucked behind the furniture, and posed between the candles on the kitchen table. We stop here. Quaa pulls out a chair, presses me into it, and pushes another so close I have to move my fingers before they are pinched. Quaa has something in her hands, beneath the table, and I pretend I cannot see it.

"Christmas tea," Iiluuna says, as she joins us. She places a pot on the table and slides a mug across the heart-themed table cloth. The air is spiced with cinnamon, orange and steam as she pours.

"Thank you."

"She can't wait," she says, as Quaa slips the present from her lap to the table.

"Is this for me?"

"*Aap.*"

The small box is heavy in my hands. Quaa's eyes are bright like stars as she watches my face. The bows are loose, and the wrapping is torn in places, but the paper filling inside the cardboard box is generous and I tease Quaa with an astonished smile.

"Paper. Oh, Quaa, it's just what I wanted."

Her hands jerk from her lap. She can't help herself, and then the top layer of paper is loose on the table and I see a small dark soapstone figure inside. It's a hunter sitting on his sledge. Quaa helps me take him out of the box. There are two dogs, and they clink together at the end of thick cotton threads as if they are pulling the hunter across the ice.

"It's David," she says. "We bought it at the Christmas market."

I don't even try to hide the tears, as I push back my chair to make room for Quaa to crawl into my lap.

"Thank you," I whisper into her hair.

Iiluuna reaches around the candles on the table and places an ornamental flag pole made of wood beside the hunter on his sledge. Her eyes sparkle and widen, tugging the corners of her mouth into a smile. I can feel my brow tighten as I frown at the flag.

"*Erfalasorput*," she says. "Our flag."

I've forgotten something. Quaa wriggles in my lap and slides across to her chair as I stare at the red and white flag, the symbol of the red sun rising over the white ice. And then it comes to me, and I see the hunter, picture him sledging across the ice towards the sun, and I realise that the people of Greenland have voted.

Iiluuna turns on the radio and I hear a mix of Greenlandic and Danish chatter, comments spliced between and around the First Minister's speech. Iiluuna turns up the volume.

"My favourite bit," she says, and we listen.

… Greenland for all Greenlanders, for our children, their children and all our futures.

We both look at Quaa as she plays with the hunter on his sledge, moving the dogs across the heart-patterned ice, one in both hands, her long black hair framing her cheeks, and the flag of Greenland, *Erfalasorput*, reflected in her eyes.

Later, we will sing Christmas carols and hymns as we hold hands and dance around the tree – a Danish tradition, loved and unlikely to be forgotten, like so many Greenlandic things rooted in a colonial history. We will remember the good things, and the bad, and look to the future. But I need some fresh air before then, and I need to buy gifts for Iiluuna and Quaa, and I need a quiet time, just for David and me.

It is quiet at the graveyard. I stuff my hands inside the deep pockets of David's jacket and fiddle with the twine between my fingers. The sky is grey with snow, and I can feel the first flakes as they fall softly onto my hair. Everything is still and quiet, and I don't hear the footsteps behind me, only the cough as Qitu clears his throat not to startle me.

"I haven't seen you for a while," I say, as he smiles.

"You've kept me busy though."

"*I* have?"

"*Aap*," he says, and then points to the small metal Greenlandic flag pinned to his collar. "There was a tiny bit of other news. I have a meeting with the First Minister later."

"It's a big day."

"It doesn't get much bigger."

Qitu reaches into his pocket and takes out a gift. The wrapping, and the bow, is only slightly neater than Quaa's.

"For you," he says.

"I didn't get you anything, Qitu."

"You don't have to."

He watches my face as I unwrap a small photo frame, hinged in the middle. I stuff the paper into my pocket and slowly open the frame. The boy in the picture on the right is Ooqi. I recognise his nose, and his eyes. He's wearing the furs of a hunter and holding a huge fish between his hands. It's too heavy for him and he grins at the weight of it. Natuk is in the picture on the left, also in furs – perhaps from the same day. I can just see Ooqi behind her. She is laughing at something.

"Atti asked me to see what I could find," Qitu says. "This is from Upernavik. Their family is from there. They must have visited one time. A happier time," he says. "I thought you might want to remember him like that."

"You're going to write a longer piece about him, aren't you?"

"*Aap.*"

"You have to use this photo," I say. "Both of them."

"I will."

"Thank you."

Qitu slips quietly through the snow after I hug him, and I slip the photo frame inside David's cavernous pockets. It really is amazing how deep they are, and I have a sudden image of Âmo, pressing his abnormally long arms into deep pockets, all the way to his toes. The thought makes me laugh.

It's good to hear you laugh, Piitalaat.

"It feels good," I say.

You're going to be alright.

"I think I might be, someday."

I know you will.

I can feel a tear on my cheek and I wipe it away with my finger.

"I have to leave you now. You know that."

Iiji.

"I'll come back, when I can."

I know.

I wipe away a second tear and crouch in the snow beside David's gravestone. The plastic flowers are bright against the snow and I brush a dusting of fresh snowflakes from the leaves. David is quiet as

I sit there, my bottom on my heels, my knees pressed into the snow, and my hands stuffed into David's pockets. That's when I see it, the black cylinder resting on the granite shelf at the bottom of the gravestone.

The cylinder is metal. If we were further north, if it was colder, it might stick to my fingers. But the cylinder has a coat of paint, and the cap unscrews without protest, without the cold bite and stiffness I expect. Perhaps it was left here recently. Perhaps someone left it here today.

"Did you see them, David?" I ask. But he is silent. *I* am silent, and sad that I am ready to move on.

Not so the person who left the note rolled tight inside the cylinder.

And what should I do in Illyria? My brother he is in Elysium.

The text is printed on one line, lengthways, small. It is almost lost in the middle of the sheet of paper.

She was here. Natuk. She left this, I'm sure of it.

I roll the paper between my fingers and seal it inside the cylinder. It might be evidence one day, and I sigh at the thought of my fingerprints smearing the cylinder, contaminating it. But then my fingerprints are all over this case, and any future case that might be linked to it.

"I can't worry about that now," I say, as I stand up and brush the snow from my knees. It is falling heavier now, as the day grows darker. I should get back. I should help Iiluuna with the Christmas dinner.

I put the cylinder in my pocket, lift the flowers above the snow, and press my fingers on the cold granite headstone.

"I'll be back, David. Often," I say.

A pillow of wind fluffs at the snow as I leave the graveyard and wait in line for one of Nuuk's yellow buses. The passengers chatter and smile, and it is more than just the magic of Christmas. There is a streak of independence in the air, tempered with the unknown, yet light, buoyed by optimism and dreams.

I can hear the First Minister's words on the radio, but my thoughts settle on Quaa's gift, the hunter on the kitchen table, the hunter on the ice, the sun rising in the north, shining red on its return. Christmas in Greenland marks the turning of the year, when the nights grow shorter. It is still pitch black in the far north, but even there, people can see a shade of grey growing lighter at end of each night.

After so many dark days, the light is returning, for the hunter and his dogs, for me, and for the people of Greenland – independent and free.

The Twelfth Night

A Scandinavian Dark Advent novel set in Greenland

~ Petra *Piitalaat* Jensen Book 2 ~

And what should I do in Illyria?
My brother he is in Elysium.

— *Twelfth Night, Act I, Sc. II*

William Shakespeare (1564-1616)

Introduction

I remember walking with my wife to the hospital in Uummannaq, one long, dark winter night. It was pitch black. The sea ice was almost thick enough to walk on, and hardy hunters had been sledging to their fishing lines for about a week. Jane was on night shift at the hospital, and I said goodnight to her at the door. As soon as the door closed, I heard a shout and the slap of feet on the ice covering the road. I stopped a few feet from the entrance to the hospital and watched a group of Greenlanders, three men in their twenties, run down the hill from the police station, past the hospital.

They didn't stop.

Then I saw the masked figure chasing them. Its upper body was padded like an upturned triangle, and it was carrying a large stick. Its face bulged and twisted, and there was steam chuffing out of the slit between the carved wooden teeth.

It was January 6th.

It was *mitaartut*.

It was the Twelfth Night.

Chris
December 2018
Denmark

CHRISTOFFER PETERSEN

Ataasinngorneq

Monday, 5th January 2043
Nuuk, Greenland

Chapter 1

The coloured paste was thin and sticky between her fingers, like blood. Natuk Petersen smoothed it into her hair, working it to the roots. She braced herself against the plastic veneer covering the bulkhead as the captain drove the trawler through the waves at the mouth of Nuuk fjord. They would be at the tourist dock within twenty minutes. Natuk worked more paste into her hair, turning and dipping her head to see as much of it as possible in the greasy mirror, cracked and scabbed at the edges with rust. Gone were the shiny black locks that turned people's heads on the street, replaced with a rough-hewn bob of blonde that seemed to repel her coffee-cream skin. Natuk washed her fingers and rinsed her hair. She left her thick eyebrows black.

There was a bump, and the slow scrape of the metal hull along the thick sea-greened wood of the dock. Natuk dressed, anticipating the knock on the door as she pulled a thick woollen sweater over her head, tucked the FNS-40 compact pistol into the back of her jeans and buttoned the fly.

"See you on deck," she called out at the quick rap of knuckles on the bathroom door.

There was a twist of magic in the early morning darkness pressing the wooden houses, the high rises, and the commercial and industrial units of Nuuk into the granite. The very weight of the darkness, the dense cold – it could almost be seen bearing down on old eaves, arches and roofs, mocking the newer buildings. Natuk tugged on her retro brown duvet jacket as she climbed onto the deck, studying the horizon as she lifted her foot and pressed it onto the railings to tie her laces. She could just see the lights of Little Amsterdam in the distance, sparkling above the city of Nuuk. Beyond that, a little to the south, she imagined the dragon tails and lanterns of Chinatown, and then the bridge across the fjord to the American Coast Guard base – out of sight and out of bounds.

"We'll see about that," she said.

Natuk adjusted the grip of the pistol pressing into the small of her back, nodded at the man waiting by the gangplank onto the dock and followed him off the trawler.

The lights of Little Amsterdam were lost as Natuk walked behind the tall Greenlander, Angut Samuelsen, her protection for the evening. He wore a pair of thick glasses, and Natuk caught the flicker of his eyes as Angut scanned the local security data streaming onto the lens. Natuk's brother had streamed his own death with a similar pair of glasses just two weeks earlier. Natuk bit her lip, shook the thought out of her mind, and slipped her own glasses onto her face. The thick black rims complemented her thick black brows, accentuated by the short blonde cut of her hair and the tight set of her jaw. *Tonight isn't about appearances*, she thought, as she logged into the same DataStream as Angut, flicking her eyes through the options on the navigation screen and selecting the shortest and least populated route to the first location on a short list of two.

Angut stopped at the bottom of a long set of concrete steps leading to the road. He frowned at the sound of voices and reached for his Beretta APX pistol, heavier and bulkier than Natuk's. She slapped at his hand and shook her head. Pressing him against a streetlamp, her hands on his cheeks and her lips on his mouth as a party of three late-night revellers, stumbled down the steps towards the dock. They cheered as they passed, and Natuk framed a shy smile on her lips until they were gone.

"Keep your pistol in your pants," she said and nodded towards the steps.

She followed Angut to the top, checked their route, and blinked to trigger the *confirm* command on the lens view screen. A pulse of music turned her head, and another blink on the map projected onto the lens confirmed that the beat came from the second and final location on the list. She centred the map with another blink, tucked her hands inside the voluminous pockets of her jacket, crunching the snow beneath the thick tread of her boots as she picked up the pace. Angut followed, a single pace behind her as they walked deeper into Nuuk, passing the outlying buildings, their faces glowing with neon reds and greens, the Christmas stars shining on their glasses from the windows, and the litter of the holidays drifting past their heels as a thin wind spindrifted down Nuuk's main pedestrianised street.

The vacant store with metal plates bolted over the windows, and burn marks scoring the edges, was at the end of the street, on the left, within spitting distance of Greenland's National Library. Natuk waited for another clump of Greenlanders enjoying the prolonged Christmas and Independence celebrations to weave past them, smiling coyly as she slipped her arm around Angut, dragging him away from the more amorous of the group.

"He's mine," she said, when a woman reached for him, spilling her drink on the snow.

"There's more than enough to share," the woman said.

Natuk gave the woman a lingering glance. "Maybe later," she said, smiling at the jeers and cat-calling as they moved on. She pulled Angut into the scarred entrance to the store as soon as they were gone and knocked on the door. It creaked open a second later, a hand's width, the length of the thick security chain. A small nut-brown hand pressed a retinal scanner through the gap. Natuk removed her glasses and slipped them inside her jacket. She pressed her eye to the screen and waited for the man to unchain the door and let them in.

The man turned on the lights as soon as the door was closed, revealing a sterile surface of thick clear plastic covering the burned walls and floor. Three rows of plastic tables dominated the centre of the room, with more tables pressed against the walls. Slim screens and computers plugged into suitcase-like battery packs glowed from the wall tables, casting a soft light onto the centre tables covered in drone parts and spares spilling onto the surfaces.

"You realise these have to be ready by morning?" Natuk said.

"*Aap.*"

"Will they be?"

The man scratched at the thin stubble on his cheek and nodded. "I have more people helping me."

"Where are they?"

"Out back." He frowned. "I didn't think you wanted them to see you."

"Whatever." Natuk shrugged.

"Keep them there," Angut said. He reached for a packet of propellers on the table. "What about the cold?"

"They are polar oiled, and the batteries are Arctic-grade," the man said. "They'll work."

"And you'll sync them with the glasses?" Natuk asked, pointing at the banks of computers along the wall.

"We're syncing them as we build them. You'll have full control."

"Then we're done," she said.

Natuk walked to the door, waited for Angut to join her, and then stepped outside. She heard the chain snick into place a second after the man shut the door behind them.

"This was one of the buildings Ooqi paid someone to torch before Christmas," Natuk said.

The thought of her brother, and his campaign to spoil the referendum for Greenlandic independence chilled her more than the cold pressing down from the winter sky. She considered the difference in their approaches, how his had been the spectacular campaign of terror, making dramatic use of dead bodies. Natuk smiled as they walked to the second location, following Angut's lead via the map on his view screen. Her campaign was a last-ditch effort designed to sour all thoughts of independence and play on the young and their distrust of the older corrupt ministers in government. It would be more explosive than Ooqi's campaign. It had to be. *Besides,* she thought, *they brought this on themselves. They deserve it – for their ignorance, and for my brother, for he is in Elysium.*

Angut stopped and pointed towards a building across the street. "They're here," he said.

Natuk waited for Angut to gather the small group of young Greenlanders, all of them aged within a year or two of Natuk's twenty-five years. All of them selected because of their dissident attitudes and comments posted across the social media and message boards connecting them across the city, and in the private cyber arena Natuk had created for them. She watched as they pulled spray cans of black paint from their pockets and showed Angut the acetate stencils tucked between the layers of their clothes. He nodded, gave them their instructions, and waited for them to disperse before walking back to Natuk.

"They're ready," he said. "They've cached stencils and paint across the city. They'll post the locations on the forums as soon as they have finished."

"I counted seven," Natuk said. "That's not enough."

Angut grinned. "They were the *team leaders.* There's more waiting."

"Okay."

Angut reached for Natuk's arm, pressing his thick fingers around her bicep as he lowered his glasses.

"What?"

"Are you sure about the next step?" he said. "I don't think you should go alone."

Natuk brushed his hand away and took a step back. "Just meet me at the dock. I'll be back within two hours."

Angut pressed his glasses onto his nose and gestured for Natuk to do the same.

"No," she said. "I'm going offline for a bit."

She tugged the pistol from her jeans and pressed it into Angut's hand, turning her back on him before he could protest. Natuk walked along the street, past the library, tuning into the pulse of music and following it to a heavily-guarded door, allowing herself to be frisked and groped by the Âmo security guards before pushing past the bouncers and kicking the snow from her boots. She walked into the nightclub as the third and last of the guards at the door opened it and nodded for her to go inside.

The music shuddered and phased up the narrow stairs as Natuk squinted into the dark, compensating for the vibrant neon blues and purples blitzing in waves across the walls to the beat, the thud and stutter of the most notorious of Greenland's nightclubs: *Amâgaiat* – the troll that eats lonely travellers. *Or tourists and foreigners*, Natuk thought as she scanned the crowds of dancers. She looked beyond the throng of bodies on the dance floor, stepping onto a raised platform beside the bar to see past the young men and women teasing at each other's hair and slipping their hands over each other's bodies in the booths beyond the dance floor. She could have put on her glasses. She could have run a quick facial scan and located her mark within seconds, but Natuk knew it wasn't necessary. The girl she was looking for would stand out from the crowd – any crowd – always.

"Hey. Staff only."

Natuk glanced at the young man behind the bar as he shooed her away and into the crowd. She turned away, pausing as a twist of three bodies bumped into her. Natuk recovered her balance, lifted her head, and looked right into the eyes of a young woman – Natuk knew she was twenty years old – perched on the edge of a seat at the booth furthest from the dance floor. The girl's eyes softened as she recognised Natuk. She started to rise, but Natuk lifted her hand.

"Stay there," Natuk mouthed, as she slid between the dancers writhing like snakes on the dance floor, until she reached the steps to the boothed area. Natuk smiled at the young woman as she walked past the booths and reached out with her hand.

"Natuk?" the woman asked.

"*Aap.*"

"I recognised you – your smile – from the photo you sent."

"*All* of them?"

"No," the woman said. She blushed as Natuk tugged at her hand and pulled her to her feet.

"Maybe later," Natuk said with a raised eyebrow, as she guided the woman to an empty table along the wall leading to the toilets.

They sat down, and Natuk pressed her fingers into the woman's hands, squeezing her fingers into a lattice, catching them in a web. The woman's cheeks coloured, her eyes soft in the neon light, her hair long and black, clinging to Natuk's cheeks as they kissed.

Natuk pulled back with a laugh.

The woman frowned, her eyes darting with confused flecks of fear and arousal.

"What is it? What have I done?"

"Done?" Natuk said. "You've haven't *done* anything."

"Then why are you laughing?"

"Because, Tiina Markussen," Natuk said. "I don't think I have ever met anyone so perfect."

"Is that a bad thing?"

"No, Tiina, it's not."

Natuk slipped her hand around Tiina's neck, felt the heat of her skin prickle against her palm, and pulled her close, pressing her lips on Tiina's, teasing her with a single lingering bite, and the promise of so much more.

Chapter 2

The bathroom tiles of the hotel suite warmed the soles of her feet as Pipaluk Uutaaq, Greenland's First Minister, leaned over the bathroom sink to brush her cheeks with a medium blush. She tiptoed for a closer look at her mouth, pressing the lipstick into the creases of her lips as she lightly gripped the edge of the bathroom unit. She heard a man's voice call out from the bedroom and ignored him, focusing instead on her lips, a crisp touch of eyeliner and some shadow. She rested on her feet, enjoying the warmth of the under floor heating, as she fastened her black bra around her stomach, turned it so the clasp was behind her back and slipped the lacy cups over her small breasts. The light around the mirror lit the straps on her dark skin, and she smiled as she brushed her bobbed hair into stylish layers with a sharp cut of the fringe framing her chin. Model-chic with just the right amount of colour for the cameras, set off by a white blouse. She tugged at the silk, lifting the blouse from her bra, wondering if black was too much, deciding that she didn't care.

"Daddy would have been proud of his little girl," she said, assuming a younger voice and a childish tilt of her chin. She altered her voice to a more ministerial pitch. "My father would be so proud of us, our people, our land, on the cusp of freedom from colonial influence, only months away from true independence."

Pipaluk frowned, plucking her tablet from the towel shelf. She highlighted the word *cusp* and searched for an alternative. *Pinnacle* sounded wrong, *zenith* too obscure. She settled on *eve*.

"On the *eve* of our independence."

"Pipaluk? Can I come in?"

"*Naamik*," she said, as she scrolled through her speech.

"I need to pee."

"There's a bathroom down the hall, by the bar."

"Pipaluk?"

She opened the door, glanced at the man's pale skin and handed him a towel.

"You might want to cover yourself up."

Pipaluk closed the door, ignored the man's curse, and reminded herself that the next time her husband was out of town, she would choose an older lover for the weekend, more robust, less Danish. She smiled at the sound of the door closing.

She sat on the toilet to pull on a pair of tights, stood up to fasten her skirt around her waist, and grabbed her tablet on the way out of the bathroom. Pipaluk stuffed the tablet into her briefcase, slipped her feet inside fleece-lined boots and her arms into the thick *Canada Goose* quilted jacket – still Greenland's favourite after all these years. She stopped at the door, remembered her shoes, and tucked them under her arm as she left the suite.

Pipaluk met her weekend lover in the corridor, returning from the toilets by the bar.

"I'll have someone from reception check the room in twenty minutes. Try not to forget anything," she said, as she brushed past him.

"You're a real bitch, First Minister."

Pipaluk stopped. "You think so?"

"I do," the man said. "Lots of people do."

"Yours or mine?"

"What?"

She rolled her eyes. "Danes or Greenlanders?"

"Does it matter?"

"Not anymore," she said, as she turned her back on him. Pipaluk heard him slam the door to the suite as she waited for the elevator. "Like father like daughter," she said, as the doors opened. She caught the reflection of her smile in the polished tiles inside the elevator, pressed the button to go down, and let the smile grow for at least another two floors. By the time she reached the lobby, Greenland's First Minister was all business.

"Your first meeting with the minister for fishing and hunting has been cancelled," her assistant said, as soon as the elevator doors opened.

"Really?"

Juuarsi Fleischer swiped the tablet in his hands. "The minister said he was feeling sick. Although, there are conflicting accounts as to what *kind* of sickness."

"It can wait, Juuarsi," Pipaluk said, as she stopped by the reception desk. "Let him enjoy the celebrations. He's earned it," she said, and smiled at the receptionist. "We all have."

"Yes, First Minister," the receptionist said.

"There's a man in my room. He needs to leave. Will you check for me?"

"Of course." The young woman smiled. "When should I check?"

"Give him ten minutes. No longer." Pipaluk smiled and followed her assistant to the door.

Juuarsi waved for the First Minister's driver to approach the entrance, and then held the door for Pipaluk to get inside the spacious electric SUV. The interior matched her outfit, and she shrugged her jacket off and onto the seat as Juuarsi sat opposite her.

"So, I bumped up the interview," he said, as Pipaluk stared out of the window. "First Minister?"

"What's that?" she said. "On the bus window – all of them."

"Graffiti?" Juuarsi pressed his face to the window as the driver pulled away from the hotel.

"The same one on every window? It's a stencil of some kind. *Freedom is a lie*," she read aloud as they passed the bus. Pipaluk turned her head. "*Ignorance is darkness.*"

The words were familiar, wrapped around the image of a Greenlandic mask, and covering every window on every bus they passed. Pipaluk saw the same stencil, in various sizes, on every shop, café and office window they passed on the way to the NMG studio. Juuarsi made a note as Pipaluk reached for her mobile.

"She's not answering," she said, tossing her mobile onto her jacket.

"Who?"

"The Commissioner, Petra Jensen."

"Perhaps she's busy, First Minister."

"She'd better be," Pipaluk said, tapping her nail on the window as they passed another bus. "I don't want this to colour the interview. Make sure they know that at the studio."

"I'll talk to the presenter while you prepare."

"That mask," she said.

"Traditional."

Pipaluk checked the date on her mobile. "Tomorrow is *mitaartut*."

"Yes, First Minister."

"So, the mask, Juuarsi, is not coincidental. It's deliberate." Pipaluk swore. "Just when I thought we had got past the whole *Calendar Man* episode. Just when I thought we could relax and enjoy the moment." She sighed. "I just want to enjoy this. Just for a little while."

"It might not be related…"

"No? Overnight, anti-independence graffiti appears on every window in the city. You don't think it's related?"

Juuarsi shrank into his seat, clutching the tablet in front of his chest – a shield against the First Minister's growing fury.

The driver slowed the car to a stop outside the studio, and Pipaluk grabbed her phone, clutching it between her fingers as she pointed at her assistant.

"Get everyone in. I don't care if they are hung-over; I want a full cabinet meeting just as soon as I am done with this interview. And get the Commissioner on the phone."

"Yes, First Minister."

Pipaluk tucked her jacket over her arm, steeling herself in the cold air as the driver opened the door. Juuarsi handed her her shoes and briefcase.

"Call the meeting," she said. "Call the Commissioner."

She didn't wait for his response, Pipaluk stomped through the snow, pulling her jacket around her shoulders as the driver opened the door to the Nuuk Media Group building and held it for her as she walked inside. Pipaluk waited for the security man to buzz her into the studio. She gripped the handle of the door and paused, expelling the irritation from her body, and working her lips into a confident smile as she greeted the presenter's assistant, and let herself be guided to the green room prior to the interview. Pipaluk made herself comfortable, raised her eyebrows in a Greenlandic *yes* for a cup of coffee, and sat down to look through her speech, teasing the appropriate sentences into a highlighted sound bite with a pinch of her finger and thumb. The coffee cooled on the table in front of her and then the assistant called her through to the studio.

"We're recording this segment," she said. "It's good that you came in early. It means we can use more time to edit before we put it out with the main programme."

Pipaluk nodded and sat down in the seat at the desk in front of the cameras. They were smaller than the ones used to record her father's speeches and interviews. It seemed to her that time had shrunk everything, everything but cars. They got bigger each year. *And more expensive.* The thought reminded her that independence meant new trade agreements, and higher taxes, such as VAT. There was a lot of work to be done.

She stiffened at the sudden buzz of an incoming message, glanced at the screen and read the concise morning message from her husband, although it would be midday in Denmark. Pipaluk texted a short reply and turned off her phone.

"All set?" the presenter said, as he sat down beside Pipaluk.

"I'm ready when you are..."

"Klemens Edvardsen," he said, and shook her hand. "I'm new. You're my big break."

"Qitu Kalia hired you?"

"Just before Christmas. I should have been on the programme earlier, but the Calendar Man affected scheduling."

"He affected everything," Pipaluk said.

"Yes." Klemens swiped at the screen set in a recess in the surface of the desk. "I was hoping to ask you about it."

"Really? I think we should focus on the future, not dwell on the past, Klemens."

Klemens smiled. "How about we settle on the present. We'll take Greenland's temperature and work in some responses from people on the street."

"Have you spoken with my assistant?"

"Yes. He suggested a few things, but I'd like to keep it light and casual to begin with."

Pipaluk studied the man's face, looking for some sign or *tell* beneath his confident and manicured composure. *Qitu chose him well,* she thought, reminding herself that she needed to be careful. The assistant keyed in the intro, and Pipaluk turned to face the cameras, working on her own composure, and the confident smile that would be her signature as she led Greenland into an independent future.

"First Minister," Klemens said, as he turned to face her. "In the interests of cutting to the chase, I'd like to start by getting your opinion on recent events."

Pipaluk scanned his face again before dipping her head in a brief nod. "Of course."

Klemens made a show of reading from his tablet, quoting as he read the first line of the graffiti stencilled across the city, before focusing on the last. "*Ignorance is darkness.* First Minister, do you agree?"

"As you know, Klemens, my party is the most transparent of any Greenlandic political party, past and present. We hide nothing. There are no dark corners to fear, and we fight ignorance with a continued policy of clear and simple language…"

"As simple as the words *freedom is a lie?* That's pretty clear."

"Is it?" Pipaluk leaned into her answer, turning her head slightly for the benefit of the camera, as she composed her response. "It's an ambiguous statement, designed to confuse. Show me the clarity in those words. Better yet," she said, as she straightened her back and looked into the cameras, "show me the people responsible. Let them have their say in a fair and measured debate. This is not the time for confusion or fear. We have had more than our fair share of that this Christmas. This is a time for unity, a time when we need to speak openly, to discuss our fears and hopes for the future of Greenland."

"Yes, but…"

"Just a minute, Klemens," Pipaluk said. She paused to consider what the studio might edit out of the interview, and what they would want to keep. "Let me be clear. Let me be transparent. I only want the best for Greenland, and its people. If someone disagrees, and clearly *someone* does disagree, then let's be open about this. Don't hide in the shadows. There is no reason to hide in Greenland. Not now, not ever. Show yourselves."

Chapter 3

Police Commissioner Petra Jensen missed the first call, and the second. She reached for her mobile the third time it rang, cursing as she pushed it onto the floor. It didn't ring again. Once the room was her own again, she rubbed her eyes and listened to the sound of the neighbours waking, running water through the pipes, calling for a sister to wake a brother to wake their dad. The new family on the floor above Petra's was louder than the one below. They couldn't know that Petra had arranged a late start this Monday morning. She wished she had told them.

Petra pulled back the duvet and slid one leg over the side of the bed. She forced herself to move, rolling onto her side, and pressing herself into a sitting position with a knuckled hand that sank into the soft mattress. She tugged the t-shirt over her stomach, pushed the paperback books on the floor to one side, and stood up. She paused in the hall outside her room to pinch the sleeve of the old and worn police jacket hanging from the peg. She pressed the sleeve to her face, as she did each morning on the way to the bathroom and breathed the smell of north Greenland into her nose. She caught the musk of huskies, the oil of fish, seal blubber and the coppery tang of blood.

"It's alright, David," she said. "It's just a ritual. A little something to remind me of you." She laughed at the books strewn on the bed and the floor – his books. The toothbrush in the glass beside hers – his toothbrush. The jacket – his. The boots in the hall – his, two pairs. The list went on, and she put it to one side, washing her face with his facecloth, and making coffee to pour into David's favourite mug. "I'm working on it," she said, as she blew on the surface of the coffee, rolling her eyes at the thought of David's ghost shaking his head, a wry smile on its lips.

The phone rang again, and Petra ignored it, sipping her coffee as she sat on the couch, her ankles tucked up beneath her bottom, her eyes fixed on the view of Nuuk city docks across the fjord beyond her balcony. She caught a blur of movement and peered through the glass to see the massive carpet-like tasselled shadow of a sea eagle circling above the tower blocks of Qinngorput, just eight minutes' drive from the city centre, and an hour and a half to the summit of Ukkusissaq with its grand views of Nuuk and the surrounding fjords.

"That's why I'll keep the flat," she said, as she finished her coffee.

Petra carried her mug into the kitchen and placed it on the counter beside a thin folder. She tapped the cover, thought of her request for early retirement tucked inside it, and then thought of Aron Ulloriaq, her assistant, and the expression on his face when she had taken it home for the weekend.

"I just need to think," she had said, when she caught him glancing at the folder. "I'll make a decision this weekend. You'll be the first to know."

Once the Calendar Man case had been resolved and the media shifted their focus to the results of the referendum on Greenland's independence, Petra had plenty of time to dwell on the loss of a good police officer – however twisted and corrupted – and her own personal loss of her partner, David. The invitation to spend time in Inussuk was an open one, and Petra drew strength from the thought of fixing up the dark blue house that she and David had lived in, through the good and difficult times associated with their life in the north. She caught a trace of husky in her nose, thought of David's jacket, how he always wore it, on and off duty, in the patrol car, out on the sledge. She was ready to go back, to visit Karl and Buuti, to dip out of the hectic life of a city preparing to enter the global market as an independent country for the very first time.

Petra shook her head at the thought, imagining for a moment the magnitude of the task facing Pipaluk Uutaaq. Eleven years her junior, Petra admired Greenland's First Minister, even if they didn't always get along. It didn't surprise her then, when she retrieved her mobile from between the books on the bedroom floor, that the first call had been from Pipaluk and the following calls were from the First Minister's assistant.

Petra dressed, pinched the sleeve of David's jacket one last time, and then left her apartment. She waited for the bus in a short line of thickly-insulated Greenlanders, their noses, mouths and cheeks hidden behind wool scarves and fleece neckies. Only their eyes were visible, shining brightly, deep within the funnel of their hoods, the tips of the fur ruff flicking in the wind.

The bus was almost empty as the new passengers found their seats. The chatter of greeting and exchange of weekend news rustled through the bus to the sound of zips being opened, scarves unwound, and Velcro tabs unstuck. As the bus drove past the bright lights of the local supermarket the talk changed to that of surprise and exclamation as the lights captured the cautionary stencils on all the bus windows. Petra turned her head, examined the stencil closest to her seat, and then studied the others – identical and numerous. She photographed the one on the window beside her and studied it on the drive into Nuuk.

"Is it just your bus?" she asked the driver, before her stop.

"All the buses in Nuuk. Most of the taxis too."

"When?"

"Must have been early this morning. But it's not vandalism," he said, and pointed at the windscreen. "All the windscreens and mirrors have been untouched. They wanted us to be able to see out. As soon as the boss realised that, he let us drive. It would have taken all morning to clean the windows."

Petra nodded and stepped off the bus. She walked past several windows on her way to the police station and found a smaller stencil with the same letters and motif on the station's ground floor windows. A closer inspection showed the stencil was less defined, perhaps painted in haste, but the station was tagged just the same, just like the buses, taxis and public buildings.

No houses or private cars, she thought, as she entered the station.

Aron met her at the door to her office, took her jacket and hung it on the rack behind the door. He had started doing that just after Christmas, when the initial inquiry had begun to examine the circumstances concerned with Petra shooting a fellow police officer. She recognised Aron's concern, and accommodated his need to protect her.

David would approve, she thought. In his own quiet way, Aron reminded her of a younger Constable David Maratse, although no-one would ever call David *shy*. Grumpy and withdrawn, perhaps. The thought brought a brief smile to Petra's lips, until she noticed the look on Aron's face, and then she realised she had left the retirement papers on the kitchen counter.

"I forgot them," she said.

"Okay." Aron's shoulders relaxed.

"But I haven't changed my mind."

"Yes, ma'am."

"You know what that means?"

"*Aap.*"

"Right." Petra walked to her desk and sat down. "I have a feeling I know how today is going to go," she said. "But tell me anyway."

"The First Minister's assistant – the new one – has called a few times."

"How many?"

"Six. I think. I may have missed one of the calls."

Petra sighed and then nodded for Aron to continue.

"It's about the graffiti. The First Minister..."

"Wants me to look into it *personally*," Petra said.

"Yes."

Petra tapped the edge of her desk. "Where's Aqqa?"

"Still on leave. He had some overtime."

"He had a lot of overtime, Aron." She tilted her head to one side and looked at him. "So do you."

"Yes, ma'am."

"What about Atii? Is she also on leave?"

"She has some time off, but rumour has it she is doing an evening shift. She swapped with one of the SRU officers."

"Because he's also overworked." Petra nodded. "I'll talk to the duty officer. Or not," she said, as she caught the brief grimace that pinched Aron's cheeks.

"He does want to talk to you. The department is stretched thin, he says."

"I know. It's been a hell of a December."

"And now that Natuk has gone missing." Aron paused for a moment. "Now that she..."

"It's okay, Aron," Petra said. "I liked her too."

"But what if she was involved, you know, with what Ooqi was doing?"

Petra remembered Natuk's note, rolled up in a cylinder and tucked beside David's gravestone for her to find. There was no doubt that Natuk was involved with the campaign of terror her brother carried out in the run up to Christmas. But to what extent? The details were sparse, and the one person who had the answers, Ombudsman Anna Riis, was proving most uncooperative, due in part to her continued detention at a facility just north of the city centre.

"We might never know. But that doesn't mean we will stop looking. We just need time, Aron."

Petra buried the guilty thoughts of a simple life in the tiny settlement of Inussuk, and hoped Aron believed her. Others might look, but Petra planned to retire, with or without the First Minister's blessing.

"Tell me the rest of the day's schedule – besides the First Minister's graffiti and the duty officer's woes."

"Ma'am." Aron took a breath. "It's not on the schedule, but I thought it was time to visit the detention centre. I could come with you," he said. "I thought we could ask the Ombudsman some questions. If anyone knows where Natuk is…"

"She does. I agree. But she's saying nothing."

"I thought…"

"It's fine, Aron. If there's time, you'll come with me. But let me do the talking."

Petra suppressed a shiver at the thought of Aron blurting out inappropriate questions, and then wondered if she was any different at his age. *Yes*, she realised, *I was*. But Aron's concern was, apparently, boundless, although a little misguided.

Aron excused himself to make coffee and Petra decided to visit the duty officer. She regretted the thought as soon as she entered Tavik Aipe's office. There were red and black stains on Tavik's fingers and the whiteboard was cursed with thick stripes of ink and smudges of names and abbreviations.

"I thought we had a computer programme for that," Petra said, as she knocked and entered the room. The chemical bite of ink pricked at her nose as she perched on the edge of the duty officer's desk.

"It can't cope," he said. "And the boxes are too bloody small." Tavik tossed the red ink pen into the wastepaper basket, cursing as it bounced off the edge and the last drop of ink splashed onto the skirting board. "Sorry, ma'am," he said, as he bent down to pick up the pen.

"It's okay, Tavik."

"No, ma'am, it's not." Tavik capped the pens in his hand and placed them on the small shelf beneath the whiteboard. "This whole Calendar Man incident… it stretched us beyond what's practical. I've got officers calling in sick, all of them are stressed, and some are close to burnout. Royal Arctic has been sniffing around again, trying to poach the younger officers with promises of better pay and much better hours." Tavik slumped in his chair. "I hope you have some ideas, Commissioner, because we're bleeding, and it won't take much for us to bleed out."

Petra thought of the graffiti stencils pasted across the city, and realised Tavik was right, it wouldn't take much at all.

"Talk me through it," she said.

Chapter 4

Custody did not suit Anna Riis. The bed was too hard, the walls too stark. The room lacked even the most basic creature comforts she had spent the latter part of her sixty-two years cultivating in Greenland. Whereas the other ingrates – she refused to call them *inmates* – complained about the DataStream connection rates and restrictions on their browsing habits, Anna missed her throw blankets, the rough base of the kiln-fired mug that prickled the tips of her arthritic fingers, and her bookshelves with the bruised spines of worn and loved books. She missed Shakespeare, and the smell of the print and the pages. Tracing favourite quotes and passages across a screen was not the same. Some things just didn't translate well to the modern age, just like Greenland, and its aspirations to succeed and surpass its colonial status.

"More ingrates," she whispered as she rubbed her fingers and pressed her feet onto the cold cell floor.

She dressed quickly, pressing the creases from her trousers and tugging the hems of her cardigan, before crossing the floor to tap the screen hanging on the wall to confirm the time of the meeting with her lawyer. She had thirty minutes before breakfast, and one hour to kill before Mia Kiberg talked her through the statement she was to give about her relationship to Ooqi Kleemann, the so-called *Calendar Man*, deceased, killed by a bullet from the Police Commissioner's gun, and the shotgun blast from Petra Jensen's pit bull, Gaba Alatak.

"Ooqi," she said. "My little Ooqi."

The walls were too slick and white to absorb the name, and it hung there, in the air above her bed, as Anna smoothed the sheets, folded them beneath the mattress, tutting as she tugged and tucked the loose corners into place.

She paused as the memory of a younger, carefree Ooqi flickered into her thoughts. She remembered the press of his knees and his bottom on her thighs as he wriggled onto her lap to listen to one more story before bedtime. At twelve, he was too big for her lap, something his sister, Natuk, reminded him of, chiding him in Greenlandic, until Anna opened the first page of her beloved bard's most famous comedy and began to read.

"If music be the food of love, play on."

That was Ooqi's cue to stop fidgeting, and Natuk would drift from the doorway to Anna's feet, twisting the ends of her long black hair into her mouth and then curling them around her fingers as she listened. Anna did her best to read each part with a different voice, eliciting giggles from Ooqi, and reluctant smiles from his sister. Anna knew the lines off by heart, allowing her to peer over the book and catch the creases at the corners of Natuk's mouth, until the girl emerged from the layers of trauma from her childhood, relaxed and listened and laughed.

It was on Anna's lap and at her feet that the twins travelled to distant lands, discovered politics and the natural law and order of government, the intrigues of deceit and the consequences of action and inaction. It was a master class in manipulation, and once the challenges of the language were overcome, Ooqi and Natuk absorbed each lesson and quizzed Anna to a degree which delighted her, and, through some of Natuk's more astute enquiries, titillated Anna's fundamentalist ideals.

The seeds were sown, quietly cultivated.

It was Anna who encouraged the twins to work hard at school in Denmark. She pushed them equally hard at home, spending her own money on private tuition to ensure that they did not lose their mother tongue, and that they understood the power of language.

It was Natuk that imagined a Greenlandic Shakespeare – a complicated plot with characters tugged out of the crevices in the granite, magma-hot, moulded and beaten into twisted personages until they cooled and were ready to enter the scene, stage right and stage left. They would swoop from the eaves and crawl out of trapdoors, masked, bent, hideous to look at, like the shaman's *tupilaq*. Anna could not read the words, but the crude images Natuk drew of each character appalled and enthralled her.

"Who is this?" she asked, perhaps a year before Natuk and her brother returned to Greenland, to finish their studies at a Greenlandic gymnasium.

"That's the king of Denmark."

Anna peered closely at the figure, nodding as Natuk tapped the king's warped crown with the tip of her finger.

"Is he a good king?"

"He's the best," Natuk said. "But the people don't know it. They have lost their way, and he needs help to help them understand."

"Lost their way? How?"

"They have turned their back on him."

"Hm."

Anna rarely made sounds, and Natuk lifted her head to study her foster mother's face.

"Grunting is for animals," she said, repeating one of Anna's oft-quoted comments.

"Sound is for words and song," Anna said, and smiled. "You're quite right." She smoothed her hand through Natuk's hair, pulling her close as she sat down beside her. "Tell me more about your play."

The plot was at once complicated and compelling, as was to be expected from a student of Shakespeare. Anna listened as Natuk explained what happened, to whom, and when. The conclusion was tragic and poignant. It sparked a cascade of thoughts and ideas in Anna's mind, a world of possibilities, a trigger to be activated if necessary.

"When necessary," she said aloud, and the walls of the cell replaced the more comfortable and intriguing borders of her memory. Anna lurched from Natuk's teenage attempts at Greenlandic Shakespeare into her present confines of detention. The knock on her door, the crack of the hermetic seal as the door opened, and the curt command to attend breakfast came shortly after. Anna slipped on her soft laceless shoes and followed the guard along the corridor to the canteen. The sounds of plastic plates sliding onto plastic tables drifted along the corridor towards her, souring Anna's thoughts as she imagined the taste of plastic food on her tongue.

The human grunts, farts and breakfast belches over pallid plates of reconstituted eggs and tired bread, pressed Anna further and deeper into a sense of depression. This was detention. This was her penance for the crimes of passion and preservation. Passion for her country and its protective and protectorate ideals to preserve a society, its people and its culture. *Ooqi had given his life for these people*, she thought, as she stood in line for her breakfast. *And still they had turned their back on him, and the king of Denmark.*

"Ingrates," she whispered.

"What's that?"

It was the guard. Female. Short and stocky. A Greenlander. Short black hair. Glasses. A photo fit caricature of the many Greenlanders over forty. Anna tried not to sneer, but she felt her lips crease, and blamed it on the eggs.

"Nothing," she said, and carried her tray to an empty table.

Breakfast was followed by obligatory recreation, the polishing of the wooden floor of the handball court in the centre of the detention centre. They polished it each day for forty minutes. Polished it until it shone. It was so slippery she doubted it would ever be used for training or even the promised tournaments, regularly advertised on the cell media screens. But the shush of the dry mop on the wood was therapeutic, and Anna imagined the rocky Illyrian coastline, or the battlements of Elsinore castle, until a shrill whistle announced that the day's recreational requirements had been met, and all inmates should return to their cells.

Anna pressed her mop into the clasp on the wall and followed a guard to one of four meeting rooms. She waited for a second as the guard entered the code for the door, and then stepped inside.

Mia Kiberg was half Anna's age, and worth less than half the money Anna paid for her services. Any other lawyer, she believed, would have found just cause for bail, and Anna would be preparing for her hearing at home, rather than in the custody of the Greenlandic Prison Service – a poor model of the superior Danish institution.

Any further thoughts Anna had were dispelled as Mia tried to break the ice with morning pleasantries.

"Have you had coffee?" Mia asked. "I've arranged for coffee."

"I prefer tea," Anna said.

"Of course." Mia gestured for Anna to sit. "I've run through your statement and had my colleagues in Copenhagen look at it." She placed a tablet on the table in front of Anna. "We've made a few revisions."

Anna skimmed the document, and then tapped the screen to close it. She pushed the tablet towards Mia.

"I'm not saying that."

"What part?"

"Any of it," Anna said. "Revisions? You've changed everything."

Mia nodded as she sat down. "Yes. My colleagues and I..."

"Who?"

"Sorry?"

"Which colleague? Was it Harfeld?" Anna pointed at the tablet.

"It doesn't read like Harfeld. If he had been here, I would be home by now."

"Anna…"

"Who was it?"

Mia sighed. "It was me."

"You made all the revisions?"

"Yes."

"You didn't even show it your *colleagues*, did you?"

"Yes, I did. And they agree with me. We believe it is important that you adopt a more conciliatory tone."

"Conciliatory?"

"Less offensive."

"I didn't feel I was being offensive."

"You are *on* the offensive, Anna. It makes it difficult to argue your position of *not-guilty* in connection with the Calendar Man case."

"It wasn't me placing the bodies on the streets."

"I understand that. But it would help your defence if you adopted a more empathetic tone. Less accusatory."

"You're going to have to explain that," Anna said. She folded her arms across her chest.

"Your initial statement, the notes you gave me – there is a sense of satisfaction in the events to which you are being linked, by association."

"They didn't listen," Anna said. "They didn't try to communicate."

"With who? Ooqi Kleemann? You see, Anna, that's what makes it difficult to represent you here. By all accounts, and with the Jonkheer's statement…"

"The Jonkheer?"

"Yes. It's Coenraad Kuijpers' statement that has made it so difficult to have you released prior to the hearing." Mia paused as a guard entered the meeting room carrying a tray of coffee. She waited until she was gone before continuing. "The Jonkheer's testimony will be the most difficult to argue against. He says it was your idea to wage a campaign of terror to alter the outcome of the referendum."

"An outcome he desired."

"And admits to," Mia said. "But it doesn't change the implication that you inspired Ooqi Kleemann – your foster child for several formative years."

"Formative?"

"That's what the prosecutor will say, Anna. They believe you encouraged Ooqi Kleemann to procure dead bodies and instil fear and chaos to disrupt the voting. We believe they will suggest and try to prove that you not only encouraged Ooqi Kleemann, but that you trained him, and ordered him to influence the referendum."

"Hm," Anna said.

A stray thought pricked at her conscience, reminding her that *grunting is for animals.*

"Ooqi Kleemann is dead, Anna."

"You don't have to remind me of that."

"No, I don't. But it's important that you understand that prior to his death, and before the police realised his involvement in the case, he was a respected young police officer. There are some within the police department, that even now express regret for his death. They are looking for some measure of understanding; one might even call it sympathy."

"You're talking about the Police Commissioner," Anna said.

"Amongst others, yes, that's correct."

"Her sympathy is misguided. Her regret is just another word for guilt. Ooqi was twice the Greenlander she will ever be, twice the *human.* Petra *Piitalaat* Jensen killed my little boy, and she will pay for that." Anna stood up. She slapped the coffee mug with her hand and it shattered against the wall. "Just wait," she said. "Petra Jensen is going to pay. They all will."

Chapter 5

The image of Tavik's whiteboard schedule lingered as Petra walked back to her office. She heard the metallic clack of equipment as she passed the Special Response Unit's ready room. She resisted the impulse to check-in, concerned that she might see the same lines of fatigue that stretched the skin around the duty officer's eyes and tugged at his cheeks. But then she heard a familiar voice, and Atii stuck her head around the door.

"Commissioner," she said, as she stepped out into the corridor. "How are you, Petra?"

"I'm fine, Atii."

"We missed you at New Year's."

"I know. I wanted a quiet evening."

"Who with?"

"No-one," Petra said, and smiled. "Well, I tried reading one of David's books. And then I spent most of the night telling him just what I thought of science fiction. Honestly, budget reports are lighter reading."

"Petra." It was Atii's turn to smile.

"Yes?"

"Come inside and have a coffee. You need to be around people."

"Not ghosts, you mean?"

Atii shrugged and nodded for Petra to follow her inside. If anyone new to the department wondered at the informality of their relationship, an old hand would mention the name Gaba Alatak, and, once the newcomer connected the dots and they realised that Atii was Gaba's wife, a wave of understanding would wash over them. Petra might be the Commissioner, but Gaba was a living legend in the Greenlandic police force. Arrogant, with an ego like an upturned iceberg with the tip hidden just beneath the surface. Atii had married Gaba only a few years after the Commissioner had ditched him. It was public knowledge, as was Gaba's service record. It made sense that the Commissioner had chosen him to accompany her when she tried to arrest the Calendar Man, although the board of inquiry might disagree.

"How's Gaba doing?" Petra asked, as Atii poured her a coffee. The five men and women of the SRU continued to check their gear once they had acknowledged the Commissioner's presence.

"You mean with the inquiry? He's fine. It's not the first time he's been roasted for his actions."

"But it's the first time as a civilian."

"He's pleading self-defence." Atii frowned. "I'm surprised you haven't heard."

"I have a meeting at the end of the week. They're keeping me in the dark until then, I suppose." Petra gestured at the team. "What's all this? Routine?"

"Partly. I think we're going to get a call pretty soon."

"About what?"

"The First Minister was interviewed this morning. The presenter is new. He pushed her about the graffiti all over town."

"I haven't heard it yet," Petra said. "I had a meeting with Tavik."

"Right," Atii said. "Well, she's called a press conference. Âmo security has been paid until the end of January, but I want to be ready. Just in case."

"Is there something you want to tell me?"

Atii picked up her mug and nodded towards her office at the rear of the ready room. Petra followed her inside. There was a moment of quiet as the SRU team members stopped working. Atii frowned at them, and then shut the door.

"They're just grouchy," she said.

"Tired?"

"Pretty much bombed, like the rest of us. But they don't get paid to sit on the sofa."

Petra waited as Atii walked around her desk. The wheels on the chair squealed as she pulled it out and sat down. Petra ignored the chair in front of the desk, choosing to lean against the wall instead. Atii took a sip of coffee, and then began.

"Gaba has been nagging me for days to tell you about this, but I've got nothing conclusive, no evidence."

"Tell me, Atii."

Atii nodded. "Commissioner," she said, changing the tone of her voice. "I don't think we've heard the last of Ooqi Kleemann."

"He's dead, Sergeant."

"*Aap*, I know, but that's not what I mean. I think there's more to this."

"More? It was a pretty elaborate terror campaign. He had us running all over the city."

"He did, but I don't think he acted alone."

"You're talking about Natuk?"

Atii nodded. "She was his brother, something they kept hidden from all of us. Why?"

"That's a question for the Ombudsman, Anna Riis." Petra put her mug down on a shelf. "Although, I can't imagine she will tell us anything. Aron suggested I visit her later. Perhaps you want to come with me?"

"No," Atii said. "I need to be in the city. I want to be available if something happens." She shrugged. "*When* it happens."

"You think Natuk is still in Greenland?"

"I think she could be anywhere, but I'm betting she's close. Gaba is tired of hearing about it. He says if I'm so sure of it, then I should get permission to go looking for her."

Petra laughed at the look on Atii's face. She imagined the discussion Atii had with Gaba, and his exasperation. She'd seen a similar look on his face, all too often. There was a reason those two were made for each other, once an idea took hold, neither of them could ever let it go.

"Are you asking for my permission, Sergeant?"

"Yes, ma'am. I want to start a search for Natuk Petersen, starting with a wide sweep of Nuuk, Little Amsterdam, and Chinatown."

"We're quite stretched at the moment, Atii."

"We are."

"I'm not sure we have the resources."

"What about Aron?"

"My assistant?"

"He spent time with Ooqi. I think they were friends. Rumour has it that he was quite taken with Natuk, although he was too shy to do anything about it." It was Atii's turn to laugh. "That's probably a good thing. Anyway," she said, "he's pretty competent with computers, whereas my guys are all action. I think Aron could narrow the search parameters, lighten the load."

Petra remembered Aron picking up the slack when Ooqi disappeared from the Calendar Man task force, revealing a quiet technological confidence that amused Petra. It would have confused David, despite his interest in science fiction.

"Don't work him too hard," Petra said, as she moved towards the door. "And keep me posted."

"Thank you, ma'am."

Petra's mobile buzzed as she left Atii's office. She slipped it out of her pocket as she walked along the corridor, answering it with a swipe of her thumb as she reached the bottom of the stairs.

"Commissioner Jensen?"

The accent was American. Petra pressed the phone closer to her ear and stepped to one side to make room for two officers and a young man with a t-shirt spattered in vomit.

"Yes," she answered, in English.

"My name is Joshua Seabloom. I'm the new station Commander at the USCG base in Nuuk. I wondered if we could meet."

"I'd like that," Petra said.

"How about now? I'm right outside."

Petra turned to face the main entrance and saw a tall man in uniform wave from where he stood behind the glass. Petra ended the call and walked to the door. She nodded for the officer sitting at the security desk to buzz the Commander into the building.

"I'm sorry to come unannounced," Seabloom said, as he walked past the security guard. He shook Petra's hand, and then stamped the snow from his boots on the rough mat in front of the door.

"It's fine," Petra said, as she studied the Commander. The grey tinge to his closely-cropped hair suggested they were the same age, but his height made him look younger. He was almost as tall as Gaba. She felt a brief flood of heat to her neck and tugged at her collar. The Americans changed Commanders at the base faster than the Chinese changed security officers. The previous Commanders had been too busy to make an impression, but Petra thought she might just remember Joshua Seabloom.

"Are you alright?" he asked.

"Yes, I'm fine," she said.

"You're sure? You look a little flushed."

"I'm fine." Petra gestured towards the stairs. "Shall we meet in my office?"

"Yes," he said. "I'll follow you."

Aron looked up from his desk as Petra entered the outer office. He stared at the American until Petra waved her hand in front of his face, and gestured for Seabloom to wait for her inside.

"Aron," she said. "Can you find us some coffee?"

"Yes, ma'am."

"And," she said, as he turned away."

"*Aap?*"

"Sergeant Napa needs your help with something. Don't let her work you too hard."

Petra waited until Aron was busy with the coffee before joining Seabloom. She found him studying the map of Greenland hanging on her wall.

"It's such a huge country," he said. "And now, with the retreating ice sheet, it's just getting bigger. Huge potential for real estate," he said, and grinned.

"But still no roads," Petra said.

"Yeah, that's an issue, right there."

Seabloom hung his winter coat on the stand beside the door and sat down at the table. Petra waited for Aron to bring the coffee. She took the tray from his hands, placed it on the table, and then closed the door.

"This is unusual," she said, as she poured the coffee. "We don't usually hear much from your side of the fjord."

"We're good at that," he said. "We want the world to adopt our ways, buy all our products, and leave us the hell alone." Seabloom grinned. "Does that fit?"

"A little." Petra laughed. "How can I help you?"

"Actually, I've come to help you." Seabloom tugged a medium-sized tablet from his jacket pocket and placed it in front of Petra. He tapped the glass and swiped an image until it filled the screen. "You've got an epidemic," he said, as Petra stared at a photograph of the graffiti she had seen on her way into work.

"It's on the to-do list," she said.

Petra leaned back in her seat. She took a sip of coffee as Seabloom selected another image from a folder and enlarged it.

"What about her?" he asked. "Isn't she one of yours?"

The image of Constable Natuk Petersen in uniform, her long black hair tied in a ponytail at the back of her head, jolted Petra's thoughts from the graffiti to the all too familiar scene of Ooqi's death, when she pulled the trigger of her pistol and Gaba blasted him with his shotgun. Petra replayed the scene often, in the quiet, empty moments of her flat when David's ghost allowed her. There was a moment during each re-enactment, when she remembered Ooqi placing his glasses on the table, recording his last moments, and she wondered just how many times Natuk had watched her brother die.

"What's this about?" she asked.

Seabloom poured a dash of cream into his coffee and crumbled a cube of sugar onto the surface. He looked at Petra as he stirred it, nodding at the tablet as he started to speak.

"We have several cutters based at the station in Nuuk. One of them is a little old now, a National Security Cutter called the *Stratford*. She was on her way back from a patrol when she spotted a Greenlandic trawler that wasn't trawling."

"What do you mean?"

"It was behaving erratically, as if the Captain was asleep at the wheel. The *Stratford*'s Captain hailed the trawler, and, when she received no response, she sent a boarding party across to inspect the boat. The crew were not asleep, but there was a heated argument below decks. The boarding party made the crew aware of their presence," Seabloom smiled. "They might have fired off a round or two – there was quite a ruckus. Anyway, once they got the crew's attention and identified the Captain of the boat, they interviewed him. The trawler was based in Nuuk but had just dropped someone off in Ilulissat. The Captain was pretty pissed about it. He said his boat had been commandeered by a police officer. One of the crew took that picture when your officer wasn't looking." Seabloom took a sip of coffee. "I thought you might want to know."

"When was this?"

"December twenty-third."

Petra looked at the image of Natuk, picturing for a moment her escape from Nuuk, on the same day that Petra killed her brother.

"What has this got to do with the graffiti?"

"The same crewman who took the picture said that he heard Natuk muttering something as she forced the Captain to sail north."

"Forced him?"

"The crewman said her pistol was unholstered, and that she seemed agitated. He said she repeated a phrase a couple times: *darkness is ignorance*. Or something like that. I wouldn't have thought any more of it, until someone tagged the bridge across the fjord with that stencil, and the same words. One of my ensigns made the connection. He was on the *Stratford* that day, and he reported it to his Captain, and she reported it to me." Seabloom leaned back in his seat and crossed his legs. "Now, I don't know the circumstances. I arrived just after Christmas, so I've only been here a few days. But I understand you had a situation over the holidays, and that things got quite out of hand. Once we put these things together," he said, as he swapped the image of Natuk with that of the graffiti, "I thought it best to come straight to you. Then I saw the same image all over town."

"You think Natuk is connected to the graffiti?"

"I think it's a good bet. Don't you?"

"My SRU leader thinks so," Petra said. She took a long breath and looked at Seabloom. "Thank you for this."

"You're very welcome."

Petra watched as Seabloom finished his coffee. She frowned as he poured another.

"What?" he said. "Only one coffee per meeting?"

"No," she said. "I just thought you would be leaving."

"I told my driver I would be at least an hour. Your coffee is stronger than ours; I thought I'd have another cup while we discuss matters."

"What matters?"

"In the interests of international relations, I'd like to offer my assistance, and," he said, with a nod towards the tablet, "from the looks of things, I think you might just need it."

Petra swiped the tablet to look at the image of Natuk one more time, remembering Tavik's whiteboard and his fractured schedule of tired officers.

"Yes," she said. "I think we might."

Chapter 6

Natuk surprised the small group of men and women assembling drones with a second visit. She moved between the tables with barely a nod of acknowledgment as the last components of each drone was assembled and they were put to one side to make space for the next. The parts were mostly plastic, and the sound of a metal click, and clack caught Natuk's attention. She moved away from the drones and watched a young man assemble a pistol. She pulled it from his hands as he slid the magazine into place.

"You don't need it," she said, reducing the pistol to a pile of components and an empty magazine in just a few seconds. The man stared at her as she flicked the bullets from the magazine with her thumb, one by one, as she returned the man's stare until he withered to a safer distance and pressed his back against the wall.

"We won't win this campaign with bullets and guns," Natuk said. She tossed the magazine onto the table and took a moment to look at each of the men and women at the tables. There were five of them, including Assa, the man that had unlocked the door on her first visit earlier that morning. The late morning sun pressed at the edges of the metal plates covering the broken windows and burned window frames. "To get the outcome we want, to truly move the people, we have to let them lead. All we have to do," she said, with a nod at the drones on the tables, "is show them the way."

"You want to change people's minds with a few drones?" The man leaning against the wall pushed away from it and squared his shoulders. "It won't make a difference."

"Each drone has a camera. Once this thing kicks off, we feed those images – all of them – into the DataStream, hacking into the mainstream media, the independents, even the government channels. It will be a feeding frenzy, and we need to keep them hungry."

"Them," the man said. "Just who are they? Eh? You don't even know them."

Natuk glanced at the leader of the group, the man with the keys.

"You told me to find people to assemble drones," Assa said, with a shrug.

"I assumed you would find believers," she said.

"Hey, I believe." The man pointed at the two men and one woman standing between the tables. "Just ask them."

"What's your name?" Natuk asked, as she took a step towards the man.

"Qallu."

"And what do you believe in, Qallu?"

"The same as everyone else," he said. He waited for Natuk to respond, continuing when she didn't. "I want a strong Greenland, one my children can be proud of."

"But not you?"

"Not right now," Qallu said. "Right now, we're weak."

"And your children?"

"I don't have any yet."

Natuk picked up the magazine from the pistol. "Tonight, you're going to forge a new direction for your country. Would you want your children to know you did it with a gun, or that you inspired people – young Greenlanders, the future – that you inspired them to rise up and make a stand?"

"But it's not a new direction. Is it?" he said. "You're trying to change the vote, to keep us under Danish rule."

"Not rule," Natuk said. "Just under their wing, just a little longer, until we're ready to forge our own path."

"Under their wing?" Qallu laughed. "Under their thumb, more like."

"So, you want freedom, Qallu? The kind Pipaluk Uutaaq says she can give you?"

"At least she keeps her promises. She did what she said she would do, what her father said *he* would do. She got us this far, even when that crazy Calendar Man ripped through Nuuk with his..."

The words died on Qallu's lips as Natuk placed the pistol magazine quietly on the table and took a small step towards him.

"I don't think," she whispered, "you're the best fit for this operation, Qallu."

"It's a job," he said. "I did this for the money."

"There's no money," Natuk said.

"What?" Qallu looked around her. Natuk moved to block his view of the other people in the room.

"We do this because it's the right thing to do, Qallu. We do this because we believe Greenland needs protecting, and we're not ready to go it alone, not yet. Maybe one day. Soon, I hope. You want your children that see a truly independent and free Greenland? So do I. I look forward to that, Qallu, I really do. But right now, you have to decide what role you will play in Greenland's future."

"What role?"

"You said you believe. You said you wanted a stronger Greenland, a country your children – the ones you hope to have – can be proud of. So, I ask you again, Qallu, what are you going to do about it?"

Qallu frowned. He focused on Natuk's face, on her eyes, and he missed the subtle shift of her stance, the slight bend to her knees, the flattening of her palms and the straightening of her fingers. He missed all the signs that hushed the other people in the room.

"Listen," he said, as he tried once again to look around Natuk. "I'll just take my money and go."

"There's no money," Natuk said.

"Then I'll just go," Qallu said, as the hush finally reached him, and the cool air inside the room settled between them.

"Not before you answer my question."

Qallu stiffened. He straightened his shoulders, clenched his teeth and stared down at Natuk. She had seen it before when on patrol, especially on Friday and Saturday nights, that moment when *they*, usually a man, attempted to dominate the situation, confusing assertiveness with arrogance as they reassessed the distribution of power, scoffing at the sight of the woman in front of them, perhaps a head shorter than they were. Natuk could forgive the drunks their moment of manliness. But even though Qallu was not drunk, he made the same mistake as men often do, he forgot that when the roles were reversed, women tended to skip over the testosterone pump and bristle, and strike, hard and fast. Just as Natuk did, slamming the blade of her right hand hard into Qallu's collar bone. She pinned him against the wall, trapping his left arm against his body as she punched him three times on the side of his face with her left fist. The small ridges of her knuckles, like tiny granite peaks, dimpled Qallu's cheek as he groaned and slumped against the wall.

"You're weak," she said, as she lowered her fist, gripped Qallu's jacket and lifted him. "Just like Greenland. "How long do you think we would last with people like you at the helm? Tell me that, Qallu."

"Just let me go," he whispered. "Let me go."

"After you've seen all this?"

"I won't tell anyone."

"It's not that simple," Natuk said, as she let go of Qallu. He slid down the wall to slump at her feet. Natuk turned her head to look at the others in the room. She caught Angut's eye as he entered the store, locking the door behind him. "A minute ago, Qallu was ready to use a gun to force the people to change their minds, but he can't even defend himself. Do you really want a man like that carrying a weapon?"

Qallu squirmed as Natuk pressed the toe of her boot into his stomach. He slid across the soot-black tiles, inching towards the door at the rear of the store as Natuk spat on the floor.

"Violence doesn't work," Natuk said. "Fear doesn't work." Natuk glanced at Angut. "It's been tried. You all know what happened this Christmas. The referendum went ahead anyway, because the voters were not informed. They were just *told* what was best for them. Some ideological idea was dumbed-down and served. There was no information. Tonight, we're going to change that. We're going to *inform* the people, the youth of Greenland. We are going to give them the power to…"

Natuk paused at the sound of a door opening. She flicked her head to look at the rear of the store, saw the door creak to a close, and then heard a second door slam. She heard the crunch of a table behind her as she raced into the back room and Angut barged passed the drone assembly line. She held out her hand as she reached the back door and Angut pressed her pistol into her hands. She slid it into her jacket pocket as she exited the store.

"I'll go around front," Angut said, as he scanned the short alleyway behind the store.

"No," Natuk said. "He's still here."

"I don't see him."

"Shush. Listen."

A raven cawed from the roof above them, claws clacking on the metal gutter. Natuk ignored it, focusing on the garbage piled against the alley wall, waiting for collection. She pulled the pistol from her pocket, gripped it in two hands, and walked forwards. The raven cawed again, flapping its great wings in protest as Natuk kicked at a pile of cardboard boxes, scattering snow and paper waste to reveal an empty hiding space.

"I was sure he was still here," she said.

"He ran," Angut said. "You scared him pretty good." He nodded at the electric motorcycle leaning against the wall. "So much, he didn't even take the bike."

"Shit."

Natuk kicked at another box and then slipped the pistol inside her pocket. The raven cackled on the rooftop. Natuk glared at it.

"I'll find him," Angut said.

"*Naamik.* I have another job for you." Natuk took a last look at the raven and then nodded for Angut to follow her to the end of the alleyway. "I need you to pick up my mother."

"Your mother?"

"Foster mother."

"Okay, where is she?"

"She is in the detention centre. Her name is Anna Riis."

"Natuk…"

"Yes, it *is* possible. Once I ignite the city, you'll have plenty of time to get in and get her out. Assa will help you bypass security. I've already patched him in through a back door breach. The police will have their hands full. Just get her to the boat, and then come and find me."

"And what will you do, about him?" Angut said, with a nod towards the street. The sun had brought out the mid-morning shoppers, and their increasing numbers slowly replaced the last of the late-night revellers.

"Once I float his picture in the DataStream, I'll let the people bring him to me."

"And if they don't?"

"They will, Angut. Have a little faith. This is an important night. We need to trust the people to make it *their* night. As soon as they feel they own it they won't let anything jeopardise it, and our work will be done."

"Huh," Angut said. "They'll still need a leader. If it's not going to be you, then who?"

"I've found someone," Natuk said. She smiled at the memory of the few hours she had spent with Tiina Markussen. Brief but enjoyable. Tiina had speed-talked for two hours without a break, hiding her nervousness with passionate strains of patriotism, balanced with the need to do things at the right speed, with the right foundations. Natuk had guided her with a measured comment her and there to keep her on course, to strengthen the pillars of her foundations, supporting her fundamental beliefs that Greenland would be independent when the time was right, and not before.

"The girl at the nightclub?"

"*Aap.*"

"And you can trust her?"

"She's committed, Angut. She understands, perhaps even more than we do. The people will respond to her, and *her* people, her generation, even more so."

"What's her name?"

"I'm going to call her Viola, and by the end of the night, all of Greenland will know her, and the young people of Nuuk will follow her, all the way to the end."

Angut laughed.

"What?"

"The light in your eyes," he said. "It's so bright, it's like they're on fire."

"And?"

"Just don't let it go out."

Chapter 7

Viola. The name was as exciting as it was unfamiliar, Tiina thought, as she boiled water for tea in the closet-sized kitchen of her one room apartment. She waited for the water to boil and stared at the sofa bed pressed into the corner of the room. The duvet and blankets were ruffled, and her pillow still had the shape of Natuk's head. If she pressed her nose to the pillow, she could smell her shampoo. Tiina closed her eyes and remembered their hushed conversation, Natuk's soft lips pressed to her ear, nibbling her lobe when she expected a response from Tiina. It had been hard to breathe, and it had nothing to do with Tiina's asthma, or the radiators turned up to the max. It was as if Natuk's presence stole the air from her lungs, she kept her breathless, feeding Tiina with small pockets of air, between words, between promises sealed with kisses.

Soft lips.

Sharp teeth on her lobes, her lips.

The scratch of clipped nails across Tiina's skin, tracing the shape of her ear, removing her librarian-thick glasses, such a cliché.

"I can't see without them," Tiina had said.

"You don't need to see. Just listen, feel, smell, taste," Natuk had said. "Use your senses. Let go."

Tiina gasped at the memory, and the bubbling of the water popped against the side of the pan, splashing on the hotplate, tugging her back into the moment. But the thought of Natuk, just a few hours earlier, stayed with her, and the smell of the tea, a cinnamon blend, jolted another thought, the soothing caresses Natuk had given and the gentle words she had said after they had used each of the senses to explore all of their bodies.

"You will be Viola," Natuk had said.

"*Viola?*"

"It's your new identity."

"Don't you like my name?"

"I love your name, Tiina, but you can't be Tiina Markussen tonight. I need you to be Viola, from now until the end."

"What end?"

Tiina remembered Natuk's touch, the way she curled Tiina's hair through her thin fingers, tucking errant lengths behind Tiina's ear as she leaned in to whisper.

"The course we are on is not healthy, it is not free. Viola needs to change that. Viola can change it, with my help."

"Viola can?"

"*Aap.*"

"How?"

That was when Natuk had stood up, the blanket slipping from her body as she leaned over the table, the one Tiina studied at, and plucked the mask from the wall. Natuk lifted it in front of her face, found the string and tugged it over her head. She stood there, her face hideously masked, her naked skin warm in the last glow of Christmas lights. Natuk danced, lifting one leg high, bent at the knee. She straightened her arms, swung her forearms at right angles, dangling like a puppet as she alternated the high steps, first her left leg, then her right. Her small breasts barely moved, the triangle of thick hair between her legs was dark in the shadows as Natuk twirled out of the light. There was more hair and more shadows beneath her arms, adding to the magic and mystery of the masked dance. Tiina was captivated, her lungs caught between breathless gasps and heaves of laughter. She knew the game. She knew what was required of her. It was *mitaartut*, when Greenlanders in masks and padded clothes knocked on doors and danced their way inside people's homes, carrying a skin drum, challenging them to recognise them, hitting them with the drumstick if they didn't. Natuk being to tease Tiina, grasping a pillow and beating her with it until Tiina held up her hands and danced around Natuk and into the kitchen where she found a bag of sweets, spilling them into Natuk's hands and onto the floor, carrying on the tradition with the gift of candy, as she pretended not to know Natuk's name.

"Kiss me," Natuk said.

"No, not with that mask."

Natuk lifted the mask over her face, letting it rest on her head, the hideous chin just above her thick black brows.

"Kiss me, Viola," she said.

Tiina remembered the kiss, the touch, the taste of Natuk's skin, and she remembered the mask. She carried her tea into the room and found the mask on the table. She put down the mug and carried the mask to the bed. It was black as soot, with thick red paint accentuating the contorted shapes and curves that distorted the face around the eyes, puffed the cheeks beyond the chin, and spread the mouth. The teeth were chiselled, wood-grained with a splash of yellow paint. Tiina pressed the tip of her finger into the thin hole cut between the top and bottom row of teeth. She remembered Natuk's pink tongue peeping through it, remembered the taste of it.

Tiina flopped back on the bed, closed her eyes, and sighed. This was love. She was sure of it. And she would do anything and everything for it. For just one more dance, with or without the mask.

"I am Viola," she whispered. "I am yours to command."

Natuk's first command had been for Viola – not Tiina – to attend the First Minister's press conference, to use her student journalist credentials to sit at the back, and to ask a specific question, to be brave, and to insist.

You speak for your generation, Viola. You are their voice.

That was the last thing Natuk had written in the DataStream, just half an hour earlier.

Viola got up off the bed. *Viola* changed out of her pyjamas and t-shirt into jeans and a body-hugging fleece. It was *Viola* that practiced her question in front of the bathroom mirror, and *Viola* that switched her librarian glasses for the slightly thicker rims of Natuk's glasses, the ones she had slipped on Tiina's face when she left her apartment.

"Now you can see," she had said, "and I will show you the world."

The lenses were expensive, adjusting and auto-correcting to accommodate Tiina's reduced vision.

"Not Tiina," she reminded herself. "I am Viola."

Viola flicked her eyes around the lenses, testing the functions of each icon, trying the blink, track and slip method of retinal navigation. It was awkward and exciting. She felt free, she felt whole, and, she realised, she felt empowered.

An icon in the bottom field of the right lens flashed, and she blinked it into the centre. The image window had a reduced opacity, and Viola walked from the bathroom to the kitchen, looking through the image and reading it simultaneously. She smiled at the thought that – glasses on – she was Viola. She removed the glasses for a second, wondering who would return.

"Still Viola," she said, and pressed the glasses onto her face.

The window was a message box, and she read the message confirming the time and place of the First Minister's press conference. Viola finished dressing, laced her quilted boots and grabbed her jacket. She was crunching through the snow on the footpath outside her apartment just a few minutes later.

She saw the graffiti on the bus, focused on the stencil on the window closest too her, and blinked as the glasses scanned the image, triggering a stream of data that cascaded down the left lens of her glasses. Viola slowed the stream with the blink and track technique. She transferred one item in the stream onto the right lens, positioning it with another blink. The stream in the other lens slowed as Viola focused on the right, holding her breath as she read the confirmation from the team leaders that the preparations for *mitaartut* were in place, and that they were waiting for further orders.

The words *Viola will confirm* flickered onto the lens at the bottom of the message.

Who?

Viola. Wait for her signal.

"My signal?" Viola whispered.

She glanced at the other passengers on the bus. She relaxed. Viola, it seemed, was just as anonymous and unremarkable as Tiina Markussen. It was no wonder the team leaders did not know who she was. Nobody did.

But all that is going to change, Viola thought, as the bus slowed for her stop. *Natuk said so.*

She flashed her student card at the entrance to the community centre opposite the supermarket on the main pedestrianised street curving through Nuuk's city centre. She found a seat at the back, as instructed, and blinked the question onto the lens of her glasses, as instructed. She looked up at a hush from the audience, and the click and hum of cameras and video recording equipment.

Before her alter ego, before Natuk, Tiina had always been in awe of Greenland's First Minister, impressed by her commitment, her clothes, and, not least, her confidence. Pipaluk projected all three as she walked up to the podium in front of the journalists, politicians, and business men and women gathered for her press conference.

"Thank you for coming at such short notice," Pipaluk began. She waited a beat, letting the audience settle as she sought out the camera. Pipaluk pressed her slender hands around the sides of the podium and leaned forwards, ever so slightly, but enough to change the pitch of her voice. It was strong, balanced, determined. "Christmas is nearly over," she said. "Tomorrow is *mitaartut*. Our decorations must come down, according to tradition. But that doesn't mean that we are finished with our celebrations. It does not mean we must put the past behind us. No," she said, and shook her head. "Now, more than ever, it is important to remember our past, and to draw on many lifetimes' of experience, the good, the bad, even the memory of those times that have terrified us." She paused to look at the people in the audience. "This Christmas was one of those terrifying experiences, and I don't imagine anyone will ever forget it. But that doesn't mean we can't move on. It doesn't mean we are weak. No-one should imagine we are weak, and we must be strong, even in the face of uncertainty." Pipaluk took a sip of water and the journalists in the front row tapped a few notes into their tablets. "Many of you will have seen the graffiti on the windows of the buses and taxis this morning. You will have seen the same graffiti on the windows and walls of public buildings, your favourite café perhaps, or plastered across the library. Someone, perhaps lots of people, want you to be scared again, as if the Calendar Man or something like him has returned, and the question of our independence and freedom is in jeopardy. Well," Pipaluk said, "I'm here today, speaking to you now, to tell you that the Calendar Man is dead, and that the people of Greenland have voted. The darkness is retreating, and there is no ignorance. Not anymore, and never again," she said. "Now there is light, hope, and freedom." She smiled, relaxed her grip on the podium and looked at the camera. "This is a time for hope. Hope makes us strong, and together we are stronger."

Several in the audience clapped. Viola felt her heart race under the soft salvos echoing around the room.

Now, Viola.

The text flashed onto the lens.

You're not alone. I am with you. We all are.

"Any questions for the First Minister?"

Viola didn't see who asked. She closed her eyes for a second as she stood. When she opened them, she saw two of the three cameras pointing at her. She saw her image, her face, flash across the lens of her glasses, and she saw the DataStream spike with a stream of comments and her name tagged to her image.

"Yes?" Pipaluk said. "You have a question."

"I do, First Minister," Viola said.

"What is your name?"

"My name is Viola," she said, "and I represent my generation, and all the generations of Greenland."

"Okay," Pipaluk said. "And your question?"

Viola took a breath. Her glasses registered a flicker of movement to the right of the podium, zooming in on the raised thumb of a young man, followed by the brief nod of his head. He mouthed the name, *Viola*, and she smiled.

"My question, First Minister," she said, "concerns the future of Greenland, and everything you have done to undermine it."

Traffic in the DataStream spiked for a second time, and the heat from the lights threatened to overwhelm her. And it might have, if she had been Tiina. But she was Viola now, the voice of her generation. The DataStream slowed to a stop, and even the hum of the video cameras was hushed as everyone in the room, everyone in Nuuk, and the whole of Greenland waited for her to speak.

Chapter 8

Pipaluk waited until her assistant confirmed that the press was gone and slammed the door to the room reserved for staff at the community centre. The thin walls shook and the last of the Christmas decorations shivered against the walls, the red paper star knocked against the window pane.

"Who the hell is she?" Pipaluk said, whirling on her assistant.

Juuarsi started to speak, and then tugged his tablet to his chest as Pipaluk gripped the back of one of the chairs and ripped it out from beneath the table. She sat down, pressed her palms flat against the table edge, and glared at him.

"Well?"

"She said her name was Viola."

"I know that, Juuarsi. I was there. Remember?" Pipaluk took a breath. "I want to know her real name, the one she signed in with."

Juuarsi checked the tablet. The tips of his fingers squealed across the glass as he scrolled through the list of attendees registered before entering the hall for the press conference.

"It's not here," he said.

"Not possible. She had to show I.D. to get into the hall."

"I know, but she's not here." Juuarsi held out the tablet and waited for Pipaluk to take it. "Either she wasn't registered, or her name has been erased."

"Find out," Pipaluk said, as she pressed the tablet into Juuarsi's hands.

He paused at the door. "Can I get you anything, First Minister?"

"Her name," she said. "Now go."

Juuarsi shut the door quietly behind him. When he was gone, Pipaluk slumped in the chair, closed her eyes, and teased her fingers through her hair. She ran the Q&A session through her mind as if she had instant playback. She pictured Viola, trembling as she stood, and someone passed her a microphone. The trembling stopped with Viola's first words.

"My question, First Minister," she had said.

Pipaluk didn't want to hear it again. She checked her thoughts, but the words filtered through, anyway, echoing around her head: *undermine, undermine, undermine … Greenland's future.*

She remembered the heat in the room, the cameras – she

imagined the lens pressing against her face, boring into her eye, rooting around her mind in search of an answer.

"I'm sorry," Pipaluk had said, "what did you say your name was?"

"Viola."

"Just *Viola*?"

"*Aap.*"

It was a coping mechanism, a strategy she had learned to employ, to buy time. Everyone in the room knew it, and it would be dissected now and for the days to come by the media. *What did she have to hide?* They would ask. *Is she undermining Greenland's future? How?*

How was the question Pipaluk wanted to ask. *How did this* Viola *get into the press conference? Who was she and who put her there?*

Pipaluk recalled the second stalling strategy, knowing that it was dangerous to ask the young woman to clarify the question – the repetition was another sound bite for the media, but she needed time to think, to respond to the woman.

Girl.

Viola looked like she was barely in her twenties.

The memory of the moment, the repeated question, the spike in viewers, the explosion of comments and the buzz on the streets, made Pipaluk's head ache. She pressed her hands to her eyes, pressing harder as she remembered her non-committal response, hoping the pain of the pressure against her eyes would erase the memory.

It didn't.

Pipaluk saw the slack jaws and wide eyes of the press and Nuuk's most influential business men and women as she turned to Viola and said, "Get out. I don't have time for babysitting ill-informed students, *Viola*. I suggest that next time you sneak into a press conference, you spend a little more time preparing your questions. Do your research, because questions like that truly will undermine the future of our country."

Viola had said nothing for a moment, and Pipaluk wondered if she was communicating with someone. The lenses of her glasses were thick, but even from her position at the back of the room, Pipaluk could see that Viola's gaze was steady and trained on her.

"Is that your answer, First Minister?"

"It's all you're going to get from me today."

Pipaluk remembered gripping the podium, in preparation of another rebuke, if it was necessary. But the girl simply zipped her jacket, slid out of the row of seats, and walked slowly to the door. The cameras followed her, as if the lenses were glued to the girl's body with thin filaments of spider silk. It was the same with the audience, as the girl turned their heads; they were all caught in her web. Pipaluk could almost see it, could almost grab it, but she dared not, for then she would be caught too. She chose to flee instead, leaving the podium and exiting the stage just as Viola closed the door of the hall behind her.

"Damn it," Pipaluk said, as she slipped her hands down her cheeks and into her lap. She let her head droop, felt her chin in the space between her collar bones. Her hair tickled her cheeks and she felt them flush with blood and heat and the sheer bloody ignorance of the girl.

Ignorance is darkness.

It was happening again. Someone was trying to derail Greenland's push for independence, and it made no sense. This is what they wanted, what they voted for – a clear majority. But someone, somewhere, wanted a different outcome and they had chosen this *girl* to speak for them.

Cowards, she thought. And then: *Who is she?*

"First Minister?" Juuarsi said, as he opened the door.

"What?"

"Have you got five minutes for Sergeant Atii Napa?"

Juuarsi opened the door at a nod from Pipaluk, and Atii squeezed into the room. She tucked her fingers between her jacket and vest and waited for the First Minister to look at her.

"Do *you* know who she is, Sergeant?" Pipaluk said.

"That's not why I'm here." Atii glanced at the window. "It's hot in here, First Minister. Do you mind if I open the window for a second?"

"Whatever," Pipaluk said and waved her hand.

Atii opened the window just a crack and only for a second, but it was enough to catch Pipaluk's attention as the sound of chanting rose from the street outside. Atii closed the window and pointed at the crowd gathering between the community centre and the supermarket.

"That's why I'm here," she said. "First Minister, I'd like your permission to escort you home."

"I'm staying at the suite at the hotel," she said, and pointed towards the Hotel Hans Egede sign just visible through the window at the end of the street. Her face paled as she realised the crowds had effectively blocked her route to the hotel.

"It might be better if you went home, instead."

"It's being refurbished. Everything is packed in plastic. It's been like that since the end of November."

"I understand," Atii said, "but given the circumstances…" She paused.

"I want to go to the suite."

Atii nodded and pressed the radio microphone clipped to her vest. "Bring the car around the back. We're going to the hotel." She looked at the First Minister. "As soon as you're ready."

It took less than three minutes for Atii to get the First Minister and her assistant inside the police car parked at the rear of the community centre. Pipaluk ducked her head as she climbed into the back. Juuarsi sat next to her, still gripping his tablet. Pipaluk almost laughed, and then she saw the crowds, as the driver began to edge the car out of the alleyway towards the street.

"Stay down, please," Atii said, with a glance over her shoulder. Pipaluk ducked her head. "It's going to get a bit bumpy. But don't be alarmed. The glass is thick enough to stop bullets."

"Have they got guns?" Juuarsi said, his voice was shrill compared to the chanting of the crowd, the thumps of their palms on the glass and the taunts and jeers – strong enough to pierce the bulletproof glass.

"This is ridiculous," Pipaluk said. "The hotel is right there."

"Twenty metres," Atii said. She flinched as someone threw a plastic bottle of cola against the windscreen. It bounced off the roof. The second bottle was glass, and it smashed on the bonnet of the police car. "Keep moving," Atii said, as the driver touched the brakes. "Don't stop. Just keep it steady."

Pipaluk looked up as Atii undid the snap securing her pistol in the holster strapped to her leg.

"Sergeant," Pipaluk said.

"Not now, First Minister."

"You have my permission to fire on the crowd, Sergeant."

Atii shifted her gaze between the crowd bumping and pressing the car as the driver inched towards the hotel.

"With all due respect, First Minister," Atii said, "that's not your decision to make."

"But these people are threatening my life, Sergeant."

"They are making your life uncomfortable. I agree."

"What are you going to do about it?"

Atii leaned forwards, tapped the driver on his arm, and pointed to the right.

"Sergeant?"

Pipaluk turned her head at the wail of sirens descending on the hotel from both directions, two cars on each side of the street. She watched as they slowed to let officers out of the back. As the police interlocked their riot shields, the cars peeled off to the sides, blocking the road and forming a channel through which Atii guided the driver. The shouting and jeering grew louder, and several glass bottles smashed against the police shields, but the thumping and jostling of Pipaluk's car stopped as the police forced the crowd away from the vehicle.

"That's it. There's your space," Atii said. "Go."

The driver floored the accelerator, forcing Pipaluk and Juuarsi back into their seats, as he raced through the police cordon, swerving around the first taxi in the rank outside the hotel entrance, and darting through the gap between the hotel and the shops beneath the five floors of rooms.

"Slow it down," Atii said, as she gripped the door handle. "Now stop," she said. "Stop."

A gust of wind caught Pipaluk's hair as the passenger doors burst open and two members of the SRU pulled the First Minister and her assistant out of the car. A third SRU officer, armed with an assault rifle, watched the crowd from his position at the rear of the car. Pipaluk resisted the urge to complain at the police officer's grip on her arm and let him drag her inside the rear entrance of the hotel. His partner pushed Juuarsi through the same door a second later.

"You're safe, First Minister," Atii said. "Now, if we can just get you to your room."

"I want guards on the door," Pipaluk said, as Atii guided her through the lobby and into the elevator. "And I want to speak to Commissioner Jensen."

"Yes, First Minister." Atii pressed the button to close the elevator door as soon as Pipaluk's assistant was inside. Pipaluk noticed the Sergeant's hand had not left the grip of her pistol, but that the weapon was still inside the holster.

"Who were they?" Pipaluk asked, as Atii led her out of the elevator to her suite at the end of the corridor.

"We don't know yet."

"Why don't you know?"

"The situation is developing, First Minister," Atii said, as she knocked on the suite door. The police officer inside stepped to one side as they entered.

"That's not good enough, Sergeant."

"Please feel free to complain," Atii said, as she turned in the middle of the room. "I'm sure my boss will take your complaint very seriously."

"Seriously? Sergeant..." Pipaluk said. The words froze in her mouth as she looked around Atii and noticed the man and woman seated at the table by the window.

"First Minister," Petra said, as she stood up. "I'd like to introduce Commander Joshua Seabloom from the United States Coast Guard; he has something to tell you."

Chapter 9

Petra stood to one side as Joshua Seabloom pulled out a chair for the First Minister, poured her a glass of water, and fixed her a smaller, stronger drink from the mini bar. His charms were not lost on the First Minister, and Petra frowned at an unfamiliar feeling that caught her unawares, something she hadn't felt in a long time, a pang of jealousy. Petra almost missed Joshua's initial outlining of their shared concerns for the safety of the city's residents, as she dealt with another feeling, stronger than the first, it cut deeper, right to the bone.

I feel guilty, she thought. *David. I feel guilty because of David.*

Petra dismissed the thought. Now wasn't the time. Joshua caught her eye, and she nodded for him to continue.

"I had my tech guy at the base analyse the stencil. I take it you've seen it?"

"They're all over the city," Pipaluk said.

Joshua nodded and picked up his tablet from the table. He swiped an image of the stencil onto the screen and enlarged it.

"The cultural stuff I'll leave to you," he said, "but technically I can tell you that the stencil was printed from a template on several 3D printers. We've analysed about fifty of the images. A lot of them match, with the same tiny striations – especially along the curved edges. Here and here," he said, as he pointed at the screen. "We found four separate stencil patterns, suggesting four different printers. Considering the reduced flights over Christmas, and the lockdown you had because of the Calendar Man incident, we're guessing these printers are located in the city, and that the template was downloaded to them."

"It couldn't just be four different stencils printed from one printer?" Pipaluk asked.

"No," Joshua said. "Like old fashioned laser printers and even typewriters before them, they are unique, especially if they have been damaged, or tagged by the manufacturer – something so tiny it can only be discovered with intense magnification, and time." He smiled. "My tech guy at the base has plenty of time."

Pipaluk reached for the glass of water, and then pushed it to one side in favour of the clear spirits and the soft splintering of the rough chunk of glacier ice bobbing within it. The ice clicked on the bottom of the glass as Pipaluk finished her drink. She placed the glass on the table and looked at Petra.

"We agree with the Coast Guard," Petra said, taking her cue. "Given the extent of the graffiti that has been spray-painted all over the city, we believe there are many stencils in play, which would suggest that lots of copies were made from each printer." She took a breath. "It also means this is well coordinated, with many people involved. To cover all the public windows and the windows of all the buses and taxis in one night, we estimate there has to be at least forty people working through the night."

"Forty people who are trying to derail Greenland's independence," Pipaluk said. She reached for the shorter glass, tapping her fingernail against it as she remembered it was empty. "What about this girl? Viola?"

"We have a name, based on her photo – we had a hit from the University database. She studies journalism. Her name is Tiina Markussen."

"Markussen?"

"No relations of interest," Petra said. She waited for Pipaluk to look at her before adding, "We do, however, think she might be connected with someone we are very interested in."

"Who?"

"Constable Natuk Petersen," Petra said. "She went missing shortly before we tried to apprehend Constable Ooqi Kleemann."

"Constables," Pipaluk said. "Both of them."

"Yes."

Petra glanced at Joshua as the First Minister stood up. She wondered what he knew of the Calendar Man case, and how much she should tell him. She was reluctant to tell him too much, not only because it was embarrassing that two officers with the Nuuk Police Department were responsible for creating such chaos in the city, but also because she liked Natuk and Ooqi. Regardless of what Ooqi had done and what Natuk might be doing, Petra was sad that the department had lost two competent and intelligent officers. *Perhaps too intelligent,* she thought. *And yet not intelligent enough to know when they were being used and manipulated.* Petra chided herself at the thought; Ooqi and Natuk were children when Anna Riis took them in. *And what's my excuse? I was an adult when they used and manipulated me.*

A light touch on Petra's arm made her look up. Joshua showed her his mobile and then pointed at Pipaluk standing at the window.

"I have to take this," he said.

"I'll talk to the First Minister."

Joshua walked to the adjoining room and closed the door. The door muffled his response as Petra walked over to Pipaluk. She smiled as the First Minister continued to talk in English as if Joshua was still in the room.

"Petra," she said, "I'm sorry about my quip about your Constables. I do realise they acted alone, or together." She frowned as she turned to look at Petra. "However they acted, the Calendar Man brought this city to a standstill, and he was just one man. You think there are forty people running around Nuuk, tagging all the public buildings?"

"At least," Petra said.

"And why only the public buildings?"

"I think they want to keep the people on their side. They can't do that if they deface private property."

Pipaluk pressed her hand to her mouth as she looked out of the window. It was still light, and the police on the street below were clearly visible as they mopped up the last of the protesters and sent them on their way.

"They look tired," she said.

"They are."

"And you, Petra. Are you tired?"

"Yes, I am." Petra gestured at the door to the room Joshua was using to take his call. "That's why I'm pleased the new Commander wants to help."

"And why is that?" Pipaluk asked. "Forgive me, Petra, but I *am* a politician. What does he want?"

"Want?"

Pipaluk placed her hand on Petra's arm and smiled.

"There are times when you are gorgeously naïve, Commissioner. You do your job, and you ignore politics as much as possible."

"Politics gets in the way of policing, First Minister."

"You're right, and until now it has been Danish politics determining what happens with Greenlandic policing, but once Greenland is independent, Petra, you'll have to deal directly with me and my staff, with policies that affect Greenland *directly*. I wonder, can you do that?"

Petra thought about her retirement papers in the folder on the kitchen counter. She had read through the fine print. All that remained to do was sign them. Even Aron, her assistant, was ready for her to sign, as if his need to process paperwork overruled his previous concerns about Petra leaving her post.

"I'm ready to do what I have to do, for as long as I have to do it," Petra said.

"I'm glad, Petra," Pipaluk said.

They both turned at the click of the door opening, and they both watched Joshua stride across the room to the join them.

"They've blocked the bridge," he said.

"What bridge?" Pipaluk asked.

"The one across the fjord to the Coast Guard base. It's off limits, as you know. I have two Seamen and a Petty Officer squaring off against a group of about thirty Greenlanders in their late-teens to mid-twenties. They commandeered a bus. They are right outside the guardhouse." Joshua stuffed his mobile into his pocket and reached for his winter coat draped over the back of one of the chairs at the table. "My men are following protocol and Standard Operating Procedures," he said.

"Which means what, exactly?" Petra asked.

"It means, if the crowd doesn't back down, they will open fire with warning shots. After which, if there is no sign of de-escalation and they consider themselves and their position to be under continued threat, they will defend themselves, and they will shoot to wound, before shooting to kill."

"You can't kill Greenlanders in Greenland, Commander," Pipaluk said.

"It's alright, First Minister," Petra said, as she caught Joshua's eye. "I won't let him."

Petra felt a surge of strength, the same kind that flooded through her body each time she realised that the time for discussion was over, and definitive action was required. She glanced at Atii, caught the subtle dip of the Sergeant's head, and then turned to the First Minister.

"Sergeant Napa has arranged for security, you'll be safe here," she said. "Commander?"

"Yes?"

"Can I escort you to the bridge?"

"Escort me? Hey, Petra, this is your shitstorm, I don't need *escorting* anywhere. It's your people on the bridge. Your responsibility. My men – they're *my* responsibility. You can escort me to the bridge, or you can drive me there, but it has to happen now."

"Agreed," Petra said. "Let's go."

Atii caught Petra's arm as she walked out of the suite and into the corridor. Joshua continued to the elevator.

"What is it, Sergeant?"

"We're stretched pretty thin, ma'am," Atii said.

"I know, Atii."

"I can talk to Gaba… He's started recruiting already to expand his team."

"No, Sergeant. We've already eaten into next year's budget. Until the situation demands otherwise, we're going to have to manage with what we've got."

"*Aap*, ma'am."

Petra nodded towards Joshua as the elevator doors opened. "I have to go."

"SRU will meet you at the door. They'll *escort* you to the bridge," Atii said, and grinned.

"Thank you, Sergeant."

Petra lost count of the graffiti obscuring windows and blistering the sides of the buildings they flashed past in the small convoy of police cars. The same police officers that cleared the protesters from the street outside the hotel were jammed into the back of each car, helmets in their laps, flak vests and additional armour pressing into their joints. Petra glanced over her shoulder at the two men and one woman on the back seat.

"Busy shift," she said.

"Yes, ma'am," the female officer said.

Petra pressed her palm against the dashboard, bracing as the driver flung the car around the last corner before accelerating towards the bridge. The wheels spun for a second on a smooth patch of ice. The driver recovered, grinned at Petra, and then increased speed.

"SRU have tactical command," Petra said to the officers on the back seat. "The Americans are concerned about the security of the base. We need to get you between the protesters and the guardhouse."

Petra waited for the officers to respond and then looked out of the windscreen. The group had swelled to about sixty young Greenlanders and two buses, their collective breath hung in a cloud above them as they chanted and waved banners and placards. Petra recognised the mask from the stencil, and, as the driver slowed, she noticed that several members of the crowd were wearing actual masks. She wondered if Natuk was among the crowd, and the thought propelled her out of the vehicle as the driver slid to a stop.

"Commissioner, stop."

An SRU officer leaped from the car in front of Petra's, curling his arm around her as he pulled her to the rear of the vehicle. Joshua climbed out of the passenger seat and joined them a moment later.

"I need you to wait here, ma'am," the SRU officer said. "Just until we get a perimeter set up."

"She might be here," Petra said, and pointed at one of the masked protesters.

"Who are we looking for, ma'am?"

"Constable Natuk Petersen."

The SRU officer nodded, raised his arm and spun one finger in the air instructing the police officers to form up and link their shields. He pressed the submachine gun to his chest and raised his voice as the crowd turned to face them.

"I'd like you to get in the car, ma'am," he said.

"I'm staying right here."

"I can't leave you here alone, ma'am. Atii will have my balls."

"She's not alone, officer," Joshua said. "I'll stay with the Commissioner. Now go do your job, before my men are forced to do theirs."

Petra almost laughed as the two men glared at each other, but a sudden flash of black above her head and the buzz of quad motors caught her attention, and Petra stared at the sight of a sleek drone equipped with a bank of camera lenses.

"That's one of yours," Joshua said. "Right?"

"Not ours," Petra said.

She glanced at the crowd, flicked her gaze across the faces – with and without masks – and then stared at the drone. With no proof, and little more than a fisherman's word to suggest Natuk Petersen was in Greenland, Petra couldn't shake the feeling that the renegade

Constable had just arrived.

Chapter 10

Natuk leaned between the two Greenlanders sitting at the table along the wall, the bank of computer screens lit their faces with a stream of code cascading down the right-hand side of the screen with real-time drone feed windowed on the left. She pointed at one of the windows.

"Enlarge that one," she said.

The window expanded to fill the screen and the image of the bridge across Kangerluarsunnguaq Fjord sharpened. Natuk tapped the screen to focus on one section of the image and the camera on the drone zoomed in. She smiled when she recognised the mask from Viola's apartment. *Viola*, she could have named her Jeanne d'Arc, but the Shakespearian name was more familiar, and it suited her purpose. Viola was in disguise; her true intent was hidden. Natuk corrected her thoughts; it was Natuk's true intent that was disguised. For the moment, at least.

"Pull back and pan to the right," she said.

The blue emergency lights of the police cordon flashed and swirled across the faces of the protesters, illuminating the masked and unmasked protesters alike. Natuk tapped the screen again, zooming in on the police officers assembling their shield wall. She tapped the screen, pinched the image of two faces standing at the rear of a police car, the one furthest from the protestors. Natuk slid her finger and thumb across the screen and the faces sharpened, she could almost hear the drone clicking through the focus range of its camera. Then she paused and took a step back from the screen as the face of Police Commissioner Petra Jensen overlapped the other feed from the drone's camera array.

"*Piitalaat*," she whispered. "That's what he called you."

"What's that?" said the Greenlander to her right.

"Nothing," Natuk said, as she pointed to the adjacent screen. "Give me the image of the man standing next to the Commissioner." She waited as the man's white face filled the screen. "Enhance and save a copy. Cast it to me. Good. Now run it through the identification suite. I want to know who he is."

Natuk pulled her glasses from her pocket and put them on. She blinked her way through the start-up icons, scanned her messages and then swiped the image of the man onto the left lens as she studied his career and biography details on the right. Commander

Joshua Seabloom, age fifty-two, was married with three children, the eldest of which was about to start high-school. He owned a modest house on East Cherry Street, not far from the USCG Seattle Base on Alaskan Way. Natuk scrolled though the details with an upwards flick of her eye until she found what she was looking for. She nibbled at her lips, clamped the tip of her tongue between her small white teeth and blinked to zoom on one particular detail. According to the details gleaned and assembled from open sources and the USCG magazine and New York Times articles, Seabloom was a Coast Guard Intelligence Officer. Natuk tasted blood on her tongue, swallowed and blinked an icon to the right of Seabloom's details to begin a deeper background scan. *You might be trouble*, she thought, and wondered why he should be assigned to Nuuk now, and what his real purpose might be? Base Commander might be a significant rung on the promotional ladder, but the modest house on Cherry Street, Squire Park, suggested that promotion and moving up the ladder were not the kinds of things to motivate Seabloom. Natuk decided he could be dangerous, detrimental to her plans, but there was nothing more to do until the scan was finished. Natuk looked at Seabloom's image for a few seconds, appreciated the handsome cut of his jaw and the steel glint in his eye, and then blinked the image into a folder.

She reached up to remove her glasses, and then stopped, remembering one more thing she had to do before she returned to the drone feed from the bridge. Natuk searched for the image she had captured of Qallu and pasted it onto the message boards for her network of enthusiastic young Greenlanders in Nuuk and tagged the image with a high-priority search icon, something to occupy the more passive *truth seekers* not currently involved with the protest on the bridge. Of course, once they found Qallu, it was up to Natuk to deal with him. She slipped her hand around the grip of the FNS compact pistol in her jacket pocket and removed her glasses.

Natuk walked back to the table and watched the drone feed from the bridge. One of the cameras was programmed to seek and follow exaggerated activity, and it zoomed onto a scuffle at the shield wall. The image blurred for a second as the drone responded and flew to a better position to observe and record the first line of protesters bashing their fists on the police shields. A second camera zoomed in on the Coast Guard officer and his men standing in front of the guardhouse. Natuk noted their weapons were drawn, as was

Seabloom's. She snapped her head to the left as the drone beeped a warning through the computer speakers. There was a flash and the camera angle wobbled for a second as Seabloom fired three bullets at the drone.

"Send another drone," Natuk said.

She knew the ballistic armour of the drone was capable of withstanding more than a few shots from a handgun, but she didn't want to miss anything from the bridge. The live feed she pushed into the DataStream was valuable propaganda that she would use to incite more young, impressionable Greenlanders out of their homes and onto the streets. And now, thanks to Seabloom, shots had been fired. The situation had just escalated.

Natuk frowned as she wondered why he would do that. Then she saw a hand raised in front of his face. She leaned forwards, pressed her finger and thumb onto the screen and zoomed out, just as Petra pressed her hand on Seabloom's arm and he lowered his weapon. Natuk flattened her lips into a thin smile. It was a nice show for the cameras, something she would edit in the DataStream. She would twist the Commissioner's concern over the use of firearms with the video footage of her brother's death. The image of the Commissioner holding her pistol in two hands as she murdered Ooqi Danielsen was a powerful one, something Natuk could use, no matter how painful the memory.

"I think you should see this," said the taller of the two Greenlanders.

"What?"

"You told us to fix her image and build into the drone's facial imagery software."

"*Aap.*"

"The woman."

"Viola," Natuk said. She looked at the third screen as the Greenlander tapped it.

A group of protesters had turned away from the Nuuk police, as if they had realised that the police were trying to get between them and the Americans. Viola was just visible at the head of the group, fist raised, and a confident energy in her stride. She seemed to draw power from the mask and was channelling it into her legs as she strode across the bridge towards the guardhouse. *This isn't the time for martyrs*, Natuk thought as she saw the Coast Guard officer order his men to ready their weapons. Assault rifles would make short work of Viola and the small group of protesters that had split up from the main demonstration.

"Where's that other drone?" she asked.

"On its way."

"Not fast enough."

Natuk gripped the back of the Greenlander's chair and wheeled him away from the table. She slid the keyboard across the table and hunched over it, the keys cowered beneath the stab of her fingers, as the windows of footage from each camera fused into just two feeds – one of Viola and her small group, and a close-up of the Americans on the other.

There was a hush inside the store, punctuated by the staccato commands Natuk punched into the keyboard and the imagined burr of the drone's propellers as it churned through the frigid air above the bridge into a position between the two groups.

The first flashes of gunfire obscured the camera image focused on the Americans. The drone rocked as a volley of bullets threatened to knock it out of the sky.

"ETA drone two?" Natuk said as she shifted her focus from the images on the screen and the keyboard.

"Eighteen minutes. There's a headwind."

"Too slow," she said, and cursed. Natuk grabbed the Greenlander by the shoulder. "Take over. Keep that drone between Viola and the Americans, and the second one, when it gets there." Natuk moved away from the table, pulling her glasses from her pocket and slipping them over her nose as she ran to the back door.

"What are you going to do?"

Natuk didn't answer. The door slammed against the wall as she burst into the alleyway. Natuk leaped onto the back of the motorbike, pressed her knees against the sides as she checked the battery and short-circuited the power sequence with a blink of the emergency start-up icon in the right-hand lens of her glasses. The rear wheel spun until the Natuk depressed the ice spikes with a flick of a switch on the handlebars, and then she buzzed down the alleyway and onto the street.

As soon as she was clear of the pedestrian street, Natuk cursed at the lack of gloves and hat as the cold air rushed against her exposed skin, biting at her earlobes and pinching her fingers. She raced through the city, blinking the drone feed onto the lens. The drone was lower in the sky, jerking upwards with bursts of power as it laboured under the repeated onslaught of Coast Guard bullets. But the Americans had done two things right, at least. Viola's group had stopped and was huddled at the side of the bridge, and, behind them, it was just possible for Natuk to see the protesters renewing their assault on the police, invigorated and incensed by the gunfire.

Natuk flashed through Little Amsterdam and Chinatown as the road dipped down to the fjord. She stopped the bike short of the bridge, two hundred metres from the police cordon and the shield wall. Natuk tugged the pistol from her pocket and held it in a loose grip at her side. She felt a rush of cold air over her head at the same time as a new feed patched into the stream of data on the lenses of her glasses. The second drone had arrived and started harrying the Americans. The last image from the first drone showed Viola running away from the Americans. Natuk scanned the crowd and used her glasses to identify Viola. She fixed her with a targeting crosshair as she inched the bike towards the police cordon.

"Don't turn around," she whispered, as she saw Petra's long hair twisting in a cold draught barrelling up the fjord. "Not now."

The police beat the protesters back against the side of the bridge, leaving a gap between them and the police cars, wide enough for Viola to slip through if she took it, if Seabloom and the Commissioner didn't stop her. They were the only ones between Viola and Natuk.

Natuk gripped the throttle on the handlebars with one hand as she aimed at the rear window of the police car, just to the right of Petra's head. *Just a distraction*, she thought, although the temptation for murder and revenge made her finger tremble and she had to fight to steady her aim.

"Viola," Natuk shouted, as she fired her first shot. She gunned the bike forwards as the bullet shattered the rear window of the police car. "Viola, run."

Seabloom slipped on the ice as he dragged Petra to the ground, pressing his body over hers as Natuk accelerated onto the bridge. Natuk turned her head away from Petra, stuffed the pistol into her pocket and wrapped her arm around Viola's slim waist. She dragged her onto the bike, clutching her to her chest as she turned the bike. The heels of Viola's boots scraped across the ice as Natuk accelerated.

There was a shout, in English, a deep American voice that fit so well with the chiselled image of the Coast Guard Intelligence Officer. The shout was followed by a warning shot. Natuk anticipated the hot fire of impact, waited for the second when she would be thrown from her bike and the plans she had for Greenland's Twelfth Night, *mitaartut*, would be over, spoiled in a sprawl of bodies and blood beneath a bike on the bridge. But there was no impact, and no further shots, just the squeal of tyres and the wail of the police siren that blistered across the fjord.

Natuk glanced at the drone feed in her glasses, saw Petra behind the wheel of the police car and Seabloom holstering his pistol as he climbed into the passenger seat. Natuk grinned as she helped Viola into a more comfortable position on the bike. She corralled the second drone with a series of blinks, slaving it to her bike, and flicked the feed onto the left-hand lens as she accelerated up the hill and away from the bridge. The drone followed the police car, as Petra and Seabloom chased Natuk back to the city.

Chapter 11

The electric SUV was faster than Petra anticipated. She spun into the first corner, forcing Seabloom to press his hands against the dashboard as she corrected, downshifted, and powered out of the corner and into the straight leading into the city. Petra could feel the smile tugging at the corners of her lips, curling her mouth upwards. She wondered if it was appropriate and realised that she didn't care. A combined effort of sickness, grief, terror and concern had kept Petra bottled up for most of November and December, it was time to let go, to let it out, and to get results. Petra's smile stiffened as she thought about the result she wanted most, in that moment, as the motorbike leaped ahead of her and charged into Chinatown. In the adrenaline-spiked moment between Seabloom knocking her to the ground and the girl jumping onto the motorbike, Petra had caught a glimpse of the biker's eyes, and she thought she recognised them. Such intelligent eyes, almost obscured behind think-rimmed glasses. She had seen them before – the same eyes and the same glasses. The rider might have blonde hair, but there was no mistaking the family likeness – Petra was convinced she had just seen Ooqi's sister, at large and alive and dangerous in Greenland.

In my city, she thought, as she reached for the radio.

"Wait a second," Seabloom said, as he leaned back in his seat. "You want to tell me what's going on?"

"We're in pursuit of a person of interest."

"I can see that," he said, "and I can feel it with every corner." He held his breath as Petra accelerated through a gap between a bus and a delivery van. "But I need to know why we left my men on the bridge to chase a blonde on a bike?"

"She's not blonde."

"Yes, Petra, she is. I saw her."

"I mean it's not natural. She's dyed it."

"Who has?"

"Natuk Petersen," Petra said, with a quick glance at Seabloom. "The young Constable your man learned about. The one in the picture you showed me."

Seabloom frowned for a second, and Petra waited as he recalled the image of the woman he had shown her.

"Think about her stature," Petra said, as she saw a space in the road up ahead and slipped the SUV into it. The emergency lights flashed along the side of a second bus, lighting the faces of the passengers peering past the graffiti on the windows for a better look at the chase.

"Yeah, okay," Seabloom said. "Suppose it is her. What was she doing on the bridge?" He twisted in his seat to look out of the shattered rear window. "And who the hell is controlling these drones?"

"It has to be her," Petra said. "And I think that young woman is the key."

"The one clinging to the front of the bike? It's a wonder she hasn't fallen off."

"No, it's not," Petra said. "Natuk won't let her fall."

Seabloom leaned back in his seat as Petra tugged the radio handset off the dashboard.

"You admire her," he said.

"Yes."

"Regardless of what she may or may not be involved in?"

Petra nodded and pushed the button to transmit.

"This is Commissioner Jensen. I need a roadblock between Chinatown and Little Amsterdam. Two female suspects. The driver has blonde hair, and the passenger is wearing a mask – traditional, Greenlandic. The passenger might be Tiina Markussen." Petra paused. "The rider is Constable Natuk Petersen."

There was a crackle of static as Petra clipped the old-fashioned handset into place and pressed the button for hands-free.

"Ma'am, this is Sergeant Napa."

"Go ahead, Atii."

"Did you say the rider is Natuk?"

"I believe so, yes."

There was a pause, and then Atii's voice burst through the radio chatter. Petra imagined her running as she heard the Sergeant's breathy response.

"On my way."

Petra stomped on the brakes as a group of Chinese miners wobbled into the street. Natuk disappeared into the distance, the glow of the motorbike's taillight merged with red, yellow and orange dragon tails stretched across Chinatown's main street.

"You don't have a helicopter?" Seabloom asked, as Petra weaved around the miners.

"There's no budget for that."

Seabloom reached into his pocket and pulled out his mobile. He glanced at the drone pacing the SUV as he dialled.

"Put me through to Wilkie in the hangar."

"Wilkie?" Petra said.

"Yes." Seabloom smiled. "I think you might have met his mother when you were attached to Polarpol."

"That was a long time ago," she said, as she drove beneath dragon's tails on the main street. "How do you know about that?"

"It's my job, Petra," Seabloom said. He smiled for a second as the Seaman in the hangar connected his call. "Wilkie? I need you to spin up the chopper. We've got an active manhunt in the city. You'll be coordinating with the local police. Alert the airport and let me know when you're in the air."

Petra pulled over to the side of the road. The drone hovered three metres ahead of them, its cameras fixed on the windscreen. Seabloom's fingers twitched as he pocketed his mobile and reached for his pistol.

"It won't do any good," Petra said.

"I know, but I really want to shoot it." He looked out of the windows. "Why have you stopped?"

"I lost her when the miners drifted into the road. I thought we would wait for the helicopter. And she might double-back once she hits the roadblock." Petra nodded. "I know," she said. It's unlikely.""

"You're sure it's her?"

"As sure as I can be."

The snow on the mountains was just visible through the Chinese lanterns and lights bobbing along the side of the road. The wind from the fjord threatened to rip the lightest of the lanterns from their fittings. A raven flapped its wings for balance as it swung back and forth on a dragon's tail wrapped around a streetlight.

"They're amazing," Seabloom said.

"Dragons?"

"Ravens." He pointed at the bird's wingspan, tracing it with a finger in front of him. "It amazes me that they don't go south for the winter." He rested his hand on the door. "It amazes me that you don't."

"This is my home. I can't leave it for six months of the year."

"Six months?"

"Eight, further north."

"Is that where he came from? Maratse?"

Petra turned. "You really do know everything."

"It's my…"

"Job. Yes, I get that. But *everything*?"

"Not everything," Seabloom said. "There are always some blanks, gaps that we have to fill with our best educated guesses."

"You're wrong though," Petra said. "David came from Ittoqqortoormiit, on the east coast."

"But you lived in the north?"

"For a time, yes." Petra took a long, slow breath, almost a whisper. "It was intense – tragic and wonderful at the same time. I want to go back."

"When you retire?"

"How do you…" Petra stopped talking and pressed her lips into a flat smile. *He doesn't know*, she thought. *He's just filling in the blanks.*

The radio display lit up with a burst of chatter at the same time as Seabloom's mobile began to vibrate. He pulled it out of his pocket and turned the screen towards Petra to confirm that Wilkie was in the air and on his way across the fjord.

"ETA thirty seconds," Seabloom said. He pointed at the drone as it twitched in the air above them. The rotors tilted as the drone changed attitude and began to lift into the air. "And we're not the only ones that know. She must be patched into all the channels and frequencies."

"I would bet money on it," Petra said, as she remembered how proficient Ooqi was at intercepting information. Anna Riis had mentioned how Ooqi and Natuk were coding at a young age when they were in her care. "She only has to be half as smart as her brother to run rings around us," she said.

"You don't think she's just half as smart, do you?"

"No, I don't." Petra turned her head to one side as she tried to catch some of the more urgent exchanges on the radio. The officers were talking in Danish – it was faster than communicating in Greenlandic – but the occasional expression slipped through with bursts of excitement. "They've spotted her," Petra said, as she pulled away from the snow-packed curb and accelerated.

The rotor chop of the Coast Guard helicopter shuddered

through the air above them, fracturing the shattered edges of the SUV's rear window as Wilkie hovered above Petra and Seabloom. The last of the safety glass clinging to the rubber weather strip fell with a soft tinkle onto the backseat. Petra might have heard it if it wasn't for the chop of the helicopter, the buzz of the drone, and the excited chatter on the radio. Natuk – if it was her – had just bumped the motorbike up the bonnet and over the roof of one of the police cars. Guns had been drawn, but no shots fired.

"Why aren't they shooting?" Seabloom said. "Why won't they stop her?"

"Because it *is* Natuk," Petra said. "They must have recognised her."

The air stilled as the helicopter flew on towards the roadblock and the drone received a new tasking. Petra watched as it raced towards the roadblock. She imagined that Natuk would programme it to follow the first car to give chase. She almost smiled when the drone locked on to the lead police car. The lights of the Coast Guard helicopter blinked in the sky above the street.

"It's getting dark," Seabloom said.

"*Mitaartut,*" Petra said.

"What?"

"Twelfth Night. It starts soon."

"That's January sixth. We've only got the fifth today."

"But if we don't catch her before tomorrow night, there's no telling what she might do."

"Why?"

"Because tomorrow is Natuk's birthday. She was a twin, before I killed her brother. She's also working to an agenda laid out by her foster mother."

"Anna Riis?"

"Yes," Petra said. She stopped herself from asking how he might know that. "We've got her in custody at the detention centre." Petra increased speed, closing the distance between them and the last car in the line of three police cars chasing Natuk.

"I think we need to go pay her a visit," Seabloom said. "With your permission of course."

Petra smiled. "You've provided us with a helicopter, I'm pretty sure I can argue why you should be present at an interview."

"Good," Seabloom said. His mobile vibrated with an incoming

call and he answered it, nodding and giving brief commands as Petra increased speed. "She's gone off road," he said.

"I can see that." Petra pointed at the police cars sliding to a stop in a bluster of snow that pillowed around each car. Petra stopped the car and got out. She pointed at the helicopter as Seabloom got out of the passenger side. "There," she said.

"Got it." Seabloom nodded. He rested his mobile on the roof of the car as he tugged on a pair of gloves and a hat. "Talk to me Wilkie," he said, as a cone of glacial light jerked across the slope of snow and granite as the helicopter crew searched for Natuk. "The tracks stop," Seabloom said. "She must be on foot, but they can't see any footprints."

"Then she must be hiding, somewhere close to the bike," Petra said.

Seabloom shook his head. "Wilkie says no. It's pretty flat there. But no tracks."

"What about the rocks?" Petra asked. "Are they black?"

"Some of them." Seabloom pressed his hand to one ear. "More now that Wilkie is hovering lower."

Petra could see drifts of snow curling and swirling, tornado-like, as the Coast Guard helicopter began a slow circle of the area. Natuk had gone to ground between Chinatown and Little Amsterdam. *But where will she go now?*

"There," Seabloom shouted. He pulled the mobile from his ear and pointed, finger extended, at two black shapes running across the closest ridge of rocks, just above the road.

The police raced along the road, hands on their holstered pistols, as they ordered the two fugitives off the ridge. Petra saw hands being raised, and then the lights from the helicopter blinked once as Wilkie flew to a position high above the road. The cone of light lit the two women as they slid down the rocks and into the arms of the police.

"It's not them," Petra said, as they walked towards the police. "Look at their hair."

Petra held her hand to her eyes to shield them from the intense light streaming from the helicopter. The black sheen of the Greenlanders' hair was unmistakeable, as were the masks they wore – replicas of the mask Petra had seen on Viola's face. The two young Greenlanders grinned as Petra approached. They laughed at the look on Seabloom's face until the police officers cuffed them and marched them back to the police cars parked at crazy angles on the side of the road, stepping over one of the masks that fell from the face of the youngest of the two suspects.

Seabloom glanced up at the helicopter, ordering the pilot to do one more sweep as Petra stooped to pick up the mask. She turned it in the light, until the helicopter was gone. The light of day was fading fast. Petra handed the mask to Seabloom.

"What are they usually made of?" he asked.

"Clay and wood," Petra said. "You can get replicas in plaster and plastic.

"But not printed," he said, as he scratched his nail against an anomalous ridge between the holes for the eyes. The rest of the inside of the mask was smooth. "We're going to see more of these," he said.

Chapter 12

Anna Riis caught a glimpse of the waiting room of the detention centre as she was escorted to one of the larger meeting rooms. She remembered that it resembled a mini courtroom, with raised seats curving around the walls on tiers either side of the judge's seat in the middle. There was a platform below it, and a table each for the defendant and the prosecutor. Behind them was a single row for the public, journalists and assorted visitors that Anna had no time for. She wondered if this was it, that her hearing had been bumped up by a matter of hours instead of days, but the mini courtroom was empty but for the two people seated at the table reserved for the prosecution. Anna sneered as she recognised the Commissioner's long black hair, tied haphazardly in a ponytail at the back of her head. The white man beside her was new.

"Hello, Anna," Petra said. She gestured at a third chair at the table. "Will you sit down?"

Anna ignored the man and glared at Petra as the guard removed her cuffs. She looked over her shoulder as the guard left the courtroom and locked the door behind her.

"I suppose I could sit," she said. "You've got a new dog?" Anna said, as she sat down.

"What?"

"Where's your pit bull? The stupid Greenlander with the shotgun?"

"I assume the dog you're referring to is me," Seabloom said. "I'm with the United States Coast Guard, and I have a few questions for you."

"An American?" Anna almost cursed as she heard the light tone in her voice. It was almost girlish. She adjusted her pitch, switched to English, and said, "What's your interest, Commander?"

"You know my rank?"

"I used to be in politics. I brokered the deal for the Dutch to establish a climate colony south of Nuuk, and I heard enough whispers about the Coast Guard and their interest in a base in Nuuk in the corridors of Christiansborg long before that. Yes, I know your rank, and I know the kind of man who possesses it." Anna glanced at Petra as she said the word *man*.

"Christiansborg?" Seabloom said.

"The Danish Houses of Parliament," Petra said.

"Where the real seat of power is." Anna allowed herself a grin as she turned to face Petra. "Just how long do you think Pipaluk Uutaaq's fledgling government will be able to run this country? How long before they start begging the Chinese or the Americans for money, and help, and then more money?"

"As long as it takes," Petra said.

"Oh, you're a believer now. Is that it?" Anna laughed. "You're just one more Greenlander with a warped sense of independence. And you, a Commissioner. You should know better, Petra Jensen, with your Danish name and your puppet position."

Petra waited a beat as she absorbed the blow. She raised her hand as Seabloom started to speak. "It's alright, let her have her say."

"My say?" Anna spat. "You can't even speak Greenlandic."

"And yet, my name is *Piitalaat*," Petra said, as she looked at Seabloom. "It's Greenlandic for..."

"Petra," he said. "I've done my homework."

Anna started to clap.

"This is so sweet. You don't need me at all. Why don't I go back to my cell and the two of you can continue this charming little chat without me. Three really is a crowd, as they say." Anna pressed her hands on the table and turned her head to call for the guard.

"I saw Natuk today," Petra said.

Anna felt her body shrink. Her shoulders hunched over the table and her head dipped. The rough weave of the prison cardigan scratched her chin, but it could have been silk for all the reaction it elicited. Anna sighed and then raised her head. She ignored Seabloom and focused on Petra.

"Where?"

"On the bridge across Kangerluarsunnguaq Fjord. And then again as we chased her through Chinatown."

"We thought you might be interested in filling in the blanks," Seabloom said.

"What blanks?"

"Gaps in our information." He stood up and placed the tablet in front of Anna. "This is Natuk, isn't it?"

"Yes."

"This was taken around the time of Ooqi Kleemann's death. What would she be doing on a fishing trawler?"

Anna moved her tongue around her mouth. "Is there any water?"

"I'll get some in a minute," Seabloom said. "Answer the question, Anna."

"Why do you want to know?"

"That's not important right now."

"Of course, it is," Anna said, and laughed. "Why else would you be here?" She looked at Petra. "Why else would the *Commissioner* pay me a visit?"

"Enough."

Anna stopped when Seabloom slammed his hand on the surface of the table. She jerked back in her seat and looked at him.

"Not so different from your pit bull after all, eh, *Piitalaat*."

"Your evasiveness is going to add years to your sentence," Seabloom said.

"Maybe, but you won't get a word out of me about Natuk." Anna looked at Petra. "You took one of my children from me, already. I won't help you take the other one."

Her words hung in the air as the guard unlocked the door and looked inside the room. Seabloom waved her away and Petra nodded. Once the door was locked, it was Petra's turn to talk. She stood up and moved away from the table. Petra leaned against the wood panel separating the first row of tiered seats from the defendant's table.

"Ombudsman Anna Riis was Natuk and Ooqi's foster mother," she said to Seabloom. "She loved them, I don't doubt that, and they could feel it. It was perhaps the first time an adult showed them true love. In Natuk's case it, Anna was the first adult to touch her without leaving a scar – physical or mental." Petra paused at the thought of her own scars, both kinds, and realised that she and Natuk had so many things in common. *Which is probably what makes this so difficult*, she thought.

"You're forgetting something," Anna said. "They were malnourished. I was the first adult to give them the food they needed. Ooqi, especially, was small for his age."

"You gave them decent clothes, too," Petra said. "And you helped them with their schooling." She looked at Seabloom. "Anna used her own money to supplement the twin's education. She taught them to code."

Seabloom snorted. "Yeah, that makes sense."

"But you had a purpose, Anna," Petra said. "Didn't you?"

Anna caught Petra's eye and then looked away.

"You see," Petra continued, "Anna saw something in those kids, something she could use, if she sowed the right seeds. So, she showed them the very best of what Denmark had to offer, and she compared that with a poisonous image of the country of their birth. She turned them against Greenland."

"But they lived here?" Seabloom said. "They were police officers."

"She put them there," Petra said. "Encouraged them to do well, and to work hard, until she needed them."

"She turned the kids into sleeper agents," Seabloom said. He looked down at Anna. "That's harsh. Your own children."

"Foster children," Anna said. "I gave them a good life."

"And in return, you asked them to give theirs," Petra said. She walked towards the table and stood in front of Anna. "The city is plastered with graffiti. A mask and text in Greenlandic. The text translates into passages from Shakespeare." Petra paused as Anna looked at her. "*Twelfth Night*," she said. "Your favourite play, and the twin's birthday. There's no doubt in my mind that you orchestrated Ooqi's campaign of terror…"

"You can't prove that," Anna said.

"Not yet. But the difference is that this time, you're behind bars, locked away. If Natuk is working to fulfil your agenda, she's doing it alone, Anna."

"She's a clever girl. She doesn't need me."

"That's right. She doesn't," Petra said. "So, what happens when she deviates from your plan? What happens when she takes matters into her own hands? Will you be able to live with Natuk's version of the future you want Greenland to inherit? Have you thought about that?" Petra took a step backwards and waited.

Anna looked over her shoulder at the door.

"The guard isn't coming, Anna," Petra said. "No-one is."

The table creaked as Seabloom stood up. He walked to Petra's side and whispered in her ear. The corners of Anna's eyes creased as she tried to hear what was said. It was about Natuk. *More lies*, she thought. Natuk is a good girl. She will succeed where her brother failed. She was always the smarter of the two. *And that should worry you, Anna.* The voice was her own, inside her head, and it only made

Petra's words more convincing.

Natuk unleashed and unchecked. There was no telling what she was capable of.

Anna recalled the Greenlandic play Natuk had written in the style of Shakespeare. She remembered the crudely-drawn figures, and the passionate flecks darting across Natuk's eyes as she explained what happened to whom and why. Natuk always had a *why* as if every action, no matter how small, always had a counter reaction. It was nature's way. It was Natuk's way. The Greenlanders were physically and emotionally closer to nature than most of the people on the Earth. What if Natuk allowed her Greenlandic roots to filter through the years of preparation and conviction Anna had instilled in her? She might be dangerous. She might derail the whole thing.

Anna felt sweat begin to bead on her brow, and a cold hand seemed to clasp her heart. It began to squeeze. She felt faint. Anna started to rise, pressing her hands on the table, but it slid across the floor, and she fell. She felt hands grip and turn her, laying her on her back. Then there was something cool on her lips – a cold glass – and water dribbled into her mouth. She looked up. She reached for Petra with a trembling hand and pinched the sleeves of the Commissioner's jacket between weak fingers. So weak.

"Slowly now, Anna," Petra said.

"You have to…"

"Have to what, Anna?"

"You have to stop her."

"Stop Natuk?"

"Yes," Anna said. "You're right, she's out of control. Out of my control." Anna's voice tapered to a whisper and Petra leaned closer.

"You're going to have to help us," she said

"But she needs to rest first," Seabloom said.

He nodded for the guard to remove the glass of water. And then, when a second guard arrived, he helped Anna to her feet. The guards supported her to the door as Anna shuffled between them. She didn't look back, only forwards, straight ahead and along the corridor. She stopped at the first security door, leaning against the second guard as the first fumbled her keycard from her pocket.

"Allow me."

The voice was gruff, male, Greenlandic. Anna didn't recognise the man, and from the way her guards stiffened, neither did they. A closer look revealed that his prison guard uniform was a little too short; Anna could see a hand's width of his blue shirt between the top of his belt and the bottom of his sweater. His keycard didn't work, and Anna heard him apologise, just a split second before he struck the first guard with his elbow. She sprawled to the floor with blood gushing from her nose. Anna felt a spatter of blood land on her cheeks, and then more as the man used his fist to the same effect on the second guard. Both of them lay sprawled on the floor, as the man gripped Anna by the arm and switched to Danish.

"Anna Riis," he said. "My name is Angut. Natuk sent me."

"Natuk?"

"*Aap*. I'm going to take you to her."

"No," Anna said.

The muscles in Anna's legs jellied. She cried out as Angut lifted her in his arms and carried her over the guards sprawled in the corridor. She heard the sound of the door to the courtroom opening, and then a shout – something in English, an American accent. And then Angut started to run, pressing Anna's nose into the smoky wool of his tight-fitting sweater. She could hardly breathe, as he clamped her body to his and kicked, punched and elbowed his way through the outer layer of security. Anna heard him grunt several times, recognising a single word here and there, often in the pause at a secure door, as he waited for someone to open it.

Not someone, she realised. *It was Natuk*.

Chapter 13

They waited inside the hollow beneath the boulder until the helicopter had returned to the Coast Guard base and the police had left with the two suspects in custody. The snow filled the tread of their boots and plastered their overtrousers as Natuk led Viola between boulders of granite above the dragon-lit streets of Chinatown. The mining town was a bitter pill for many Greenlanders to swallow. Natuk remembered the initial argument to build the town for the Chinese miners needed for the mine located in the very north of Nuuk fjord. The original plans located the town close to the mine, but it proved easier to house the miners at the mine, and their families and the families of the additional workers closer to the city of Nuuk. The arrival of three thousand new residents with a variety of ailments not shared by the Greenlanders threatened to overwhelm the existing hospital and medical services. The announcement and building of Kong Frederik's Hospital, a very modern and sophisticated institution, made the lack of mining jobs for Greenlanders a little more palatable. Greenland was used to buying in or trading for foreign expertise, but the initial excitement surrounding the promise of *some* jobs for the locals proved to be nothing more than noise and political bluster. A couple of cleaning jobs and the obligatory translator position was the extent of the Greenlandic roster of workers at the Chinese mine. Natuk paused to look down at the pretty lights and dragons and tried to remember her foster mother's comments when the deal had been struck – something about *ignorant enthusiasm* and *nothing new*.

"Greenland," Anna Riis had said, "just isn't ready to make deals on this scale."

The Greenland Self Rule government had argued for the right to negotiate their own terms, and Denmark had agreed. When plans for the Kong Frederik's Hospital had been leaked, Anna had scoffed, encouraging Natuk and her brother to look closely, and not be distracted by the political smokescreen.

"It's like *Twelfth Night*," she said. "A flattering letter left in the right place to be found at the right time. You can be sure that Denmark has negotiated that on behalf of the Greenland government, and the so-called leak has been seized by that upstart Malik Uutaaq. But," Anna said over dinner that night, "credit where credit is due, he handled the leak masterfully, and now the people are placated, once again, revelling in the shrewdness of their politicians, once again."

But for how long? Natuk wondered, as she slipped her glasses into the inside pocket of her jacket. Greenland couldn't be ruled by a government that profited from opportunists. When Denmark retreated, and the real playmakers and dealmakers were gone, what then? How long would it take before Greenland was railroaded by a more mature government from a country with a history of colonisation and manipulation? Perhaps even more chequered than the Danes?

Natuk stopped as Viola stumbled over a stretch of ice-filmed boulders. She took her hand and guided her to the deeper snow on the other side.

"Are you alright?" she asked.

"Cold," Viola said.

Natuk pressed her hands against Viola's cheeks and brushed clumps of snow from her hair. She kissed her nose, nibbled at her lips, slipping her tongue briefly between them.

"Your hands are so warm," Viola said, as Natuk brushed at another clump of snow. "How can that be? You have no gloves."

"You know what they say," Natuk said. "Warm hands, cold heart." The light of the late afternoon moon lit her teeth and turned her blonde hair white.

Viola took her hand. "I don't believe that."

Natuk kissed her and tugged at her hand. "We have to keep moving. There's a car waiting for us."

Natuk led the way, breaking a trail through the deep snow and the deeper drifts. It was wetter and denser than the snow she remembered from the north of Greenland, when she and Ooqi had lived in Upernavik with relations. The snow on the mountains around Nuuk required more effort, pumping more blood around her body as she pushed forwards, it kept her hands warm. She smiled at the thought, but her lips flattened when she saw the lights of Little Amsterdam ahead of them.

The lights reminded her that her foster mother wasn't always right. In fact, there were times when Natuk had questioned her reasoning. There had been arguments. Anna blamed it on Natuk's teenage temper, tossing her comments and political naivety to one side – chaff to be discarded and ignored.

"One day you will understand," Anna had said when the initial ideas for the Dutch climate colony in Greenland had been discussed.

They were still in Denmark at the time, and Natuk remembered slamming the front door of the house, and the bewildered look in Ooqi's eyes. He always had been more impressionable. Anna's favourite.

"And now he is dead," she said, as she stopped at the top of the slope leading down to the road. The streets of Little Amsterdam were littered with artificial trees. Draped in strings of white lights, they glittered beneath the black winter sky.

"Are you alright?" Viola asked. She took Natuk's hand.

"You did well at the bridge," Natuk said.

"I did?"

Natuk turned to look at Viola. "You showed your face. You rallied people."

"I was wearing a mask," Viola said, tapping the cargo pocket of her jacket.

"It's not a mask anymore, Viola, it's a symbol. *You* are a symbol." She pressed her hands around Viola's shoulders, turning her south to look at Chinatown. "Greenland has made some poor decisions since you were born. Decisions that you and your children have to live with." Natuk turned Viola to the north to face Little Amsterdam. "Some of the decisions were made for Greenland, supposedly in Greenland's favour. There are some people who would argue that Greenland is not mature enough to make its own decisions."

"That's what you believe?"

Natuk shook her head. "Not exactly. But it's what I was brought up to believe. My brother died for that belief." Natuk paused. She slipped her hands down Viola's arms and pressed her fingers into Viola's gloved palms. "I loved my brother. I always will. He was convinced that the people of Greenland need someone strong to guide them."

"But you don't?"

"I did once, but not anymore."

"Then what do you believe?"

Natuk looked up as thick clumps of snow started to fall, plastering Viola's head and clinging to her hair.

"I believe we need to make a change. We can't trust the

governments of Greenland or Denmark to make decisions for us —
we will have to live with those decisions long after they are dead and
gone. It's time for us to make a difference. If Greenland is going to
be independent, if we are to be the youngest government in the
world, then the young need to lead it. We're going to need a leader,"
she said. "Someone to follow." Natuk gripped Viola's hands. "*You.*"

"Me?"

Viola shivered. She stumbled backwards, but Natuk caught her.

"You led the people on the bridge."

"I was excited by the crowd. I didn't know what I was doing."

"They followed you anyway."

Viola shook her head. "I don't know…"

"You made the First Minister stumble at the press conference."

"Only because I asked *your* question."

"I wasn't there, Viola. It was you. You asked the question."
Natuk pulled Viola close, pressed her forehead against Viola's and
caressed her cheek. "Greenland's youth needs a leader. They will
follow you."

"But why me? Why can't they follow you?"

"*Naamik*," Natuk said. "I'm not a leader. I work better behind
the scenes."

"Pulling the strings?" Viola shivered again, stronger this time,
"Are you pulling my strings? Are you manipulating me?"

Natuk pressed her cheek against Viola's. She nibbled at her ear,
melting snowflakes with her warm breath as she whispered, "You are
not a puppet, Viola. You are the future."

"I'm scared," she said.

"Of what?"

"Of leading people," Viola pulled away from Natuk. "Those two
girls, the ones the police arrested. One of them was pretending to be
me. And now she is in trouble."

"She's not in trouble," Natuk said. "The police will let her go —
they'll let both of them go — as soon as they have asked them a few
questions."

"How do you know?"

"Because I used to be a police officer," Natuk said. She frowned
for a second. "I suppose I still am."

"But they sacrificed themselves to protect us…"

"Sacrifice is a strong word, Viola."

"And you keep calling me *Viola*. Stop that. You have to stop." Viola wrenched free of Natuk's hands and stepped backwards onto a crust of snow. "I'm not who you think I am. I'm not even who you want me to be. I can't be that person. I don't want to lead people. I don't want to run the country."

Natuk laughed. "You're sweet when you're upset," she said. Natuk held out her arms. "Viola, please."

"I don't know," Viola said. She stamped her foot and sank into the snow to her knee. She leaned to one side, wobbled for a second, and then fell, driving her arms deep into the snow as she tried to stop her fall.

Natuk giggled.

"Stop it," Viola said.

"You're even sweeter now."

"Stop laughing and help me." Viola rolled onto her side and pulled one arm free. "Natuk."

Natuk took a step forwards, spread her weight evenly, and took another step towards Viola. She gripped her by the arm and slowly pulled her out of the snow and onto her feet. Natuk led Viola onto the top of a flat boulder. She brushed the snow from her back and sides. When she was done, Natuk reached forwards and tucked a strand of Viola's hair behind her ear.

"You don't have to run the country, Viola," she said. "You just have to inspire people."

"I can't do that."

"It's too late," Natuk said. "You've already begun."

Natuk reached inside her jacket and tugged her glasses out of her pocket. She slipped them onto her face and checked the battery icon. The short time she had kept the glasses close to her body had been enough to preserve the battery long enough to check the status of the drones and to confirm that a car had been sent to pick them up.

"They're waiting for us," she said, and took Viola's hand.

"How do you pay for all this?"

"I don't. All the technology is paid for from a fund set up many years ago."

"What fund?" Viola stumbled over a boulder and leaned against Natuk.

"Someone has been preparing for this day for a long time."

"Who?"

"You'll meet her, soon," Natuk said. She pointed at the road below them. "There's our car."

Natuk didn't say another word until they were sat on the back seat. The driver, one of the young Greenlanders who had assembled and steered the drones from the abandoned store in Nuuk, turned up the heat and drove through Little Amsterdam towards Nuuk. Natuk scrolled through the DataStream in her glasses. She opened an encrypted message with a blink, holding her eye open for a retinal scan. Her hand shook as she read the message from Angut.

"What's wrong?" Viola asked.

"Nothing."

"Your hand is shaking." Viola squeezed Natuk's fingers. "And it's cold."

"I'm fine."

Viola laughed. "A minute ago, on the mountain, you were comforting me. It was me that needed reassuring."

Natuk shrugged. "I'm fine." She closed the message and slipped her glasses into her pocket. "We'll be there soon, and I'll tell you what happens next."

Natuk looked out of the window and thought about Angut's message. Anna Riis was free. He would take her to the fishing trawler, as agreed. But it was his last comment that worried Natuk.

She knows.

Two words, but enough for Natuk to lose control, if only for a second. Viola had felt it. *It can't happen again*, she thought.

"What's next?" Viola asked, as the driver looped around the block to check they weren't being followed, before backing into the alleyway at the rear of the store.

"*Next* is *mitaartut*," Natuk said. "Twelfth Night." She smoothed her hand through Viola's hair. "January 6th is also my birthday. There's going to be a party, and all of Greenland is invited."

Chapter 14

Pipaluk put her mobile on mute and hid it beneath the towels she had piled on the toilet seat. She slipped into the bath, wincing as the water scalded her skin. She held onto the sides, slipped her legs all the way into the tub and felt the water melt the outer layers of her skin as she lay down. It was too early for a bath. There were a hundred things she had to do, but since the first reports came in of the disturbance on the bridge, and when the police bustled outside her door and her security was downgraded from the leader of the SRU to a Constable, Pipaluk decided nothing really mattered anymore, at least not for the next hour, an hour she planned to enjoy.

As the bath bubbles popped and the water singed her exposed knees, breasts and neck, Pipaluk remembered her father's belief that Greenland had to stay primitive in order to appeal to the tourists. He worked hard to promote the image of the Greenlanders before they were *civilised*, encouraging the building of sod and turf houses on historical sites within an hour's journey by boat of each of the main towns and villages. He encouraged the tourist companies to populate the fake settlements each summer with traditionally clad *natives*, funding the projects with government support. When the tourists asked if people really lived like that in modern Greenland, the guides were instructed to be ambiguous. Pipaluk worked as a guide in one of the settlements one summer, and soon discovered that the more ambiguous she was, the greater the tip. The bathwater rippled, and the bubbles popped as she smiled at the memory of spending that summer's earnings on designer clothes and make-up.

Anything for the money, she thought, as she moved her legs.

The thought soured her luxurious mood, and Pipaluk tried to flush it away with more hot water. She turned the taps with her toes, cursing at the hot metal faucet that burned her skin. It wasn't the only thing that burned. The demonstrators, and that *girl*'s insinuations that Pipaluk was hiding something, that she had ulterior motives and designs for an independent Greenland. *How dare she*, she thought. *She has no idea how hard I have worked for this.* The Calendar Man and his campaign of terror had nearly been the end of Pipaluk's term as First Minister, *and nearly the end of an independent Greenland*, she thought. But the dream of independence survived. It gathered even more support, and grew stronger, bigger, and more realistic. *Until today.*

Pipaluk turned the tap and stopped the flow of water. She bent her legs and slipped under the water, pressing her fingers to the sides of the bath as she slid deeper into the tub.

She didn't hear the first vibrations of an incoming message, and she didn't check either. Pipaluk waited until the water began to cool and her skin changed colour from lava red to European white. She felt goose bumps prickle her skin and had to rub the colour back into her legs, her stomach and her arms with the towel. She glimpsed the first message on the screen of her mobile as it fell onto the floor.

Pipaluk let the towel fall and bent down to pick up her mobile. Her wet hair clung to her cheeks, damp and slightly cold. She brushed it behind her ear as she read the first message – an update from the bridge.

The second message was more interesting. Juuarsi had been contacted by someone who knew the girl responsible for inciting the young Greenlanders to act, at the press conference and later, on the bridge.

His next message encouraged Pipaluk to dry herself and dress quickly. Juuarsi had brought the contact to the hotel, and they were waiting for her in the Skyline bar.

Pipaluk pulled a pair of jeans over her panties, stuffed her feet into thick socks and pulled on a pair of sealskin boots. She left the boot zips open halfway. She found a thick cotton shirt and buttoned it over her bare chest. She stuffed her mobile in her back pocket and pulled on a black sealskin gilet. She smiled at her reflection in the mirror as she fixed her hair with a patterned headband. If it wasn't for the years, she might have been looking at a younger version of herself, ready to take on the world, and the tourists.

"The world first," she said, as she grabbed the keycard for the suite. "The tourists can wait."

There was no telling what Juuarsi's source might reveal about Tiina Markussen – the so-called *Viola*. But the potential to change the status quo and for damage control buoyed Pipaluk along the corridor; the Constable guarding her had to jog to keep up.

She paused at the entrance to the bar, spotted Juuarsi as he raised his hand to wave to her and walked to his table. Pipaluk checked the frown she felt wrinkling her forehead beneath her headband when she saw the man sitting next to Juuarsi. He looked like one of the demonstrators she had seen at the press conference. He could easily have been one of the people jostling her car or thumping on the windows. She decided there wasn't much that she liked about his appearance, or his behaviour. He cast furtive glances around Pipaluk, barely registering her as he scanned the bar. She almost turned her head to see what he was so afraid of. When he did look at her, Pipaluk forced a smile and sat down. She waved the Constable away to a nearby table and nodded when Juuarsi asked if he should order more drinks.

"The usual," Pipaluk said, as Juuarsi caught the eye of the waiter.

"This is the man I told you about," Juuarsi said, once the waiter had gone.

"What's your name?" Pipaluk asked.

"No names," the man said.

He tilted his head to one side and looked around Pipaluk. The frown hidden beneath Pipaluk's headband deepened, pinching the skin around her eyes as she looked at her assistant.

"Perhaps you can tell the First Minister what you told me," he said.

"About her?" the man said.

"Yes."

The man paused as the waiter returned with their drinks, and then leaned over the table, beckoning for Pipaluk to lean closer.

"She's well organised," he said. "And a real bitch. If she saw me with you, or with them." He nodded at the police Constable. "She'd gut me. I'm sure of it."

"Gut you?" Pipaluk struggled at the thought of Viola carrying a knife, let alone sticking it into the stomach of the man sitting opposite her.

"*Aap*," he said. "That's right."

"Tell her about the drones," Juuarsi said.

"There's lots of them. We built them not far from here."

"Drones?"

"Expensive ones. They've got four or five cameras on each one."

Pipaluk leaned back in her seat. She studied the man as he scanned the bar once more. He was about the same age as Viola. He dressed like a student, but his eyes lacked something – there was no spark to them, just a dull glow that pulsed with tension.

"I don't understand," Pipaluk said. "What are you talking about?"

"Your assistant said you wanted to know about the girl."

"I do."

"I know all about her. I know where she is, where the drones are." He paused to lower his voice. "I even know what she plans to do."

"And what's that?"

"*Mitaartut*," he said.

"That's tomorrow night," Pipaluk said. "What about it?"

"That's when she's going to strike."

"Viola?"

"Who?" It was the man's turn to frown.

"You said Viola is going to strike tomorrow night."

"I don't know anyone called Viola."

"Then who are you talking about?"

"The girl. The woman with the blonde hair and the black eyebrows. She's going to cause a riot. She's going to get everyone to march on the streets with masks and sticks, just like you do on *mitaartut*, but everyone."

"Juuarsi," Pipaluk said. "I honestly don't know what this man is talking about." She stood up to leave. "I think it's best if you take him to the police. He can tell them all about it."

"No," the man said. "I can't talk to the police. She *is* the police. She'll know. Then she'll find me and kill me."

"Pipaluk," Juuarsi said. "I think this is important. It must be connected with the graffiti."

"It is," the man said.

"Fine." Pipaluk sat down. "But I want to know your name before I hear another word. I won't act on the words of a stranger."

The man glanced around the room for the fourth time since she had arrived. He took a breath. "My name is Qallu," he said.

"And your surname?"

"Just Qallu."

"Okay," Pipaluk said. "The blonde woman you described, the one who's not Viola."

"*Aap.*"

"You say she's a policewoman?"

"I think she used to be."

Pipaluk looked at her assistant. She beckoned for him to lean closer and whispered in his ear, "I think he means Natuk Petersen."

"I think so too."

"You told me he knew Viola."

"I was mistaken," Juuarsi said. "But maybe this is even more important? Unless they're connected?"

"They're definitely connected," Pipaluk said.

Pipaluk took a sip of her wine, watching Qallu over the lip of her glass. It was coming back to her now. The woman Qallu described, the woman he was so clearly frightened of, was one of Petra's own officers, gone rogue, and determined to destroy everything Pipaluk had achieved so far. He knew where she was, but it seemed unlikely that she would still be there. Unless, of course, she didn't know he was here.

"How did you get away, Qallu? Did you just walk away or sneak out the back?"

"What?"

"You said you know where she is, this woman. I think you're talking about Natuk Petersen, and if it *is* her, then I really need you to tell me where she is. I can send people there to get her, and we can protect you."

"You can't protect me," he said. "She has eyes everywhere."

"They why did you come to me?" Juuarsi said.

"I want a plane ticket to Denmark."

"There are no flights today," Juuarsi said.

"I want to be on the first flight tomorrow. When I'm on the plane, I'll send you a text with her location. Not before."

"You said she was planning something for *mitaartut*," Pipaluk said. "That's tomorrow. We need to act now."

"It's tomorrow *night*," Qallu said. "I'll tell you where she is when I am on the plane."

And she'll be long gone, Pipaluk thought. She took another sip of wine and looked around the bar as Qallu scanned the patrons for a fifth time. *He feels safer here*, she thought. *Why?* Pipaluk looked at the couple at the table nearest them. They were in their late thirties, the same as her. The two men drinking at the bar, judging by the size of their guts and their jowls, were closer to fifty, maybe older. The other patrons were aged somewhere in-between. They had the money to drink in the hotel bar, or their employer was paying for the room and the drinks. This was a different crowd to the one Qallu was a part of, different in age and intensity. *That's why he feels safe here.* Pipaluk finished her wine.

"Juuarsi will get you a room for the night. I want you to stay in it."

"And the flight?"

"We'll pay for your ticket, but you will tell us where she is tomorrow morning, at breakfast." Pipaluk held up her hand as Qallu opened his mouth to speak. "No exceptions. Your other option is to leave now and take your chances on the street." She stood up. "It's up to you."

Qallu glanced at Juuarsi and nodded. "I'll take the room," he said.

"Good." Pipaluk turned to Juuarsi. "Call the Commissioner. Arrange a breakfast meeting in my suite." Pipaluk paused as she remembered how Petra had reacted in the presence of the American. "Tell her to bring the Coast Guard Commander."

Pipaluk nodded for the Constable to follow her as she passed his table. He didn't have to jog to catch up, but he lengthened his stride to match Pipaluk's. The long soak in the bath had been relaxing, but there was nothing like a shift in the balance of power to rejuvenate Greenland's First Minister. *Viola can wait*, she thought, as she entered her suite. *There are bigger fish in the ocean, and once they are caught, we are back on track.* She stopped in front of the mirror as she removed her gilet. She recognised the same smile from her youth. It was her father's smile, the one that creased his lips when he dreamed of an independent Greenland.

"I'm going to make it happen, *ata*," Pipaluk said. "I'm not going to let anyone get in the way of a free and independent Greenland. Not a silly girl and certainly not some crooked cop."

Pipaluk removed her headband, smoothed her fingers through her hair, and fixed herself a celebratory drink. She turned off the lights and sat at the table by the window as the Northern Lights drifted over her city.

Chapter 15

Petra listened as the Governor explained for the third time that he *couldn't* explain how someone had hacked the detention centre's security system. Nor did he have an explanation as to how someone could overpower a guard and change into their uniform just a few minutes before walking through the front gate and past security without being caught on camera.

"It's a glitch," he said.

"You were hacked," Petra said.

"With respect, Commissioner," the Governor said, "you don't know that for sure."

Petra held up her hands as the Governor opened his mouth to say more. "Please," she said, "let's move on. Just tell me you have at least one image of the man."

"We've got nothing," the Governor said. "The glitch affected all…"

Petra walked away. She waited for the guard to buzz her through the security door, and then joined Seabloom outside. There was a layer of rime ice on the thick collar of his coat where his breath had frozen to the edges. Tiny pearls of ice beaded in the rough wool of the lapels of his jacket, and smaller beads clung to the stubble on his cheeks. Petra chided herself for noticing.

It's alright, Piitalaat.

"No, it's not alright, David. It's too soon."

"What's that?" Seabloom asked, as he pulled his mobile away from his ear.

"What?"

"You said it was too soon."

"I was talking to myself," Petra said. "Have you found anything?"

"A trail of sorts," Seabloom said. He pointed at a single thick tread pressed into the snow. It snaked up the road towards the runway. "Another motorbike," he said. "It will be long gone by now. And by the time the helicopter gets here, any heat signature will be invisible, just like when we lost your Constable."

Petra nodded. She didn't like to be reminded of losing Natuk. The two youths they had arrested knew just enough to tease the police and nothing more. The message on her phone from Atii revealed they had been released less than an hour after being taken to the police station.

A swirl of blue emergency lights swathed across the snow. Petra heard the siren next and ran through a series of actions in her head as she waited for the two police SUVs to slow to a stop in front of her and Seabloom. Atii was the first out of the vehicle, followed by Aron.

"I had no-one else, ma'am," Atii said, as Petra started to frown. "You wouldn't believe how many officers have called in sick today. Three of them right after they were finished on the bridge. Tavik is losing it."

"Alright," Petra said. She smiled at Aron. "I need you to have a word with the Governor, Aron."

"Yes, ma'am." Aron glanced at the entrance to the detention centre.

"He's going to tell you it was a glitch that allowed someone to walk into the centre and to break out with Anna Riis. But even I know that's not the case. I want you to find out how and who, if you can."

"I thought…" Aron stopped speaking and looked at Atii.

"There is a high chance it was Natuk," Petra said. "But we left her on the side of a mountain somewhere between Chinatown and Little Amsterdam. She's either constantly online or someone else is helping her. I want you to find out."

Petra pulled Atii to one side as Aron walked towards the detention centre. Seabloom followed him, clapping his hands together and brushing the layer of ice from the front of his coat.

"I realise we're short staffed," Petra said, "but what resources do you have here and now?"

"With me?"

"Yes."

"Aron's inside, that leaves me and two officers."

"That's not enough to find Anna Riis."

"*Naamik*," Atii said. "Not nearly enough. We have the regular patrols out, but with two protests in one day, we are feeling it. Everyone's tired. Just one more demonstration will push us to breaking point." She nodded at the detention centre. "What about the Americans?"

"I think that's what Joshua – the Commander – is trying to negotiate," Petra said. "He exhausted the goodwill funds when he ordered the helicopter to assist in the search. I'm not sure he can help us." Petra pressed her hand on Atii's arm. "Sergeant," she said, "Why are you laughing?"

"Sorry, ma'am," Atii said. "I'm not laughing at the situation. It's just…" Atii grinned.

"Come on, Atii. Tell me," Petra said. "At least stop laughing."

Atii shrugged as a civilian car sped into the parking area and skidded to a stop just a few metres from where they stood.

"I tried to stop him," Atii said. "But you know Gaba…"

Yes, Petra thought. *I know Gaba.*

She watched as Gaba Alatak opened the car door and climbed out from behind the steering wheel. He stood up, smoothed a bare hand over his bald head and walked towards them. Atii pushed him away as he tried to kiss her.

"I can't kiss my wife?" he said.

"Right now, I'm a Sergeant on duty. You can kiss me later," she said. "If you've cleaned up after yourself."

"The boys and I got a new toy for Christmas," Gaba said, as he kissed Petra on the cheek. "Atii thinks outboard motors belong on boats, not kitchen tables."

"I'm not having this discussion," Atii said.

She turned to leave.

"Sergeant?" Petra said.

"I'm going to coordinate the search. I'll call Tavik and see who he can spare. Besides," she said, and looked at Gaba, "I think the fewer people that hear your conversation, the better."

Gaba grinned as he watched his wife walk away.

"What's she talking about, Gaba?"

"I have a proposal."

"No," Petra said. "You are under investigation for your role in Ooqi's death. I'm still waiting for the inquiry to reach a decision about my role, and how responsible I am for involving you. If it wasn't for the circumstances surrounding the Calendar Man, I would be suspended, already. I can't have you anywhere near any police investigation, Gaba. Not now, and not in the future, either."

Gaba waited until Petra was finished. He hitched his thumbs into his belt as if he was still wearing a utility belt like the one he wore as leader of Greenland's SRU, the same position his wife now held. Petra sighed as he looked down at her. She consoled herself with the thought that it wasn't personal, Gaba Alatak looked down on everybody. She couldn't even remember a Dane who was as tall as he was. He was a Greenlandic anomaly, and a very old friend.

"Petra," he said. "Do you know how much Âmo Security earned in December?"

"No."

"Enough to give the entire team a Christmas bonus, even the junior members of the team. The Calendar Man might have been bad for Nuuk, but he was good for business. The First Minister paid for two months in advance. But when the threat level dropped, I gave half the team a week's paid leave on the condition that they stay in Nuuk, ready to respond if I need them. That's twenty of my best men and women."

"I'm pleased for you, Gaba, but this is not the time to discuss business." Petra pointed at the detention centre. "I've got an escaped suspect and her crazy foster daughter to find, and…"

"A police department that is overworked, underpaid, and on the edge," Gaba said. "I know. That's why you need my help."

"I can't."

"Off the books."

"What?"

"This is an exceptional situation, Petra. You don't have the resources to get the job done. I'm offering you my help."

"I don't have the resources to hire Âmo either, Gaba."

"I don't mean my company. I mean me."

Petra pressed her hands to her temples.

"Gaba," she said. "I thought I just told you that I couldn't have you anywhere near an official police investigation. What part don't you understand?"

"The *official* part," he said.

Gaba waved as Atii shouted that she was leaving. He waited until her police car had left the parking area and then shrugged.

"I'm bored, Petra," he said. "Running a business is one thing, but I miss the action. The blue lights."

"You're as bad as David," she said.

"Then I'm in good company." Gaba reached out to pull a length of Petra's hair stuck to the corner of her mouth. "Whatever you need done, I'll get it done."

"By the book?"

"Don't ask that, Petra. Just tell me what you need." Gaba glanced at the detention centre as the door opened and a tall man walked towards them. "Just tell me quickly," he said.

Petra glanced over her shoulder as Seabloom approached. She took Gaba's hand, and said, "Find Anna Riis." She let go as soon as Seabloom reached them.

She waited as the two men bristled for a moment. It reminded her of David's sledge dogs. The snow where he kept them was stained with the daily pissing of the Alpha dog's territory, followed by the more physical display of dominance that followed any discretion or opportunity to test the Alpha's ability to lead. It was the same with men and women, but men were less subtle about it. In some ways that made it easier, but Petra didn't have time for two men in their fifties to display their Alpha potential.

"Commander Seabloom," she said, short-circuiting the canine formalities, "this is Gaba Alatak. He used to be leader of the Special Response Unit." Petra waited as the two men shook hands. "He's married to Atii," she added.

Petra couldn't decide if she should read anything into Seabloom's sudden relaxed attitude, or just enjoy the peeved expression on Gaba's face. *Either way*, she thought, *we just don't have time for this.*

"I'll leave you to it," Gaba said. He kissed Petra on the cheek. He waved as he walked to his car.

What have I done? Petra wondered, as Gaba drove away.

"You worked together, I presume," Seabloom said.

"Yes."

"For quite a while?"

"Yes. A long time."

"I don't know how you do it."

"It wasn't easy," Petra said. She smiled at the thought, and the memory of how arrogant and frustrating Gaba could be. It didn't matter if he was an ex-lover, colleague or friend, he would always be *Gaba*.

"I meant, I don't know how you can stand out in the cold so long," Seabloom said. "I'm freezing. Again."

"I'm sorry. I didn't think about it. We can go back inside."

"No," he said. "I have to get back to the base." Seabloom looked up as it started snowing. "Whatever happened to it being too cold to snow?"

"This is Greenland," Petra said, and smiled.

"It is, and I'm sorry to say that my government is not quite ready to provide any more assistance. Not for the time being. That's why I need to get back, to see if I can move a little money within the budget."

"You don't have to do that."

"Commissioner," he said. "I think we both know that you can use all the help you can get."

"You're right," Petra said. She looked at the road and watched the taillights of Gaba's car disappear around the bend. When they were gone, she started walking back to the detention centre. "I do appreciate all you have done already. I will be grateful for any extra assistance."

"That sounds pretty damned formal, Commissioner. Did I miss something?"

"I don't think so," Petra said, and frowned.

She stopped by her car. The snow fell through the shattered rear window, layering the back seat with a blanket of thick flakes.

"Can I drive you back to the base?"

"I've got a car on the way," Seabloom said. He scratched a clump of snow from his cheek. "I'm sorry, Petra, I'm not very good at this."

"At what?"

"Nothing," he said. "Don't think about it." Seabloom pointed at a large American SUV as it rumbled into the parking area. "That's my ride." He walked to the car and opened the door. "I'll call you as soon as I know more," he said.

"I appreciate it."

I like him, Piitalaat.

"Not now, David. It's not a good time."

Petra's mobile rang as she walked to the entrance of the detention centre. She recognised the number of the First Minister's assistant and sighed. *It's never a good time,* she thought as she answered the call.

Chapter 16

Viola waited in the car in the alleyway as Natuk slipped through the back door of the store. The driver glanced at her a few times in the mirror but said nothing. He smelled of cigarettes and Viola covered her nose with her jacket sleeve. The driver looked at her again, staring this time. Viola turned her head. She could just see the back door.

"She'll be a while," the driver said.

"What?" Viola moved her hand from her nose to her lap.

"Your friend. The blonde."

"Oh."

The seat creaked as the driver turned around to look at her. His hand was just a few inches from Viola's knee. He flicked his finger and it caught the hem of her jacket.

"You're her, aren't you?"

"Who?" Viola said. She shivered as he plucked the jacket between his fingers.

"The girl. The one who's meant to inspire us." The driver grinned, flicking his tongue between brown gums and yellow teeth. "We could get to know each other while she's gone," he said.

He tugged one more time at Viola's jacket, laughing as she twitched. The movement lifted her jacket and exposed her knee. The weave of her overtrousers was coarse and the material was thick, but Viola could feel his fingers burning circles on her skin.

"Stop," she said.

"Why?"

"Because I don't like it."

The driver reached between the car seats and pressed his hand between Viola's knees. She twisted away, and he reached further, grinning as he pawed at her. A sudden rap on the window made him stop, and he pulled his arm away from Viola's legs, twisting in his seat as the passenger door opened.

"Did I scare you?" Natuk asked as she sat on the backseat and closed the door.

Viola stared straight ahead. She caught the driver's look in the mirror, and the tiny shake of his head.

"Viola?" Natuk said. "What's wrong?" Natuk grasped Viola's fingers, squeezing them once to get her attention. "Hey? You there?"

"Yes," Viola whispered. She turned her head and looked at

Natuk. She tried to smile. "I'm here."

"You must have been colder than I thought," Natuk said. "We've got one more stop, and then I'll take you somewhere you can rest before *mitaartut*. There won't be any time once we start." Natuk pressed her hand against Viola's cheek. "Hey, relax. You're going to be a star." Natuk looked at the driver. "Take us to the den. You know where."

"*Aap.*"

When Natuk looked away the driver winked at Viola and then started the car. He pulled away from the store and drifted down the alleyway. Natuk leaned back in the seat and put her glasses on. She held Viola's hand as she blinked her way through the DataStream. Viola looked out of the window. She could feel the heat of the driver's look, the intensity of his gaze, but so long as she could also feel Natuk's fingers, slender and strong, she felt safe.

They drove for ten minutes, turning through a series of narrow snow-lined streets until the driver stopped beside a low wooden house shaped like a long letter L. The roof closest to the street sagged with a winter's worth of wind-blown snow.

"I'll be a few minutes," Natuk said.

Viola caught the driver's eye in the mirror, as Natuk started to open the door. She gripped Natuk's hand and moved to follow her.

"I'll come with you," she said.

"I'm not so sure. It's not exactly the nicest of places."

"I don't mind. I'll come anyway."

Viola opened her door as Natuk hesitated. She zipped her jacket to her chin as Natuk walked around the car to join her.

"You won't have seen anything like this before," Natuk said.

"I'll be okay."

"If you're sure." Natuk plucked at a length of Viola's hair that was caught in her jacket zip. "Okay, but I need you to wait while I talk to someone inside. He's got some information I need. Something he doesn't want to share in the DataStream." She took her glasses off and slipped them into her jacket pocket.

Natuk led Viola to the front door. It was jammed open with a drift of snow. She pushed it open and tugged Viola by the hand, leading her through the doorway and into a cold room with black plastic taped to the windows and a thin crust of ice on the walls. There was snow on the floor, and a broken wooden pallet with half a rusted oil drum positioned in the middle of it. A low flame licked at the solid fuel bricks inside it. Natuk pointed at the sofa and the woman bent over the arm at one end. Viola frowned at the rattling sound the woman was making as she breathed.

"You can wait there," Natuk said. "She won't bother you."

Viola nodded and picked her way across the floor, weaving between a litter of bottles and food wrappers. The woman's wheeze deepened, and the rattle in her lungs became a click like a set of rusty cogs as Viola sat down at the other end of the sofa. Natuk waited for Viola to nod before pointing at a door at the end of a long corridor.

"I'll be ten minutes," she said.

Viola watched her walk down the corridor and enter the far room. Natuk closed the door behind her leaving Viola sitting in the gloom with dirty snow and a woman with rattle lung for company.

The driver entered the room half a minute later.

Viola stiffened at the sound of the front door scraping over the drift of packed snow. The smell of his cigarettes seeped into the room ahead of him, followed by his shadow, his sneer, and the dull glint of the knife in his hand.

"I thought we could finish what we started," he said, as he walked across the room. He moved quickly, pressing his hand on Viola's shoulder as she tried to stand, and the blade at her throat as she opened her mouth to scream. "Not a word," he said. "Or I'll cut you."

The blade scraped up and down Viola's skin as she trembled, half standing, her knees bent, fingers stiff and useless at her sides.

"Now," the driver said, "unzip your trousers." He looked over his shoulder, staring at the door at the end of the corridor for a second, before stepping closer to Viola. "Faster," he said, as she fumbled with the zip of her jacket.

The driver's breathing changed to a kind of huffing, bestial, like a bear, as he unsnapped his jeans and reached inside his pants. Viola choked on the draught of stale cigarette smoke that he breathed in her face. She felt tears well in her eyes, and then she gasped, choking on a sob as the driver grew tired of waiting and gripped a fistful of her trousers and tugged them down her legs.

It was the last thing he did.

Viola didn't see or hear Natuk enter the room, but she felt the brush of air on her face and across her thighs as the driver toppled onto his side. The tip of the knife nicked the hem of her jacket, catching in the stitches for a second until the driver jerked it free and slashed at the air in front of Viola.

"Idiot," Natuk said, as she bent the driver's wrist until he dropped the knife.

He kicked out at her, and then cursed as Natuk curled the toe of her boots into his knee. He cursed her again as she pressed the muzzle of her pistol into his cheek.

"Hey, no mess."

Natuk paused to glance at the man who entered the room. She nodded at the litter on the floor.

"Mess?"

"Body fluids then," the man said. "Take it outside."

"You hear that?" Natuk said, as she pressed the muzzle deeper into the driver's cheek. "I've got to take the trash out."

"Police bitch," the driver said.

"You're half right," she said, and gripped the driver's jacket.

Natuk pulled the driver to his feet and shifted the muzzle to the back of his neck. She nodded for Viola to follow, waited for her to zip up her overtrousers, and then shoved the driver towards the door. He stumbled over the lip of the door and sprawled onto the snow. Natuk knelt on his back, forcing the air out of his lungs as she pressed the muzzle into the back of his head.

"You can't kill me," he said.

"Why not?"

"If you kill me, people will know. They won't follow you anymore."

"They don't have to follow me," Natuk said. "Just her." She nodded at Viola as she stepped out of the doorway.

"Natuk," Viola said. "What are you going to do?"

"Hey, girl," the driver said. He squirmed beneath Natuk's knee to look at Viola. "I wasn't going to hurt you. You know that. Right?"

"Shut up," Natuk said. She gritted her teeth, as a ripple of energy shuddered through her body.

"*Girl*, believe me."

"That's enough."

Viola stepped over the lip of the door. She reached out to touch Natuk's shoulder, only to recoil as Natuk pushed her away. The driver felt the shift in Natuk's weight and he twisted beneath her, reaching for the pistol. Natuk bounced onto her heels, slipping on the ice as the driver reared up above her.

"No," Viola shouted.

Natuk fell onto her back and fired. The first bullet went through the driver's stomach and he buckled above Natuk's head. She straightened her arms and fired twice, snapping the driver's head backwards. His body flipped in the air. Viola pressed her hands to her mouth at the sound of the man's head slamming into the side of the car. His body slid down the door and crumpled in the snow as Natuk rolled onto her knees and stood up. She slipped the pistol into the waistband of her trousers and grabbed the driver's trousers at his ankle.

"Help me, Viola," she said.

Together they dragged the driver's body around the side of the house and rolled it into the shadow behind the empty oil tank.

"You just gonna leave him there?" the man from the house asked. "The neighbours is going to find him. Then they is going to come looking for me." He spat on the snow. "That's not fair," he said.

"No-one's going to find him," Natuk said. "Come tomorrow night, they'll be too busy. You've got the whole winter to hide him."

"It's still not fair," the man said. "I gave you good information, and you is giving me a body in return."

"I paid you plenty," she said. "Enough to hide him." She pointed at the oil tank. "Stick him in there. You don't use it."

The man spat again, glared at Natuk, and then went back inside the house. Viola stared at the driver's body.

"Don't look at him," Natuk said. "He can't hurt you now."

"You killed him."

"He was going to hurt you."

"No," Viola said. She shook her head. "That's not why you killed him. I saw your face. You were trembling."

"It was adrenaline."

"It was more than that," Viola said. "Someone did something to you. Not him. Someone else. They did the same to you that he wanted to do to me." Viola looked at Natuk. "I'm right. That's why you killed him."

Natuk pressed her finger to her face and wiped a spot of blood from her cheek. She stared at the blood on her finger, and then used her sleeve to wipe her face. Viola watched her. Natuk looked up and down the street. She stared at a window in a small apartment block opposite the house. Viola turned to see the curtain move. She thought she saw a face, and then Natuk took her arm and walked her to the car.

"I've got what I need. We have to go."

"No," Viola said. "Not before you answer me." She pulled free of Natuk's grip and took a step away from the car. "I'm not going with you until you tell me."

"Viola…"

"My name is *Tiina*," she said.

"Fine," Natuk said. She pointed at the oil tank and the shadow beside it. "My father abused me when I was a girl. He raped me. More than once. I told myself that once I was strong enough, I would never let it happen again. Not to me. Not to anyone." She stabbed her finger in the air between her and the driver's body. "*He* was going to hurt you. I stopped him," she said. "Now can we go? We have a long night and a long day ahead of us, and I have to go see somebody."

"Someone else?" Viola frowned. "Who?"

"My mother."

Chapter 17

There were devils outside Petra's apartment. She heard them scuffing the floor in the stairwell, stubbing Petra's doormat with oversized boots to match their oversized bodies. Petra paused at the last step and studied the monsters. She took out her key as she watched them begin their dance. One of the devils was tall, adult-sized. Its shoulders were uneven, as was the triangular body that tapered toward its waist. Petra looked at its face, black and sooty. There were red welts crumbling in thick red paint beneath its eyes, and its hair, thick and black, was tied in a tight bun at the very top of the devil's head; small whalebones protruded from it at crazy angles. The second devil was shorter with a more vigorous dance. Its face was masked, not painted, and its hair was pigtailed and pinned with more bones, white against the black mask. The teeth of the mask were stubby and brown, but it was the clawed fingers that impressed Petra the most, as the devil pawed at the air between them, dancing towards Petra and then giggling and shrieking back to the bigger devil at the door.

"I wonder who it is." Petra said. She creased her forehead with an appropriate frown.

The tall devil cocked its head and struck an ungainly pose, while the shorter devil giggled once again.

"I just don't know," Petra said. She took a step towards her apartment door. "Perhaps if I let you in, and find some candy, maybe I will remember your names?"

The devils pawed and clawed at Petra's shoulders as she unlocked the door. Compared to the devils on the street, the uneven pair with their bulky upper bodies and grotesque faces were a welcome relief. Petra stood back to let them inside.

The shorter devil kicked off her boots and ran to the sofa, shrieking as she climbed up and over the back to roll onto the thick cushions. The other devil shrugged as if she was not responsible for the child-sized devil. Petra laughed and filled a glass bowl with sweets.

"You have to come closer," she said, and beckoned for the shorter devil to come and sit on her lap. Petra placed the bowl of candy on the kitchen table and sat down on a chair beside it, the shorter devil squirmed onto her lap. "Now, who are you?"

When the devil reached for the candy, Petra tickled its stomach.

The devil giggled.

"I didn't think you were supposed to say anything," Petra said.

"I'm not," the devil said, and giggled again.

"You just did."

Petra tickled the devil a second time, and its mask slipped down to its nose.

"You're cheating," the devil said, its voice shrill, the words bouncing as it giggled.

"I know who you are," Petra said. "You're not a devil, you're a little boy."

"*Naamik*," the devil said as it squirmed on Petra's thighs.

"Your name is Johannes."

The devil shook its head.

"It's Karl."

"*Naamik*. I'm not a boy."

"Ah, so, you must be Gertrude."

"I'm not Gertrude."

"No," Petra said, as she pulled the devil into a long, tight hug. She pressed her cheeks against the devil's mask and whispered in her ear. "Your name is Quaa," she said.

"*Aap*." Quaa lifted her mask and pushed it up onto the top of her head. There was soot around her eyes, Petra smeared it with her fingers as she clasped her hands to Quaa's cheeks and kissed her on the nose. Quaa pointed at the tall devil standing behind her.

"That's right. There's another devil in my kitchen," Petra said. "Do you know who she is?"

Quaa shook her head and pushed two wine gums into her mouth.

"I think I do," Petra said, as the other devil stuck out its tongue, raised its arms and twirled around the kitchen. "Hello Iiluuna."

"Finally," Iiluuna said, as she dropped her arms to her side and slumped on a chair at the table.

"It's a good mask," Petra said.

"It will never come off."

"No, it won't." Petra laughed.

"We're a day early," Iiluuna said. "We're flying to Denmark tomorrow. Quaa desperately wanted to visit you on *mitaartut*, so I said we would come today." Iiluuna sighed. "I should have called. I didn't think you would be so late."

"I'm sorry you had to wait, but I enjoyed the surprise." Petra turned Quaa on her knee. "Why are you going to Denmark?"

Quaa looked at Iiluuna. She pushed the sweets around her mouth and waited for her to answer.

"The doctors at Kong Frederik's Hospital found an Atrial Septal Defect in Quaa's heart. A tiny hole. She's never shown any symptoms, no shortness of breath, but they were checking the kids in Quaa's class for tuberculosis, and they wanted to see Quaa again. They think she has a tiny hole in her heart. The specialist is off sick, but they don't want to wait, so we fly to Denmark tomorrow."

"Hey," Petra said, as she pulled Quaa to her chest. "I'm sorry."

"It's okay," Quaa said. She shrugged. "I can't feel anything."

"They just want to check." Iiluuna reached across the table and took Petra's hand. "She's alright, Piitalaat. Really."

"I know." Petra pressed her cheek against Quaa's hair, sniffing at the familiar coconut shampoo, and hiding her tears in the tangle of Quaa's hair. She pulled back as the tip of a whalebone pressed into her forehead. "Ow," she said. "You're all spiky."

"I'm a monster," Quaa said. "Monsters are spiky."

Petra nodded. She brushed Quaa's cheek with her hand, and then pushed her gently off her lap.

"I'm going to make some coffee," she said. "For the other monster."

Quaa took a handful of candy and skipped to the sofa. Petra watched her and then filled the coffee maker with water.

"She really is okay," Iiluuna said, as she stood up. She pressed her hand on Petra's shoulder and pulled her close.

"I know," Petra said. She pulled her head back as something smeared her cheek. "You're covering me in soot," she said.

"I'll never get it off."

"You know where the bathroom is."

Petra dumped four scoops of coffee into the filter and then pressed her hands on the lid of the coffee can. She took a breath, wiped another tear from her eye, and then pressed the start button. The coffee maker spluttered as the water warmed.

Quaa is going to be alright, Piitalaat.

"I know, David. It's just…"

You're going to be alright.

Petra nodded, dried her eyes, and joined Quaa on the sofa. They found a Christmas film to stream on the wall screen as Iiluuna wiped the soot from her face.

Iiluuna emerged from the bathroom with a grey face and slimmer shoulders. She filled two mugs of coffee and handed one to Petra as she sat down in the armchair next to the sofa. Quaa slid onto Petra's lap, twirling a wheel of liquorice slowly around her finger as her eyelids blinked slower and slower. Petra tugged the whalebones from Quaa's hair and stroked her head until Quaa started to snore.

"She's excited about flying tomorrow," Iiluuna said. "It's her first time to Denmark. I want her to go before…"

"Before we become independent?"

Iiluuna shrugged. "Things will change."

"A lot of things," Petra said. "Are you nervous?"

"*Naamik*," Iiluuna said. "Not for me." She looked at Quaa. "Maybe a little for her."

"Pipaluk is strong," Petra said. "She'll make it work."

"You think so? I thought you didn't like her."

Petra teased a knot out of Quaa's hair as she thought for a moment. "We don't always see eye to eye, that's for sure. But I am impressed. She has strength and a sense of conviction. I think she will make a good President."

"President?" Iiluuna laughed. "I suppose we could be a republic."

"If that's what the people want," Petra said. She looked out of the window at the lights of the city just across the fjord. *But I don't know what they want*, she thought, *not really*.

"We should go," Iiluuna said.

"It's okay. You can stay."

"You've got that look in your eye, Piitalaat. I can see you're busy – thinking."

"I have a meeting with the First Minister in the morning." Petra found another knot in Quaa's hair. "I'd like to enjoy tonight. Please stay," she said. "You can sleep in the guestroom. The bed is made up."

"If you're sure?"

"I am."

The Christmas film finished and Iiluuna lifted Quaa from Petra's lap. She carried her into the guestroom and Petra pulled back the covers. She kissed Quaa goodnight and hugged Iiluuna.

"I met you on the saddest day in my life," she said, as she splayed her fingers on Iiluuna's back. "But I'm so pleased you're in my life. David is too, you know, I can feel it."

"I know," Iiluuna said. She smiled as Petra let go.

Petra tidied her hair, smoothing long strands behind her ears.

"I'll be up for a bit," she said. "Reading."

"You're reading David's books?"

"I'm trying." Petra frowned. "They're not really my thing, but I think it amuses him, wherever he is, that I am trying. Don't worry if you hear me padding about for a bit. I just need to unwind. It's been a long day."

Petra closed the door quietly behind her, topped up her mug of coffee, and found a cold beer in the fridge; she carried both to the armchair, sat down and picked up the book on the table next to the chair.

"This is for you," she whispered, as she glanced upwards.

She read until midnight, cradling the bottle of beer against her chin between sips. She let her coffee cool in the mug on the table. Petra turned another page, frowned at the start of yet another battle in space, and then paused at the sound of her phone vibrating. She put the book down and pulled her mobile out of her pocket. The screen flickered with cascading windows, message boxes glowing with a series of reports of masked people on the streets of Nuuk. Several of the reports indicated that the people were armed with sticks. Petra read a pinned message from Tavik as he called for calm, reminding all the officers on duty that it was January 6th, and *mitaartut* had begun, albeit much earlier than usual.

They're supposed to wait until the evening, Petra thought.

She read a string of three more messages, before opening a fourth from Gaba asking her to call.

"It's late, Gaba," she said, as he answered. "You should be at home."

"Atii is with the boys. She's resting. She wants to be up early."

"We have a meeting…"

"With the First Minister. I know." Gaba paused. "I told her I was looking for Anna Riis. She pretended not to hear me, but she's focused on finding Natuk now. I thought you might want to know."

"I have a feeling that if you find one, you'll find the other," Petra said.

"This is why I'm calling. I'm pretty sure I can bring in the Ombudsman without too much trouble."

"But you're worried about Natuk?"

"*Aap*," he said.

Petra fidgeted on the chair, tucking her heels beneath her bottom as she considered what Gaba was really asking.

"You want to know how far I'll go," she said.

"I want to know how far you'll let *me* go. What are my limits?"

"Limits?" Petra almost laughed. "I didn't think you had any."

"I don't, that's why I'm calling."

Gaba waited as Petra thought about how well she knew Natuk. Beyond the fact that she was young, intelligent, and committed, Petra realised she didn't know her very well at all. But those three things were enough. Natuk had the energy, the commitment to do anything, and the mental capacity to see it through. Just like her brother, Ooqi. The irony of Gaba being investigated for his role in Ooqi's death as he secretly hunted a woman that might lead him to Ooqi's sister dried Petra's mouth. She took a last sip of beer and pressed her mobile to her ear.

"Gaba," she said.

"*Aap?*"

"Do what you have to do. Just be safe."

"You know me, Petra."

"Yes, and that's what worries me."

Chapter 18

The bow of the trawler bumped through the ice littering the fjord as the captain returned to the dock. Natuk waved at the tall Greenlander on the deck and wrapped her arm around Viola as she shivered beside her. Natuk frowned at the blue tinge to Viola's lips and wondered if she had a fever. It had taken longer to get her away from the bridge than Natuk had anticipated. The snow on the slopes of the mountains was wet and deep. She looked at Viola's boots and wondered if her feet were cold. The leather on the sides and above Viola's toes was darker than the leather around her ankles.

"It's warm on the boat," Natuk said. "You can rest, change your clothes and dry your boots."

"I'm fine."

"We'll see. Not long now."

Natuk let go of Viola as the trawler slowed and bumped along the wooden dock. There was a damp squeal of metal and the slow pop of a rubber fender. Natuk caught the line that Angut cast from the deck and wrapped it once through a cleat. She held one end as Angut helped Viola onboard, and then climbed over the side, letting the line run through her fingers and the cleat as the captain steered the trawler away from the dock towards the mouth of the fjord.

"You did well," Natuk said, as she slapped Angut on the shoulder.

"And you?" he asked. "I heard there was some trouble."

"The bridge?"

"*Naamik*." He shook his head. "Something about one of the drivers."

"I dealt with it." Natuk looked down as she coiled the line at her feet.

"And Qallu?"

"Natsi's going to get back to me, as soon as Qallu comes up for air."

"We should move the drones."

"Not yet," Natuk said. "I want them airborne first, and then we can relocate the computers and the controllers." She gripped Angut's wrist and turned it to look at his watch. "Another hour, then we fly. The batteries will keep them airborne for twenty-four hours. That's long enough."

Natuk smiled at Viola and took a step towards the door to the cabin. Angut caught her arm and stopped her.

"What is it?"

"Your foster mother is below."

"I know. You did well."

"It's not that. She's spooked. I wanted to warn you."

Natuk caught the smile creasing the corner of her mouth and took a breath of cold air to flatten it. The balance of power was shifting, finally. *But it's too soon for her to realise that*, she thought.

"How?"

"How did she get spooked?" Angut shrugged. "I don't know. But when I picked her up, she had just been in a room with the Police Commissioner."

"Petra," Natuk said. She bit her bottom lip as she stared past Viola towards the wide mouth of the fjord. "Of course."

It was just possible that Petra Jensen might be the one person who could see through Natuk. She remembered the way Petra cut through the concerns of the police officers around her and tried to convince everyone that the Calendar Man's terror campaign had nothing to do with her, it wasn't personal, it was a smokescreen. Natuk thought about how she had worked with Ooqi to ensure that Petra and the task force understood the links to Petra's past, and yet, she had still seen through them. Perhaps the only thing that Petra failed to see through was her own belief that Ooqi and Natuk were victims, that someone else was pulling the strings. She was right, of course, Ooqi was acting under orders and increasing pressure from their foster mother. *But I'm not like my brother*, Natuk thought. Anna might have seen it, glimpsed what Natuk has capable of, glimpsed her commitment. Petra would just have to find out the hard way.

Natuk took Viola's hand and led her inside the cabin of the trawler. She caught and held her as the captain turned into a wave, and then helped her down the ladder to the crew quarters below.

"Have a seat, Viola," she said.

Natuk helped Viola out of her jacket. She smiled as she unzipped her salopettes. She would have lingered and taken her time, teasing Viola as she removed more clothing, but she was still unnerved by the incident with the driver.

"He'll never hurt you again," Natuk said.

"I know."

Natuk unlaced Viola's boots, tugged them off her feet and tossed them to one side. She removed Viola's socks, pulling a face as she twisted them in her hands, squeezing water onto the deck below the table.

"Your feet are ice cold," she said. "Come on. Let's find you a bunk. You'll feel better after some sleep, and then a meal and a hot drink."

Natuk opened a thin wooden door and led Viola inside a dingy cabin. There was a soft light glowing above the pillow on the bottom bunk bed. Natuk pulled back the sheets and pressed Viola onto the bed. She tucked the sheets around Viola's body, covering her to the neck, and kissed her forehead, her nose and lips when she was done. Viola took her hand as Natuk turned to leave.

"You said he would never hurt me," Viola said.

"He can't."

"I know, but would you?"

"Me? Would I what?"

"Would you ever hurt me?"

"No," Natuk said. "Never."

She kneeled by the bed and stroked Viola's hair across her cheek.

"It's just, sometimes, you get this look in your eye," Viola said. "It scares me."

"There's nothing to be scared of," Natuk said, although she knew the look Viola had seen. It was the same look she gave herself in the mirror when a little extra effort and commitment were required to get through a difficult day, or an hour, *or the next few minutes*, she thought as she kissed Viola, plucked her fingers from the young woman's grasp, and turned out the light.

Natuk shut the door on the way out of the cabin, caught her reflection in the polished metal sheet screwed into the wall, and saw the look, that steely-eyed glare that gave her a sense of superhuman strength. It gave her the edge she needed to open the door to the next cabin, the one reserved for her foster mother.

"Hello, Anna," she said, as she stepped into the cabin.

The same lamp glowed above the pillow of the bunk in Anna's cabin, as it had in the cabin next door, but the light was lost in the stark and bright illumination of the overhead light, the lamps on the walls, and the flare of light reflected in the mirror. Anna Riis stood in the room, bathed in light from all angles. It shone through the thin cardigan from the detention centre, and Natuk almost gasped at how frail she had become.

"I'm Anna now, am I?" Anna said. "Am I not your mother?"

"You never were."

Natuk closed the door and leaned against it. She studied the firm set of Anna's jaw, right-angled like the sleeves of her cardigan and the crease in her trousers. She might look frail, but she was still as sharp as a razor.

"Ungrateful child. After all I did for you and your brother."

"My brother is dead," Natuk said. "You killed him."

"It wasn't me that pulled the trigger."

"It might as well have been. You put him there."

"For a purpose, Natuk. He had a job to do, just as you do. He failed. What about you? Are you going to fail too?" Anna tensed. She gritted her teeth. The harsh light caught the lines of muscle beneath her thin and pallid skin.

It was a good act, Natuk decided. She almost clapped. *Not yet*, she thought. *I want to see how far she will go.*

"I won't fail," Natuk said. She pushed away from the door and opened the cupboard. She slipped her hand between two towels and pulled out a pistol. "I'll look after this," she said. "I don't want you to hurt yourself."

"What are you up to, Natuk?" Anna took a slow step towards her. She reached out to touch Natuk's arm, only to let her hand fall as Natuk pulled away. "What are you doing with that girl?"

"You mean Viola?"

"You called her *Viola*?" Anna laughed. "What have I done?" she said. "I knew you were impressionable, you both were, but I never knew just how much."

"What can I say, *mother*? You taught me well."

"I taught you politics, and administration. I taught you how to manipulate and convince people to think one thing while you did another. I taught you the art of deception." Anna stabbed a wrinkled finger towards the bulkhead separating her cabin from Viola's. "I didn't teach you to get someone else to do your dirty work."

"Dirty work?"

"Or whatever else it is you have planned for that pathetic waif."

"You saw her?"

"I saw her picture in the DataStream. I heard the questions she asked at the First Minister's press conference, and I saw her at the bridge wearing the same mask you have plastered all over the city."

"You saw all that from your cell?"

Anna sneered. "That's what's so perverse about this country. I was supposed to be in detention, yet I have access to the news, current events. I saw your first moves, Natuk. I watched them develop."

"And what about now?"

Anna pressed her lips together. She looked over her shoulder and sat on the edge of the bed. She watched as Natuk removed the magazine from the pistol and the bullet from the chamber. Natuk tossed the magazine and the bullet onto the bed. She slid her right hand to the stop beneath the sights and gripped the tear-down switches with the fingers of her other hand. She pulled the pistol apart and tossed the parts onto the bed.

Natuk stared at her foster mother. "I asked you a question, *mother.*"

"Is that supposed to impress me?" Anna said. "That you can handle a gun?"

"It's not the only thing I can handle." Natuk pointed at the bulkhead. "That pathetic girl you mentioned is the face of the new campaign. *My* campaign. She might even be the face of the new Greenland."

"A new Greenland?" Anna scoffed. "What are you talking about? I thought I made it very clear that there is only one thing that can benefit this country, and that is continued influence from Denmark. Your brother understood that. Why can't you?"

"This patriotism of yours," Natuk said. "I don't understand that. I mean, is it rewarded? Do you feel rewarded or maybe even admired or appreciated by your beloved country? I can't see it."

"You can't see the appreciation?" Anna stood up. "Just who do you think funds all this? Your drones, the weapons, this boat. Where do you think the money comes from?"

"It's not the Danish government."

"Of course not, stupid child. Really, Natuk, I thought you were smarter than that. Now I realise I was stupid to worry. Clearly, Ooqi was the more intelligent twin. It's such a shame that he died, and now it's up to you to complete his work."

Natuk clenched her fists at her sides. She pressed her teeth together as she glared at Anna.

"You can call me anything you want," she said.

"But not stupid?" Anna laughed. "Stupid children think that governments support radical campaigns, when really it is far more complex than that. You won't find any links to the Danish government in any of the supplies you have received. But neither will you hear them denounce Greenland's independence games in public. They have to be seen to be supportive. It's all about public opinion and popularity. But the real agenda can be seen beneath the surface, or even in the cabin of a fishing trawler, if people knew where to look." Anna reached out and brushed her hand against Natuk's face. "Child," she said. "My child. I was rash. Forgive me. Let's start again. Tell me what you have planned, and what progress you have made. I can see you have been busy, and I am sure that the girl is a crucial part of your campaign. She has already put the First Minister on the back foot and should be commended for that. You both should. I know it was you that orchestrated it. I just want to understand why. Tell me so I can reassure our backers."

"You want me to tell you everything?" Natuk asked.

"I want you to convince me that you are on the right path. Because for a moment, I was concerned that you had strayed."

"Did the Commissioner make you think that?"

Anna frowned. "How did you know about that?"

"Angut."

"Yes, of course." Anna nodded. "He is more perceptive than I imagined." She sat down and swept the gun parts to one side. "Sit with me, Natuk. Tell me everything. Show me your vision for our Greenland, one that our friends in Denmark can be proud of."

"I can bring you up to speed," Natuk said, as she sat down. *But it's not your vision for our Greenland anymore*, she thought. *It's mine.*

Marlunngorneq

Tuesday, 6th January 2043
Mitaartut

Chapter 19

Gaba bumped his car over the ridge of ice by the side of the road and parked in a space between the drifts of snow on the street. He turned off the engine and lowered the window. The sound of chanting drifted along the street from the main road, Gaba could just see the blur of masked figures passing the entrance, he noted the sticks and baseball bats they carried. Gaba opened the glove compartment and took out the extendable police baton. He would prefer a pistol, but the inquiry into Ooqi Kleemann's death was ongoing, and Gaba decided the chance of being caught with a pistol was not worth the risk of jeopardizing the outcome. *If this crowd gets ugly*, he thought, *I'll just have to get physical.* Gaba smiled at the thought. He slipped the baton into the inside pocket of his jacket, closed the window and opened the door. The sound of chanting and jeering was louder now, and the crowd passing the street entrance was denser. *Mitaartut* had begun.

"About twelve hours too early," Gaba said, as he closed the car door.

Gaba jogged to the end of the street and then slipped into the crowd. He took the baton out of his jacket and jerked it to its full length. One of the crowd nodded at the baton and then pointed at Gaba's face.

"Where's your mask?"

The mask obscured the person's mouth and muffled their words, but the deep tones suggested it was a man. Gaba paused for a second to study the man's body and noted the thick leather jacket he wore over a fleece hoodie. The man carried a length of metal that looked like a railing from a fishing boat.

"I left it at home," Gaba said.

"Talk to Kuupik, he's got loads in his pack."

"Right." Gaba gestured at the group flowing around them like a steam of armoured fish around an island of coral. "Which one."

"He's the one with the red backpack." The man laughed. "All the leaders have red backpacks. Didn't you read the message in the DataStream?"

"I must have missed it."

The man leaned in close to Gaba, tilting his head as if the mask restricted his vision.

"You're a little old for this."

"But young at heart," Gaba said. "Red backpack?"

"Over there." The man pointed. "At the back of this group.

Gaba estimated that *this group* included about thirty people. All of them were armed and wore some kind of padded top, varying in size and thickness. They wouldn't stop a bullet but might deflect the first or second strike of a police baton, giving enough time for a second wave or *group* of demonstrators to rush the police line. Gaba wondered if the police had enough officers to form a line, and where? Just one group of thirty could close a street. It wouldn't take many groups to shut down the city.

This is going to get ugly, he thought.

The man in the mask drifted away, and Gaba pushed his way through the group to the man wearing a red backpack. He walked at the rear, with the next group about two hundred metres behind him. They rounded the corner in the main road as Gaba approached him.

"Kuupik?" Gaba asked.

"*Aap.*"

"I need a mask."

Kuupik stopped walking, shrugged the backpack off his back and unzipped it. Gaba glanced up and down the road. As Kuupik reached into the backpack, Gaba hooked his arm around the shorter man's neck and dragged him into the shadows between two buildings. Gaba kicked Kuupik's legs and dropped him to the floor. He pulled the mask off Kuupik's face, as he pressed his knee into the young man's chest.

"What's your last name?"

"What?"

"Your last name, *idiot*. What is it?"

"Heilmann."

"That's better," Gaba said. He lifted his knee a little to let Kuupik breathe. "What's in the backpack?"

"Masks."

"Anything else? Any weapons?"

Kuupik shook his head.

"You're sure? What about a knife? If I find anything in there, it's just going to make me mad. This..." Gaba pressed his knee into Kuupik's sternum. "This is just mildly irritated. I guarantee you don't want to see me mad." He lifted his knee and Kuupik gasped cold air into his lungs.

"I've got flares," Kuupik said.

"Like signal flares?" Gaba opened the backpack.

"*Aap.*"

Gaba emptied the backpack onto the snow beside Kuupik's head. The sound of the second group approaching turned Gaba's head. He gripped Kuupik's jacket and dragged him deeper into the shadows, pressing both knees onto the man's chest as the first of the group passed the entrance to the alleyway. When the last member of the group – a short person carrying a red backpack – disappeared out of sight, Gaba released the pressure on Kuupik's chest and let the man breathe. Gaba stabbed the police baton into the snow beside Kuupik's head and leaned close to whisper in the man's ear.

"Don't even think about shouting."

Kuupik shook his head.

Gaba plucked the mask from Kuupik's head, turning it in the light as he studied it. The form was identical to the stack of four masks pressed together in the snow, only the colour was different. Each mask was painted black but with different accents of red smeared beneath bulbous cheeks and twisted lips. It was the same mask pasted onto every public window in Nuuk. Gaba tossed it into the snow.

"How many groups are there, Kuupik?"

"What?"

"Don't make me mad," Gaba said. He slapped Kuupik's cheek.

"Are you police?"

"I'm retired," he said. Gaba smiled at the thought of an old friend who used to say the same.

"Then why do you want to know?"

"That's two questions too many," Gaba said. He slapped Kuupik a second time. "How about you try again. How many groups?"

"Fifteen," Kuupik said.

"And thirty people in each?"

Kuupik nodded.

"About thirty," he said.

Gaba did the math. He plucked the baton from the snow and tapped Kuupik's head as he counted.

"You're telling me, that there's over four hundred idiots like you with masks and sticks running around in my city?"

Kuupik stared at him, and Gaba tapped his head one more time, hard.

"*Aap*," Kuupik said. "But it's not *your* city. Not for much longer."

"No?"

"We're taking it back."

Kuupik glanced at the baton as Gaba stabbed it into the snow.

"You're taking it back?" Gaba nodded. "Okay, you've got my attention. Enlighten me. Just who are you taking it back from?"

"The corrupt politicians."

"Corrupt?"

"All of them. Especially that bitch, Uutaaq."

"You mean the bitch that has been working towards Greenlandic independence since she left high school? That *bitch*?"

"She's not doing it for us. It's all for her. She just wants the spotlight on her. She wants the rewards too. All the…"

Gaba slapped Kuupik hard. He pressed his fingers into his cheeks, prising his teeth apart.

"See that kind of talk does make me a little mad. But you're entitled to be stupid. I might even forgive you if you co-operate." Gaba relaxed his grip. "You said you are one of the leaders. How about you tell me where I can find your boss?"

Kuupik's face twisted beneath Gaba's grip, his eyes widened. Gaba let go and studied his face. He peered into Kuupik's eyes and leaned in close. Gaba sniffed twice and pulled back.

"You're scared, Kuupik. Is it your boss who scares you? More than I do? Now, that's interesting. How about you tell me about her?"

"I don't know anything," Kuupik said, as Gaba reached for the baton. "Hey, you can hit me as hard as you want, and I still won't know anything."

"You're that scared of him?" Gaba paused as Kuupik looked away. "Or maybe it's not a *he*? Who's your boss, Kuupik? Who's calling the shots?"

"I don't know her name."

"No?" Gaba shifted his knee onto Kuupik's chest.

"I don't." Kuupik gasped for air and Gaba lifted his knee. "I don't even know where she is. Not in Nuuk. Not all the time. We get messages in the DataStream. If we meet with anyone, it's her partner."

"Her partner?" Gaba reached for the baton.

"He's our contact. His name is Angut," Kuupik said, his voice louder.

Gaba glanced over his shoulder, and then leaned closer.

"Angut *who?*" he asked.

"Just Angut."

"Describe him."

"Tall, like you," Kuupik said. "And mean…"

"Like me?" Gaba laughed. "I'm actually beginning to like you, Kuupik. Maybe I'll let you go, so you can have some fun with your friends tonight. If you just tell me a little more, a few details. We'll keep it between you and me." Gaba lowered his voice. "Angut doesn't need to know. Neither does your boss. What was her name? Natuk, maybe?"

Gaba smiled as Kuupik squirmed beneath him.

"How do you know her name?" he asked.

"So, I'm right?"

"I didn't say that," Kuupik said. "I didn't say anything."

"No," Gaba said. "I have to do all the work."

Gaba cursed at a sudden crick in his knee and shifted his weight to one side. Kuupik felt him move and grabbed a handful of snow. He cast it into Gaba's face as he jerked his body to one side and rolled free of Gaba's body. Kuupik scrambled to his feet. He turned and kicked Gaba in the chest as the older man rocked back onto his heels. Kuupik sprinted for the main road as Gaba fell back into the snow.

"That was all kinds of stupid," Gaba said, as he watched Kuupik run around the corner. Gaba picked up the baton and brushed the snow from the shaft. He tucked it into his jacket, slipped a mask over his head, and ran after Kuupik.

Gaba slid at the corner. He grabbed a wooden fence for support and scanned the road. He saw Kuupik flailing with the gait of a weekend warrior. Gaba grinned behind the mask and ran after him. Kuupik looked over his shoulder as Gaba closed the distance between them, stumbling and slipping on the compacted snow, he sprawled onto the road. Gaba grabbed the back of Kuupik's jacket and pulled him to his feet. He pushed him across the road, slapping his head with his free hand.

"I'm mad now, Kuupik," he said.

Slap.

"You know what that means?"

Slap.

Gaba dragged Kuupik around an SUV parked in the snow. He slammed the younger man's body against the side of the car and pressed the palm of his hand beneath his chin, pushing upwards as he spread Kuupik's legs with a swift kick to each ankle.

"You know what people call me?" Gaba said, as Kuupik trembled. "They call me the *pit bull*." Gaba's breath was hot behind the mask and he pushed it up over his face and onto his bald head. "I don't mind the name; it kind of fits," he said. "Something you're about to find out."

"I don't know anything," Kuupik said.

"You're lying."

Gaba pushed Kuupik's head backwards into the snow on the roof of the SUV.

"You've told me how many. Now I want to know where, when… Tell me the plan, Kuupik, or your part in it ends right now, right here."

"They'll kill me if I tell you."

"And I'll kill you if you don't. Your choice."

Gaba turned his head at the sight of a third group of demonstrators. Kuupik followed his gaze and began to laugh.

"You think this is funny?" Gaba said. He pressed his face close to Kuupik's. "We just have to work faster, that's all." Gaba looked at the group again, judging the distance. There was about forty metres of road between them. Not enough. He let go of Kuupik when the demonstrators at the front of the group began to shout and point.

"Who's the idiot now," Kuupik said, as he slid down the side of the car.

Gaba reached inside his jacket and silenced him with a swift blow from the baton. He extended the baton and then pulled his mobile from his pocket. Gaba swiped through the list of contacts and pressed Petra's avatar. He pressed his mobile to his ear and started to run.

"Petra," he said, when she answered. "We've got a problem."

Chapter 20

The broad utility belt pressed down on Natuk's hips as she slipped the regulation Heckler and Koch USP Compact pistol into the holster and her own FNS 40 into a holster strapped above her left ankle. Natuk adjusted the belt, tugged her police sweater over the light blue shirt and pulled her jacket off the hook beside the bathroom mirror. She stared at her reflection as she pulled on the jacket. She had worn the uniform for much of her adult life, and, regardless of her foster mother's ulterior motives, Natuk had been proud to wear it, and privately pleased with the role of keeper of the peace in Greenland. *Except now, on my birthday*, she thought, *I intend to disturb that peace in the worst way.* Natuk zipped her jacket and stepped out of the bathroom, it was time to wake Viola.

Natuk stepped lightly into Viola's cabin. She held her breath as she watched her sleep, pushing a darker stream of thoughts from her mind. Natuk stooped beneath the cot, and pressed her lips to Viola's forehead. She kissed her nose and brushed her cheek, sitting down on the bed as Viola stirred. Natuk smoothed Viola's hair against her head and smiled as Viola opened her eyes.

"What time is it?"

"Early."

Viola blinked as she propped herself up on one elbow. The smile on her lips faded as she looked at Natuk. "Why are you looking at me like that?"

"Like what?"

"Like you're sad or something."

"I'm not sad," Natuk said.

"But you look it."

Natuk leaned over and kissed Viola on the lips, teasing Viola's bottom lip between her teeth. She pulled away and stood up.

"I promised you breakfast," she said. "You've got five minutes."

"Ah, you're so evil," Viola said.

Natuk paused at the door. "Am I?" she whispered.

She turned away as Viola slipped her slim legs over the side of the bed and walked into the kitchen area. The door to her foster mother's cabin was closed, locked from the outside. Natuk allowed herself a smile at the thought. She had busted her out of the detention centre only to lock her away onboard the trawler. She remembered arguing the logic with Angut, that it was a matter of control.

"Timing is key if the play is to be a success," she had said. "I need all the actors to perform their lines at the precise moment. I can't do that if they are beyond my reach."

Angut had grunted something about him just being an actor in some stupid play, but Natuk had ignored him, just as he was ignoring her now, choosing to stay up top with the Captain, leaving Natuk and the women below decks.

"It's just as well," she said, as she turned the eggs on the pan. She pressed two slices of bread into the toaster. "There's no use complicating things by giving him more lines."

"What about *lines*?" Viola asked. She squirmed onto the bench seat and slid into the corner. Viola rested one arm on the table as she picked at a crumb of sleep in the corner of her eye. Natuk pulled a pair of thick-rimmed glasses from her jacket pocket and slid them across the table.

"I've prepared your speech," she said, as she carried two plates of bacon, eggs and toast to the table. "Just put your glasses on. You'll find the icon at the bottom of the lens on the right.

"These things give me a headache," Viola said.

"You get used to it."

Natuk made coffee as Viola ate. She listened as the younger woman rehearsed a little of the speech, encouraging her with tips for more stress on some of the words, less on others.

"Is this what you believe?" Viola asked when she was finished. She let the autocorrect function adjust the lenses to compensate for her eyesight and looked at Natuk.

"*Aap.*"

"You think the current government is corrupt."

"Corrupt or corrupted," Natuk said. "It's the same thing."

"But why do you want me to say it? Why not you?"

Natuk smiled. She handed Viola a mug of coffee and then gestured at her police jacket. "Look at me, Viola. I represent the *system*. I can't make that speech."

"Then take it off."

"Now?" Natuk raised her eyebrows. "Here?"

"You know what I mean," Viola said. She turned the mug on the table, as if searching for words with each revolution. "I just don't understand why it has to be me?"

"Because you're the face of the future." Natuk slid onto the seat beside Viola. She took her hand. "You're young, pretty and strong."

"I'm a student."

"You're clever, smart..."

"I'm going to be a journalist."

"The voice of the people."

A strand of Viola's hair slipped across her cheek as she shook her head. "I've got nothing to say."

"They'll listen anyway," Natuk said. She brushed the hair from Viola's cheek. "Stick to the speech. You can read it from the glasses. I'll be with you, in the DataStream, in the left lens."

"You're not going to be with me? I mean, physically?" Viola pushed away from Natuk and pressed her finger into Natuk's chest, the jacket pillowed at her touch. "Why are you wearing a uniform?"

"We each have our parts to play today. This is mine."

"A police officer?"

"Representing the system and the government, yes."

"I don't understand." Viola took off the glasses and pointed at the DataStream on the lens. "You created all this. You've got people protesting all over the city. It should be you leading the people. You're the one they will follow. Not me."

"You're wrong, Viola. But you're also right, about some things at least. I might be able to pull some strings, but I can't do everything. Once people find out that I am a police officer, then all this will be for nothing. I can't let that happen. I need you to lead them..."

"I can't..."

"Yes, you can. Just far enough for them to begin to lead themselves. This is about giving power to the people, giving them the chance to ask questions and make demands. It's all about the future, Viola, a future you can give them. They'll listen to you. They'll follow you, and, when they're ready, they will take matters into their own hands."

"When will that be?"

"Soon," Natuk said. "Sooner than you think."

"They'll take over?"

"*Aap*. I promise you they will."

"How?"

Natuk bit her bottom lip. She stared at Viola and said, "Don't think about it. Not now." Natuk slid off the seat and stood up. She glanced at the door to Anna's cabin, and then pointed at Viola's jacket hanging from a hook on the bulkhead between the cabins. "It's cold outside," she said.

Viola pushed her mug to one side and slid around the seat. She crossed the deck and stuffed her arms into her thick quilted jacket.

"What about my mask?" she said, pointing at the mask on the hook.

"You won't need it today," Natuk said, stuffing the mask into the cargo pocket of her trousers.

Natuk pulled on her boots and tied the laces as she waited for Viola to do the same. When Viola nodded that she was ready, Natuk took her hand and led her up the stairs to the wheelhouse. She whispered to Angut that they were ready and told the Captain to stay at the dock until she got back. Angut stopped her at the door.

"You haven't seen the feed?" he asked, tapping the rim of his glasses.

"What about?"

"Natsi's been trying to contact you. He found him."

"Qallu?" Natuk said.

"*Aap*. He's got a room at the Hotel Hans Egede. The night porter saw him."

Natuk dipped her head once at Angut, and then opened the door to the deck. Viola cringed at the sudden breath of cold that flicked at the loose strands of hair beneath her hat. Natuk took a deep breath and stepped over the lip of the door. She beckoned for Viola to come, and then led her down the gangplank to the SUV parked beside the dock.

"We have a short stop to make," she said, as she climbed in behind the wheel and Viola sat down on the passenger seat. "Stay in the car and rehearse your speech."

Natuk drove to the hotel, turning quickly onto a back road to avoid a group of masked revellers marching down the street and parked around the back. Viola shivered as Natuk opened the car door.

"You'll be fine," Natuk said. "Just rehearse your lines."

"Where will you be?"

"There's something I have to do. It won't take long."

Natuk closed the door and jogged around the car to the hotel's rear entrance. She waved her police ID card at the camera and waited for the night manager to buzz her in.

"Can I help you, officer?" he said, as Natuk approached the desk.

"I need to leave a message for one of my colleagues."

The night manager nodded and tapped the screen of his computer to open a new document. "What's the message?" he asked.

"It's more of a *thing*," Natuk said. She pulled Viola's mask from her pocket and placed it on the night manager's desk. "It's evidence. They'll know what to do with it." Natuk shrugged as the night manager frowned at the mask. "I'm on a call. I don't have the time to get it to the station. The duty officer said I could leave it here on my way."

"You can't take it up to your colleague?"

"I don't have time. They know it's here. I'm sure they'll be down soon to pick it up."

The night manager turned his head and looked out of the window. Natuk nodded as he gestured at the revellers passing on the street.

"*Aap,*" she said. "It's related." Natuk tapped the desk and took a step backwards.

"I'll send the night porter up and ask your colleague to come down and pick it up."

"It's important that they collect it. I trust you to give it them personally."

"You can rely on me."

"*Qujanaq,*" Natuk said. She walked towards the rear entrance, and, when the night manager turned away, she slipped into the hall and pressed the button for the elevator. Natuk stepped inside as the doors opened and slipped her glasses onto her face. She found the message from the porter in the DataStream. Qallu had a room on the fourth floor. Natuk pressed the button for the third. She turned her head away from the camera in the ceiling of the elevator, flicked her eyes onto the messaging icon and dialled Assa at the store.

"What do you need?" he asked.

"I'm at Hotel Hans Egede. I need you to loop the security feed from all cameras thirty minutes ago. A ten-minute loop should be sufficient."

"You want me to patch it in now?"

"*Aap.* Override the recording function and erase the last ten minutes and the next five."

"Is that all you need?"

"That's all."

Natuk slipped her glasses into her pocket as the elevator slowed. She peered into the corridor as the elevator doors opened. Natuk stepped into the corridor and checked the display above the elevator as the doors closed. She waited for it to continue to the fourth floor and then took the stairs. Natuk saw the police officer guarding Qallu's door step into the elevator on the fourth floor. She waited for the doors to close and then drew the FNS 40 pistol from her ankle holster. Natuk stood to one side of the door to Qallu's room and knocked. She took a breath as he padded to the door. She breathed out as he opened it.

"What is it?" he said, as he looked out of the room.

Natuk twisted around the door and slapped Qallu's chest with the palm of her hand. She pointed the pistol at his head as he recoiled into the room. She slapped him again, harder, forcing him onto his bed. Natuk grabbed a pillow from the chair beside the desk and pressed it against Qallu's chest as she straddled his body. Natuk shoved the barrel of the pistol into the pillow and fired once before moving the pillow and firing a second time into Qallu's face. Natuk took a second to search for the bullet casings, slipping them into her jacket pocket as she stepped off Qallu's body and walked to the door. She stepped into the corridor and closed the door softly behind her. Natuk slipped the pistol into the ankle holster, walked down the corridor and took the stairs to the rear entrance of the hotel. She opened the door and jogged to the car.

"That was quick," Viola said, as Natuk closed got in and closed the driver's door.

"Yep."

"Are you alright?"

"I'm fine."

Natuk glanced in the mirror, saw a spot of blood on her cheek and wiped it off with the back of her hand. She started the engine and pulled away from the hotel.

"Where are we going now?" Viola asked.

"To join the demonstration. It's time for you to make your speech."

Chapter 21

Petra wrote a note for Quaa and her mother as she drank her morning coffee. She left it on the kitchen table, grabbed her keys and pulled on her jacket. Petra stopped as she felt the jacket's familiar greasy texture beneath her fingers. *Not today*, she thought, pushing the stray feelings of guilt to one side as she hung Maratse's old police jacket on the hook and took her own. She left the apartment and locked the door before she could change her mind.

The bus was busier than she had expected, but then most people were back at work now, and school would start soon. Petra stared through the stencil of the mask on the window at the dirty snow lining the street. Someone had tried to remove the stencil, but the image remained, only thinner, more translucent. Petra pressed the button to get off the bus as it neared Hotel Hans Egede. She stepped out of the middle door and into a shallow drift of snow, zipped her jacket to her chin and walked towards the entrance. A shout and the clump of a car door shutting turned her head.

"Don't you have a car?" Seabloom asked as he negotiated a patch of ice between his car and Petra.

"I like the bus," she said. "It makes me feel closer to the…"

"City?"

"I was going to say people, but I guess it's the same." Petra waited for Seabloom to join her. "Is this a pleasant coincidence or are you here on business?"

"Business? I don't know about that, but it is always a pleasure to see you, Petra."

Petra shook her head slightly, shaking thick snowflakes from her hair and a small flurry of guilty thoughts from her mind. *It's too soon,* she thought.

I was sick for a long time, Piitalaat.

"I know, but…"

"What do you know?" Seabloom asked.

"Nothing," Petra said. She started to say more but stopped at the sight of a group of people in masks at the top of the street. *Aqqusinersuaq* rose slightly in elevation from the hotel to the Post Office at the top of a small hill, and a group of about thirty people stood to one side of the street. It looked like they were waiting for something and Petra wondered if the officers on the night shift knew about them. She spotted a patrol car on the opposite side of the street. Petra checked her watch. It was close to the end of their shift.

"You've seen them then?" Seabloom said.

"Just now."

"They are all over the city. They're wearing the same masks as the protestors on the bridge." He gestured at his car with a wave of a thickly-mittened hand. "We've ratcheted the base security up a notch, and I have three men in the car, including the driver." Seabloom turned to look at the masked figures on the hill. "What do you think?"

"It's a little early for *mitaartut*," Petra said. She smiled at the thought of Quaa and Iiluuna surprising her the evening before. They were early too, but the figures on the hill didn't move, making them that bit more sinister.

"What?"

"It's a tradition. Normally, I wouldn't be worried, but they're not supposed to be out before the evening, and they usually don't go around in such big groups."

"Well, they've spooked your neighbours. We passed guards on the road in and out of Chinatown and Little Amsterdam. I think the incident at the bridge has everyone on edge." Seabloom grinned. "Which is a good thing."

"It is?"

"Based on the unrest we experienced yesterday, I was able to tap into a whole new budget. The three guys in the car are just one part of it."

"I don't understand," Petra said.

"It means the US Coast Guard is ready to assist. I'm here to help, Petra," he said. "I think your First Minister will be pleased to hear that." He nodded at the hotel. "Shall we go inside?"

"You're here to meet with Pipaluk?"

"I've been summoned," Seabloom said. He waited for Petra to walk inside the building and walked beside her to the lift. The night manager waved at her from behind his desk.

"Excuse me," he said. "May I speak with you for a moment?"

"I'll be right there," Petra said to Seabloom. She walked to the desk as he waited by the lift.

"Is this about the First Minister?" Petra asked. "I'm supposed to meet her in her suite."

"No, Commissioner," the night manager said. Colour rushed to his cheeks. "I wasn't thinking. I thought you were a police officer."

"I *am* a police officer," Petra said. She glanced at the man's hands as he tucked something into one of the alcoves on the desk. "What's that?"

"It's a mask. I thought you had been sent to pick this up. The officer said the station would send someone to collect it. He wasn't supposed to leave the hotel."

"Slow down," Petra said, and held up her hand. "Which officer?"

"The one guarding the room on the fourth floor."

"The First Minister is on the fifth floor." Petra frowned. She turned as Seabloom approached the desk, switching to English to explain the situation.

"So, your officer is guarding the wrong door?"

"No," the duty manager said. His English was broad and soft like Seabloom's. "There are currently two officers guarding rooms in the hotel. The First Minister is in one of them. I apologize for any confusion."

"And the second?" Petra asked.

"I don't know his name."

"His?"

"Yes. The police officer on the fourth floor is guarding a man."

"And he told you that someone would be in to pick up the mask?"

"The police officer did, yes." The night manager sighed. "My shift is nearly over. I'm sorry, it has been a long night. What with the breach in our security and…"

"What breach?" Seabloom asked.

"We have lost ten minutes of video footage," the night manager said. "He tapped the mask. "Actually, it was about the time that the police officer delivered this."

"Another police officer?"

"Yes, a woman."

"Can I see it?" Petra held out her hand and the night manager gave her the mask. She turned it in her fingers and tugged a single short hair from beneath the elastic strap. "Blonde," she said, as she held it up to the light. "I'll take this with me." Petra studied the mask as she walked to the elevator.

"You need a bag for that hair?" Seabloom asked. "An evidence bag," he said, as Petra frowned.

Petra shook her head and tucked the hair inside a small zipped pocket on the front of her jacket. She turned the mask towards Seabloom as he pressed the button for the fifth floor.

"It's the same as the stencil," she said.

"It's pretty ugly."

Petra smiled as she held it up in front of her face. The elevator stopped, and the doors opened, followed by a shriek. Petra lowered the mask to see the First Minister take a step back into the corridor.

"Commissioner," she said, as she recovered. The police officer beside her hid a smile behind his hand. "You're late. I was just on my way down to see if you were in the lobby."

"I thought we should meet in your suite?"

Petra lowered the mask and shot a look at the officer. He took a second to compose himself and then stepped back into the corridor.

"Well, now you're here," Pipaluk said, "we may as well continue." She stepped into the elevator, nodding at Seabloom as he made space for her. The police officer squeezed in as Petra moved back.

"We're not meeting in your suite?" she asked.

"I want to introduce you to someone first," Pipaluk said.

"On the fourth floor?"

"How did you know?"

"First Minister," Petra said. "How you manage your own people is up to you but assigning police officers to special duties is way beyond your remit." Petra unzipped her jacket as the elevator warmed up with the heat of four bodies. The elevator doors opened, and she followed the police officer into the corridor.

"I made an executive decision," Pipaluk said, as she exited the elevator. "I have that privilege."

"Not with my people, you don't." Petra spotted the police officer guarding a room at the end of the corridor. She walked towards him.

"Exceptional circumstances demand immediate action," Pipaluk said. "I found myself in an exceptional situation and I acted. Which is far more than I can say about you and your police force, *Commissioner*. If the rumours of your pending retirement are true, I suggest you hurry it along before I'm forced to make more decisions without your knowledge."

"You can't…"

"Can't I?" Pipaluk stopped outside the door, shoving the police officers to one side with a single look. "Once this country is truly independent, I think you'll find there are many things I can do, with or without your knowledge."

"Excuse me," Seabloom said. "I might not have understood a word of what you have been *discussing*." Seabloom let the last word linger before adding, "But I would like to know why I am here, and what we're doing outside this hotel room?"

Pipaluk changed her tone and softened the smile on her face. She took a moment and then lifted her hand to the door to knock. She knocked three times.

"My assistant was given a tip yesterday. The man in this room came to us with information about the ringleader of this little uprising." Pipaluk gestured at the mask in Petra's hand. "He was concerned for his own safety, and I took the decision to protect him."

"How long have you had this information?" Petra asked.

"I haven't got it yet. He wanted to be assured of his safety before telling me."

"Telling you what?" Seabloom asked.

"The name of the ringleader." Pipaluk's forehead creased as she knocked on the door a second time. "I can't believe he is sleeping. We promised to put him on a plane to Denmark a few hours from now." She stepped back as the police officer entered a code into the number pad on the door. He drew the pistol from his holster a second after he opened the door.

"First Minister," Petra said. "I think you should wait with your protection officer."

Seabloom unsnapped the buttons of his coat and pulled a large pistol from a shoulder holster. He followed the police officer inside the room.

"Ma'am, I think you'd better see this."

Petra stepped into the room, squinting in the darkness. She reached for the switch on the wall and turned on the light. There was relatively little blood compared to the mess one might expect from the bullet holes in the man's head and chest. Petra looked at the pillow tossed to one side when Seabloom pointed at it.

"A silencer?" he said, with a shrug.

"Call it in," Petra said to the officer. "First Minister, would you come in here, please."

"Petra," Seabloom said. "Is that smart?"

"She took an executive decision. I think she should see the consequences."

Pipaluk pressed her hand to her mouth as she stepped into the room. She looked at Petra and turned to leave.

"Not yet," Petra said, as she took the First Minister's hand. "I want you to look at him."

"But your police officer was outside the door," Pipaluk said, her voice quieter than it had been in the corridor. "He's your responsibility."

"And *he* was yours," Petra said with a wave at the dead man on the bed. "If I had known about this, I could have protected him down at the station."

"He didn't want the police to be involved."

"Well, they are now," Seabloom said. He opened his coat and slid the large pistol back into the holster. He flicked his gaze to the media screen mounted on the wall as it turned itself on and the image of the protestors at the top of the street flickered into focus. "What's that?"

A young woman's voice drifted into the room, and the rooms above, opposite and to each side of them as all the media screens in every room of the hotel tuned into the same broadcast.

"That's the girl from the press conference," Pipaluk said.

Petra watched as the young woman, the only one not wearing a mask, stood in front of a group of what looked like hundreds of protestors.

"My name is Viola," she said, as she brushed a snowflake from the lens of her thick-rimmed glasses, "and I have something to say."

Chapter 22

A fresh wind curled a cloud of snow from the rooftop above the back of the nightclub, dumping it on top of Gaba Alatak as he pressed his body against the wall. A group of revellers ran past, the soles of their winter boots thudding across the hard snow pressed into the road, their breath streaming through the holes in their masks like dragon steam. Gaba waited until they had passed, brushed the snow from his shoulders and head, and then stepped out from beneath the roof and onto the street. The corners of his lips wrinkled as he remembered running down a similar street in his youth as the older boys in the town chased him on *mitaartut*. Gaba struggled to remember if it was thirty-five or forty years ago. Probably both. He let the memory linger as far as the corner of the street.

The sounds of the revellers disappeared as he moved deeper into a residential area, further from the centre of Nuuk, and further from the more affluent areas. The grey dawn pushed the black of night into the shadows and cast an eerie light onto the tired apartment blocks, smaller wooden houses, and one L-shaped house in particular. Gaba wiped a soft clump of snow from his bushy eyebrows and stared at what looked like a man dragging a body by the ankles. Gaba almost laughed as he realised the man was wearing some kind of Japanese housecoat. His long hair was bound in a bun at the back of his head, and smoke poured from his lips as he huffed his way across the snow surrounding the house, ploughing a line to the road with the torso and head of the body.

Drunk, Gaba thought, and then he saw the trail of blood in the snow. He took several quiet steps towards the man and then stopped beside a car, waiting for the man to drag the body towards him.

"Natsi?" Gaba said, as the man drew close enough for him to recognise him. "Natsi Hermansen?"

Natsi let go of the dead man's ankles. The cigarette fell from his lips and smoked on the snow as he squinted at Gaba and then looked left and right as if he might start to run.

"Don't," Gaba said.

Natsi darted to the right. Gaba leaped forwards and planted the sole of his boot on the tail of Natsi's housecoat, stopping the middle-aged man in his tracks as he slipped and fell onto the ground. Gaba loomed over him and knelt beside him.

"I told you not to run."

"But you're a cop." Natsi's eyes darted to the left where the body lay in the snow.

"I used to be," Gaba said. He pointed at the body. "Who's your friend?"

"Not my friend. Never met him before tonight."

"No?" Gaba shook his head. "So, you killed a man the very first time you met him? That's not very nice, *Nasty*."

"No-one calls me that anymore."

"But no-one knows you like I do."

Natsi started to rise but Gaba placed his hand on his chest.

"I have a few questions."

"I'm cold."

"Then answer them quickly."

Natsi sighed and lay back in the snow.

"Who killed him?"

"A woman."

"When?"

"Earlier."

"Why?"

"I don't know. I just walked into the living room and she had a gun to his head, shouting. I think he tried to get it on with her friend." Natsi shivered for a second before he continued. "She was with this girl."

"Girl?"

"Young. Twenty-years-old, maybe."

"Okay, now I'm confused, Natsi. Start again. Were there two women?"

"*Aap.*"

"One of them was about twenty?"

"And she was the one he tried to screw," Natsi said. He jerked his thumb towards the dead body.

"And the other woman? You know her?"

Natsi nodded his head.

"What's her name?"

"Natuk."

Gaba looked away as he mouthed the name. Natsi tried to sit up, but he pushed him down again.

"Describe her."

"About twenty-five. Pretty, or she used to be, before she did her hair blonde."

"And how do you know her?"

"We had business together. She used to come around before. She'd help me out if I needed it, I returned the favour."

"What kind of help did you need?"

"You know, man, like when I had trouble with you and your kind."

"Police?"

"*Aap.*" Natsi laughed. "It was crazy, man. I mean she was one of you."

Gaba stood up and pulled Natsi to his feet. He nodded at the body, and said, "Where are you taking it?"

"I was going to put it in the skip, so no-one pinned it on me."

Gaba dipped his head and stared at Natsi. He pointed at the track of red snow leading from the house to the road.

"Shit, man, I'm not stupid. It's snowing. Now's the time to move it." He kicked one of the ankles. "You could help."

"Natsi."

"Sure, man," Natsi said. "If you help, then I'll tell you where to find Natuk. I can see you want to know. You've got that look in your eye, the old Sergeant Gaba hunting look. Everyone knows it. And I can see you got it bad for this girl. She's crazy like you. You'd make a good pair. Maybe you want to get it on and..."

Gaba clasped his hand around Natsi's thin throat. He choked the last of Natsi's sentence with a firm squeeze.

"I think you're going to tell me what you know, and then you're going to call the police." He loosened his grip. "Understand?"

"*Aap.*"

Gaba waited. Natsi looked down at the dead man's feet, then at Gaba, and down again.

"You're kidding?"

Natsi shook his head and Gaba let him go. He grabbed one of the dead man's ankles and waited for Natsi to do the same. Natsi smiled as they dragged the body towards the rubbish skip.

"Stop smiling, Natsi."

"I can't help it," he said, and laughed. "It just feels so good to be working together for a change, Sergeant."

Gaba let go of the body and pulled his mobile out of his pocket.

He dialled Petra's number as Natsi rolled the dead body up against the skip.

"Petra?" Gaba said, as she answered. "I've got a lead on Natuk. She's…" Gaba reached out to slap Natsi's arm. "Where's Natuk?"

"She's on a boat," Natsi said. "If she's not in the city."

"In Nuuk?"

"*Aap.* A fishing trawler. She moves around, but I seen her once down by the old dock."

Gaba took a step away from Natsi and pressed the phone against his ear. "She might be on a trawler at the other end of town. Can you send a patrol?"

"Did you say *might*," Petra said.

"What's that noise?" Gaba's forehead creased as he concentrated. "It sounds like you're in a crowd."

"Of protestors, yes. The city is full of them. We're stretched thin again, Gaba. I need everyone I've got on duty. I've pulled Atii off the search for the Ombudsman and Natuk."

"Listen, Petra, I'll check it out. I'll call if I find anything."

The call ended and Gaba stared at his phone. He looked up, tilting his head towards the centre of the city as the sound of shouting and chanting drifted towards him.

"The city's falling apart," Natsi said, and grinned.

Gaba glanced at the dead body and stabbed his finger into Natsi's chest.

"Call it in, today."

"Sure. Later today." Natsi pulled a crumpled packet of cigarettes from his pocket and shook a cigarette out of it. He lit it as Gaba walked away. "Let's do this again, Sergeant," Natsi called out. He grinned again and puffed a cloud of smoke into the snowflakes tumbling onto the street and covering the body by the skip.

Gaba started to jog towards the street on which he parked his car. The sound of hundreds of protestors grew louder as he jogged across a connecting street. He spotted his car, pulled out his keys and slowed to a stop beside it. Gaba opened the door and climbed behind the wheel. His mobile rang as he started the car and he put the call through the speakers.

"This is Gaba," he said, as he drove along the street, turning once, away from the protestors, on his way to the docks in the oldest part of the city, close to the church and the statue of Hans Egede.

"This is officer Aron Ulloriaq. We met in December. I'm the Commissioner's assistant."

"I remember. What do you want, Aron?"

"The Commissioner said you were looking for Natuk. I've been working through the DataStream, trying to find her."

"And?"

"If you're looking for a trawler at the docks, you want one with a hexagon at the top of the mast. It's a Stream booster."

"Like a box?"

"More like a star, open, you can put your hands through it."

"So, like more shrouds?"

"Shrouds?"

"Lines and cables. It won't stand out much, but thanks, anyway." Gaba pressed his finger on top of the button to end the call, and then hesitated. "Aron?"

"*Aap.*"

"Go and find Petra. She needs you."

Gaba ended the call as he spotted the church. He parked the car in the parking area and locked it. He paused to look at the fjord to the right of the church, and then turned his head slowly to the left. Several old wooden buildings obscured his view, but as he started to walk towards the water, he spotted the top of a mast peeping above the roofs. Gaba smiled when he saw thick cables shaped like a hexagon at the top.

"Well done, Aron," he whispered.

He stopped beside a rack of skin-on-frame *qajaq*s in front of the old medical station built in colonial times. Gaba had always been too big to fit inside the tiny round cockpit of a *qajaq*. At least, that's what he would tell people when they asked. The truth had more to do with not wanting to be so close to the water, preferring the stability of a boat to a thin, pointy hunting kayak.

Gaba brushed the snow from the bench next to the rack and studied the trawler. The wheelhouse was lit with a soft red glow and he could see the silhouette of a man sitting in the Captain's chair. The other man, taller with the same build as Gaba, was more interesting. Gaba watched the man walk across the deck to the bow. The distance was too great for details, but the man walked with the attitude of one employed to be the muscle.

"Or leader of the SRU," Gaba said with a smile. "Now, what are you doing onboard that ship and why aren't you in the city stirring up trouble with Natuk and her friends?"

It occurred to Gaba that Natuk might even be below decks on the trawler. *But then she would be missing out on the fun in the city.* He dismissed the thought, and stood up, intending to move closer once the Greenlandic gorilla on the deck returned to the wheelhouse.

Gaba retreated to the shadow of the *qajaq* rack as the grey sky lightened and the snowfall slowed to a light dusting of soft powdery crystals. A second silhouette inside the wheelhouse caught Gaba's eye and he watched as a third person stepped onto the deck. The man at the bow pointed at the wheelhouse. If he had been closer, Gaba imagined he might have heard the man shout something. The third person, a woman, strode defiantly across the deck until the man grabbed her by the shoulders and turned her around.

"Got you," Gaba said, as he caught a glimpse of the woman's face before the man pushed her inside the wheelhouse. It was a brief, but enough to convince Gaba that he had found Natuk's trawler, and he had found Ombudsman Anna Riis. Now all he had to do was get onboard. Gaba straightened at the thought, flexing his fingers in anticipation of another bout of action to stave off the boredom. His childhood memories of *mitaartut* resurfaced, but he tossed them aside in favour of the thought of a bigger, more powerful opponent.

Chapter 23

The city of Nuuk had grown over the years since Petra lived there, first as a child at the children's home, later as a police student, and now as Police Commissioner, but she could not remember ever seeing so many young people gathered in one place at the same time. She did a quick head count of the first row of protestors, ignoring the masks and sticks as she stepped out of the police SUV at the top of *Aqqusinersuaq*. Petra counted just under sixty people in the first row, and, if she stepped onto the bottom rim of the car, she could see four more rows of people behind the first, and a large gathering of people behind the last. They filled the road from the Post Office to the graveyard, blocking traffic, intimidating shoppers, office workers and the few tourists hardy enough to withstand a Greenlandic winter. Only the children seemed unafraid, the school-aged ones, they stared and pointed with wide-eyed fascination. Some of the braver boys and girls challenged the front row with mock charges, only to scurry away when they lifted their sticks.

Petra ignored the children for a moment and studied the sea of masks, all of them identical, all of them fierce. Only one protestor was unmasked, the young woman they called Viola. Petra watched as she took a step forwards, clasped her hands in front of her, and prepared to speak. That was when Petra noticed the drones, flitting into position to cover all the angles; they began broadcasting to the DataStream the moment Viola stepped forwards.

"I honestly don't know what to do, ma'am," Atii said as she joined Petra by the side of the SUV, she acknowledged Seabloom with a brief nod. She switched to English for his benefit. "I thought about forming a line as we did at the bridge, but we haven't got the numbers to resist."

"And even if I emptied the base," Seabloom said, "I'm not sure it would make much difference. Do you have water cannons?"

Petra almost laughed. "No," she said. "And we don't want to turn the street into an ice rink."

"No," he said. "I didn't think of that."

"Tear gas is out, too," Atii said. "We've just never had to deal with a demonstration on this scale." She shook her head. "I don't like it."

"I think," Petra said, "the decision has been made for us. We will just have to hear what she wants to say and take it from there. However…" She scanned the ranks of police officers and vehicles assembled in a hatched formation across the street. "I suggest equipping all officers with riot shields and body armour. Just do it quietly, Atii. I don't want to force their hand."

Atii nodded and jogged around the car to give the order. Petra watched as the Sergeants dispersed to organise the remaining officers. Seabloom stamped his feet as he watched the line. He grinned at Petra and she saw tiny beads of frost pearl around the hairs above his lip. There was a hush, and then Viola began to speak.

"I speak for the dispossessed," she said, her voice amplified by the drone hovering directly above her. "Those too old to be cared for, and too young to be heard. We are the middle generation of students and apprentices, the untrained and uneducated, the poorly paid, the homeless and the unemployed. We are Greenlanders, all of us, though we have no common tongue. We are Greenlanders, all, though we do not look the same, act the same, nor live the same way as our ancestors, not even our parents and grandparents. We are the post-colonials, the refuse and the unwanted, but we are the future. Ignore us at your peril, for we are not placid or weak. Our parents and grandparents agreed to laws that will outlive them and poison our future. They supported outdated ideas and older referendums when we were too young to vote, and they voted with their hearts, when they should have voted with their heads. Our heads may be young, but our minds are bright, and our hearts big enough to embrace the whole of Greenland, its mountains, the ice, glaciers, the rocks, the birds, beasts, the men, women and children of Greenland, now and in the future, ours, and theirs. But we will not be unheard, we will not be unseen, and we will not be idle." The rows of young men and women bristled, and their masks steamed with appreciative comments and enthusiastic laughs together with the turning and nodding of heads. Viola continued, "January 6th is the Epiphany, the manifestation of Christ. But it is also the day of *mitaartut* when we embrace our Greenlandic traditions and call upon our friends and our family to recognise us, challenging them to call us by our true names, no matter the disguise, the masks, or the paint. Today," she said, "we have had our epiphany, we have come to that great realisation that the future is ours, that we have more at stake than ever before, and that we will have our say, we will be heard." Viola paused as the young Greenlanders roared and shrieked. "We will decide our future, for us, for them," she said and pointed at the children, "and for you. Gone is the day of corrupt governments and hushed deals. Gone too is the day of the colonial power, the casual oppressors." She raised her fist, and said, "On this day, our *mitaartut*, we will call on you and you will recognise us. We will be recognised."

The front row took a step forward.

"We will be seen."

They raised the sticks in their hands.

"We will be heard."

Viola shuffled forwards as the front row parted to each side of her. Petra glanced at Atii and the police formed a line, two ranks deep. Gloved hands flexed around shields. Visors were pulled down to cover the officers' faces as the protestors took another step forward. Viola joined them.

"We will not be forgotten…"

Viola paused as a police officer, a woman, broke through the ranks of police shields. The officer stepped in front of Viola and placed her hand on the pistol holstered at her waist. Two drones flew in on either side of Viola, the dull light of day reflected in the large round camera lenses as the police officer drew her sidearm.

"Atii," Petra shouted, pointing at the police officer aiming her pistol at Viola's face. "Stop her."

Viola's eyes widened as she stared through the visor obscuring the police officer's face. The creases of fear on Viola's forehead softened as she recognised the face behind the gun. Atii burst through the police line as the officer held her pistol in a two-handed grip and fired.

"No," Petra shouted.

She took a step forward. Seabloom grabbed her arm and she jerked it free, stumbling towards the protestors as Viola slumped to the ground. Her blood pooled beneath her head, spreading across the smooth snow covering the road. The officer fired three more shots into the air above the crowd and the protestors scattered for a second, long enough for her to turn and kick Atii to the ground, before darting across the street, and disappearing between two patrol cars blocking a side street.

The protestors rallied, surging towards Atii as she scrambled to her feet. The police rushed forwards to meet them, locking their shields together to protect their Sergeant from an onslaught of sticks, boots and venom.

"Wait, Petra," Seabloom said. He reached for her again, but again she pulled free of his grasp.

Petra twisted to see Viola's body being dragged away from the clash of sticks and riot shields. She turned again to glimpse the back of the police officer running away from the street and picking her way between the rocks towards a long low block of apartments. Petra ran after her.

"Commissioner, wait."

Petra slowed long enough to see a police SUV skid to a stop a few metres to her right. Aron's breath steamed out of the open window as he fumbled with his seatbelt, opened the door and scrambled out of the driver's seat.

"Aron," she shouted, "you're with me."

"Don't be stupid, Petra."

Petra heard Seabloom's voice and ignored him. She focused on the distance between her and the police officer leaping between outcrops of rock poking out of the snow between the houses and apartments. The officer stopped to aim her pistol at the drone following her, disabling it with just a few shots, suggesting an intimacy with the design, and a flair for accuracy. She holstered her pistol and removed her helmet, tossing it to one side as the drone crashed into the side of the Post Office building. The shock of blonde hair surprised Petra, her breath catching in her throat as she recognised Natuk. The rogue officer's face was wet with tears, her lips wrenched with pain, and she glared at Petra for a split-second, before jumping off the rocky outcrop and skidding onto the icy street below. Petra caught her breath and gave chase.

"Ma'am," Aron said as he ran beside her. "Permission to run faster?"

"Granted," Petra said. She cursed her lack of activity during the winter months as Aron peeled away from her and chased Natuk deeper into the residential area. Petra jogged after him, pausing at the side of a building to rest, and then cursing again as she saw Natuk use a frozen drainpipe to climb onto a low asphalt roof, scattering ravens as she climbed onto the next longer roof covering the apartment block. Petra kept running.

"Ma'am."

Petra looked up as Aron reached down from the first low roof to take her hand. Her feet slipped on the drainpipe as she climbed, causing Aron to grunt as he pulled her up. They ran to the next roof together, the ravens cawing and flapping about their heads as Aron laced his fingers into a step for Petra to step onto. He lifted her up and she scrambled onto the roof. Aron joined her a second later and they pounded across the bare bitumen just as Natuk reached the gap between two roofs.

"She'll jump," Aron said, as she slowed to a jog. Petra slowed beside him. "I don't want to force her, ma'am," he said.

"Neither do I," Petra said.

She stopped as Natuk turned and drew her pistol. Aron reached for his, but Petra stopped him with a shake of her head and a cautionary wave of her hand.

"She's armed, ma'am."

"I'm not blind, Aron."

"I know, but…"

"There has to be another way," Petra said.

Natuk shifted her stance and took aim. Petra stopped. She looked at the young police officer, the woman she imagined to be a younger version of herself, so full of energy and opinions. *But I was but a shadow of Natuk*, she thought, as she considered just how determined Natuk was. *Determined enough to kill me*, she realised, *the one who murdered her brother.*

"Can we talk, Natuk?" Petra said. She motioned for Aron to stay on her right.

"I've got nothing to say, *ma'am*."

Her last word surprised Petra. It could be an act, some kind of diversion. But Petra hoped it was something else, a last vestige of hope, that Natuk – deep down – might still be the exemplary officer that she was, before she was corrupted and poisoned to pursue such a dangerous and tragic path. Petra remembered the photos on the Ombudsman's wall, the ones of Natuk and her twin brother sharing a birthday, several birthdays. She was reminded that the poisoning of Natuk's mind had begun long before she wore the uniform of a police officer, and long before she shot and killed that young woman in the street, only moments ago.

"Help me, Aron," Petra whispered. "Give me something."

Aron scuffed his shoe as he shifted his balance from one foot to the other. He stared at Natuk, and then whispered out of the corner of his mouth. "Today is her birthday," he said. "She's twenty-six."

Twenty-six, Petra thought, *and already she is a murderer and a revolutionary.* Petra pressed her hands to her sides and took a deep breath. *She's also one of mine*, she thought, and took a step forwards.

Chapter 24

Gaba waited until the big Greenlander disappeared below decks, pushing the smaller, frailer figure of Ombudsman Anna Riis in front of him. Gaba could have walked towards the trawler, but he decided that when the Captain noticed him, he would have plenty of time to decide if he should leave the dock and drive out to sea. *No*, Gaba thought, *I may as well run. If nothing else, it might make him panic.* Gaba jogged across the short beach to the rocks beneath the parking area and the old wooden dock. The pounding of his boots on the slippery wooden slats vibrated through the dock and into the hull of the trawler, the Captain looked up just as Gaba gripped the rail and vaulted onto the deck. He slid on the icy surface all the way to the wheelhouse and wrenched the door open.

The Captain grabbed a pistol from a holster glued to the side of a wood panel below the windows of the bridge; he turned and fired, clipping Gaba's shoulder. Gaba cursed as he crossed the short deck to the Captain's chair. He closed his fist around the pistol, pulled it free of the Captain's grip, and slammed it into the man's forehead. The Captain slumped to the deck, as Gaba held the pistol in front of him on his way to the stairs leading below decks.

A short burst of bullets ripped through the door at the bottom of the stairs forcing Gaba to take cover behind the nearest bulkhead. He held the pistol in a tight two-handed grip and peered around the bulkhead only to snap his head back at the sight of the Greenlander below decks taking aim. Gaba slid away from the stairs and rolled to the door as a second, longer burst of fire forced him to open the door to the working area of the trawler behind the wheelhouse. Gaba slipped on the rime ice coating the steps and roared as he scraped his shin on the last step. He stumbled across the deck towards the thick plastic fish bins lashed to the trawler's starboard side. The Greenlander shoved the rear door open with the muzzle of a submachine gun – a Heckler and Koch MP5, Gaba's preferred weapon of choice.

Gaba leaned against the fish bin and allowed himself a short chuckle. The last few years running Âmo Security had been dull compared to the last few minutes. He had tried convincing himself that he was a father now, that he was getting too old for this game, but he missed it. He might even admit to being more or less addicted to the thrill of action. Atii knew it, and she told him about it at every opportunity.

"One day it will get the better of you," she had said, "and where will that leave me and the boys?"

She was right, Gaba just hadn't realised that day had come. He listened for the Greenlander's footsteps, some indication that he was moving across the deck. But it was quiet, apart from the distant sounds of cheering, or shouting, coming from the city centre.

He's waiting, Gaba thought. *Clever man.*

"That's what I'd do," Gaba called out. "Find a good position and wait."

"What do you know about it?" the Greenlander said.

Gaba turned his head slightly and imagined the man to be hiding in cover on the port side of the trawler, somewhere beneath the wheelhouse.

"I used to do this for a living," Gaba said.

"And now?"

"Now?" Gaba laughed. "More of a hobby really."

"Dangerous hobby."

"Tell me about it. My wife wants me to quit." Gaba waited for the man to speak, or move, perhaps both. When nothing happened, he tried again. "My name's Gaba Alatak."

"Angut."

"Just Angut?"

"Samuelsen."

Gaba checked the magazine in the pistol. The weight of it suggested it was half full, with another round in the chamber. About six shots, if he was being generous. More likely there were just five.

Not enough.

"Samuelsen? You related to Sammy Samuelsen?"

"*Naamik.*"

"No? How about Jens Jensen?"

Gaba flicked his head at the sound of movement, footsteps, a slow, almost silent shuffle across the deck.

"You're starting to annoy me," Angut said.

His voice was closer, as if he had crossed the deck. Gaba stuck the barrel of the pistol over the lip of the bin and fired a snapshot before rolling to his left. Gaba fired again, clipping Angut's knee. Gaba's third shot caught him in the shin and the fourth in his thigh as he worked his way up the man's body. Gaba aimed at Angut's chest as the Greenlander raised the MP5. The pistol was lighter in Gaba's hand, he should have known that all his bullets were spent, but he pulled the trigger anyway, and then launched himself at Angut as the MP5 stuttered another three-round burst. The bark was worse than the bite as the cold air seemed to press the rapid crack of the submachine gun down upon the deck, the weapons fire echoed around the sides of the trawler as Gaba landed on Angut's body and slammed his fist into the Greenlander's knee. He reached for the MP5 but received an elbow in his face instead. Gaba spluttered a gob full of blood from his mouth and scrabbled across the slippery deck as Angut cursed his mangled leg, reached for the railings and pulled himself to his feet. He kicked Gaba in the head as he crawled towards him.

"I've heard of you," Angut said, as he aimed a second kick at Gaba, catching the retired SRU Sergeant in the jaw. "You're the dog that killed Ooqi."

Gaba rolled out of Angut's reach, scrabbling to his feet as Angut pulled himself along the railings towards the rear door of the wheelhouse. Gaba wondered why he didn't fire. He saw Angut wince as he reached for a spare magazine in the cargo pocket of his trousers. Gaba wiped the blood from his face with the back of his hand and launched himself at Angut, slamming him into the railing. The magazine splashed into the water. Gaba ignored Angut's blows to his head and grabbed Angut's good leg, the one without the bullet holes and blood. He lifted it as Angut shifted his grip on the railing and used his elbow to beat down on Gaba's neck. Gaba roared as he lifted Angut up and over the side of the railing. He kicked at Angut's bloody shin, and again as Angut faltered. Gaba twisted and shoved Angut over the side. The big Greenlander slammed into the side of the trawler, gripping the railing with one hand, reaching with the other.

"I was wrong," Gaba said, as he grabbed the MP5 by the sling and pulled it over Angut's head. "I never heard of you." He held the submachine gun by the barrel and slammed the butt into Angut's fingers. "I don't know you." He hit Angut's fingers a second time. "And I don't need to know you, either." Angut spat as he slid down the side of the trawler. The splash he made in the water sent a small wave that rippled into the smooth chunks of ice bobbing by the side of the boat. Gaba lowered the MP5 and waited for Angut to slip beneath the surface. "It *is* a dangerous hobby," he said, as he gritted his teeth and walked to the wheelhouse door.

Gaba tossed the submachine gun onto a bench just inside the door. He checked the wound on his arm, explored his jaw and nose with tentative fingers, stopping when he heard the bone in his nose crackle. He wiped the blood on his trousers and shuffled to the top of the stairs, tilting his head at the sound of raised voices and a single shot. There was another shot and more voices, identical to the first, almost as if they were looped. Gaba climbed down the stairs and pushed at the door into the living area below decks.

Anna Riis was thinner than Gaba remembered. The last time he had seen her, she was entertaining the Dutch Jonkheer in her cosy wooden residence close to the water. She was even closer to the water now, but there was nothing cosy about her surroundings. Anna Riis' legs were sprawled on the floor at odd angles, as if she had been shoved and did not have the strength to stand. She leaned against the side of the bench seat beside the table and watched a video sequence looping on the media screen mounted to the bulkhead. Gaba heard the shot, saw the close-up of the police officer, a woman in full riot gear, her pistol extended in front of her in a two-handed grip. The camera switched to a different angle catching a young woman's fall as the bullet from the police officer's gun punctured her skull and removed the better part of the back of her head. Gaba saw the mess on the snow beneath the young woman's head, recognised it for what it was, and then stared at the screen as the camera switched to a third angle, showing the police rushing forwards to protect an officer on the ground.

"Atii," he said, and took a step towards the screen.

"It's alright," Anna said. "They save her. Although the police take a beating. You'll see it in the next sequence, after another close-up of the girl." She turned her head to look at Gaba. "They call her Viola. She's a martyr now. Greenland's first."

Anna took Gaba's hand when he offered it to her. She pushed down on the seat as he pulled her up. Anna perched at the edge of the seat, her back to the media screen, as Gaba slumped onto the bench opposite her.

"Is he dead?" she asked. "Angut?"

Gaba nodded.

"And the Captain."

Gaba cursed as he realised he had forgotten all about the Captain.

"Not dead. Knocked out, maybe."

Anna shrugged. "It doesn't matter anymore. It's all over." She glanced at the screen before looking at Gaba. "She was supposed to turn the people against the government, to make them question the First Minister, to sour and stall the move to independence." Anna shook her head. "Anarchy wasn't part of the plan. I underestimated her."

"Who?"

"Natuk. My foster daughter."

"You think she wants to turn Greenland on itself?"

"What do *you* think she's done, Sergeant?"

"I'm not a police officer."

"Not anymore, maybe, but you know how this looks. She has made a martyr and turned the youth of Greenland against the very institution that remains fully Danish – the police and the justice system. They will tear this country apart."

"You don't know that."

"Hah, forgive me," Anna said, "I forgot for a moment who I was talking to. You're the Commissioner's pit bull. The one that killed my boy."

"It's funny," Gaba said. He pointed at the image of Natuk pointing and firing her pistol as it flashed onto the screen. "You call her your *foster* daughter, but Ooqi Kleemann is your boy. I might not mix in the same social circles as you and your Danish cronies, but even I can imagine how a good dollop of favouritism might split a family, and turn a daughter against her own mother, foster or not."

Gaba stood up. He pulled a winter jacket from a hook behind the door and tossed it at the Ombudsman.

"Put it on," he said.

"Are we going somewhere?"

Gaba pointed at the screen. "We're going into the city. We're going to stop this."

"Really, Sergeant. And how do you imagine we're going to do that?"

"Oh, I don't know. You're the clever, devious, one. I'm sure you'll figure something out."

Gaba waited for Anna to pull on the jacket and then pushed her towards the stairs. The Captain groaned as Gaba searched his pockets. He tugged a pair of car keys out of the man's shirt pocket and slapped him on the cheek. Gaba pulled the keys for the boat out of the ignition and stuffed them into his pocket.

"Don't leave town, Captain," he said, as he gripped Anna by the arm and guided her to the wheelhouse door.

"You really think I can stop this?" Anna laughed, as she slid across the icy deck. "You're mad."

"That's right," Gaba said. "It's Petra that is the brains in this partnership. Don't underestimate her, like you did your daughter." Gaba helped the Ombudsman onto the dock and clicked the Captain's car keys. The lights of a small electric town car flashed and Gaba sighed, thankful that he didn't have to walk back to his own car, thankful for the small things. Petra would have to deal with the bigger things, like saving the country.

Chapter 25

The distance between Petra and Natuk could be measured in ravens. The wingtip scratches in the snow shadowed from the sun stretched between them, perhaps three ravens, or one flapping and hopping over the other. Petra could hear them scratching across the roof, their claws biting into the bitumen as they stalked and hopped their way towards the three police officers staring at one another at the edge of the roof, the ravens' domain. They weren't alone; a drone hovered nearby, darting backwards and forwards and then holding its position, as if uncertain as to how to proceed. Natuk waved her pistol at Petra, forcing her to stop as she put on a pair of thick-rimmed glasses. Her left eye flickered back and forth while her right focused on Petra. The drone retreated and Natuk slipped the glasses into her pocket.

"It's the cold," she said. "I have to keep them warm."

Petra nodded, as if it was perfectly normal to discuss practical matters during a standoff that was Mexican by nature, and yet typically Greenlandic; the ravens seemed happy to perform the role of desert vultures, and Petra knew Aron had his hand curled around the grip of his police issue pistol. A thin sheet of snow curled across the roof, dusting their boots as Natuk shifted her grip on her pistol.

"I've been here before, Natuk," Petra said. "Two weeks ago."

"Don't," Natuk said. Her aim wavered as she shook her head. "Don't tell me about my brother."

"It was like this." Petra gestured at Aron behind her with a subtle wave of her hand. "Three of us. It didn't have to end in his death." Petra took a breath and a tiny step towards Natuk.

"I saw what happened." Natuk swallowed. She flexed her fingers around the grip of her pistol.

"Yes, but do you know why he reached for his gun?"

"I know why. It was for the cause. He did it for our foster mother. She put him there," Natuk said. She raised the gun, changing her aim from Petra's chest to her head. "But you killed him."

"I don't agree," Petra said. "I know I killed him, I have to live with that, but that's not why he died, why he chose to die. He was sending a message, Natuk. He put his glasses on the table so that you could see what happened. That message, tragic and brutal – it was for his sister. It was for you."

Natuk laughed. "You think so? Alright, *ma'am*. What was he trying to tell me? What was the message?"

"I think it was a warning," Petra said. "I think he was trying to tell you not to follow him. He wanted you to know the consequences of listening to your foster mother, to show you how she had poisoned him, so that he could save you." Petra took another step forward. "He loved you, Natuk."

Natuk lowered the pistol and glanced over her shoulder. She shuffled closer to the edge of the roof. The boldest of the three ravens stalked closer, tapping its claws on the metal gutter as it stared at Natuk.

"He always was the more emotional one." Natuk looked at the gap between the roofs, judging the distance.

"Was he older than you?"

"What?"

"You were twins. Was he born first?"

"We never knew," Natuk said. "Our parents never told us. But I think I was the firstborn. I was oldest."

"He would have been twenty-six today," Petra said. "Just like you."

"Hey," Natuk said. She raised her arm as she leaned to one side, pointing her pistol at Aron as he inched closer to Petra. "Stop there, Aron."

"He's your friend, Natuk."

"I don't have *friends*," she said. "I use people, until they are no longer useful."

"Like Tiina Markussen?"

"What?" Natuk's eyes narrowed as she switched her gaze and the pistol from Aron back to Petra.

"You called her Viola. But her name was Tiina."

"I know what her name was."

"Was she not a friend, or was she just *useful*?"

"Tiina was a friend. I liked her," Natuk said. The pistol wavered as she took a breath. "But Viola is very useful."

"*Is?*"

Natuk nodded towards the main street running through the city, just behind Petra. The cool air rumbled with protest. "What do you think?"

"I can see that," Petra said. "But what now? You've created a martyr and sowed the seeds of anarchy. What's next?"

"I don't need a next," Natuk said. She turned her head slightly, flicking her gaze from the edge to the roof opposite. "I'm just looking for a way out."

"You mean you're done? You're finished?" It was Petra's turn to laugh. "Not only have you killed a friend, Natuk, you've dishonoured your brother. He might have been misguided, but he wasn't a coward..."

"Ma'am," Aron said, his words soft, closer than Petra anticipated. "Be careful."

"You're calling *me* a coward?"

"Because you've given up on Greenland," Petra said. "If you truly loved your country, and if you believed in what your brother was doing, then you wouldn't stop now, now that there is so much work to be done."

"You understand *nothing*," Natuk said. Spittle flew from her mouth and the pistol shook in her hand. "What have *you* done for your country? When did you stand up for something? I don't remember hearing you challenge the First Minister when she signed the deal with the Chinese, or again, when my so-called foster mother brokered another shitty deal with the Dutch. Where were you? What would Maratse think of you?"

Petra shuddered for a second as Natuk hurled David's name at her.

"That's what I thought," Natuk said. "You're ashamed. You never spoke up." She laughed. "I heard a rumour once that you never voted. That the referendum was your first time. Imagine that, a Police Commissioner that doesn't vote."

"It's not my place to..."

"Not your place? It's *exactly* your place – as a Greenlander, you have to vote. You can't sit on the fence, you have to be active, to take a stand, like them," she said, and pointed the pistol towards the protestors clashing with the police less than half a kilometre away. "But no, you waited to cast the first real vote of your professional life when Greenland was weakest, when the whole country voted with their heart, not their heads. Someone should have used their head. Someone should have challenged the government, forced them to clean up their act before committing to a future that will have us on our knees before we reach the end of our first year of independence."

"That's what you think?"

"It's what I *know*," Natuk said. "It's what you know too."

"You call me a coward, but you could have done something about it."

"I did." Natuk jabbed the muzzle of the pistol towards the city.

"From behind a mask, Natuk. It's not the same."

"Sometimes you need to use a mask to send a message. One face can make a difference. I gave them two. I gave Greenland the mask for the people, and Viola's face – her memory – to lead them. I've played my part. I just need to exit now."

"This is not a play, Natuk."

"You're wrong, ma'am." Natuk spread her arms like raven wings. *"All the world's a stage,"* she said. *"And all the men and women merely players; They have their exits and their entrances..."* She bowed once, turning the gun back towards Petra as she applied pressure to the trigger. "This is my exit," she said. "And yours."

Petra heard Aron's boots scrape across the roof as Natuk squeezed the trigger. She felt his hand on her shoulder as he shoved her to the ground, and she heard the *whoomph* of the air escaping from his lungs as Natuk's bullet punched into his chest. He had never been a frontline officer, he never wore body armour, and he never fully understood, like Petra did, that his devotion to duty might one day get him killed. Aron's body crumpled onto the roof and his pistol skittered onto a patch of wind-blown snow as Petra slid onto her side. She saw Natuk run towards her, and then watched her turn, tossing her pistol to one side as she ran for the edge of the roof, arms pumping. Natuk leaped, slamming into the roof opposite, the toes of her boots scraping against the building's wooden façade as she gripped the gutter and clawed her way onto the roof.

Natuk rolled onto her side and rested for a second. Her chest heaved, and she pressed her hand to her ribs, grimacing as she probed the part of her body that had been the first to strike the side of the building. She didn't see or hear Petra pick up Aron's pistol, and the first bullet flipped her onto her back as she tried to stand.

"Stay down, Natuk," Petra shouted. "Just stay down."

Petra kicked at the snow on the roof. She kicked at the ravens, cursing them as they flapped out of reach, taunting her just like their cousins had taunted Maratse's dogs further north, in Inussuk, where she should be, where they should have stayed. It was Petra who had pushed for them to move back to the city. It was Petra who had accepted the job as Commissioner.

"And I'm the one responsible for the dead," she said, pressing the grip of the gun to the side of her head as blinked away the tears cooling on her eyelashes to look at Aron's body.

You're not responsible, Piitalaat.

"Yes, David, I am."

Eeqqi. You're not.

Petra palmed the tears from her eyes and took a deep breath of cool air.

"You don't understand, David. I *am* responsible. These are *my* officers." She looked across the gap between the roofs and watched as Natuk pressed a hand to her bloody shoulder and tried to stand. "All of them."

David's voice retreated to the last quiet place in her mind. She imagined he was brooding, although he never brooded. He would just observe, quietly, biding his time, until it was time to act. She bit back another tear and smiled at the thought. People always underestimated Constable David Maratse. That's what she loved about him. That and many other things.

It's time to act, Piitalaat.

"I know," she said.

Just be careful.

"I will," she said, as she took three steps back, stuffed the pistol into her pocket and ran towards the edge of the roof.

Petra's fingers slapped against the side of the gutter on the opposite roof with a dull thud. She grasped the gutter with just three fingers of her left hand as gravity tugged at her body, her legs flailing as the ravens flapped and cawed in the gap between the roofs. The pistol slipped out of her pocket as Petra twisted. She cried out as she felt her fingers slip and the metal gutter begin to bend. She looked down, saw the snow plume where the pistol fell, and imagined landing on top of it, her back broken by the fall and Greenland in pieces.

She felt cold fingers wrap around her wrist, and a fierce energy that trembled into her arm. Petra lifted her head and looked into Natuk's eyes as the rogue police officer leaned over the edge of the roof.

"You have to reach up with your other hand," she said. "I can only use one arm. You shot the other."

Petra raised her right hand, stretching her fingers until she felt the cold bite of metal and gripped it. She scraped her boots against the wall as Natuk pulled her up until Petra could hook her elbow over the edge. Natuk shifted her grip, grabbing Petra's belt as she shifted her position to kneel on the roof and drag Petra's body up and over the gutter.

"You're too old to jump, ma'am," Natuk said, as she clawed Petra onto her lap.

"I know," Petra said, as she caught her breath. She looked at Natuk. "You could have let me fall. Why didn't you?"

"Aron," she said, with a nod towards the opposite roof. "He was Ooqi's friend. He was kind to him, to both of us. He was never meant to die." Natuk wiped a bloody hand over her face, hiding the tears welling in her eyes. "I don't know what to do next. I don't know where to go, or what to do when I get there."

Petra sat on the roof and pulled Natuk into her body. She wrapped her arms around her, brushed the grit and snow from Natuk's short blonde hair and held her as she sobbed. Petra stared at Aron's body, and then shifted her gaze to the city and the clash of police and protestors – the clash of *Greenlanders*, fighting for their future and the survival of their country. Petra looked at the rough bands of ink tattooed into the joints between her fingers.

I know all about survival, she thought. *And now it's time to act. To make a difference. To fight for Greenland's future.*

Chapter 26

The Fire Chief beckoned for Petra to join him beside the fire engine as two voluntary firefighters strapped Aron's body onto a spinal board and prepared to move him to the ground.

"You never checked his body, did you?" the Fire Chief asked, when Petra joined him.

"No," she said. "I jumped off the roof just a few minutes after he was shot."

"You jumped off the roof…" the Chief laughed. "Well, if you'd *stayed* on the roof, you might have noticed he was breathing." He pointed at the ambulance where the paramedics wrapped a dressing around Natuk's shoulder. "She didn't kill him." He pointed at the firefighters passing Aron over the railings of the bucket lift. "He's unconscious, but he will recover. They're expecting him at Kong Frederik's."

"That's good," Petra said. Her shoulders sagged as she smiled. "What about you, Commissioner, you look tired. Are you hurt?"

"I don't have time to be tired or hurt, Chief." Petra nodded towards a thin twist of smoke rising above Nuuk's main street. "I've got to sort this mess out."

"It is a mess," he said. "Honestly, I don't know what they're all fighting over. We all want the same thing. Don't we?"

"What *do* we want?" Petra pressed her hand on the Chief's bulky sleeve and smiled. "Look after Aron for me." She took a last look at the firefighters in the bucket lift, and then beckoned to the officer guarding Natuk. "What's the situation on *Aqqusinersuaq*?"

"Ugly," he said, and then, "lots of shouting. The smoke is from a burning car – one of ours."

"Any casualties?"

"Lots of bruises. Sergeant Napa has a concussion but try telling her that."

Petra smiled at the thought of Atii brushing off any concerns for her health as she cursed and coordinated her colleagues into order.

"I can imagine. What about the protestors?"

"They are mad as hell, and they just got madder when the Americans arrived. They've moved back down the street, but they are rallying. Atii… Sergeant Napa thinks they are going to charge again. She's not sure they can stop them a second time."

Petra struggled to imagine a charge. She thought the disturbance would be more sporadic, with a constant push backwards and forwards between small groups probing the police lines. But so long as their aggression was directed at the police, Petra thought there was a chance to keep innocent bystanders out of harm's way.

But we're all in this together, she thought, as she walked with the officer to the back of the ambulance.

"Are you ready, Natuk?" she asked.

"I thought I was taking her into custody," the officer said.

"Not yet." Petra held out her hand to steady Natuk as she stepped out of the ambulance. "We've got work to do."

The officer drove them to the end of the side street, parking as close to the police lines as possible. He held the door for Petra as she got out of the car. He fumbled with the cuffs on his belt and gestured towards Natuk, but Petra shook her head.

"You've got her gun," she said. "And she won't run. Not this time."

Natuk nodded and followed Petra to the back of the police lines.

"Have you still got control of the drones?" Petra asked.

"If you let me put my glasses on."

"I want you to film this, so, yes, put your glasses on and have two drones follow us."

"Where are we going?"

"To talk to them," Petra said. She pointed at the line of protestors.

Atii stepped away from the police line as soon as she saw Petra. She stopped beside a body lying on the ground between two police patrol vehicles. The corner of the thin sheet covering it snapped gently in the wind, and Natuk stared at it. Strands of Viola's hair were just visible clinging to the edge of the sheet. Petra took Natuk's arm and held her gently as Atii approached.

"I heard you found her," Atii said. Her lip curled slightly as she looked at Natuk. "I heard she shot Aron."

"He needs help, but he's going to be okay."

"What are we going to do with her?"

"I honestly don't know," Petra said. "We're going to go down there and see what happens."

"I don't think that's a good idea, ma'am," Atii said. "And I'm pretty sure Seabloom will agree with me."

"Where is he?"

"On the right side of the street. He has two groups of Seamen like wedges on each side. They're armed, and they're aggressive. I don't like it, but the protestors have backed off."

"Greenlanders," Petra said. "We have to look beyond the masks, Atii."

Atii started to speak but the words hung in her mouth as she looked around Petra at the car approaching the rear of the police lines. Gaba grinned from behind the wheel. He was still grinning as he opened the door and got out of the car.

"What happened to you?" Atii said. "And why are you bleeding?"

"I'm still bleeding?"

Gaba opened the passenger door and helped Anna Riis out of the car. She tensed at the sight of Natuk, and Gaba gripped her arm.

"I guess this is a family reunion," he said, and grinned at Petra. "Told you I'd find her."

"Yes, you did," she said.

Natuk bent down as if to tie the laces of her boots. She lifted the cuff of her trouser leg and pulled the compact pistol from her ankle holster. Atii reached for her sidearm as Natuk pointed her backup pistol at her foster mother.

"Stand down, Natuk," Petra said, as she stepped between them, cursing herself for not having searched her for hidden weapons.

"Step aside, ma'am," Natuk said.

Petra shook her head, waving a discreet hand at Atii as the SRU Sergeant started to move around Natuk's flank.

"I will shoot you if you get in my way," Natuk said.

"Killing her won't help," Petra said. She pointed towards the young Greenlanders regrouping further down the street. "They need to hear what she has to say. They need to know what she has done. If you kill her, there's no turning back. Greenland will be lost. There will be no future, only pain." Petra walked towards Natuk. "There's been enough pain, already. Don't you think, Natuk?"

Petra heard heavy feet sliding and scuffing across the snow and imagined Gaba moving in front of Anna Riis, shielding her from Natuk. The look on Atii's face confirmed it.

"I should have killed her on the boat," Natuk said, as she lowered the pistol. She dropped the pistol onto the ground. The wind flapped at the sheet, and the corner lifted to reveal Viola's face and the neat black hole in her forehead. Her eyes were open, frozen wide in disbelief.

Atii covered Petra as she stooped to pick up the pistol. Petra handed it to Atii and then turned to look at the Ombudsman.

"It's time to tell the people what you have done," she said. "It's time to stop this, to put an end to your machinations."

"Machinations?" Anna laughed. "That's a fine word coming from you, *Commissioner.*"

Petra nodded. She picked at a spot of blood on her fingers, studied the bands between the joints. "That's what you think, isn't it? That we're all simple. That Greenland can't survive without the help of another, more sophisticated people watching over them." The winter sun broke through the clouds and the corners of Petra's mouth curled as if they were attached to the sun's rays like strings. She smiled, stuffing her hands into her pockets, just as she had seen Maratse do so many times when they were out on the ice, or even when walking through the city. *My city*, she thought.

"My dear Commissioner," Anna said. "Is this going to be your moment, your speech, when you tell me just how strong and independent Greenlanders can be, how they must be allowed to make their own mistakes? It's all very touching, and boring. I've heard it before. Too many times. The people I represent…"

"Are standing right over there," Petra said. "You were employed as Ombudsman in Greenland. You were the supposed to be the voice of the people. If they had concerns or grievances regarding the government, it was you they were meant to come to. You were the people's advocate, and you failed. You are not the check and balance. You were not supposed to play God or take on the role of a secret dictator. You were supposed to listen and serve."

Petra paused at the sight of a government car approaching from the hotel at the bottom of the hill. It stopped just behind the Ombudsman, and Greenland's First Minister stepped out. Petra gestured for Natuk to put on her glasses and looked up as a ring of drones moved into position above them.

"The people are listening," Petra said. "It's time for you to serve."

"It's cold, Commissioner," Anna said. She shivered for effect. "Perhaps if we did this inside?"

Petra turned at the sound of boots padding, sliding and scuffing on the snow as the young people of Greenland filled the spaces between the police and their patrol cars. They removed their masks and dropped their sticks as the police lifted their visors and lowered their shields.

"This is interesting, Petra," Seabloom said, as he pushed through the crowd to stand beside her. "It's also potentially dangerous." He lowered his voice. "I can get you out, but it has to be now."

"No," she said. "I want to hear what she has to say."

"I don't think she's going to say anything at all."

"She will," Petra said. "We're not leaving until she does."

Gaba let go of Anna's arm and stepped to one side. He walked over to a police car and leaned against it, grimacing as he moved his leg until it was comfortable. He smiled at Petra and took Atii's hand as she joined him.

"You're in trouble," she said.

"I usually am," he said.

"But you enjoyed yourself, didn't you?"

"More than you want to know."

Gaba stopped talking as the First Minister stepped into a gap as two of the protestors made room for her in a tight circle around the Ombudsman. The drones pulled back as Natuk positioned them, dragging, dropping, and blinking icons in her lenses as she broadcast the drone feed into the DataStream.

"You are under arrest, and you will answer for Tiina's murder..."

"I understand."

"But I want you to record this moment. Make sure that Greenland gets the whole story, and that they understand what has happened here, and why." Petra took Natuk's hand. "I can't and won't pretend that you haven't done the things you have done, Natuk, but neither can I ignore your intelligence and your passion, albeit misguided. You will be punished. You will be imprisoned, but you are going to serve your country one way or another. You owe Greenland that much."

"And what about you, ma'am?" Natuk asked.

What about me? Petra mused.

She looked at Anna Riis, shivering inside a ring of Greenlanders, the future of the country. She looked at the First Minister, at Gaba and Atii, and she looked at the faces of the young men and women, the children squeezing between their legs, and the older generations gathering behind them. A future Greenland, independent of Denmark, free to make its own mistakes, and create its own opportunities, would need its own police force, to serve the people, and lend a helping hand where needed, to do the heavy lifting when required.

"What about me?" Petra said.

Natuk let go of Petra's hand as a small girl pushed through the ring of people and walked right up to Petra. Quaa grinned as Petra lifted her into her arms.

"I thought you were on your way to Denmark?" Petra said. She smiled at Iiluuna standing on the opposite side of the circle.

Quaa shook her head. "The doctor came back to work today. We're staying in Nuuk," she said.

Petra pulled her close and kissed her forehead. "What a coincidence. So am I."

Snow drifted through the sun's rays, glistening as it fell, dusting the crowd's heads and shoulders. Petra wondered at Anna Riis' stubborn streak, and how long it would take before she cracked. The look on Pipaluk's face suggested she was thinking the same thing. They were not alone.

"I'm curious, Petra," Seabloom said. "Just how long is this going to take?"

Petra shrugged. "As long as necessary," she said. "We're a patient people. We're not going anywhere."

The thought of sticking around and doing her job just a little longer brought a smile to Petra's lips. She felt a sense of peace settle in her mind, like a thick blanket she could curl up in. She closed her eyes for a moment, searching the darkness until she saw his image and heard his voice.

That's good, Piitalaat. I'm happy for you.

Petra clung to Maratse's last words for as long as she could, sad at the thought that they were his last, but happy that he was ready to leave her, happy that they both might find peace. When the Ombudsman finally opened her mouth to speak, Petra smiled at the thought that Greenland might now be able to settle, and that a new sense of peace and understanding would allow them to face whatever challenges lay ahead. For one thing was certain, there would be plenty of them.

About the Author

Christoffer Petersen is the author's pen name. He lives in Denmark. Chris started writing stories about Greenland while teaching in Qaanaaq, the largest village in the very north of Greenland – the population peaked at 600 during the two years he lived there. Chris spent a total of seven years in Greenland, teaching in remote communities and at the Police Academy in the capital of Nuuk.

Chris continues to be inspired by the vast icy wilderness of the Arctic and his books have a common setting in the region, with a Scandinavian influence. He has also watched enough Bourne movies to no longer be surprised by the plot, but not enough to get bored.

You can find Chris in Denmark or online here:

www.christoffer-petersen.com

By the same author:

THE GREENLAND CRIME SERIES
featuring Constable David Maratse

Book 1
SEVEN GRAVES, ONE WINTER

Book 2
BLOOD FLOE

Book 3
WE SHALL BE MONSTERS

Short stories from the same series
KATABATIC
CONTAINER
TUPILAQ
THE LAST FLIGHT
THE HEART THAT WAS A WILD GARDEN

and

THE GREENLAND TRILOGY
featuring Konstabel Fenna Brongaard

Book 1
THE ICE STAR

Book 2
IN THE SHADOW OF THE MOUNTAIN

Book 3
THE SHAMAN'S HOUSE

www.ingramcontent.com/pod-product-compliance
Lightning Source LLC
Chambersburg PA
CBHW031945260626
47157CB00017B/2369